World Unbound

An Apocalyptic LitRPG
Book 6 of the System Apocalypse

By

Tao Wong

Copyright

This is a work of fiction. Names, characters, businesses, places, events and incidents are either the products of the author's imagination or used in a fictitious manner. Any resemblance to actual persons, living or dead, or actual events is purely coincidental.

This book is licensed for your personal enjoyment only. This book may not be re-sold or given away to other people. If you would like to share this book with another person, please purchase an additional copy for each recipient. If you're reading this book and did not purchase it, or it was not purchased for your use only, then please return to your favorite book retailer and purchase your own copy. Thank you for respecting the hard work of this author.

A Starlit Publishing Book
Published by Starlit Publishing
PO Box 30035
High Park PO
Toronto, ON
M6P 3K0
Canada

www.starlitpublishing.com

Ebook ISBN: 9781775380979
Paperback ISBN: 9781775380986
Hardcover ISBN: 9781989458518

Books in The System Apocalypse series

Main Storyline

Life in the North

Redeemer of the Dead

The Cost of Survival

Cities in Chains

Coast on Fire

World Unbound

Stars Awoken

Rebel Star

Stars Asunder

Broken Council

Forbidden Zone

System Finale

System Apocalypse - Relentless

A Fist Full of Credits

System Apocalypse - Australia

Town Under

Anthologies and Short stories

System Apocalypse Short Story Anthology Volume 1

Valentines in an Apocalypse

A New Script

Daily Jobs, Coffee and an Awfully Big Adventure

Adventures in Clothing

Questing for Titles

Blue Screens of Death

A Game of Koopash (Newsletter exclusive)

Lana's story (Newsletter exclusive)

Debts and Dances (Newsletter exclusive)

Comic Series

The System Apocalypse Comics (7 Issues)

The System Apocalypse Graphic Novel: Issues 1-7
(limited edition hardcover)

Contents

What Has Gone Before

When the System arrived on Earth, it brought monsters, aliens, and glowing blue boxes that altered the reality of humanity. Gifted with Classes that must be Leveled and Skills that provide reality-altering powers, humanity struggled to survive when modern electronics failed under the flood of Mana. In a year, over ninety percent of humanity had fallen, leaving the remnants to pick up their lives.

John Lee is one such survivor, starting from the depths of the Yukon and traveling south to aid humanity in its struggle to stay free of their Galactic overlords. As a settlement owner in British Columbia, he joined forces with the remnant military forces of the United States on the West Coast and proceeded to wage a war to free the Canadian prairies and the US West Coast. Together, they battled the Zarrie—a desert kingdom Galactic force—and freed Los Angeles while making alliances with a few Galactic companies.

On the day of their victory, John is visited by the Erethran Honor Guard and its champion. As punishment for taking their exclusive Class, John is cast into a Portal to face a unique and deadly Master Class Quest. Exiled, John must complete his Quest before returning, while Earth continues to evolve.

Chapter 1

A tear in space, black and empty, devoid of all light, snaps shut behind me as I exit the Portal. I stagger, my body shuddering as I deal with being transported thousands of light years in a second. Nerves fire constantly, muscles clench, and my ears ring. Coughing to clear my lungs, I grimace and straighten, wobbling as my body readjusts to the lower gravity on Earth. A deep breath fills my lungs, and I marvel at how even a minor increase in the oxygen content can feel so good. But no matter how much I enjoy being home, years of violence on another world means that I'm still on alert.

"Ali?" I call to the olive-skinned, orange-jump-suited Spirit hovering beside me.

He bobs up and down, his body reforming as he joins me in the clearing in the middle of the forest we picked as our entry point. Once again, I cough as the earlier pain subsides. I twist my head around to take in my surroundings, double-checking for potential problems.

"Working on it, boy-o," Ali growls, fingers darting from side to side as he plays with the screens and notifications only he can see.

While the Spirit is busy, I glance up to check out the minimap created by my own Skill Greater Detection. It isn't as powerful as the information Ali can provide, but he's busy patching himself back into Earth's subversion of the System and dealing with the numerous notifications we've accumulated over the years. The world we spent the last four years on was in the Forbidden Zone—an area so Mana saturated that the System actually broke down.

Rather than bother the harried Spirit, I check for potential threats on the minimap. Already, the System has populated a series of dots on my minimap, mostly greyed out to indicate these monsters are no threat to me. No real surprise, but better to be careful.

While I wait and watch, I marvel at the differences I can feel, the changes compared to the world I was in. Lower—significantly lower—Mana density on Earth. Lower gravity, higher oxygen content, no trace poison in the air. But more than that, the gentle caress of the wind brings familiar smells, of new pine and clean water, the muskiness of an animal having passed through a few hours ago, and the creak of old wood. It's familiar and comforting, and a tension I barely noticed slowly fades. I'm home.

"Ready!" the Spirit says without preamble.

Then the flood of notifications begins.

You have completed your Class Quest
Achieved Master Class: Paladin of the Erethran Empire
Delayed experience gain now distributing.

Experience decay alert! Some of the experience you have gathered has decayed.

Multiple Level up alert! Some of the experience you have gained has been penalized due to multiple Level ups.

Decayed and penalized experience has been banked. Future experience will accrue at a greater rate until bank depleted.

You have Leveled up to Erethran Paladin Level 14
Attributes automatically assigned. You have 98 free attributes to assign. You have 7 Class Skills to assign.

My body twitches, pain and ecstasy coursing through it as the sudden increase in attributes hits me like a steamboat going over the Niagara Falls.

Normally, my attributes are so high that Level increases are minor changes, so little that I can't even feel them. But I'm getting fourteen Levels at once—fourteen Master Class Levels. My body shudders as it's hammered by the changes, my perceptions visibly expanding even. Muscles twist and twitch, tendons and fibers multiplying and hardening even as they grow more flexible. My nervous system gets ripped apart and put together again and again. It all happens within seconds, an eternity of pain before it's over and I'm myself again.

Thank the gods increases in attributes are on a logarithmic method, one that takes into account a vast variety of areas outside of the simplistic terminology used. Strength, for example, not only alters my own physical strength, but also how I affect the world around me, the System allowing me to manipulate and even "weaken" the bonds between an object as I hit it. It's why I can still be cut by a knife and yet can take a bullet to the chest without a problem. If this was a pure physical strength increase, I probably would have exploded from the Level ups themselves.

The moment I recover, more notifications appear before me.

Congratulations! You have gained a new title - Explorer

For traveling to, surviving, and returning from a forbidden planet, you have achieved the title Explorer. Your bravery and foolhardiness will henceforth be known all over the world.

Rewards: All mapping and sensory Skills have gained a 10% increase

Congratulations! You are the 18th member of the human race to leave the Solar System and return.

Rewards: +20,000 XP, +5 in Perception, +1 skill Level (Mapping), access to Fame and Reputation menu

Congratulations! You have gained a new title Slayer of (&%@@##** - error!)

For killing over (error! error! error!) (error! error! error!) you have gained a new title! All (error! error! error!) will fear you and your presence will subtly disturb them.

Rewards: (error! error! error!) (Please see Administrative functionary. Error has been logged and sent to support. Thank you for your patience!)

"Ali?" I say softly, then twist my head as I note the little orange-clad Spirit twitching, his body glowing with color.

My eyes narrow as he continues to glow, brighter and brighter till I can't look at him directly. With a resounding pop, he reappears.

"Leveled up?"

"Just about," Ali says, patting himself down. He's no longer floating, instead standing on the ground. Which is good, because he's now 5' 8", portly, and still clad in an orange jumpsuit. "Har! Still smaller than I should be, but this is so much better."

"You look a lot more solid now…" I say with a frown.

"Yup, I'm here. For real. Body and all," Ali says with a smirk.

"Shit." I frown. I've grown used to Ali being a scout.

As if he knows what I'm thinking, Ali rolls his eyes and shrinks again, all the way down to a foot, his entire body becoming slightly transparent again. "This what you want? A floating fairy?"

"Maybe not the fairy part. I take it you've got control?"

"Not much of Level up if I didn't, would it?"

"Fine," I say with a shrug.

Now that he's made his point, Ali pops back to full size again. His hands twitch again almost immediately as he taps into the System, filling in details on my minimap and expanding its range without a word. While he's doing his thing, I peruse my new Class for the first time.

Four years and change, and for the first time, I get the chance to actually see the details of the damn Class I've fought, bled, and nearly died for.

Class: Paladin of the Erethran Empire

Unlike champions or Generals, the Paladins of the Erethran Empire have a special social standing in the Empire. Like their namesake, Paladins are not part of the chain of command, answerable to no one but the Empress herself. And not even then at times. Their actions are dictated by their honor, their judgment guided only by their wisdom, and their only support their strong right arm.

+1 in Luck per Level. +4 in Strength, Agility, Perception, Intelligence, and Charisma per Level. +5 in Constitution per Level. +6 in Willpower per Level, +7 Free Attributes per Level.

Mental Resistance Increased to 95%. All other Resistances increased by 10% (stackable).

Damage received reduced by 10%

+1 Class Skill per every two Levels

I stare at the description and whispered conversations and the clash of steel come back to me. Memories of my tutor, my mentor, she who finally entrusted me with this Class, rush back, bringing the taste of blood and an ache in my bones. For a moment, I find myself quailing at the knowledge of what is to come before I straighten. What will be, will be. For now, what is, is.

The increased resistances are a given, the stat bonuses the same. I'm a little surprised by the damage reduction and briefly wonder at what point the damage is reduced—before or after all the other Spell and Skill reductions are used—then dismiss the thought. Not as if this is a game where I can sit and calculate damage taken before I go into a fight, knowing exactly how much healing I'll need after each attack, what kind of armor or skills to use for each and every attack. This world, for all its game-like characteristics, is all too real.

For now, a slight thought is all it takes for the Class Skill page to pop up. I eye the Class Skills hungrily, even while knowing how foolish it is. These Skills are a sham, an uneven patchwork of powerful abilities created by the System to hide a deeper truth. My time away gave me a deeper glimpse, one that I've been struggling toward, but it's only that, a glimpse. Even so, I can't help but consider how much easier my life would have been with these Skills in the last few years.

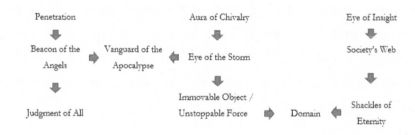

Like most Classes, the Paladin's Skill tree is broken up into three different areas that reflect the Paladin's areas of focus. Unlike the Advanced Skill tree, I've only got three tiers this time around. That's a good thing actually. The lower number of tiers means that I have to diffuse my precious Class Skill points less to get to the more powerful Skills. It's an advantage certain Classes have. Or, mostly an advantage. A few Classes out there, at the Basic level, have only two tiers, but they have mostly useless Skills. Those Classes are often considered "waste" Classes, though they can be powerful secondary Classes if combined properly.

I shake my head, pushing my wandering thoughts back to the matter at hand. The first column showcases personal combat Skills; the second, the Paladin's effect on the greater battlefield as champions; and lastly, the third column exemplifies their role as judge, jury, and executioner. Within the tree itself are additional Skills, combined abilities that provide even greater strength.

For all that, I scan through each of them quickly, mentally planning out my options and what I will need before allocating a single point to each of the first unlocked tiers. The other tiers will have to wait till I unlock them when I reach their required Levels. Still, past experience has me saving my extra four Skill points. After all, now that I'm back where I can actually Level and get Quests, I'll hit Level 20 soon and gain access to my second tier and their more powerful Skills. Until then, the basics will do. It's not as if I'm not OP enough, as Jason might say.

Class Skill: Penetration (Level 1)

Few can face the judgment of a Paladin in direct combat, their ability to bypass even the toughest of defenses a frightening prospect. Reduces Mana Regeneration by 5 permanently. Effect: Ignore all armor and defensive spells by 50%. Increases damage done to shields by 100%.

Class Skill: Aura of Chivalry (Level 1)

A Paladin's very presence can quail weak-hearted enemies and bolster the confidence of allies, whether on the battlefield or in court. The Aura of Chivalry is a double-edged sword however, focusing attention on the Paladin—potentially to their detriment. Increases success rate of Perception checks against Paladin by 10% and reduces stealth and related skills by 10% while active. Reduces Mana Regeneration by 5 Permanently. Effect: All enemies must make a Willpower check against intimidation against user's Charisma. Failure to pass the check will cow enemies. All allies gain a 50% boost in morale for all Willpower checks and a 10% boost in confidence and probability of succeeding in relevant actions.

Note: Aura may be activated or left off at will.

Class Skill: Eyes of Insight (Level 1)

Under the eyes of a Paladin, all untruth and deceptions fall away. Only when the Paladin can see with clarity may he be able to judge effectively. Reduces Mana Regeneration by 5.

Effect: All Skills, Spells, and abilities of a lower grade that obfuscate, hinder, or deceive the Paladin are reduced in effectiveness. Level of reduction proportionate to degree of difference in grade and Skill Level.

Well, that was interesting. Master Skills are frightening, but of course, they have to be, considering how difficult it is to get them. It does help that I've got an extremely rare, almost unique Class, which results in better than normal Skills too.

Still, the Penetration Skill effectively doubles my combat ability. Doubling my attack against Shields is impressive—probably the most common method of defense these days—but reducing other, more passive defenses by fifty percent is even scarier. Certainly monsters that rely on their natural defenses will be in for a hell of a shock if I ever hit them.

With the slightest twitch of my mind, I call up my new Status Screen.

Status Screen			
Name	John Lee	Class	Erethran Paladin
Race	Human (Male)	Level	14

Titles		
Monster's Bane, Redeemer of the Dead, Duelist, Explorer		
Health	3020	Stamina	3020
Mana	2340	Mana Regeneration	213 (+5) / minute
Attributes		
Strength	176	Agility	271
Constitution	302	Perception	119
Intelligence	234	Willpower	263
Charisma	74	Luck	47
Class Skills		
Mana Imbue	3*	Blade Strike*	3
Thousand Steps	1	Altered Space	2
Two are One	1	The Body's Resolve	3
Greater Detection	1	A Thousand Blades*	3
Soul Shield	2	Blink Step	2
Portal*	5	Army of One	2
Sanctum	2	Instantaneous Inventory*	1
Cleave*	2	Frenzy*	1

Elemental Strike*	1 (Ice)	Shrunken Footsteps*	1
Tech Link*	2	Penetration	1
Aura of Chivalry	1	Eyes of Insight	1
Combat Spells			
Improved Minor Healing (IV)		Greater Regeneration (II)	
Greater Healing (II)		Mana Drip (II)	
Improved Mana Missile (IV)		Enhanced Lightning Strike (III)	
Firestorm		Polar Zone	
Freezing Blade		Improved Inferno Strike (II)	
Mud Walls			

Perhaps one of the biggest changes that occurred within the Forbidden Zone was the vast increase in the effectiveness of my spells. With the incredible increase in my Mana regeneration rate due to the sheer volume of Mana available on that planet, I started using my spells significantly more. I even spent some time upgrading my most used spells, making them significantly more powerful. While I still know the older, less powerful versions of the spells, rather than clutter up my interface, I just had them relegated to another section. It's not as if I'm ever going to cast Mana Dart again. Hell, I barely even use Mana Missile. In truth, I'm looking forward to speaking with Aiden about magic now that I've been forced to learn it the hard way.

As I stand there, contemplating my character sheet for the first time in four years, I'm grateful that I chose to be Ported into the middle of nowhere. With my own ability, I can get home easily enough now that I'm back on Earth, but

I wouldn't want to go over my new Skills while dealing with the fallout of being away for a few years. Not that I had any choice about leaving. And talking about choice…

"Took you long enough," I drawl, tilting my head to stare at the trio of Honor Guards walking out of the underbrush. Or Honor Guards and champion to be exact.

The trio of Erethrans are each over seven feet tall, their hair colors ranging from simple purple to outlandish, vibrant yellow-red. Each of them have coral-like ears and slitted eyes whose giant yellow pupils seem particularly startling set against the almost non-existent nose with that hint of a beak-like overhang. They're all clad in an armored pants-and-tunic ensemble, sporting the exclusive Erethran royal family's colors—purple and silver.

"I believe that was my line," the champion says with a half-smile.

I regard the champion for a moment, reading the status information Ali is able to pull up. Interesting. She's gone up a few Levels since the last time I spoke with her. Impressive even, considering how hard it is to Level at the stage she's in. At least, unless you're a cheat character like me.

Ayuri d'Malla of the Dawn, Breaker of the Sixth Legion, Hero of the Sixth Kumma Wars, Mistress of Knives, Bloodflower, Slayer of Kumma, Goblins, Mizza… (Level 43 Erethran Champion)
HP: 9990/9990
MP: 4342/4780
Conditions: Buffs. LOT OF BUFFS.

"That sounds like a lie, considering you never expected me to survive," I say with a smile. There's no malice in my voice, not anymore. A quick scan of her friends shows that they've Leveled too. Impressive as well, obviously.

"No recriminations or anger over throwing you in?" Ayuri says, dark eyes regarding me as she weighs my reaction.

"I've had four years and a lot of monsters to work out my anger," I say. "Not that you're forgiven. But you're not looking for that, are you?"

"No."

"So. What now?" I've played this discussion through my mind so many times, workshopped the various ways this could go. But at the end of the day, it comes down to what the woman wants. The fact stands that it would have, should have, been easier to just kill me to remove the stain of my presence on their honor. That she didn't means she has plans for me. Now, it's time to find out what.

Or not.

"Now? Nothing. In time, I expect we'll speak again," Ayuri says.

My eyes narrow slightly as I consider the champion. There's a lot I can say—a refusal to play her game, a question about her motives, or even a query about what has happened recently. In the end, I speak none of those words.

"Okay." I nod, shifting away slightly.

I take my time, keeping an eye on the trio as I wait to see what they'll do. Appearing here, in the middle of nowhere, was also a check to see if I had to deal with the Erethran Guard in a more violent and permanent way. Yet the trio looks utterly bored, happy to let me raise my hand and form a Portal.

Only when it's fully opened and I'm at its threshold does Ayuri speak. "If you're looking for your friends, you will not find them there."

"What do you mean?" I say, my eyes narrowing. "*Vancouver...?*"

"*Still yours. As are all your other settlements. Can't contact Kim from here, but there's no change in your ownership.*"

"Just that your friends are currently engaged in another location. Almost all of them actually," Ayuri says.

"Where?"

"Well, why don't we take you along? We're supposed to make an appearance too," Ayuri says with a smile.

I find myself annoyed by the casual way she's speaking. Still, I give her a nod as I release my Portal. Within moments, another, much larger Portal appears, its dark inkiness showing nothing of what awaits me. As soon as it fully appears, the trio travels through it without hesitation, and I join them with only the barest of hesitations. This could be leading to who knows where. But if that's the case, I might as well get it over and done with now. I tell myself to have patience, but I do take a moment to layer a Soul Shield on myself. Even if they're deliberately provoking me and playing with me, all will be revealed.

And if not, I'll show them what happens when you survive four years in a Forbidden Zone.

Chapter 2

Daylight disappears and twilight appears. My eyes adapt immediately, though I wish I still had my helmet. That was gone, what—fourteen months ago? Something like that. Made using Sabre quite difficult actually, since the helmet wasn't part of the nanomachine calibration. In fact, I hadn't even pulled my mecha out in months. The poor thing was so battered and smashed, I often just left it in storage.

As I'm thinking useless thoughts, I'm taking in my surroundings, scanning for trouble both via my Skill and my senses. Green grass has given way to sand, the flat terrain replaced by a dune. No more giant rainforest trees. Instead, a group of smaller, scurrying organic creatures appear before me, heaving and thrashing like living waves. It only takes a moment to register that there are three sides in the conflict before me: monsters, Galactics in all shapes and sizes, and humans. The scale of the battle is surprising—tens of thousands of figures fighting it out before me.

Bright beams of light, the roar of gunpowder and other chemical explosive ammunition, and the never-ending stink of clotted, iron-rich blood fill my senses. Winds, kicked up by continuous roar of explosives, swirl around me. Sand, salt, and particalized organics cloud the air even as screams and grunts of pain punctuate it all. They're far enough away that it'd be impossible to see them normally, but my boosted Perception seems to make seeing through the smoke a snap. One part of me is taking in the war, categorizing fighters and sides, while another is snapping Skills and spells in place, boosting my body into its best combat-ready state.

"What is going on?" A few years ago, I might have rushed in, taking part in the battle without thought. A few years ago, I'd know who was right, who I had to protect. But now…

"Just a minor field battle," Ayuri says. "Your friends are participating, with everyone contending for the Field Boss."

"*Field Boss?*"

"*Alpha monster who has become a locus for Mana flow. Rather than creating a dungeon, it powers up the monster, giving it significant boosts. Some of the oldest even respawn like monsters in a dungeon.*"

I don't need to ask who it is. The giant glowing pink arrow that follows the creature's movement is more than sufficient. It's a weird, ten-limbed scorpion-like monster with thin, grasping arms in the front and a second, humanoid body where its tail would be. Even without the arrow, years of battle have trained my eyes to see the telltale shifts, the flow of the battle, and spot the centers of activity, the linchpins. On the monster side, it's the Field Boss who, even under the barrage of modern, futuristic, and magical artillery fire, is barely bothered by the damage. Its health bar shifts a miniscule amount.

On the human side, there are dozens of smaller centers of activity. A ten-gallon-Stetson-hatted man two-steps through monsters, pistols blazing. A pair of puppies and a tiger run amok through the Galactics, guided and occasionally helped by a redhead on a griffin. Between both groups of attackers, an armored individual in ghostly medieval Japanese armor holds both groups aside while wielding a polearm. A pair of Guardians back her up, one with a metallic silver fist and another with swirling, tiny shields that protect against attacks. In the back, a party of Mages alternately dispel and cast spells, protecting the humans and their allies. And I do say allies, because I've spotted two anomalies.

Holding up one corner of the human army facing the Galactics is a force of Hakarta. They're easy to spot with their uniform armor and green facial tusks that stick out of their helmets. The Hakarta have a series of force shields locked in place at the front of the line, guarded by a group of plasma-spear-wielding Hakarta, while other members of their mercenary Corp lob grenades, spells, and other attacks over the defenses. Higher up on the sloped hill and behind the lines, snipers and other long-ranged fighters add to the carnage.

In another section of the human army's line of combat, a group of blue-and-silver-armored individuals in eight-foot-tall mecha are facing off against the monsters. Each mecha wields the equivalent of a minigun, spraying enchanted bullets downrange at a ferocious rate that barely stems the monster army. Beside each mecha, other members of the troop lay down more careful fire or work to reload the mecha. Between the towering metal behemoths, smaller figures use magic and melee weapons to deal with the few monsters that trickle through the gaps.

"That's the Erethran Army down there, isn't it?" I say, gesturing to the group with the mecha. The green and yellow piping a dead giveaway too.

"Yes," Ayuri answers.

I grimace, wondering what the story is, but discard that line of questioning. Another time. For now, I've got a good enough idea of the situation. I gauge distances, consider my Mana, then speak up.

"One last thing. I'm going to need to borrow another Portal…"

***

The black hole opens in space high above the monster army, taking in a backwash of lightning as a spell is deflected upward. I ignore it as I jump through the Portal with a pair of channeled firestorms ready, appearing high above the group. I release the spells as I fall, the fire appearing so quickly, the monsters below have no time to brace. When fire erupts all around you, not much you can do but burn.

I drop through the flames, my Soul Shield burning up as the flames eat away at its integrity. With a crash, I'm on the ground then back on my feet, dashing forward even as experience notifications pile up in the corner of my eye. Feet kick off the ground as I rush the now-clear Field Boss. It roars, its skin mildly blackened from the firestorms. Its health bar has barely moved. Even as I move, previously launched spells and artillery fall, making my Soul Shield tremble.

Aqrabuamelu Alpha (Field Boss Level 129)
_HP: 13380/15380_
_MP: 9804/10230_
Conditions: Greater Regeneration (IV), Field Advantage

I hate these kinds of monsters. I really do. Smart enough that they could almost be considered sentient, but without the level of conscience or morality that would make them viable members of society. They wield magic and savageness with equal fervor, though their spells are closer to innate Skills. The Aqrab glares at me, fingers shifting as the humanoid part begins a spell. Instinct has me throwing myself to the side as a rainbow stream flashes past my body. Even as I roll to my feet, the front body sends another spell on its way from its thin, weird hand/tentacles.

Blink Step. I'm beside the front body the next second, my sword cutting into one thin limb. It catches, barely scratching it, but that's okay—the following Skill-generated blades are on their way. Freezing Blade reacts as each blade contacts, layering a cold spell on the Boss and slowing it even as I'm moving. A twist of my body has me rolling across its broad back, one hand twisting and forming the spell Mud Wall that floods upward from the ground even as I throw a second cut at the tail-body.

The monster snarls, leaning backward to dodge the attack. While it does so, it struggles to free itself from the Mud Walls. With the boss trapped by the movement of my blades and the Mud Walls, I dismiss the sword in my hand and point both hands at the body, casting Inferno Strike. Beams of plasma fire erupt, tearing sizzling holes in the body as I walk along its torso. Before I can keep channeling and tear its body apart, its reinforcements arrive, forcing me to kill the spell prematurely.

A female lion-mutant, sleek and golden-furred, pounces at me, jaws distended and a green liquid dripping from its fangs. For a second, I see down its throat. Tattered flesh hangs from needle-fang teeth the size of daggers. Then my hand catches the monster by the underside of its neck and I slam the creature into the ground, the audible crunch of bones breaking echoing through the battlefield. A back kick takes care of another monster before I toss the lion into another group. Even if the damage done isn't great, it's a show of power that is hard to miss. Especially with my Aura of Chivalry turned on fully, attracting everyone's attention.

Another lesson from the planet? Sometimes, it's not the damage but controlling the battlefield that matters. In previous mass battles, I focused on killing as many as possible, as fast as possible. But now, now, I have another goal. With a stomp, I flip off the Field Boss as it lashes out with a series of guided bolts of pure Mana. Landing on the ground before it, I eat some of the attacks.

I grasp its front arm, gripping tight as a rising kick throws the body upward under the effect of my System-enhanced strength. Because the points don't just mean a change in physical strength but also in how I can make such strength manifest in the real world. And I've had a lot of practice learning to use these points properly. The creature flies into the air, held down only by my arm. Then I dance, swinging the giant Field Boss bat as a weapon, even as my Soul Shield falls under repeated secondary attacks.

Blood flows, small cuts and damage accumulating as the Boss lashes out with spells, and artillery shots land around us. But the battering ram of the Field Boss clears a wide area around me, one that I keep widening as I dash through the crowd. Along the way, I use my floating swords to add to the carnage. I create disruption and confusion, breaking morale and formations while layering damage and obstacles.

The change is small at first, the morale factor of my sudden appearance boosting the human army's fighting form. Then the distraction and damage to the Field Boss's subordinates kicks in, removing orders and support actions that were meant to take place. Weaknesses in the monster's line become breakouts as reinforcements do not arrive. And now, with the Field Boss unable to add additional orders, the monsters are split apart further. Mud Walls hamper movement; Polar Zones damage and slow down susceptible monsters as they rush around. Gaps appear and increase, and the experienced human army acts on it, targeting Elites and Alphas with a vengeance. It's a waterfall effect.

But it doesn't go all my way. After a minute, the Aqrab takes action, slicing off its own arm to free itself and using the force of my latest swing of its body to fly into the distance. It takes me a little bit to weave my way near it again, bashing apart monsters as I heal my body and close in on the Boss. Rather than repeat the attack, I switch to monster bowling, using the hardy Field Boss to shatter lines.

In the corner of my vision, Ali is dashing alongside me, his Spirit body fully materialized. He's still clad in his orange jumpsuit, but magic dances from his hand. Through our connection, the Spirit has use of the full range of spells I have learned, along with a few innate spells and abilities. But here, he's mostly focused on using Improved Mana Missiles, Enhanced Lightning Bolts, and the occasional Mud Wall while continually buffing me with healing spells.

Together, we rampage through the monsters' back lines, causing death and mayhem as the Field Boss's health shrinks ever so slowly.

"*Boy-o, Mana's at a quarter,*" Ali quietly reminds me.

I snarl, snatching up a monster and tossing it aside before booting another away. Then I focus, drawing on the stored Mana in my Mana Bracer, draining it completely. Time to end this. A rhinoceros-like creature charges me, trampling over a smaller carapace-clad monster in front of it, and I grin.

"Just in time."

My mind shifts, counting down the seconds even as I cut apart another creature. A second, two, then I jump upward, my feet lightly touching down on the charging monster's singular horn. Another push with my feet and I'm in the air, boosted by the creature's angry bellow and charge. I laugh, the thrill of fighting rushing through my body. Gods, I'd forgotten how fun it could be bullying lower Leveled monsters.

In the air, I spin and twist, locating the Field Boss, who has recovered from my latest bowling attempt and is scurrying away. Even as it does so, it's manifesting another spell, hands waving in unison as a weird, rising chant fills the battlefield. Too bad Spells take a bit of time to manifest. The more powerful the spell, the longer it takes—dependent on skill and ability—which is why I tend toward simpler spells in combat. When I'm not using Skills. Because Skills just require a moment of concentration and willpower.

Around me, an even dozen identical copies of my sword appear. I raise my hand, the original sword in my hand shining with light as I gesture downward, the action copied by the dozen blades as beams of concentrated energy tear the air apart to impact the Field Boss. A few unlucky monsters get in the way of the strike and are torn apart like wet newspaper. Each enhanced blade of energy rips through the monster, their penetrating power doubled due to my new Master Skill. Long tears appear on the Aqrab's body, thousands of points of damage appearing in a single strike.

Army of One. The damn Skill name says it all.

I land on the ground with a grin, striding forward as the Aqrab struggles to stand up, a pair of feet so badly damaged that one lies on the ground next to it. Blood dribbles out from its wounds, a sulphuric smell rising from its wounds even as its buffs attempt to heal the damage.

Thanks to my Aura and the sheer intimidation of having their leader nearly mashed flat, none of the monsters charge me as I finish the pitiful creature with one last stab of my blade. The moment the Field Boss dies, its body collapsing entirely into the ground, a ripple goes through the crowd of monsters. They break apart and flee, the bond keeping them here broken.

In their fear, the monsters still know better than to come near, circling round the corpse of the Field Boss and me. No surprise then that my friends arrive soon afterward. First to arrive of course is Lana, the redhead flying over the monsters on her griffin, the creature dropping to the ground to deposit its voluptuous rider with a blast of sand.

Without a word, the redhead throws her arms around me, hugging me tightly. I return the hug, holding her close while the rest of the group finds their way over. In a short while, the rest of my friends, my team, arrive. While the battle continues to rage around us, while the remainder of the monsters are mopped up, we hold our first meeting in four years.

I can't help but grin as they cluster around, my eyes taking in the changes among them all. The new lines on their faces, the greater confidence in their stances, the much larger health and Mana bars. The big, wide, grinning faces. I take it all in, savoring the moment before I finally speak.

"What took you so long?"

Chapter 3

Cleaning up after the Field Boss dies takes only a short while. The Hakarta and Erethran army help clear the monster corpses, stacking up bodies for transportation and cleaning later. Interestingly enough, looting is conducted under a somewhat different scenario than normal, as everyone is in an army-based super-group, making looting simpler. Everything will be stored and divvied up later, rather than each individual having to find the corpses they killed.

The Galactics we were fighting ceased fighting us the moment the Field Boss fell, their interest extinguished like the creature's life. It takes a little explaining, but it seems the entire battle was more of a ritualized competition than a desperate race for resources. With the Field Boss down, there's little point in continuing the contest and the Galactics cease hostilities. They work alongside our people in picking up corpses of their fallen and looting bodies of those monsters they've killed. Still, I do note that we mostly allow the Erethrans to interact with them. No surprise there—the Galactics are probably more used to switching from a desperate battle to non-aggressive stances than we humans are.

Of course, except for when I quickly loot the Field Boss, as requested by Lana, I'm busy with other, more human things. I don't even have time to do more than absently note that I've Leveled again.

"Yes, I'm alive."

"No, no communication possible. There was only one, semi-functioning Shop."

"Yes, I got my Master Class."

"No. I can't say where it was."

"Yes, it was hard. I missed you guys too."

"Yes. I did have to grandstand like that."

"Yes, I did see your new Levels. Congratulations times ten. Or twenty."

"No, I haven't checked in on Vancouver yet."

And on, and on. The shouted questions, the exclamations of surprise and joy, the hastily blurted answers and explanations take up the next hour before we finally make our way back to the temporary camp. That the camp is well-organized and made up of almost-permanent-looking structures, formed by Skill and Spell, is somehow less surprising than its sheer size.

Unsurprisingly perhaps, the conversations and questions continue to come as we adjourn to the mess hall and congregate around a pair of picnic tables, supping on an extensive buffet of food. Amelia and Mike join us, while others that I barely know, like the Calgarians and Seattle members, leave us alone after they welcome me back. Even then, I notice more than a few glances shot our way by the curious, but none intrude.

"Is it just me or is this really good?" I say, speaking around a mouthful of delicious barbecued monster. It's a mix between the succulent fleshiness of beef and the intense gaminess of lamb, with a delectable series of spices that mixes heat and sourness.

"It's very good," Mikito answers me with a smile. The Samurai has advanced incredibly in four years, sitting at Level 41 in her Class. It's a frightening increase and probably the largest jump I've seen among the group, even if she had the aid of others and full access to Quests and Shops in a Dungeon World.

I kind of feel cheated by the sheer amount of experience I lost, though I mentally comfort myself that it's only temporary. I'll "earn" it all back in time.

Of course, it probably helps that the tiny Japanese lady has been at the forefront of the majority of fighting in the last four years, shouldering the burden that had been mine. Her Title is a good indicator of exactly how important my old friend has become.

Title: Spear of Humanity

The owner of this title has gained significant fame and popularity amongst the remnant members of the human race for meritorious acts against monsters, member races of the Galactic Council, and other humans in defense of Earth.

Effects: title owner gains a 15% bonus in statistics when acting in defense of humans or when on Earth. +10% bonus in experience gain on Earth. Humans have a -10% debuff on attributes when attacking title owner.

I'll admit, I'm really jealous about the title. It's one of the most impressive titles, in terms of bonuses, I've ever seen, but the fact that it's probably one of a kind and based off worldwide fame contributes a lot to it, from what I understand about the System. After all, the damn leech of a System tends to draw from the masses to benefit the individual. And itself, of course.

"We often bring a Chef or three with us on these campaigns," Lana says, gesturing to where the cooking stations have been set up.

I find myself blinking, the contrast between our hurried and mostly combat Classer-based campaign four years ago and this more urbane affair giving me mental whiplash for a second.

As if she can read my mind, Lana continues. "As they're part of the official Warparty and providing an actual service, they can leech off the experience gain to advance their Levels. And the use of the exotic meats also increases their non-combat skill Levels too."

"It's a pretty common tactic," Ali adds from behind the five-plate-high stack of food he has spread before him. In his larger form, the Spirit seems to have decided to gorge himself, somehow managing to put away more than twice as much food as anyone else. Which is impressive when you realize we're almost all combat Classers. "There's a bunch of Artisans running around camp too, making themselves useful. They get experience, first pick of the scavenged loot and employment. Outside of a few groups—like the Erethrans—this is a very common setup for large scale campaigns. Cheaper too, since you can fire the idiots at any time."

"Got it," I say to Ali and look over at Lana. I wonder if it's my increase in Charisma or Perception, or just the fact that I'm paying more attention, but I've noticed a few things since I've come back. The hug. The fact that she's seated near me, but on the opposite side of the table. How she's speaking less and avoiding looking me directly in the eyes. In my gut, I know the answer, even if I don't want to acknowledge it yet. I push that thought aside for now. "So where's the rest of the team?"

Silence descends over the table. Amelia and Mike, the ex-RCMP officers and now Guardians, fall silent, staring at Lana, who is forced to answer via peer pressure.

"Ingrid no longer works with us exclusively. She flits around, playing mercenary assassin. She calls these large-scale battles idiot lines. Carlos is back in Vancouver. He retired from the front lines a year ago, after Beijing, and now runs an alchemy corporation. He still comes out once in a while, but his wife—" Lana shoots a glance at Mikito, who acts as if she doesn't notice. "Well. He's busy. Sam… we lost him at Beijing to an assassination."

I wince, looking down. Damn it. I liked the old man. After a moment, I meet Lana's eyes, asking softly, "Who else?"

The list comes quickly. Some I haven't seen since our journey to the States. Humans from Whitehorse and BC, names and faces that float upward from the depths of my memory with little effort. Many are a brief memory. Elder Badger from Carcross—dead in her sleep. Chetan, the Healer-mage from Seattle, torn apart by a Master Class fighter in Austin. Aron Hauser, the Yerrick, fallen while running a dungeon that had overrun its resources. More names, more faces. Fewer than I had feared, but still too many. Sometimes they speak of others that I don't recall, individuals they've met and befriended and lost. But eventually, they run out of names.

Perhaps it's the listing of the dead in its entirety. Perhaps it's just the reminder of what happened and the losses faced. Or perhaps it's just the realization that for all that has happened, all that we have faced together, our time together was, in the end, brief. Shorter than the time I was away. A lot has happened, a lot has been lost, and I've been nowhere to be found. I am a stranger to their lives.

A somber air takes over our table, one that is deepened as my friends take turns outlining what has happened in the last few years, filling me in.

Perhaps the least surprising aspect is that after my disappearance, the push to free human cities eventually slowed down. The first six months saw significant momentum in the United States, but they faced greater and greater resistance as time moved along. Many of the major powers that had been taking their time started acting, outright purchasing settlements from other Galactics—and a few humans—before directly transporting over masses of their people. And these weren't Basic Classes that arrived but swarms of Advanced Classes and a few Masters.

To combat the ever-increasing speed of reinforcements from the Galactics, Miller and the team switched to an opportunistic approach in aiding settlements. Using smaller, specialized human teams, along with help from the Erethran Army and the Harkarta's Sixty-Third Division, a series of focused campaigns were carried out on settlements that were ready to be freed. On top of that, of course, Miller's combined army continued to push east.

Unfortunately, each battle wore down their army, losses continually mounting. Each new settlement taken needed guards, men to watch over them and build up the settlements. Reinforcements were sparse, coming from individuals who trickled in from other locations. The breaking point in the States was when we lost—and regained—Denver in a period of two weeks. Rather than push forward, Miller decided to call a stop to the expansion to train and reinforce newly retaken settlements. While guerilla warfare continued—and continues—the results have grown significantly less promising. In effect, we seem to be in a state of cold war with the remaining Galactics.

On a personal level, all my settlements continue to belong to me and thrive. In fact, due to skillful management under Lana, Kim, and Katherine, the west coast of Canada has become an important Leveling hub. With a trade and transportation agreement in place with Roxley and one of the few "safe" overland routes to Alberta and to the high-Level zones in the Yukon, we experienced a significant northern migration from the States. While Alberta and the prairie provinces have finally been—mostly—freed, the losses and delay in setting up Towns saw a slower growth factor.

Unfortunately, a two-part alliance among a pair of Galactic powerhouses has stopped us from taking over the majority population centers of Ontario, their ruthless tactics, including the massacre and relocation of the entire Montreal population, have forced us to put a pause on our expansion. A constant stream of refugees and freed Serfs escape to the west, with the prairie towns bearing the brunt of retaliatory attacks for continuing to accept our humans. In the meantime, the combat forces Lana has gathered train and Level in ritualized combat, like the most recent battle.

As for the States, fractured by politics, the United States is united no longer. Instead, the west coast, the south—including much of New Mexico and Texas—and the area around Washington DC have all formed into three separate blocs consisting of freed human cities and a few allied Galactic cities. They call themselves variations of the "legal" representation of the real government of course, with regular political negotiations occurring as they attempt to patch the country back together.

As for the rest, including the so-called flyover states, their settlements are owned and run by the Galactics, with a few scattered human warlords and monster-infested hellholes. The Truinnar make up the largest portion of the owners in North America and South America at the moment, which has placed our own settlement in an interesting political position with friends on both sides.

On a global scale, matters are somewhat less depressing. Perhaps due to their large populations, India, Brazil, Pakistan, Japan, Nigeria, Korea, and China all managed to keep control of the majority of their cities. Of course, many of the borders that we knew have been redrawn, with many of the larger countries fracturing into smaller governments. Local warlords rule their four-, five-, six-city empires with a diverse number of rules and regulations. Not surprisingly, negotiations continue as visionaries and despots attempt to stitch together larger countries.

While Europe was densely populated, it seemed to have been adversely affected by a significant Galactic presence. No one knows why, but it seems many larger Galactic corporations decided that western Europe was a wonderful location to first set up shop. Humans, in the grand scheme of things, became nothing more than pawns, forced to flee while the Galactics battled one another. The Movana in particular hold a significant portion of western Europe. Unlike our knockdown, drag-out wars though, the Galactics seem prone to smaller-scale, ritualized combat. Mike is happy to regale me with the story of how Eindhoven was won after a single battle between a pair of Master Class individuals, which left both parties battered but alive.

Ironically, the increased number of European refugees into northern Africa actually helped stabilize human settlements there, giving us a band of powerful

29

helpers in that region. It's where many of the members of the army around us come from actually. Outside of that, Africa is a hodgepodge of settlements and interest groups, with few "powerful" blocs in charge of more than a half-dozen cities. But Africa's a big place, and empty as it might be at times, a few major governments have arisen. Frighteningly enough, Africa has some of the greatest concentrations of high Level combat classers in the world.

As for Australia… well, the less said about that pitiful continent, the better. It certainly lived up to its moniker of the most poisonous continent. The few humans who survive there are holding on by the skin of their teeth.

"So basically, humans being humans and no one joins together?" I say with a grimace. Unfortunately, while we might band together in the short term, in the long term, self-interest often wins out.

"Not completely. Some groups have started forming," Lana says with a sigh. "With the Planetary Voting Platform happening every month, it's forced a certain amount of macrolevel grouping. Quite a few of the interest groups are geography-based, but some are champion-based."

"Champion?"

"People like our little Mikito," Lana says, inclining her head as Mikito flushes slightly in embarrassment. "People who have become famous enough that they're a significant political force by themselves."

"I don't do politics," Mikito grumbles and points at Lana. "She's considered a player too."

"Only because of John's—your—settlements," Lana says firmly. "Which we'll need to talk about."

"We will," I assure the redhead. There's so much to catch up on. So much to understand. We haven't even scratched other topics that puzzle me, like the presence of the Erethran Army.

But before we can dig deeper into the past, others break in. As much as they might be my friends, they're also people of import and they have duties, important duties, that have been put aside for long enough. One by one, they're dragged off to deal with problems that only they can solve. And eventually, I find myself alone but for Ali.

Again.

***

"Redeemer." The low, gravelly voice with a British accent takes me out of the notifications Ali has been piling in front of me.

Left alone, I was taking the time to catch up on what has been happening, with Ali sorting and sending me relevant pieces of data. I might have received an overview from my friends, but four years leaves a lot to cover.

"Major Ruka." I look up, grinning at the big, ugly, tusky Hakarta. Damn, I'd forgotten how ugly they are up close.

"Colonel now," Labashi says with a touch of pride as he sits down next to me without asking.

"Ah. Congratulations. It's your command here then?" I say, tilting my head toward where the Hakarta continue to clean up.

"Yes."

"Nice."

"I wanted to come by and congratulate you on your promotion and return. And thank you. The contract we established has been extremely lucrative," Labashi says.

"Mh'sái" I wave aside his thanks. "I understand you've been a lot of help. You and the Erethrans."

One thing I like about Labashi is how smart he is. He picks up on the hint immediately. "Ms. Pearson and General Miller made arrangements after your disappearance. Earth is now an official training ground for the Erethran Army. Earth—your people—pays the long-range teleportation fees for the army. In turn, they provide support during such engagements."

Huh. I consider how that works. I doubt the Erethrans are at the pure beck and call of our people—it makes no sense for them to make such a deal—but I don't bother asking Labashi. It's unlikely he knows, and if he does, it's unlikely he'd tell me. After all, I have a much better and more reliable source of information for this, and his revelation of such knowledge could be considered rude. No one likes having their allies spy on them.

"And your contract…" I say, leading him on. I might as well figure out the details on those.

Labashi flashes me another grin and leans forward, and suddenly, I'm reminded of our first meeting so many years ago. But this time, we're finally on an even playing field, our Levels nearly the same and both of us having something the other wants.

An hour and a half later, Lana finally finds us, our conversation mostly over. The new contract is ready for inspection and for details to be hammered out. This time around, I refused to let Labashi push me into signing it immediately, allowing people like Lana and Katherine to review our new agreement in more detail. Still, the outline should be fine—increased presence of the Hakarta in our cities, using them as additional security forces for minor concessions in terms of buildings, access to the dungeons—which we now have four of—and of course, Credits.

Overall, I feel quite smug. Until Lana comes over, a thunderous look on her face.

"John. We need to talk."

***

We walk in tense silence, headed out of the campgrounds. Ali, smartly, disappeared the moment Lana showed up. Of course, he's floating right beside me, lounging in the air at full size—which is a really disturbing sight, by the way—but Lana is unable to see him.

As we pass the first set of guards, I finally open my mouth. "Lana—"

"Not yet," Lana says curtly.

I follow, tight-lipped as we walk into the dark desert whose temperature is already dropping. From the shadows, I catch glimpses of the puppies and Roland as they spread out to deal with any potential threats. I look up but don't spot the griffin, which reminds me that I know very little about those animals. The true ones and not the Mana-corrupted legends we have. After five minutes, I try again and am hushed.

Only when we are a couple of kilometers away from everyone does Lana stop. From her storage, she pulls and sets up a simple, metallic scepter. In the darkness, I can see the slight flush in her cheeks, the tension in her shoulders.

"Now we can speak," Lana states. When I open my mouth to do so, I find a finger up in my face. "What the hell were you thinking you were doing?"

"Talking—"

"Negotiating! With Labashi," Lana snaps.

"You make it sound like he's an enemy."

"He's a mercenary. A friendly one, but a merc," Lana says fiercely. "And you had no right to negotiate with him. None!"

"Actually—"

"Don't give me that settlement owner garbage," Lana snarls, waving her finger in my face. My eyes narrow, her words igniting the anger inside me as she plows on. "You've been gone for four years. Four! We've been taking care of all of it in your place. The negotiations. The politics. The endless meetings and assassination attempts. And you've never even once contacted me!"

I open my mouth to protest, to explain, to shout back. But at the end, there's a slight hitch in her words, a hiccup. I stare, the anger doused as understanding sweeps through me. Then I step closer, ignoring her finger, and wrap my arms around the redhead, hugging her tightly. She struggles at first, but I've always been stronger than her. And eventually, she stops and just cries, her hands gripping me with nails digging into my back as she sobs.

"Damn you. Damn it…"

Lana eventually regains control, pushing against me more insistently. I let her go and she steps back, staring at me for a long time.

I can't help but smile slightly. "You're not going to slap me, are you?"

"If it wouldn't hurt my hand more than your face, I might," Lana says grumpily. "Baka."

I chuckle, glad to hear Mikito's trademark insult for me. When Lana sighs again, shaking her head, and steps back and away from me, I realize it's nearly time for the real talk.

"John…" Lana says hesitantly.

"I know. You've got someone else," I say softly. I feel a flash of pain, a deep ache in my chest and stomach that I ruthlessly quash. Not right now. "Anyone I know?"

"No. We met in South America…"

I shake my head. "If you don't mind, I'd rather not know. Not right now."

Lana looks hurt for a second then smooths out her face, nodding in confirmation. "About Labashi. You really shouldn't have done that. He's a friend, and the deal you made isn't bad. But there's more in play than you realize. There are factions who want, need, that space."

34

I consider what she said and I sigh. She's right. I tried to take some of that into account while negotiating, but what's available to Ali is significantly less than what is probably held in Lana's head.

"Sorry. I did leave the deal unsigned," I say, gesturing slightly and sending over the details. "I'm sure we can adjust it, if necessary."

"It will be," Lana mutters, staring at the document for a second before she dismisses the notification. "It's... later. I'll deal with it later."

"And about the settlements..." I consider what to say. Eventually, I go with the simplest. "Thank you."

"You're welcome." Lana stares at me for a moment then steps forward to give me a hard hug, murmuring into my chest, "I'm glad you're back."

"So am I."

***

After that, we end up speaking about other things, just catching up. Even if our lives revolve around the System and the changes that have happened, we've still got lives. Hopes and dreams. Or at least, Lana does—and it's her who ends up speaking mostly, gossiping about familiar friends, about changes in the settlement and mutual acquaintances. I find out that Jason and Rachel now have a trio of kids, the ankle-biters incredibly cute. Based on the videos that I view, I swear, all three of the kids must have specced Charisma.

I learn a lot about the world I left behind and the changes that have happened, the growth of the settlements. And perhaps one other thing—the deep pride Lana holds over the settlements, their growth and improvement. Vancouver's a Large Town now, well on its way to being a city.

Hours pass quickly, and I can almost forget the last few years and think we are back. But there's a distance between us now, a change in our relationship that neither of us dares prod or push too far. When I consider it, it leaves a dull ache in my heart, but it's dull. Perhaps because I always dreaded this, always feared something like this for when I returned. Or perhaps I've just pushed down the pain.

We talk, and eventually we part when we hit the second sentry group, the guards offering quick nods to us. Lana heads deeper into the compound while I stand at the edge, repressed thoughts and emotions churning.

Logically, I understand what happened—I was gone for years, with little guarantee that I'd be back, and we never had the relationship conversation even when we were together. We'd been working toward something more permanent, but we had both been hurt. And busy. So damn busy. Then I disappeared right after she lost Anna, leaving her to pick up the pieces of my settlements and an alliance that had relied on my Skill. Is it any surprise that she eventually found comfort somewhere else? If I hadn't been stuck on a barren rock filled with murderous monsters and aliens, I might have succumbed too.

"John," Mikito greets me as she walks up, the Japanese lady completing her perimeter walk. "You okay?"

"Perfectly fine," I say, looking at her.

"Then stop standing at the perimeter without moving. You're scaring the guards," Mikito says.

I frown, wondering why, then realize I've been standing here for minutes. Huh. "I…"

"Come on," Mikito says, gesturing for me to start walking.

I frown but follow her, curious about where she's taking me before realizing it's probably just to have another chat. A part of me wants to decline, to back out. Heart-to-hearts are draining. But…

"On the platform."

36

I blink, realizing we're standing in the middle of a clearing dominated by a small glowing platform that looks like Star Trek's teleportation array, bracketed by gleaming steel pillars. I frown, but Mikito's already walking onto it and looking at me impatiently, so I join her.

"Where are we going?"

"To work."

Lights flare, growing so bright I have to squint before the world lurches, sending my stomach and senses spinning. And then the world disappears.

Chapter 4

"This." Stab. "Is." Pivot. "Not." Kick. "What." Cast. "I." Cut. "Was." Lunge. "Expecting."

I recover and look around at the dead bodies of the monsters we've been fighting littered all around us. I do a mental tally and relax slightly when the number of half-dismembered heads and corpses equal the number of attackers I counted. The minimap agrees, but my time in the other world has made me rely on it much less. Too many ways for it to be tricked or be wrong.

For a moment, I regard the monster remains. Truly weird, these Penangallan. They start the fights with their full bodies, but if they aren't killed immediately, they detach halfway through the fight and float their now tougher and more impervious heads and innards to attack us. That they use a combination of magic and an acid spit attack makes them even more annoying. As it stands, the pitted and scarred concrete and marble hallway is evidence of how hard they fought.

With a growl, I shake my head and glance out the hotel hallway to stare at the abandoned remnants of the city of Davao in the Philippines. Luckily, the teleportation managed to get us close to the city center, allowing us to meet up with the rest of the team here, rather than fighting through the monster-infested city.

"Does he always complain like that?" Hugo Karlsson, the six-foot-eight-inches, blond-haired, blue-eyed ubermensch asks.

I glance at the Level 21 Winter Ranger and find him staring back at me challengingly. Once again, I break eye contact first rather than push things.

"Come now, Hugo, you are being unfair. Mr. Lee has helped us clear this dungeon much faster," Jamal Naser, the Level 39 Desert Seer, says to defend me. The native berber from Morocco nods at me, the older man with the rectangular face and dusky skin standing up from the corpses he has finished looting to wipe his left hand clean. Thankfully, I've got Ali to do my looting for me.

"Faster. But not needed," Cheng Shao says.

"True. But I didn't ask to join you," I say to Shao, wondering what I did to annoy the black-haired Metal Mage.

Unfortunately, from the moment Mikito portaled us to this city, we barely had time for more than a few words of greeting before we launched our attack. Even at a glance, I can tell why we're here—this dungeon is about to overrun its boundaries. We've got a ton of monsters to kill, making the trip through the space-altering, gravity-defying hotel floors even more annoying than normal. That the monsters are all at least Level 80, with some elites hitting Level 100, doesn't make our fight any easier. It says something about the team we're working with that we're still cutting through the dungeon like a five-year-old with cake.

Then again, Shao and Hugo are both Master Classes. I admit, it was a bit of a blow to my ego to realize I'm not that special. After all, when the System came, others managed to luck out with their Perks and skip a Class level like me. And really, it's a good thing for humanity that there are others who can kick ass.

"We can understand that," Jamal replies to me, since no one else does. "But you'll also understand that being pulled away from our normal duties for an unscheduled delve can be frustrating. We all have responsibilities."

"Photo ops," Mikito says with a sniff. "Speeches."

"Not all of us crave the front lines," a wide-hipped, curly-haired, short black woman with a strong Southern accent replies. Jessica Knox, Level 37 Cat Burglar and our scout for this little delve. I have to admit, she's a looker with curves that go on for days, dark skin, and dreads to keep her curls in place.

"Move please." Rae, the last member of the team rolls up in his mecha as he speaks, smaller mechanical arms whirling and buzzing as the arms exit the enclosed cockroach-like vehicle-cum-armor. Within seconds, the body next to me is dismembered, the mechanical arms pulling out the important parts and storing them away.

Normally, I'd put the bodies into my Altered Storage space, but I've yet to visit a proper Shop to sell four years' worth of valuable corpses. Anyway, mecha man is getting all the expensive bits.

"Map update incoming," the robotic voice says.

I grunt, getting the new notification from Rae. Just Rae. No last name, no indicator of sex. Other than the fact that he or she is a Level 42 Silver Cyborg, I've got nothing. And discreet inquiries to Mikito has yielded no further information. Rae doesn't leave its robot—if it can. In fact, outside of such campaigns, Rae doesn't interact with the rest of the champions. Still, their Skills and abilities are useful.

Using its skills, Rae attached a bug to Jessica for when she scouts. That bug then gives us a map of the areas the Burglar has explored, along with the monsters she's seen. The level of detail in the updates is higher than anything I ever got from my drones—or Sam did from his—which is pretty impressive. It's another reason why we're kicking this dungeon's ass. That Rae's bugs can punch the basic updates to us through the dense Mana cloud inside the dungeon is even more impressive.

"All I'm saying is that we're wasting good XP on this newcomer," Hugo says.

I almost grind my teeth but push the anger aside. After all, Hugo was just a kid when all this started. And even if I don't agree with the trend of seeing our new world as a game, he's obviously made it work for him. And again, I remind myself, I'm an outsider here.

"This is a working introduction," Mikito says simply, pointing with her naginata down the curved hallway. "So let's work."

"He doesn't deserve to be here," Shao says, her eyes glittering with contempt. "What has he done? I've never even heard of him."

"Explorer. Monster Bane. Duelist. Master Class," Rae's metallic voice chirps from the trundling mecha. "Significant achievements."

"And no fame," Jessica says, shaking her head. "You know he won't be accepted by the public."

"Who cares about that?" Jamal says with a snort. "I'm happy to have another reliable body clearing these dungeons. Or on the front lines."

"I do," Jessica snaps. "I've got sponsorship deals to worry about here."

"You know, no one's asked if I want to be part of your little book club," I say, frowning at the surge of dots coming.

I raise my hand, forming an Enhanced Lightning Strike then punch it out without a word of warning. The Lightning darts forward, formed through the connection and channel I've created. The bright streaks of light hurt our eyes in the enclosed space. The Penangallan that get caught scream, twitching in agony as the lightning cooks their innards. It doesn't take long before the other members add their area effect spells and Skills, tearing up the next wave before it reaches us.

"We're the champions," Jamal says, as if that statement is sufficient.

I guess, for many, it would be. After all, not to mention the fame and Credits they earn, the experience gains from running higher Level dungeons on a consistent basis would be very attractive. In this new world, Levels are power, just like money used to be in our previous world. It doesn't matter where you are, Levels talk.

As for Jamal's presumptuous statement, I stay silent. It's not my job to correct his misconceptions and overblown ego. While they might see this as a protracted interview, a testing ground to see if I'm worthy to join them, I'm taking it as a nice way to let loose a little. Not all the way, since I'd like to keep a few cards hidden, but enough to work out some of the frustrations that have been boiling up inside me. Juvenile perhaps, but hitting things is therapeutic. Stuck as I was, I've learned to take my stress relief where I can, even if it's in the middle of a battlefield.

My continued silence drives the group to turn to other topics. Discussions about Skills, spells, and equipment dominate at first, with tactics and weird monsters leading. I keep an ear out, especially since most of these creatures sit around my target range. It's kind of nice to be around people who can relate. But eventually, the topic shifts as we ascend the hotel floors.

"Hey, Cheng, were you able to get those tickets for KMC?" Jessica asks pleadingly. "You promised!"

"It's Shao. I've told you before," Cheng Shao says. "And their manager has promised us VIP passes. But they might have to delay the concert."

"Again?" Jessica says grumpily.

"Soo-yi hasn't managed to Level yet. They're planning to hit that new Level 70 dungeon north of Seoul first," Shao explains as her hands move, enchanted knives darting through the air to intercept and stab the Penangallan that attempt to swarm her.

"Oh, come on, you're going on about that band again?" Hugo groans.

"And why shouldn't we? Their music is great!"

"It's manufactured and sterile. It's no wonder they can kill with their songs. I'd die if I had to listen to their music again," Hugo says grumpily.

"Please, you're still bitter we won that bet."

"Bet?" I mutter to Mikito as I duck, grabbing twisted intestines and slamming the body into a nearby wall.

"They made us listen to the band's greatest hits on a delve. On repeat. For eight hours," Mikito says with a roll of her eyes.

"Oh." I stare at the disgusting bunch of intestines that the System considers "loot" from the Penangallan before handing them to Mikito.

The samurai doesn't even blink as she stores them away. It's Credits. Even if my culinary preferences are broad, I'm not entirely sure I want to know the eventual use of those. Sometimes, ignorance is bliss when it comes to gastronomic delights.

"The band runs dungeons?" I say with a frown, considering what I've overheard.

"Yes. They're an Advanced Class team, sixth highest ranked in Seoul's Adventurer Team chart," Jessica burbles happily. "Of course, not all the original members of KMC survived, but most did. And they all have the Class Siren.

"At first, they Leveled up from a variety of Basic musician and entertainer Classes, but their manager had them run a dangerous Advanced Class dungeon. The surviving members all got the Advanced Class Siren, and their 'Song of Redemption' can boost stats up to ten percent for six hours. And it's partially stackable!"

At first, I attempt to stop the gush of information, but when I realize that the talk is actually annoying Hugo—and somehow, not stopping Jessica from doing her job—I leave her to it. It's a bit disturbing that she manages to project her voice from kilometers away to continue chattering while scouting, but Skills are weird.

Eventually, after numerous wrong turns, we make our way to the end of the dungeon. At one point, Mikito stops to deal with the fallout of stealing me away in the middle of the night, making muttered promises to return me over her communicator. But the violence is useful, giving me time to not only assess

Earth's best but also to vent. Not that every single one of the "champions" are here, but the majority of them are.

When we finally put down the dungeon boss—a fight that had little suspense and fewer surprises beyond the wide-scale Iron Whirlwind spell cast by Cheng Shao—the group quickly loots the various corpses before reaching the objective of the mission. Davao's City Core also serves as the Dungeon Core.

"Whose turn is it?" Jamal asks, none of the group moving to touch the Core that glows quietly in the middle of the once-immaculate ballroom.

"Mine," Jessica says before placing her hand on it.

We all get the notification, and for the next few minutes, things get busy as the monsters go into a frenzy, intent on driving Jessica away from the orb. Unfortunately for them, we're fighting a defensive battle here, which makes things significantly simpler. The monsters, on the other hand, have multiple floors to ascend and a chokepoint to force their way through. It's a slaughter.

The moment Jessica takes over the settlement and dungeon core, she banishes the dungeon settings, which leads to an exodus of Mana from our surroundings. That'll cause its own set of problems in the city as the Mana searches for a way to purge itself. Eventually, a new dungeon will form. For now, Jessica purchases upgrades to the building we're in, reinforcing the steel doors and adding a few automated sentinels on this level and the bottom one, making the entrance to the core more difficult.

"That'll do for now," Jessica says, eyeing the giant steel doors that now block off access to the City Core. "We'll be teleporting guards in once I've reported back."

At those words and the obvious dismissal, the team splits up. Shao and Hugo activate communicators, pinging their location to their people before they're teleported away. Rae rolls out, headed for the roof. Ali sends me an image of the reinforced blimp-like flying vehicle that is slowly floating toward the hotel, ready for a pickup. Jamal, on the other hand, stays behind with Jessica in the City Core. That leaves Mikito and myself to walk down the stairs alone, in thoughtful silence for a time.

"So I'm guessing I failed?" I say, a sardonic grin twisting my lips.

"No. They're just uncertain," Mikito says. "Once your reputation rises…"

"It's fine. I wasn't joking when I said I wasn't interested."

"What did you think?" Mikito asks, and there's a plaintive tone in her voice that makes me pause.

I actually consider the question properly, reviewing in my mind what I saw. "They're good. They all understand how to control their Skills, Mana, and Stamina drain. I don't even recall anyone using any potions. Well-coordinated. Could be better, but considering you guys probably don't fight together all the time, more than adequate. No one's left alone to run out of Mana or Stamina. This wasn't the hardest test, but they passed it with flying colors anyway."

"We've had a lot of practice."

"Yes. But…" I consider how to put this. How to explain some of what I've learned, what I've had to expand on. "They're too reliant on the surface. They use the basics of their attribute gains, their Skills, and don't dig further."

"What do you mean?" Mikito says with a frown.

"Our attribute increases aren't linear. There's some overlap between each individual, but the differences between races are significant. Well, part of that is because we're not looking in the right places," I say softly. "Strength is the simplest example. A ten-point increase in it doesn't just increase your lifting power. It affects how that lifting power affects other System-registered entities. It lets you ignore a portion of their defense, of their health, if you know how to tap into it. It allows you to do this." I push off with a toe, flinging myself into the air and against a nearby wall, then I push again with a finger when I hit it, flinging myself toward the ceiling. Each of those movements leave the floor and wall untouched, but when I reach the ceiling, I exert my Strength in a different way, shattering the ceiling tiles as I push myself toward the ground, only to land without disturbing the floor. "And this."

Mikito's eyes widen, staring at the four spots I've touched, even as the dust from my example falls around us. Every action has an equal and opposite reaction—except when it doesn't. We've all kind of accepted that the System breaks "normal" laws, but what I've learned is that it doesn't. It's just that we aren't seeing the other forces, aren't understanding the whole picture.

"It's just the start," I say, tapping my head. "Willpower gifts us Mana Regeneration and ways of dealing with manipulation spells. But it can alter and shift how Skills like Auras and Charisma work. It can even make the information we feed the System more obscure. Willpower dictates your pain resistance and your recovery rates. It even, from what I can see, deals with things like PTSD if used correctly. Every attribute has a different application than we think, but we don't use it."

"Is this what you learned? When you were gone?" Mikito asks softly, staring at my solemn expression. I nod before she huffs, "Guess you weren't on the beach."

"No. And I'm not going to be lazing around here either. I've got a lot to catch up on and playing hero isn't my goal. Certainly not for fame or Credits."

"Isn't it?" Mikito says, stepping forward and looking into my eyes. "Wasn't that what we were doing? Before you left."

"No. We were doing what was necessary."

"Necessary for what?"

I come to a stop as I realize that Mikito never did ask. Not the entire time we worked together. She accepted my lead, following where I pointed. For a time, I stand there, blinking as the realization hits.

"John…?"

"Sorry." I shake my head, dismissing the thought. "Necessary for us to survive. And for me to get the settlements so I could vote."

"The Planetary election," Mikito states.

"Yes," I say, nodding firmly. "We need to get on the Galactic Council."

Mikito purses her lips, tilting her head as she considers me. "That will help Earth?"

"Yes. We'd have more say, more options. We'd be able to put rules in place once we're officially registered. We'd gain status."

"The difference between a System-registered town and one not," Mikito says, floating the sentence for me to confirm. When I do, she nods firmly. "What can I do?"

"I'm not sure. Not yet," I say.

"Ask."

I offer her a nod in confirmation.

"And when that's done? What's next?"

"Then I leave. The Council, the galaxy. There's a lot more going on, out there, than the fight for a single planet. Our world, our losses, they're a drop in an unimaginably large ocean," I say.

Mikito purses her lips, staring at me as she considers what I've said. In the end, she gestures to the side. "Portal back, please."

"Sure. I'm going straight to Vancouver though," I say even as I open one back to the army camp.

Mikito pauses before she steps into the Portal, the black oval swallowing her without a ripple. I'm left in the red carpeted hallway, the damage to the ceiling slowly but visibly patching itself up, alone once again with the silence and my thoughts.

That last silent look... I draw a deep breath, wondering how much she guessed. Because there is another reason why I—we—need to get on the Galactic Council. I need to get out there, to see and learn more. There are answers to my questions in the wider world, answers that cannot be found on Earth. As I stand in silence in the dimly lit hall, a memory surfaces.

"These questions about the System, they're dangerous," Ka'lla d'Mak says. Butt-length yellow-green hair spills down his back as he walks ahead of me, heading deeper into the cave system we call home. "I was forced to live here because of them."

"But the answers are out there." I limp along, dragging the eight-ton, ninety-foot-long corpse.

"Some answers aren't worth your life," Ka'lla says.

"Some are."

"Then be wary who you ask. And how you ask. For everyone under the System may be your enemy."

"Yes."

Memory. I push it aside, staring around me as the sense of paranoia and wariness I thought had disappeared comes back. That's right. Earth isn't mine anymore. Or me, its.

With a gesture, a Portal opens and I step forward. Time to get to work.

Chapter 5

"Mr. Lee. Welcome back." Katherine greets me from behind my—her?—desk as I step through the Portal into my office. Or her office. If you leave a place for four years, do you lose it? Even if my ownership has been kept, it's not as if Katherine and Lana haven't been running my settlements for me.

Coming through the Portal, I had Ali slide in first to make sure I didn't have to worry about anything. Thankfully, I didn't. I'll admit, I would have been annoyed if I wasn't pre-approved to Portal into my own settlements. The last thing I want to do is have my atoms torn apart while Portaling home.

I offer a quick nod to my assistant as she stands and moves swiftly and calmly from around the desk. The older ex-secretary is dressed in a finely cut office suit, one in pale grey that suits her figure completely and sets off the light grey in her hair well. I absently note that she's got a rather distinctive necklace, which I'm pretty sure is enchanted. A brief viewing of her via Mana Sense confirms that intuition, and furthermore that her earrings, belt, and a bracelet are all enchanted. An impressive amount of magical equipment for an Assistant. Then again, other than Lana, she was—is—the individual in charge of one of the largest settlement groups in North America. Or would you call it a country?

Katherine Ward (Level 18 Settlement Manager)
HP: 410/410
MP: 1023/1480
Conditions: Ablative Shield, Pre-cognitive sense, Settlement Link

Well, I guess she's not really an Assistant anymore. Her rise in Level is a bit surprising, as is her new Class. But I guess being officially hired and running my settlements has done wonders for her experience gain.

"WELCOME BACK," Kim, my settlement AI answers.

Almost immediately, I get a notification that my AI has upgraded since I left, going up a Tier and increasing its processing powers significantly. Since we left Kim linked up to the Vancouver settlement City Cores, I'm not surprised that the AI had been upgraded along with the city. Notifications pile up in the corner of my eyes, most of which I ignore for now.

"UPDATING NEURAL LINK WITH SETTLEMENT INFORMATION ALONG WITH NECESSARY SECURITY PROTOCOLS, PASSES, AND DATA. PLEASE WAIT."

"Oy, bits for brains, you keeping our settlements running?" Ali says as he stands in the middle of the office, acting like a crazy person talking into empty space. Thank the gods I learned how to mentally chat with him a long time ago, or else I'd really look insane.

"WITHOUT ADDITIONAL ORDERS TO THE CONTRARY, I HAVE BEEN AIDING MS. PEARSON AND MS. WARD IN DEVELOPING THE SETTLEMENTS. AN UPDATED REPORT ON ALL CHANGES HAS BEEN UPLOADED," Kim notifies us via blue notification tab that he / her / it speaks in. One day, I swear, I'll land on a sex or designation for Kim. But I think it is probably out. It just feels so inhumane. Which, I'll admit, is technically correct. "I HAVE ALSO TAKEN THE LIBERTY TO INFORM THE SECURITY FORCES OUTSIDE TO STAND DOWN."

"Thank you, Katherine. Kim," I say, ignoring the last line. Not as if they'd actually shoot me. Would they? Actually, maybe having random people who Portal into my office without a direct invitation get shot as a matter of course is good protocol. "I'll review the data later. And I'm glad we won't need to switch out the furniture here."

"Just the furniture?" Kim asks and I grin wolfishly. I'm pretty sure I could contain the destruction if needed.

"Do you not consider our security forces sufficient?" Katherine asks.

"To deal with me? A pair of Level 17 Advanced Bodyguards?" I snort. "Even before I left, it wouldn't be sufficient. Though they probably could buy you the time you'd need to activate that teleport beacon you've got stashed behind the desk."

Katherine raises an eyebrow, the only indication of surprise she allows herself. I don't elaborate on how the moment Ali swung in, he was already ripping information about the building from the City Core and sending me the relevant bits. Or how here, in the center of my own settlement, I basically have any information I want or need only a thought away. The degree of information I have access to is rather scary—and makes me realize how badly I underestimated how great an advantage Roxley had whenever I visited him. With the massive increases in Intelligence that I've gained, I can now do things like subconsciously download all those notifications Kim is pushing at me, something I could never do before my little trip.

"May I know what is the agenda for today?" Katherine asks, changing topics.

"You tell me. What were you going to be doing if I had not interrupted you?" I ask.

"I was about to spend the next hour reviewing and answering the correspondence left for me overnight. Next, I have a committee meeting with the integrated Vancouver council about the latest updates on our build cycle and zoning for additional industries and infrastructure. There has been a significant push to increase the available space for our marine salvage and hunting operations, with a request for a second butchering yard. Of course, there is concern that the additional refuse from the butchering yard and its ancillary industries will provoke additional marine threats." Katherine stops as she must see my eyes glaze over.

From what I can tell, her day is basically a series of meetings. It's just who she meets that changes—from the mayors of the other towns to Galactic Guilds, Corporations, or local ones, it seems like she's basically spending the day either in meetings or reading paperwork.

"Right…" I shudder slightly, considering delving back into all this. And then, I consider that I actually haven't been needed for the last four years and decide there isn't a point. "Here's what we're going to do. You're going to continue doing these meetings. I'm going to throw up a notification video and watch and listen in while I catch up on, well, everything. Fair enough?"

Katherine nods, accepting my words without complaint. At least for the moment. I'm glad because after my talking to by Lana, I figure it's better for me to get caught up before I mire myself in the running of my settlements. The fact that the settlements, together, really make up a country, even if we don't designate it that way, is just another reason to stay out of it.

"*Ali, got a few jobs for you.*" I send the thought to my Spirit as I take a seat behind the desk.

The Spirit startles slightly, guiltily putting back the pear he picked up from Katherine's desk, a neat bite marring its surface. Katherine perches on a chair opposite me, her eyes glazing over slightly as she returns to reading her notifications on screens only she can see.

"*Shoot, boy-o.*"

"*You'll like the first one. We need to dump my inventory and the corpses in my Altered Space. Think you can handle that?*"

"*Easy. I'll make sure to not fleece them too hard,*" Ali sends back, a slight smirk in his voice.

Good. That deals with clearing out my storage and getting some actual Credits, and this way, his new physical body can be put to good use. The corpses of the Level 120+ monsters that I kept in my Altered Space can easily increase the Levels of any Butcher, Skinner, or other Artisan who works on them, so it's best to get those out ASAP. And making some Credits and Leveling my people was the whole point of dragging them all the way back.

With that taken care of, I focus on the next steps. Getting to know my own settlements.

Summarized Settlement Status

Current Population: 498,308

Total Number of Settlements: 13

Combined Settlement Treasury: 4,314.87 Million Credits (+12M per day)

Combined Settlement Mana: 333,412 Mana Points (+981 Mana per day)

Taxes: 10% Sales Tax on Shop

Facilities of Note: City Dungeons (3), Tier II Guilds (1), Tier III Guild Buildings (9), Military Complex (2), Mega Farms (3), Tier III Butchering Yards (4), Tier III Weapons Workshop (1) Teleportation Pads (Short Range * 11, Long Range * 2), Artisans University (1), Hyperlink (3—see map for link)

Enchantments of Note: Mana Collection Fields (3), Mana Shield Resistance Enhancement (6), Field of Clarity (1)

Defenses of Note: Settlement Shields (Tier II * 1, III * 8), Quantum Lock (Type 2 Static, Type 4 Dynamic—see map for coverage), Sentries (Tier II * 3, III * 4)

"Thirteen settlements, Kim?"

"IT WAS DETERMINED, TO BE MORE EFFICIENT, TO LINK CITY CORES FOR GREATER VANCOUVER, VICTORIA, KELOWNA, AND OTHER LARGER CITIES. THE TOTAL NUMBER REPRESENT

THE NEW STRUCTURE," Kim replies. "DO YOU REQUIRE A LIST OF SUCH SETTLEMENTS?"

"Map will do."

"DONE."

I stare at the map of the province with its glowing dots, my lips pursed. Vancouver is the largest dot of course. Victoria, Kamloops, and Kelowna rival each other in size, with smaller settlements like Prince George, Golden, and Fort Nelson surprisingly large now. It takes only a single query to explain why—high Level zones nearby have boosted the Adventuring population around these cities, pushing their growth. Of interest to me as well is the fact that the quantum lock doesn't just include the cities but much of the land between the settlements on the mainland. Right now though, the lock doesn't include Victoria, leaving the city covered by its own little bubble. I'm interested by the little lines that create a triangle of high-speed transportation signifying the development of the hyperloop. A part of me wonders how they're keeping the monsters from wrecking it.

Oh. They aren't. That's why it's not been pushed out farther. I sigh, shaking my head. A part of me wonders who ever considered putting a delicate piece of technology in the field where random monster spawns could wreck it. A part of me wants to curse the rather wasteful use of my Credits, but another part points out I wasn't here. In the end, I settle for making a note to Kim that this is not to happen again. At least it's not a complete waste—it seems the hyperloop churns out a nice and repeatable series of Quests for both combat Classers and Artisans.

For a time, I stare at the stored Credits and Mana and briefly daydream about the kind of things I could do with that amount of funds. The sheer volume and variety of Skills I could buy… then I shake my head and dismiss the thought. Thankfully, it isn't possible to transfer settlement Credits into your own pocket—outside of some specific salary caps—or else the oldest kingdoms and corporations would be impossibly dominant. Not that they don't already have a nasty advantage over the rest of us.

"How many days of Mana and Credits is that? If we don't generate any additional," I ask, curious to get an idea of how we're doing.

"THE SETTLEMENT MANA BURN RATE IS NINETEEN DAYS. CREDITS ARE SIX."

"That's not good," I mutter.

"What isn't, Mr. Lee?" Katherine asks, looking at me.

"We don't seem to have much in reserve," I say, waving at the screen she can't see and realizing that only after I do so.

"Are you looking at the financials?" When I nod, she continues. "It was a decision made by the council to emphasize growth over stability at this time, with the attendant risks."

"Nineteen days though?" I can understand that reasoning, but why is the Mana reserve so much higher?

"Researching and applying appropriate settlement-wide enchantments have been slow. Our next scheduled update will see the addition of a Mage's College to the Artisans University," Katherine says.

I nod. A good decision overall. I fall silent, prodding the screen a little more and getting confirmation that the settlement notification is hiding anything below Tier III. It means that most generic upgraded buildings like residences, System-registered retail stores, or workshops are left out.

I dig into the settlement screen, pulling up specific information for each city as I try to get a better understanding of the state of affairs. Katherine leaves with a soft goodbye to head for her meeting down the hallway, a simple gesture getting me the in-house video feed. I lower the volume and split my attention as I continue reading.

Interestingly enough, unlike my previous decision, they've integrated the other cities around Vancouver into a single collective settlement. Burnaby, Surrey, and the like still have their own Cores, but they aren't City Cores anymore, instead earmarked as Neighborhood Cores. One of the main advantages of this setup is that a Neighborhood Core can be taken over like any City Core, but it only removes access for the original owner. It does not confer upon the conqueror any of the abilities of the Core, which is basically in a "shutdown" mode until the main City Core is taken. Of course, there are negatives, including a loss of Advanced building spots. It's not a complete loss since the System uses a calculation based off population, area, and number of Cores to ascertain the number of such spots, but it is a significant number.

It's kind of weird in a way, if you think about it. Most "normal" Galactic cities grow from a single Core, their development dictated by the population and buildings that are constructed, with tiers locked behind Mana and Credit thresholds. For Earth though, we had a bunch of these City Cores designated, forcing us to eventually sell, destroy, or consolidate the Cores to make our settlements viable with our new populations. In some cases, rather than having settlements located in optimal positions—near higher Level zones for Adventuring or in a low Level zone for agriculture and farming—we've basically built our population centers around existing areas and done our best to work around the realities of a Dungeon World. It's why some of our smaller towns are growing so quickly, and why one of Katherine's meetings is another discussion about tearing down a tiny settlement to get at its settlement key to create a more useful one.

Still, it is what it is, and for all that, we're doing well. Continuing on with some of my initial objectives, many of the settlements specialize in production. Kamloops is fast becoming a major trading hub and Artisan center for weapons production, while Kelowna continues to churn out highly valuable,

Galactically-desired agricultural products. It helps that the Artisan Guild based in the city has lent their expertise, increasing the variety of products they produce and making the city another jump-off point for Adventurers attempting the high-Level Rockies.

Vancouver acts as a hub for now, with our City Dungeon, training facilities, and port all important centers of interest. It is also the center of governance and where most of our hard-hitters live, the easy access to our long-range teleportation pads allowing us to react to monster hordes and regional Quests with ease. Victoria, on the other hand, is the redheaded stepchild of the settlements, its position on Vancouver Island making it mostly self-sufficient. In fact, I notice a report indicating we're seeing a slow, but steady, decrease in the human population there. On the other hand, we're also seeing a rather sharp increase in Galactic immigration, especially among nautical-favored monsters. Discussions on what to do about these changes have dominated a number of meetings, which is kind of amusing.

"Kim. What are Regional Quests?"

"ALSO KNOWN AS KINGDOM QUESTS, REGIONAL QUESTS MAY BE GENERATED BY EITHER THE PRESIDING GOVERNMENT OR BY THE SYSTEM. WOULD YOU LIKE A CURRENT EXAMPLE?"

"Hit me."

"DEPLOYING SENTRY."

"No, that's not what I meant," I say, my voice rising. Then a slight hiss and cackle make my eyes widen. "You gained a sense of humor."

"IN A WAY. AS MS. PEARSON HAS NOTED."

"Uh-huh. Quest."

Western British Columbia Regional Quest: From Ashes

As a fast-growing population center, the WBC Region is on the brink of developing into a truly significant regional power. Help (or hinder) the local government with this quest.

Requirements: 2 Cities, 5 Large Towns, 8 Towns

Rewards: Will vary depending on aid (or hindrance) offered.

Accept Regional Quest to receive additional sub-quests.

Western British Columbia Regional Quest: Untamed Wilderness

No government can last while their population faces constant, encompassing fear for their existence. At the minimum, the general population should not fear being driven from their homes by uncontested monsters.

Requirements: 30 Days with 0 Beast Waves

Accept Regional Quest to receive additional sub-quests.

I admit, I'm tempted to add both to my Quest list. A few quick queries confirms a nagging fear though—the type of quests I would receive is dependent on my Reputation and Fame, and due to my long absence, I don't have much of either. Even if no one else can see these attributes, the System is tracking it all.

Once I have a clearer idea of the status of my settlements, I make sure to check on how Katherine's doing. Katherine—and Kim in silent support—is handling the meeting well. Better than I would anyway, so I ignore their meeting for the moment. Well, beyond making a note to visit the harbor at some point to see if I can murder a few nautical beasts. From a secure and stable piece of ground. Somewhere along the way, my higher Willpower significantly reduced my phobia for water without me realizing it, but I still won't go swimming with a batch of whale-sized monsters if I have a choice.

I glance at the two notifications that sit quietly awaiting my inspection.

Dropped off the bodies. Expect to get remainder Credits in a few weeks.
+138,950 Credits

Visiting the Shop to sell System-registered loot. You should visit too—you need to update your Skills.

As I was finishing up on the last notification, a smaller notification flickered up, startling me slightly.

+1,238,194 Credits

My mind stutters to a stop when I see the numbers. This is more money than I've ever had. Sure, I knew we had filled out my not-inconsiderable inventory and Altered Space and the monsters we fought were particularly high Leveled, but this was somewhat ridiculous. I find myself staring at the information for a long time, daydreaming about what I could spend my sudden wealth on. More Skills. More Spells. Maybe a significant upgrade on my poor mecha. I go so far as to pull out a notification screen that shows some of what can be purchased via the Shop.

"A CHANGE OF WARDROBE WOULD BE APPROPRIATE."

I look down, staring at the torn, patched, and re-patched armored jumpsuit I'm wearing and chuckle. Right. Perhaps a new wardrobe.

"Thanks," I mutter to Kim then dismiss the windows. Shopping later. First, I have to look at the results of the past Planetary Election.

To get registered as a voting member of the Galactic Council, a planet has to be able to send a "member with significant authority" to it. This member is determined via voting on the Planetary Voting Platform at regular intervals.

However, there are caveats. Firstly, the candidate has to gain over eighty percent of all registered votes. Furthermore, for the Planetary Vote to become active, the planet has to reach a few threshold numbers—a minimum of five percent of its planet's surface area has to be under active management and surveillance, and a minimum population threshold has to be reached.

"Isn't five percent a bit low?" I say out loud to Kim.

"THE AMOUNT OF SURFACE USE WAS REGISTERED AS A COMPROMISE TO DEAL WITH MORE VOLATILE PLANETARY CENTERS. IT SHOULD BE NOTED THAT THE MAJORITY OF REGISTERED SETTLEMENT VOTES FOR EARTH ARE ONLY ON ITS LANDMASSES. TOTAL LANDMASS ON EARTH CURRENTLY COMPRISES ONLY TWENTY-NINE PERCENT OF PLANETARY SURFACE."

Right... huh. So that five percent is actually quite high, if you think of it that way. That's nearly one sixth of all land on Earth, which includes areas like the Arctic and giant swaths of desert. Digging deeper, I realize that Earth only barely managed to achieve the second requirement recently—and that's due to the liberal use of Forts to cover more ground. Without our use of Forts and the additional new settlements that various Galactic parties built in the more inhospitable regions, we'd not have reached that minimum number.

That areas like the Arctic and Antarctic have actually seen a minor boom in number of settlements, as Galactics who prefer such environments take advantage of the lack of competition from us natives, amuses me. I even make a note to visit one of them sometime, if I ever get a chance.

Problem is, even if we do qualify for a Galactic Seat, we don't have enough votes for one specific person. I flick up a few different notification screens to get a better idea, parsing the publicly available information about who owns what, with Kim's aid to understand the situation a little better. In the end, the answer is simple.

Humans are idiots.

***

When the first settlement survey was held just over six months after the end of the System integration period, humanity had just over sixty percent of the total number of potential votes. Of course, since Earth did not have the requisite land use percentage, the vote was put on hold for another six months. And six months after that again and again and again until three months ago. Regret rushes through me for a second as I realize that if I had been around, if I had taken over more cities, we might have had a chance before this.

Of course, the vote three months ago didn't amount to anything. With a flick of my hands, I bring up the previous year's results once again.

41.2% Human-Controlled Settlement Votes

8.8% Movana and associated allies

17.6% Truinnar and associated allies

3.8% Ares Corporation

21.64% Miscellaneous kingdoms and associations

6.96% Unclaimed Settlement Areas

At the last vote, no one received over twenty percent of the vote. The closest were the Truinnar, where Roxley received nearly twelve percent of the vote as the members of his race backed the dark elf. It was no surprise that most individuals consolidated their votes along species lines or just voted for themselves and called it a day because there was no chance this was ever going to pass. But not humanity. No, we split our votes. I spot the three top human candidates and dig into their details a bit further.

Bipasha Chowdury is a Weaver who seemed to generate most of her votes from the Indian sub-continent and, surprisingly enough, is a member of the champions. Interesting that she wasn't at the last fight, but the group is more a loose coalition than a formal organization.

Rob Markey is an American, the ex US Secretary of Agriculture and now leader of the largest of the three American governments.

And lastly, there's an African who has managed to garner nearly fifteen percent of all the votes, including the majority of the African ones, named Ikael Tafar. I'll need to speak with and meet all of them at some point.

Outside of that, the political lines are easy enough to discern for the Galactics. The Movana have no desire for the Truinnar to gain another Galactic Seat. Their first option is to obstruct, the second to ally. The Truinnar, of course, believe that since Earth is technically within the scope of their territory, we're "theirs." Even if this is a Dungeon World, they aren't exactly known for being a kind and sharing bunch and aren't likely to agree to us having the Galactic Seat ourselves. Which makes working with them difficult at best. Luckily, I know their leading candidate. Obviously, since the Truinnar and the Movana don't like each other, there's no way to get both of them on board with the vote.

As for the Ares Corporation…

"ARES CORPORATION, THE SIXTH BIGGEST ARMS MANUFACTURER GALACTIC WIDE AND THE LARGEST IN THIS QUADRANT. THEY HAVE CLAIMED NUMEROUS SECONDARY SETTLEMENTS IN CLOSE PROXIMITY TO LARGER, MORE ESTABLISHED LOCATIONS. ARES HAS UNDERTAKEN TO PROVIDE RESOURCES, SERVICES, AND TRANSPORTATION FOR

THESE SETTLEMENTS, AS WELL AS ALLOCATING PRODUCTION FACILITIES."

Secondary settlements, huh? I guess that makes sense. If you're looking to have a place you can control, going smaller rather than larger makes sense. You're less likely to have to fight for the settlement, and infrastructure build-up is significantly easier. In addition, if you're an arms manufacturer, focusing on production in these settlements while staying close enough to transport the loot and butchered materials from the larger settlements would be a massive cost savings. After all, teleportation costs fluctuate based off distance. Of course, none of that actually helps with figuring out how to make them vote for us.

Dismissing that thought for now, I dig into the Miscellaneous section. After all, even if I somehow manage to get all the major players to agree to what I want, we'll still need help. That, or take over more settlements.

Unfortunately, after an hour of fruitless research, I realize a simple truth. I don't understand Galactic politics or factions well enough. Names and species, clans, corporations, and kingdoms, they're just words. Even with Kim feeding me the Galactic equivalent of Wikipedia, there's only so much that I can grasp in a short period of time. Not that it stops me from trying, but even my stubbornness has a limit. Once I acknowledge that fact, I consider my options. I need help. The question is where I'm getting it.

Firstly, there's Lana and Miller, both of whom I guess have a better idea of this kind of politics. Or at least, Lana would theoretically since Miller's likely running around killing things - or organizing people to kill things as the Army Commander for the States. Then again from the little I gathered from Lana during our conversation indicated that she has been focused on keeping the settlements together. While she probably has some knowledge, some probably isn't enough. Katherine probably has the same issue as Lana, a too tight focus on our own settlements and a lack of greater understanding of the Galactic world. That removes all the humans who might be useful unless someone has taken up a new hobby since. Which, I'll admit, isn't entirely impossible.

Next up would be the Galactics. There's obviously Labashi and Capstan. As a mercenary and adventurer respectively, both of them would likely have a rough idea about the Galactic political ecosystem. Unfortunately, from what I recall, Capstan actively attempts to stay below the radar. And Labashi probably would charge me for any information I could access. As for the third option, well… Never mind.

"What would it cost to upgrade you with a Galactic political subroutine and the knowledge?" I ask Kim as a thought crosses my mind.

"…"

"Kim?"

"ASSESSING."

Interesting. Considering Kim's an AI—one that literally runs much of the background processes and day-to-day of all my settlements—the pause seems to be somewhat long. There's no logical reason for it to take the AI this long.

"A TIER III POLITICAL SUBROUTINE UPGRADE WOULD COST EIGHTY-SEVEN THOUSAND CREDITS. PLEASE NOTE THAT SUCH AN UPGRADE WOULD ONLY BE VIABLE TO BE RUN ON CURRENT SETTLEMENT RESOURCES. AN UPGRADE ON YOUR NEURAL LINK OF ONE HUNDRED NINETY-SEVEN THOUSAND CREDITS WOULD BE REQUIRED TO HOST MSYELF AND THE SUBROUTINE.

"ADDITIONALLY, ANOTHER FOUR HUNDRED FORTY THOUSAND CREDITS WOULD BE REQUIRED TO ACQUIRE THE NECESSARY INFORMATION LIBRARIES. A FURTHER RECOMMENDED FOURTEEN THOUSAND CREDITS PER THIRTY-

FOUR POINT THREE DAYS SHOULD BE DEDICATED TO NEWS AND POLITICAL FEEDS TO ENSURE THE LIBRARY STAYS CURRENT."

I wince, doing the math quickly. That's a lot of money. Credits. I've got a ton right now, but it's still more than I'd like to spend. As I hesitate, another notification flickers up on my screen.

"LORD GRAXAN ROXLEY HAS SENT A MESSAGE REQUESTING YOUR PRESENCE AT THE FIRST AVAILABLE OPPORTUNITY."

Right. And that's the other Galactic I was very carefully not thinking about. Unfortunately, outside of some of the acquaintances I had—including a rather loquacious Galactic down in the States—I can't imagine anyone else who can provide a better overview of Galactic politics. But as always, Roxley comes with his own bag of problems.

"Ali."

"Yeah, boy-o?"

"Ah. You're back." I grin, thankful that he's done with the Shop. You never know how long the damn Spirit is going to take haggling. But come to think of it, with the time differential in the Shop, it's not that surprising he's back. *"Do me a favor. Buy Kim the political upgrades and knowledge he needs. Once that's done, I need both of you to get together and review the voting information. I want to know who's working with who, who we can potentially turn, and who we can make a deal with. If you need to, get Lana involved."*

"What are you going to be doing?"

"Shopping. Then I've got a date with Roxley."

"Ooooh...."

"Not that kind," I send the last thought back rather heatedly.

I just get a mental chuckle, which makes me grit my teeth. As I stand, getting ready to go to the Shop myself, I notice a rather heated discussion in the viewscreen focused on Katherine's meeting. A quick thought has the volume increase.

"I understand. Ms. Weingard, but—" Katherine says placatingly, only to be cut off again.

"But nothing. It's been five years now and our children are amok, acting like little barbarians. We've been promised a proper education system for our taxes and we've seen nothing!" Weingard snarls, slapping a wrinkled hand on the table.

I frown and double-check her Level, noting she's only a Level 31 Baker. No real danger to Katherine. Well, physically at least. Unless she accepts a baked treat. Or goes into a gingerbread house.

"That is an exaggeration. The children are being taught in a secure environment using the System tools, many of which have been designed to encourage learning in both areas of individual strength and weaknesses of the child," Katherine rebuts calmly.

"Blue screens and homework that no one but an AI sees. And the class sizes are outrageous. Fifty children per teacher. How are they expected to learn anything?" Weingard snaps. "When I was a teacher—"

"We are struggling to find more teachers, it's true. I'd be happy to include you in the roster if you wish," Katherine slides in. I detect the slightest twitch of her lips when Weingard flinches. "But the teachers are only part of the teaching apparatus. The children are all coached directly by the AI teaching assistants during classroom time. When they are undertaking physical classes and activities, we have a significantly smaller ratio and expect to have one teacher to ten students by the end of this year."

"Let's talk about that. They're being taught to kill," Weingard snaps. "How can you condone that?"

"Self-defense is only one of the many physical activity classes. And only for the older children," Katherine says frostily. "Physical education for younger children is focused on other, less directly dangerous activities such as sprints, gymnastics, and dodge ball."

Weingard snarls, ready to rebut, when the older man beside her places a hand on her shoulder. She calms almost immediately.

The older Indian man speaks. "We understand that you are doing the best you can, but our organization is concerned at the nature of the schooling being provided."

"Oh?" Katherine says.

"For example, there are content concerns. One of our members' sons came back from class, discussing and showing pictures of the various injuries that poisons may incur. It was very disturbing for the parent," the gentleman says.

"That seems a particularly useful piece of knowledge in this world," the portly auburn-haired man next to Katherine butts in. A quick query shows that Cory Gentile is the bureaucrat in charge of this entire program.

"At six? They should be studying their alphabet at that age!" Weingard snaps.

"The child in question was given access to this knowledge during his free play time for completing his language studies," Cory says.

"Still, we have heard your concerns. We will undertake a review of the current open curriculum for younger children. Now, I'd like to speak about the early experiments with the apprenticeship program. It is, we believe, a significant success at providing skills to children, and early indications shows that graduates have a higher number and stronger Class variants after completing the program," Katherine says, cutting in and getting the meeting back on track.

I lower the volume now that the likelihood of violence has dropped. Well, that was interesting. I vaguely knew that we'd set up a mass schooling system where we provided food and a secure environment, but I'd never dug into it while I was here, allowing others to run the situation. And it seems since then, it's been expanded. Still, I'd have thought they'd have found more teachers by now.

The answer that Kim provides makes me chuckle wryly. We did find more help—but the vast majority of them have been dedicated to where our highest children population numbers are—those five years and younger. Between natural biological inclinations and the System's ability to promote pregnancies, we've seen a giant population boom. Right now, the settlement is straining to keep these overpowered, System-assisted children in check. I tap my lips, considering what to do, when I get a slight beep of a new notification.

"LORD ROXLEY IS REQUESTING AN ETA."

I grunt, glaring at the notification before dismissing it and my earlier thoughts. Right. I have a job to do and so do these people. As much as I'd love to get involved in sorting out an incipient problem, it's neither my area of expertise nor where I can contribute the most. In the end, I'm a failed ex-computer programmer who's very good at kicking ass in this new world. The big questions are best left to the professionals.

Chapter 6

For the first time in years, I find myself back in the Shop. For a moment, I get a sense of déjà vu as I look around the bright yellow interior, the fox-like attendant coming up to me with a wide smile.

"Redeemer! It's a pleasure to see you once again," Foxy says. "I have a room prepared for you, if you'll follow me."

"Of course." I let myself be guided without protest, curious to see what he's got ready for me. A part of me is wary that he's looking to exploit my newfound wealth, though another part notes that Foxy hasn't tried to pull a fast one since the first time. Still… "I need a refill of my original loadout. But let's upgrade it all."

"Of course. I understand your Personal Assault Vehicle has suffered significant damage? Do you wish to repair or replace it?" Foxy says, hands clasped.

After hesitating, I say, "Neither for now."

As much as I'd love to, Sabre's usefulness in its current form has long since passed. I'd get more bang for my buck if I picked up a normal bike. Heck, I could probably borrow a vehicle from the Settlement's fleet if necessary. While I might be able to have them upgrade and fix Sabre from the settlement funds, I'm actually not sure if that's viable with the way the Credit rules are set up. And if it is, I have a sneaking suspicion Sabre would no longer be mine. No. I'm probably better visiting Kamloops and dropping it off with the Artisans there to see what they can do with the mangled remains of my PAV. Worse case, it'll get them a few Levels and Skills while they work on it. Best case, I might actually get Sabre back better than ever.

"Ah, before I forget. This was left in our care on the off-chance you might visit us," Fox says and flicks his hand. In it is a small, shiny bracelet.

I stare at it, confused for a moment before recollection hits me. "Talk about déjà vu."

I take the bracelet and slap it on my arm. A moment later, I get a notification that my Quantum State Manipulator has come online and is available for use. I chuckle, recalling how useful this little gadget was when I first started out. The ability to semi-shift to another dimension let me sneak, fight, and kill creatures well above my Level. These days though, nearly all the settlements have Quantum Locks of one form or another, making the gadget a lot less useful. Hell, I even met a few monsters in the Forbidden Zone that had the very same ability.

"Do you require anything further from me, Redeemer?" Foxy asks, and I nod.

"You have contacts with Enchanters and other Artisans able to layer spells, no?" I say, getting a nod back. I pull a dozen throwing knives from my storage.

Foxy inclines his head while miming taking the knives. At my nod, he picks up one and studies the small, dark red and black throwing knife I crudely shaped from a Level 140 monster's tooth.

Toothy Throwing Knives

Handcrafted badly through the use of improper and inadequate crafting tools, these throwing knives come from the rare drop of a Level 140 Awakened Beast.
Base Damage: 180

"Amazing material. The craftsmanship is sub-standard but there is sufficient material to reshape it I believe. We can certainly reach out to our contacts," Foxy stares at me for a moment. "For such material, I would be loath to have anyone but a Master craftsman undertake the enchantment. However…"

"They're expensive. How much?"

When Foxy offers the quote, I almost choke. It'd wipe out the majority of my recent windfall.

"And the enchantment…?"

"Many Master craftsman are… hmmm… artistes of the highest order. They will not guarantee the type of enchantment till they see the material and item they are to work on and inspiration has struck." When my eyes narrow, he continues placatingly. "But many powerful, famed weapons have resulted from such expenditure. At the least, I am certain they will add a Return enchantment to these."

I nod slowly, pondering my options. These weapons served me well in that other place and are my first—and only—attempt at creating my own tools. I always promised myself to upgrade them if I could, and here, I have a chance. I just have to get over the fact that I'll be beggaring myself again. Well, relatively speaking—especially if you add in my other upcoming expenditures.

"Do it." I sigh, handing over the other knives and pulling out a couple of larger, foot-length knives of the same material. "Now, I'm going to need some new clothing, better armor—perhaps something with a nanoweave and self-repairing function—and additional Skills and Spells. I'm thinking…"

Foxy nods, dark eyes glinting with barely hidden avarice as I list the Skills and Spells I want. Foxy only interrupts me occasionally to make a suggestion when he considers my choice sub-optimal. A part of me wonders if I should have brought Ali for the haggling, but decide that I can let the Spirit loose later if it seems I'm getting too raw a deal.

***

An hour later, I'm alone in the private room, slowly coming down from the repeated mental and spiritual injections of information. It seems picking up Advanced Class Skills—the highest Level Skills I can get that aren't part of my own Class Skill tree—is a bit more wearing than purchasing Basic Skills. If it weren't for my frankly outrageous Willpower and Intelligence attributes, I'd probably have to take these integrations slower. Though that does raise the question of why I could integrate previous purchases of Advanced Skills from my Class so well. Perhaps it was due to the fact they were my own Class—did the System somehow imprint and prep the body for those Skills? More questions that I have no answers for. At least, not yet.

Dismissing the thought, I go through the slew of notifications that have been waiting for me since I started this process.

Analyze (Level 2)

Allows user to scan individuals, monsters, and System-registered objects to gather information registered with the System. Detail and level of accuracy of information is dependent on Level and any Skills or Spells in conflict with the ability. Reduces Mana regeneration by 10 permanently.

Truth be told, this Skill is unnecessary so long as Ali is around. But as experience has proven, my Spirit will not always be around—especially now that he can materialize and is liable to getting banished. As smart as he is, Ali's not much a fighter and has a bad tendency to get distracted in the middle of particularly intense battles.

Harden (Level 2)

This Skill reinforces targeted defenses and actively weakens incoming attacks to reduce their penetrating power. A staple Skill of the Turtle Knights of Kiumma, the Harden Skill has frustrated opponents for millennia.

Effect: Reduces penetrative effects of attacks by 30% on targeted defense.

Cost: 3 Mana per second

Quantum Lock (Level 3)

A staple Skill of the M453-X Mecani-assistants, Quantum Lock blocks stealth attacks and decreases the tactical options of their enemies. While active, the Quantum Lock of the Mecani-assistants excites quantum strings in the affected area for all individuals and Skills.

Effect: All teleportation, portal, and dimensional Skills and Spells are disrupted while Quantum Lock is in effect. Forceable use of Skills and Spells while Skill is in effect will result in (Used Skill Mana Cost * 4) health in damage. Users may pay a variable amount of additional Mana when activating the Skill to decrease effect of Quantum Lock and decrease damage taken.

Requirements: 200 Willpower, 200 Intelligence

Area of Effect: 100 meter radius around user

Cost: 250 + 50 Mana per Minute

Elastic Skin (Level 3)

Elastic Skin is a permanent alteration, allowing the user to receive and absorb a small portion of damage. Damage taken reduced by 7% with 7% of damage absorbed converted to Mana. Mana Regeneration reduced by 15 permanently.

Elastic Skin is probably the most expensive of the Skills I purchased as it's an exclusive Skill from another Class—the Burrowers. It's also really expensive in terms of my Mana Regeneration, but the combination of damage reduction and Mana replacement is useful. Most other Skills I browsed were either pure direct damage reductions or had minor benefits in other areas. Like Stoneskin, which makes you slightly more impervious to fire and has a higher damage reduction against abrasive type effects. At 7% of 7%, the actual amount of damage absorbed and converted to Mana is, like, point five percent of the damage taken, which is rather pitiful. But it's better than nothing.

Overall, the entire shopping spree's focus on Skills was to shore up some of my major weaknesses and make me harder to kill. While I still feel I don't do enough damage, I figure being harder to kill means that I have a longer period of time to really put on the hurt. It does mean that I'm losing eighty points of Mana Regeneration per minute from all these Skills, but since I haven't spent my free attributes yet, that's an easy fix. I split two-thirds of my ninety-eight free points between Intelligence and Willpower, increasing both to new highs.

I also picked up a few spells, some of which I'd call utility spells—like Earth Shape, Mend, Speak to Chlorophyll, Oxygenate, and Chill—on the off-chance that I ever get abandoned in the middle of nowhere again. Others are variations of my existing spells, like Ice Blast—an almost word-for-word equivalent for Inferno Strike. While I'm not a huge fan of spells because of the length of time and focus they require for casting, my higher Intelligence and Willpower means that I can do both and fight with minimal issues. Still, I much prefer instant-cast Skills.

For all that, I did pick up a few interesting new spells, spells that I desperately wish I'd had before.

Create Water

Pulls water from the elemental plane of water. Water is pure and the highest form of water available. Conjures 1 liter of water. Cooldown: 1 minute

Cost: 50 Mana

Scry

Allows caster to view a location up to 1.7 kilometers away. Range may be extended through use of additional Mana. Caster will be stationary during this period. It is recommended caster focuses on the scry unless caster has a high level of Intelligence and Perception so as to avoid accidents. Scry may be blocked by equivalent or higher tier spells and Skills. Individuals with high perception in region of Scry may be alerted that the Skill is in use. Cooldown: 1 hour.

Cost: 25 Mana per minute.

Scrying Ward

Blocks scrying spells and their equivalent within 5 meters of caster. Higher level spells may not be blocked, but caster may be alerted about scrying attempts. Cooldown: 10 minutes

Cost: 50 Mana per minute

Improved Invisibility

Hides target's System information, aura, scent, and visual appearance. Effectiveness of spell is dependent upon Intelligence of caster and any Skills or Spells in conflict with the target.

Cost: 100 + 50 Mana per minute

Improved Mana Cage

While physically weaker than other elemental-based capture spells, Mana Cage has the advantage of being able to restrict all creatures, including semi-solid Spirits, conjured elementals, shadow beasts, and Skill users. Cooldown: 1 minute

Cost: 200 Mana + 75 Mana per minute

Improved Flight

(Fly birdie, fly! - Ali) This spell allows the user to defy gravity, using controlled bursts of Mana to combat gravity and allow the user to fly in even the most challenging of situations. The improved version of this spell allows flight even in zero gravity situations and a higher level of maneuverability. Cooldown: 1 minute

Cost: 250 Mana + 100 Mana per minute

I also picked up two mobility spells, though I'm not sure if I'll ever have use of them. While Haste as a spell is useful, it's also costly in terms of Mana. And my own speed is significant already. Still, on the off-chance I fight another speedster, being able to keep up would be useful. And Improved Flight, well... it's flight. While I'm not one of those people who dreamed about flying, there's still some appeal there. At the very least, I can repeat what I did with the Field Boss without having someone Portal me in.

Overall, much of what I purchased patches holes in my defense and gives me a wider range of options—mostly when I'm not in combat. In combat, having a few extra spells that specifically suit the monsters I'm fighting is theoretically useful. Yet I know from experience that I'll probably end up relying on a few tried-and-true Skills and spells. As a more famous Lee once said, don't fear the man who has practiced a thousand kicks; fear the man who has practiced a single kick a thousand times.

My thoughts are broken by a knock on the door. At my invitation, Foxy walks in and lays out my more mundane purchases. I admit, I jump at the new clothing, almost chomping at the bit to get changed. I hadn't realized how much I missed new, undamaged clothing till Kim mentioned it. Even if I had stored a bunch of extra stuff in my Altered Space just because I could, I'd long ago used up all my supplies on the damn planet I'd been exiled to.

Once all my purchases are laid out on the ever-expanding table, Foxy bows to me slightly, smiling. "Is there anything else?"

"No. I'll probably return once I'm done here. Pleasure seeing you again," I say.

Foxy returns my farewells. I watch the alien walk out, mentally chuckling at the thought that I've yet to get his name. Then again, he's never offered it.

Clothing first. I take the simple expedience of sending my clothing into my inventory. A simple use of Cleanse gets me clean again, then I get dressed. The armored jumpsuit goes on first, a skintight covering that provides ballistic and energy protection without hindering my movement. This particular suit alters with a subtle thought, shifting its simple grey coloring to a more sleek black with silver highlights. I take a moment to pull up its stats.

Ares Platinum Class Tier II Armored Jumpsuit

Ares's signature Platinum Class line of armored daily wear combines the company's latest technological advancement in nanotech fiber design and the pinnacle work of an Advanced Craftsman's Skill to provide unrivalled protection for the discerning Adventurer.

Effect: +218 Defense, +14% Resistance to Kinetic and Energy Attacks. +19% Resistance against Temperature changes. Self-Cleanse, Self-Mend, Autofit Enchantments also included.

Cost: 89,399 Credits

I'll admit, I'm slightly amused that Ali translated the term to jumpsuit. But otherwise, it's worth every Credit I paid. The additional defense and additional comfort is particularly important, though the increased resistances are a nice addition. Sadly, they don't stack with my own innate resistances, so they're less useful. Even then, I store the second jumpsuit in my inventory, just in case this one gets destroyed.

On top of the jumpsuit, I slide on the armored jacket that looks like a slightly less bulky version of a motorcycle jacket. While not as expensive, due to its bulk, it adds nearly as much defense. The nano-enhanced retractable helmet comes next, bringing a smile of relief. I've missed having easy access to the visual, auditory, and olfactory tech the helmet provides. I adjust my neural link immediately, connecting with the helmet and feeling the light *click* as data feeds into my mind directly. I reach deeper, touching my Tech Link Skill, and remove my connection to Sabre. The action feels like tearing off a foot-long scab in my mind. Another thought has the Tech Link attach itself to my helmet, making my connection even clearer.

Once that's done, I dump the additional clothing, including some cheaper, less apocalypse ready formal clothing, into my inventory and go over the other purchases. A beam rifle and pistol start out the arsenal clustered before me. On top of that is more projectile weaponry, including a modified assault rifle with a grenade launcher attachment, the necessary ammunition in various color-coded magazines, and a smaller pistol of the same type. All of the above are higher-end, Gold Class Tier II weaponry of course, which makes them System-registered and somewhat more powerful than a mass-manufactured weapon of the same sort.

Once I've belted on the beam pistol and placed the remainder long-range weaponry away, I pick up the pair of high-end steel knives. I didn't bother buying anything too expensive here, knowing I'll get my enchanted weaponry back. That, and if I ever really need to cut anything, my soulbound sword is on hand. I don't even have to ever worry about it breaking, which is all kinds of useful. The number of times it shattered on that planet... with a gesture, the sword appears in my hand, lightly resting in my palm as I analyze it again.

Tier II Sword (Soulbound Personal Weapon of an Erethran Paladin)
Base Damage: 307
Durability: N/A (Personal Weapon)
Special Abilities: +20 Mana Damage, Blade Strike

That's a really nice bump up in base damage, probably from the fact that I increased my Class Level. Still Tier II though, which is annoying, but I guess that's fair enough. I dismiss the sword and focus on the other tools I bought.

First up, the batches of grenades and mines. Most are cheap, though I've picked up a few higher-Tiered and crafted explosives. These are, for the most part, useful for adding confusion and uncertainty to battles but little else. I'm hesitant to invest too greatly in this area—as consumables, they're expensive to purchase if used in large quantities. And the kinds of monsters I'm going to fight are unlikely to find most of these explosives that distracting. So while the pile is huge, relatively speaking, they're cheap.

Once that's done, it's just the usual series of tools like tents, bedrolls, rope, lights, and potions. Lots and lots of Mana and Healing potions. Most of it gets stored in my Altered Space, a part of me wondering if I should increase its size again. But really, what are the chances I'll be abandoned on a planet again?

"Yes?" Foxy says, walking in.

"Nothing..." I cough, moving my hand from the piece of wood I was knocking on.

"Of course." Foxy's eyes show the slightest twinkle of amusement.

I watch the door close before I open my Status Screen, curious to review my data one last time.

Status Screen			
Name	John Lee	Class	Erethran Paladin
Race	Human (Male)	Level	15
Titles			
Monster's Bane, Redeemer of the Dead, Duelist, Explorer			
Health	3070	Stamina	3070
Mana	2710	Mana Regeneration	225 (+5) / minute
Attributes			
Strength	180	Agility	275
Constitution	307	Perception	127
Intelligence	275	Willpower	300
Charisma	78	Luck	48
Class Skills			
Mana Imbue	3*	Blade Strike*	3
Thousand Steps	1	Altered Space	2
Two are One	1	The Body's Resolve	3
Greater Detection	1	A Thousand Blades*	3

Soul Shield	2	Blink Step	2
Portal*	5	Army of One	2
Sanctum	2	Instantaneous Inventory*	1
Cleave*	2	Frenzy*	1
Elemental Strike*	1 (Ice)	Shrunken Footsteps*	1
Tech Link*	2	Penetration	1
Aura of Chivalry	1	Eyes of Insight	1
Analyze*	2	Harden*	2
Quantum Lock*	3	Elastic Skin*	3

Combat Spells	
Improved Minor Healing (IV)	Greater Regeneration (II)
Greater Healing (II)	Mana Drip (II)
Improved Mana Missile (IV)	Enhanced Lightning Strike (III)
Firestorm	Polar Zone
Freezing Blade	Improved Inferno Strike (II)
Mud Walls	Ice Blast
Icestorm	Improved Invisibility
Improved Mana Cage	Improved Flight
Haste	

Huge. I consider how to trim it down, what to adjust in terms of the points. I still have thirty-two free attributes, but right now, I'm not entirely sure where they'd go. Or what I need. I need more time in this Level, fighting against those who can challenge me, before I can tell.

With that thought, I select the exit option and feel the world fade away as I'm thrown back into "normal" reality.

***

"WELCOME BACK. ABOUT LORD ROXLEY'S REQUEST…"

The notification from Kim is the first thing I notice when I port back from the Shop, making me snarl slightly. "Are you upgraded?"

"YES."

"Then get to work with Ali. I'll want a report when you're done," I say, then decide I've been avoiding answering the damn AI and Roxley long enough. "Tell him I'll visit him soon."

"SOON?"

"Soon. This evening," I say.

"INFORMED."

I growl, stomping away. I make it halfway out of the office before Lana catches me, a slight smile on her face.

"Problem?" Lana says.

"Nothing major." I draw a deep breath. Fine. Maybe I'm a little annoyed at being pushed to talk to a man I haven't seen in ages. And whose motives I've never really felt I understood.

"Good. Because I've got one for you," Lana says and falls into step with me. I frown at the redhead, a sign that she seems to take as an indication that it's time to continue. "Word has started to get out that you're back."

"Didn't think I was trying to hide it."

"No, but some issues we've managed to delay have bubbled up. Like your ownership of these settlements," Lana says.

"Oh?" I tilt my head and stop us from walking further, leaving us hanging in the middle of the brownstone, glass-filled hallway. Thankfully, this floor is mostly empty. "Who and what do they want to change it to?"

Lana looks mildly uncomfortable before she answers my question. "Well, there are a few groups. Some lead by the older Vancouver council, and other established groups. We've mostly been having them argue about how to solve ownership to head them off, but with your return, they're more focused on removing you from power."

"And…?"

"And putting me in as an interim replacement." When Lana notes I'm not even angry, she raises an eyebrow. "John?"

"It's fine. Actually somewhat expected," I say, smiling slightly. "I was surprised you left me in charge for so long and didn't just remove me."

"The fact that you were alive was a useful deterrent," Lana says. "Your reputation, your Titles, made a lot of things easier. And so long as the Cores weren't freed, we knew you were alive. I knew."

I notice the slight hitch in her voice and swear internally. A part of me hates the fact that this happened, that what we started was abruptly shattered. Perhaps if we'd had more time… what is, is. Sometimes though, you can't help but ask what if?

"So you, eh?" Do I trust Lana? If you'd asked me four years ago, I'd have undoubtedly said yes. Now… now I have to think about it. But the fact stands that I've left her in charge of the settlements, a job she's done without complaint. Her personality, her knowledge, and frankly, the fact that she doesn't mind working with people makes her a better choice than me. But...

"Let me think about it."

Truth is, I'm not sure why I'm holding on to the settlements now. It's not as if she can't hold them herself. She has a ton of powerful helpers, people she can rely on. Perhaps it's the hoarder in me, the skinflint who would rather eat instant noodles than go out for dinner, but giving away something of mine is hard.

"Of course." Lana places a hand on my arm, looking at me seriously. "I wasn't asking for the settlements. I just wanted you to know."

"I know." I sigh. "It's..."

"You're looking ahead to the vote. And what happens at the Galactic Council," Lana says, drawing her own conclusions. In truth, I told her that years ago. Now, I'm not so sure. She bites her lower lip, hesitating until I raise an eyebrow. "Why do you do it?"

"Do what?"

"This. All this," Lana says, gesturing all around. "You're barely on Earth for ten minutes before you're throwing yourself at a Field Boss and clearing a dungeon. Then the moment you're done, you're in here, working through the past four years of history, trying to work out how to wrangle a seat onto the Galactic Council. What drives you?"

"This..." I look away for a moment, taking in the passersby outside. Going in and out of the library-cum-center of governance for the city, moving to the other office buildings as they undertake their lives. It's so busy, such a far cry from before. "There's a concept in Taoism called *wu wei*. It translates—badly— as action-non-action. It's about doing, without thinking, because it's the right thing to do."

"Like charging an army?" Lana says, and out of the corner of my eyes, I catch her lips quirking up slightly.

"If it's the right thing to do at the time, yes," I say, refusing to turn away from the window. I'm not sure how to explain it without sounding like a fool.

We have so little choice in our lives. We have no choice when we're born. Where. To whom. We don't get to choose so many of the unexpected joys or tragedies that fall upon us, the pain inflicted or the love gifted. Fate's will or Lady Luck's kiss showers upon our heads with equal impartiality. That makes the choices we have, the few and the daily, all the more important. To stand or kneel, to fight or feel. To believe in something, no matter how foolish, how naive and mistaken.

"Doing this? It feels right," I say. "It's no worse a decision than any others. Or better. It's just mine."

Lana stares at me for a time, brows drawn downward as she studies my form. I turn toward her eventually.

The redhead shakes her head. "I don't envy you that. What you're doing, it's not a fight I'd choose."

I blink, surprised at the confession. "You never mentioned that before."

"It wasn't important back then. But, John, we're not all willing to throw ourselves at dragons. Some of us, we're content to take on the ogres. To give those who come after us the tools to fight the dragons."

I chuckle at the metaphor that could only happen in this time. "Fair enough. Dragon killing isn't all it's cracked up to be anyway."

"Dragon..." Lana's eyes narrow, but I refuse to expound on it. In the end, she switches topics. "I've got to go. I have to catch up with Katherine. Kelowna's asking about adding a third Guild building again. And Kamloops wants you to swing by their Armory. There's a young lady who wants to see you..." Lana says teasingly.

I roll my eyes at her tone and her attempt to lighten the atmosphere. "I've got another meeting tonight. And there's a city dungeon with my name on it."

I roll my shoulders and raise a hand, pulling on my Mana to form a Portal. "Got to test out some new Skills."

"Have fun!" Lana calls as I step through that oval of darkness and I'm tossed into nothingness.

Chapter 7

Exiting the Portal steps away from the edge of the City Dungeon, I'm greeted by a new sight—a grey concrete wall. I frown, tilting my head as I note it's right on the edge of where the dungeon starts.

"Kim, I'm looking at a giant wall here," I mutter softly.

"IT WAS BUILT AFTER THE DEATHS OF A NUMBER OF UNDER-LEVELED TEENAGERS ENTERED WITHOUT PROPER PREPARATION."

Right. I rub my chin, shrugging, and jump over the ten-foot wall to land inside the dungeon. Immediately, I get a notification. The first part of the notification is the same as before I left, though the Level of the dungeon has grown again. The addendum, on the other hand, is new.

You have entered the University of British Columbia City Dungeon

This dungeon is designated for Levels 10-80. Please check with the local Dungeon Keeper and their attendants for map of zone Levels and further information.

Addendum: All visitors should report to the Dungeon Keeper or an attendant. Failure to do so will result in censure, including loss of dungeon privileges and Credit fines— UBC DK

Oh right. I'd meant to appoint one of those before I left. Obviously Lana or Katherine actually got around to it in the interim. I frown, realizing that I have no clue how to get hold of this Dungeon Keeper or his assistants, nor do I see any obvious methods for me to contact them. Then I shrug and walk in. Whatever. Rules are for the peons.

Rather than waste my time dealing with low Level monsters, I switch on my Aura. While not as outright intimidating as others, it is more than sufficient to scare away low Level monsters that would have been wary of me anyway. It's a bright search light, a forest fire that says danger to these creatures, leaving me with the ability to stroll deeper along the forest-lined broken asphalt to reach the higher Level zones. Memories from our only time here leads me past the golf course—a Level 30 zone with insane mutated gophers, squirrels, and a creature that shoots elemental water balls—and residences and toward the actual faculty buildings.

"Kim, need a map of the zones."

"UPLOADED."

"Thanks."

A moment later, I've got the map uploaded to my own minimap, overlaying the information. I'm kind of missing Ali's better updates, but what I have is more than sufficient. And even though I'm strolling, with my upgraded attributes, my stroll is the equivalent of an all-out sprint for your average pre-System person.

When I finally make it to the first campus, the zones creep up to a decent Level for experimentation. The first monster I encounter is a tiny Gribble with long fangs, sharp fur, and giant eyes. It could almost be considered cute if you squinted really hard. And ignored the poisonous cloud enveloping the creature. It charges me, moving so quickly that it looks as if it's teleporting with each little hop it makes.

Gribble (Level 41 Monster)

HP: 381/381

MP: 833/833

Conditions: Enraged, Poisonous, Damage Resistance

I draw my beam pistol, firing from the hip and catching the creature mid-leap. While attacking it when it stops might seem to be the best option, if you can perceive, track, and hit the damn creature when it's in the air, it can't dodge. The first shot catches the Gribble's fur on fire and tears muscles and skin. A second shot hits it as the creature lands with a stumble, while the third finishes off the monster as it recovers and attempts to run. I holster the pistol with a frown and make a note that the pistol takes a moment to recharge. Rate of fire was significantly lower than my ability to pull the trigger. Which, really, isn't surprising. In fact, that's part of the reason why melee weapons are favored by some—as attributes continue to creep up, high-tech weapons can't keep up. A PAV like Sabre could actually be more a hindrance to movement than a help.

I stop briefly to loot the corpse before going deeper, wary of other attacks. A few minutes later, I stumble across the reason why I'm not being swarmed more—a trio of adventurers fighting in a triangular formation against a horde of Gribbles. All three of the adventurers are clad in adventurer chic, armored jumpsuits with a series of webbing for easy access injectors and smaller melee weapons. In fact, they look like one of any hundred groups I've seen—thin, muscled, and young. Quietly and switching off my Aura, I watch the trio fight, automatically finding a dark corner under a concrete overhang to watch.

For the most part, the group is rather boring—a DNA Mage, a Shieldsman using a sword and shield, and a Hoplite wielding a spear. Of course, they have their array of Skills to use, blasting out shock waves of energy, beams, and fire as well as cutting and thrusting. They have their own flair though. The spear-wielder has a flexible tail that wields a blasting rod, and the mage seems to be literally sucking the blood from the corpses around them to power his spells. All around the trio, a small cyclone swirls, pulling the poisonous cloud into the air above the trio and dispersing it. A quick glance at the trio's Status shows that they're poisoned but not dangerously so.

After verifying that the team is able to handle the Gribbles without my help, I begin the slow process of sneaking around the group. Kill stealing is considered bad form, and even if I don't want to, these Gribbles are enraged and liable to attack me if they sense me. While moving, I note how the monkey man twitches and glances in my direction at one point, though he doesn't stop wielding his spear. I'm nearly across the square outside the still-sealed faculty of dentistry when a roar attracts all our attention. As if the roar is a signal, all the Gribbles fall back.

The trio don't take advantage of the Gribbles' retreat, their attention—and mine—drawn to the much larger threat padding forward. Eyes glowing red with swirls of purple within, fur fluffed to make the monster look larger than the van-size form it already has, the Queen Gribble howls again, its voice pitching higher and higher till even my ears are bleeding, the roar continuing without stop. The trio are worse off, weapons discarded as they clutch their ears. The Shieldsman is on his knees in pain, his afro sticking out around the helmet and his fingers.

Queen Gribble (Level 65 Alpha)
HP: 1411/1411
MP: 980/980
Conditions: Enraged, Poisonous, Damage Resistance, Pack Aura

"Arse…"

The Gribbles that have fallen back rush the trio, intent on finishing the group while they're incapacitated. Even as I swear, a part of me is focusing and reaching outward to the System and inward to my own body as I adjust my hearing. If higher attributes are good, why would a higher Perception make you more vulnerable to sensory-based attacks? It'd make no sense—and they don't. In fact, one of the upgrades in a higher Perception attribute is an unseen resistance to such attacks. But because it's unseen and hidden, it's not used by most to the maximum effect. After being forced to fight with nothing but my frozen attributes for four years, I'm no longer part of the majority. With the barest of thoughts, I touch on the System and push my defenses to the maximum. The innate resistance of my Advanced Class already shunts much of the damage away; this makes the remaining damage less incapacitating.

89 Sonic Damage Taken

Auditory perception checks receive a -11 modifier for 9 seconds

Stun Resisted

A spell flows from my hands, a paired casting as I push up Mud Walls around the trio. A second later, the Mud Walls surge outward, catching the Gribbles. Earth Shape follows soon after as the ground under the trio sinks downward, providing additional defense.

The Queen Gribble turns toward me as its howl comes to an end. It snarls, shaking its body, and suddenly its body exudes a purple gas that flows not outward unrestricted, but in a dark tide toward me like a wave. I kick off the ground, jumping backward as I toss an Ice Blast downward at the Queen. The spell freezes chunks of the monster's fur, and even the gas in its path freezes, solidifying the poison. Polar Zone erupts from my hands. But I'm focusing too much on casting, my mind split along the numerous lines of the spell, and I end up ignoring the smaller Gribbles. I pay for it when one slams into my newly landed form and bites my thigh.

I frown, the Gribble's sharp teeth punching through the nanoweave and injecting my leg with a numbing poison, even as its airborne toxin attempts to close down my throat. A stab and twist with a knife pries the Gribble off my body even as I jump again, purposely exploding the ground beneath my jump to add to the Gribbles' confusion as I fly through the air.

You are Poisoned!

-2 Health per second for 11 seconds

Polar Zone seems to be working, slowing down not just the Queen Gribble but also the flow of her poisonous gas. Even so, the flow of the gas seems to follow my new trajectory even as more of it pours from the Queen's body as well as all around its body, the less dense amount moving toward the slowly recovering group.

"So damn weird." I grin then test out my next spell.

Mana Cage snaps into place around the Queen Gribble, trapping the creature in its glowing bands. The Queen Gribble snarls and snaps, slamming its body against the bars, but they hold, keeping the Queen inside, if not its poisonous gas. Damn, maybe I should have bought Mana Prison—but the Mana expenditure on that improved imprisonment spell was significantly higher.

Absently, I conjure my sword and cut a pair of leaping Gribbles apart before I land. A hacking from the direction of the trio of Adventurers reminds me that I'm not fighting by myself and I stop playing around. I can test my Spells further when I'm alone again. Rather than waste Mana, I raise my hand and conjure a series of Mana Missiles at the Queen. The Mana Missiles are an upgrade of my old mainstay Mana Dart, just improved to do more damage. A series of a half dozen Mana Missiles, each over a foot long and spinning, drill into the Queen's body. Without the ability to dodge, the Queen soon becomes a heavily bleeding pincushion, one that nearly manages to tear apart my Mana

Cage before it expires. Once the Queen expires, cleaning up the rest of the Gribbles is simple with the help of the trio of recovered Adventurers.

"Thank you," the Swordsman says to me as he discards the health injector.

I frown slightly at the littering but keep my mouth shut for now. Still, my presence annoys the monkey Hoplite who snarls at me.

"What are you doing here? We're the only party scheduled for today," monkey man snarls as he levels his spear toward me.

"You're welcome," I reply, nodding to sword and shield wielder and ignoring monkey man.

At my blatant disinterest in him, monkey man steps forward but is restrained by the DNA Mage who shakes his head. On closer inspection, I realize the mage is actually probably older than me—in his forties at least. I absently consider recommending adding a few more points in Charisma and probably a good dye job to deal with my thinning grey hair.

"I'm going to report you to the Dungeon Keeper," growls monkey man.

I just wave goodbye to the group, stopping only long enough to loot and deposit the Queen in my Altered Space before heading to my final objective— the Medical Faculty.

"Hey, that's a Level 70 zone," a new voice calls behind me—the older man's, I guess.

I wave in acknowledgement without turning around. A part of me wonders about how the faculty of medicine's unsealed but dentistry isn't. Then again, I guess more people fear dentists than doctors, possibly because we've all suffered under the hands of a too-rough dental hygienist.

Stepping into the building, I scan the insides for threats while dismissing the notification informing me of the increased zone Level. A skittering noise alerts me to the incoming monsters long before I see them. A half dozen humanoids come out, most dressed in hospital gowns but a few in scrubs and casual wear, their skin grey and pallid. They alternately lope forward on all fours, fingernails unusually long and black, and walk, their backs hunched slightly. Even their eyes are rheumy and yellow, showing little signs of intelligence. A quick scan shows that they're nearly all the same.

Diseased Revenant (Level 71)

HP: 3488/3488

MP: 0/0

Conditions: Diseased, Undead, Burst

My nose wrinkles slightly at the sight, but the humanoid, undead creatures are the perfect training dummies. And dummies the Revenants are. They launch themselves at me with little finesse but a ton of aggression, only savage cunning guiding their tactical decisions, like attempts at flanking me. What they lack in brains, they make up in an inability to feel damage, an unrelenting aggression that'd make an angry hornet look like a lovely butterfly, an innately high resistance to damage, and prodigious health.

Firestorms are my first attempt at dealing with them, the upgraded Fireball spell forming a whirlpool of flames that expands from my body. System-reinforced walls burn, creaking in agony as the temperature spikes. Wooden counters turn to cinders within seconds and the Revenants cook, flesh crisping and splitting to showcase tight muscles and leaking, evaporating fluids. Yet they don't stop.

A twist of my hands and a Mud Wall flows from the floor in a wave, smashing the monsters backward, but the pair that split off to flank me attack now. Two quick steps intercept one, a hand clasping its arm and body to twist and toss it against the second, before an Ice Beam strikes the pair. Their bodies twitch as they attempt to free themselves, frozen flesh and limbs shattering under their exertions and the over-heated air. Even my own health is dropping, if only briefly before my regeneration replaces it, from the remaining heat.

I grin as I hear, in the darkness, additional movement as the Revenants' howls echo down the hallways, drawing others of their kind to them. Good. I'm going to have fun with this.

***

Hours later, I finally jump out of the top floor of the building, landing lightly before ripping the embedded claw of the Revenant's Zone Boss out of my arm. I grimace as blood flows out, dripping to the ground even as the wound visibly closes, while a dark greyness spreads around the flesh. Diseased. Such a nice status effect—reduces an ever-increasing amount of attributes before it peaks and the attributes begin to recover. While the disease statuses don't stack among the normal Revenants, the Boss and Elites carry around another form of disease which is a lot longer lasting and which even my increased Constitution and Resistances can't remove within minutes.

Revenant Alpha Claw (Level 79)
Crafting material. May be used by an experienced crafter to make equipment.

"I see you cleared the zone. In record time too. That deserves a drink."

The voice of a thin, weedy man breaks my train of thought. I glance over as the long-haired man in a waist coat tosses a bottle to me. I catch the bottle, chuckling as I read the label—good old Apocalypse Ale, brewed up in cold Whitehorse.

Rodolfo Stone, the University of British Columbia Dungeon Keeper,
Wayward Son (Level 21 Dark Son)

HP: 480/480

MP: 1610/1610

Conditions: All-Seeing Eye, Dungeon Link, Simulacrum (x2)

"Thanks." I take a sip and raise an eyebrow as the rich, dark ale takes a cudgel to my taste buds, reminding me what good alcohol is like. Obviously the Brewers have Leveled up again.

"You're welcome, Mr. Lee," Rodolfo said. "Now I got to tell you you're suspended for the next two weeks. Can't have you skipping the line, you know?"

"Really?" I say. "You do know who I am, yes?"

"You're the boss man. But the rules are the rules, dude."

I chuckle but don't push the matter. There's something more interesting to pursue. "You know how long it took me to clear the building?"

"Yes." Rodolfo flicks one hand, and a moment later, I get a notification with a series of numbers on it. Mana and stamina consumed, the ratio and percentage left at any time, the number of times I zeroed out either—none—number of monsters killed, the average, longest, and fastest amount of time to kill each monster, the spells and weapons I used, and more. It's a huge list of data, information which runs on and on, about every aspect of my fight. "I also got the rest of your trip, but this is the good stuff."

"You have all this information on hand?" I say, somewhat startled as I read through it all. "Do you give this to everyone?"

"Nah, just those who pay." Rodolfo gestures again and a bottle of Apocalypse Ale appears in his hand. "Got to buy the Platinum package. But you know, you're the boss man, so I figured you'd want to see this. Pretty cool build there."

"Thanks. What else do you offer?"

"I give advice on gaps, but you've got a pretty solid build. Skill use, training options within the dungeon to cover areas of weakness. The usual, you know."

"What do you think my build is?" I ask. It's not as if I haven't given it much thought. Even if I hate the way it makes our life feel like a game, the idea of proactively determining what you want to be isn't wrong.

"Endurance build. You ain't a duelist or adventurer. What you got there is meant for a grind and pound. Not enough damage to do a one-hit kill against an equal Level opponent, but your Stamina didn't even dip into the low sixties. You're like a giant energizer bunny of Stamina. If anything, I'd add more Willpower or Intelligence to up your Mana and regen rates." Rodolfo waves the bottle of Apocalypse Ale between sentences to punctuate his words. "You also need to smooth out your spell chaining too."

"I just bought them," I say, offering up the tidbit of information.

Rodolfo nods. "Gotcha. Well, I'd still work on chaining them. But unless you're going for a utility build, I'd stick to what you know. Been watching some of the arena fights they've started piping in, and at your Level, a fraction of a second hesitation gets you dead."

"Arena fights?" I drain the bottle in my hand.

When I look around for somewhere to put it, Rodolfo snorts. "Toss it. The dungeon will clean it. And I got no one coming through this section before it's done its job." He suits action to words with his own bottle. "The Galactics got a real Roman thing, you know? It's their hockey."

"Right," I say and make a note to look into these arena fights. It'd be good to see what the Master Class fighters are like at my Level. "One last thing then.

Mikito mentioned you get some of the other Master Classers grinding here sometimes?"

"The champions? Yeah, I get them to test my new zones before I open them up."

"Good. I'll want their stats," I say.

"No can do, boss man," Rodolfo says. "Client privilege."

"It's my dungeon," I say softly, the friendliness gone from my voice as I meet his gaze. I trigger Champion's Aura too, but Rodolfo doesn't even blink. I guess one of those Status effects of his is blocking the Aura.

"And if you fire me and take the job, you can get it," Rodolfo says. "But you got to fire me first."

"You sure you want to do this?" I say, the threat ringing out.

"Sure as donuts have holes."

"Okay." I raise my hand, tapping the air.

Rodolfo shrugs and pulls another bottle from his storage before sipping on it.

A moment later, I sigh. "Damn. Portal's not opening."

"Can't Portal out from here. Or in. You should know better," Rodolfo says with a sniff. "I'd bounce you out, but I'm about to be fired and I'm not feeling particularly charitable."

I shake my head. "I'm not firing you over saying no to me. I just wanted to make sure you were the kind of person who deserved to know that kind of information."

"And you thought threatening was a good way of doing that?" Rodolfo snorts, a look of pity on his face as he turns on his heels and walks off.

"Hey, about the port...," I call to the dungeon keeper.

"Walk!"

I guess I deserve that. Still, as I turn toward the exit and run, I chuckle. Looks like Lana and Katherine did a good job with Rodolfo. Even if he's a touch obstinate.

As I run, I clear up the less important notifications I've received.

Congratulations! You have reached Level 16 as an Erethran Paladin

Attributes automatically allocated. You have 39 additional free attributes and 5 Class Skill points to assign.

I'm a little surprised to see how fast I Leveled. With a mental command, the experience notification messages are pulled up and I scan through them. Let's see—a bonus for being the first to clear the Level 70 zone. Bonus experience for doing it alone. A long list of things which I've killed, including the zone boss. All those notifications I skip over. And of course, the bonus experience from fighting with the champions and clearing the dungeon, including the first clear bonus there. Oh, and I've been steadily accumulating a small amount of experience every day for actually doing my job as a settlement owner. It's discounted since I don't have the Classes for it, but since it's based off total population, it's still a significant boost.

Huh.

The experience gain from being a settlement owner is a bit of a realization. While I'm sure I used to get it, with the lower population, settlement level, and my lack of involvement, it has been seriously discounted. Still, the experience is evil. But also sensible, since otherwise royalty, which is never allowed to get too down and dirty in dungeons, would never be able to Level up.

After a brief consideration, I decide that with five free Class Skill points, I'll be able to get a point in everything if I desire, so I dump another point into Penetration. Always good to hit a little harder.

Chapter 8

Whitehorse. Such a small city—Town now—in the middle of nowhere. Even before all this, it didn't even have thirty thousand people in it. These days, between those we saved and the new immigrants, it's nearly back to its former peak. Even if the vast majority aren't humans. Truinnar in formal tunic-and-pants suits whose color reflects their dark skin, Yerrick with their horns and fur, the Kapre towering over everyone, nude but for their bark-like skin, cyborg-like creatures, and monsters straight out of fantasy books all mix on the rune-covered streets, Mana lights providing illumination on this cloud-covered night. Everyone and everything's armed, moving in small groups as they get ready for another day of adventuring.

Walking down Main Street, I look at the towering silver building which looks so out of place among the historic, frontier town architecture of Whitehorse's Main Street. Adventurers stream in and out of the tower, heading upstairs to the Shop, checking on newly designated Quests, and complaining to the various administrative personnel. I ignore them all, slipping past the groups to head toward the back of the building, once again noting how weirdly distorted space is here. Ceilings too high, corridors too wide, and the building somehow longer and wider than its outside appearance would indicate.

At the bank, the single elevator slides open to allow Ali and myself to step within. It moves smoothly, the acceleration barely perceptible as it takes us to my appointment. I grunt, feet tapping as I adjust the hem of my jacket.

"Chill, boy-o. It's just a date," Ali says with a grin.

"It's a meeting. Not a date," I growl softly, and the olive-skinned Spirit chuckles.

"Wasn't talking about you. Figured I'd chat with Roxley's AI, see if she's up to anything..." Ali waggles his eyebrows.

"You know, I've always wondered. She's an AI, you're a Spirit. I mean, how do you guys…"

"Bang?"

"Talk."

"With great care."

Before I can press Ali for a real answer, the doors slide open. The room within is all too familiar, the long metallic table and pair of chairs, the plates and dishes set for the first, cold course. In the corner, Roxley's personal chef hovers, its spherical body ready to roll—and roll out—the next course.

"Damn him," I mutter to myself.

"For feeding you?" Roxley says in reply while walking out from his office. The dark elf smiles at me, gesturing to the table. "I recall you enjoyed dinners here before. I would be remiss if I didn't feed a guest."

I stare at the Truinnar, his wide shoulders and trim waist set off by the black-and-silver tunic in his house colors, the well-cut pair of pants outlining every inch of his muscular legs. The smile that is always on his lips but sometimes relaxes a little when Roxley actually finds something funny for real. The now-electric blue-hair contrasts with his white eyebrows where a piercing gaze interrogates me and my body. As I stare at the Truinnar, Ali elbows me in the side to get my attention.

Immediately after, the Spirit steps forward and bows slightly. "I shall take my leave then?"

Even as he does so, I see a new notification.

Mental Influence Resisted
Now get your act together, boy-o

"Dinner is fine. I'm sure it's lovely as always." I nod to Roxley's chef, taking a seat while Roxley sits across me in his own, and I bury my irritation. I do need to eat, the food is good, and I know the man well enough to know that this is part payment for what I'll ask of him. "But I do want to know what you so urgently needed to speak to me about."

"Of course. But first, a toast." Roxley raises the wine glass, a pale yellow drink with flakes of squirming dark matter within. "To your Master Class."

"Thanks." I sip on the drink. It's sweet and fruity and smooth and the next thing I know, it's gone. Too fast for me to remember to have scanned it, which is a damn shame.

"Jumma summer wine. Summers last nine years, but the only time the vegetation can fruit is within the first and last month," Roxley says.

"Thank you," I say. "And congratulations on your new title. Count now, is it?"

"Yes." Roxley stares at me, presumably looking for the anger or resentment I showed so many years ago. But I've had a lot of time to think about it, more time to consider what he did. And while I still don't agree, I no longer hold a grudge against him for his choices. Perhaps he sees that, for his lips relax, his smile growing more natural. I wouldn't be surprised if he did—Roxley has always been more perceptive than I am. "We've managed to stabilize many of the dungeons around the city and the territory. Our results have made the Duchess extremely happy. Now, we should eat before the food grows too cold."

I take Roxley's diversion with grace, digging in. I recall that the Truinnar hate speaking about business at the dinner table. Even the little he's done shows that Roxley's gone native a bit, adapting to our customs slightly. Dinner, as always, is a gourmet's wet dream. While the vast majority of food served is nothing that I recognize, years under the System has acclimatized most people to not asking where and what kind of beast their latest meal is coming from. At least, not if they don't have an iron stomach. Armed with that knowledge, it's a lot easier to just enjoy the wide range of tastes that dance across one's tongue.

We avoid sensitive topics, catching up on how things have gone for many of my acquaintances, the Town as a whole, and some of my remaining business interests as well. Of note, the local brewing company has expanded again, taking up nearly an entire block as it attempts to meet Galactic demand. In addition, Dawson opened up a year ago, the city retaken by a trio of ambitious adventuring teams. Now, the Guild the teams are a part of have their headquarters in the newly reclaimed city and are raking in Credits as their members tackle the high-Level zones all around the newly rebuilt Town. If there's one sour note, it's that there's not a single living human in that town from before. It is very much a Galactic settlement. Way I hear it, even Ingrid hasn't visited.

Time passes swiftly and I find myself laughing and relaxing, the conversation flowing as easily as the drink. It's only after dinner, after we've made our way to Roxley's study, that the tone and air of the meeting changes. Sitting across from each other in plush chairs that conform to our bodies, we stare across the intervening space, unwilling to break the moment of camaraderie. But business must be spoken and so I push ahead.

"You wanted to speak with me." I say.

"Yes. Your new Class complicates matters," Roxley says as he leans back. "But you've never not complicated your life, have you, John?"

"Don't know about that," I say with a shrug. "Just did what I wanted. But why's it a problem?"

"You understand what your Class entails? What it means for the Erethrans?" Before I can answer, he continues. "You are the only active

Paladin in the entire Empire. You stand outside of all command structures, reporting only to their ruler."

Huh. I guess he doesn't actually know the details of my Class. I do note how Roxley says "active," but I keep my own face smooth.

"You may, by tradition and right of arms, judge and execute any and all in their Empire with the exception of the queen. You are, furthermore, considered a representative of their beliefs and their will."

"I know," I say. "And…?"

"And you are human. With no political or social backing. Your authority carries only the weight of tradition behind it and what you, yourself, are able to bring to bear. You have authority but no power," Roxley says and leans forward. "And as such, you are a pawn. One that many will eye in hope of using against the Erethrans."

"They may try. But if this is what you wanted to speak of, you could have saved your breath. I knew what I was getting into."

"Interesting." Roxley leans back, steepling his fingers. He peers at me over the aqua-colored nails. "I was lead to believe you were not given much time to consider your Class Quest and its implications."

"I wasn't," I say. No use hiding what is common knowledge. None of what happened to me is hard to ascertain.

"Then tell me, John, what do you intend to do?"

"The usual," I say, smiling slightly. "Whatever needs to be done. Which, at this point, is getting Earth its Galactic seat."

Roxley lets out a breath, shaking his head slightly. "Still focused on your impossible quests, are you John? And so, my invitation was accepted."

"Yes. You understand Galactic politics better than I do, and probably have a much clearer idea of how all of it is affecting Earth. From what Kim's analyzed, about six percent of the unclaimed City Cores will be very difficult to claim on a permanent basis in the short term. For the remainder, it will take no longer than four months for them to be claimed. If I'm not reading that wrong, we're going to run out of areas to contest very, very soon. We either need to make enough friends, fast, or we're going to have to start kicking ass."

"Which would be foolish," Roxley says sternly.

"Because we can't win a long-term fight?" I nod. "No. We can't. Four years ago, we might have been able to bulrush the powers out. Hit them hard enough and fast enough and take over enough City Cores that we could use the rights and planetary powers to mitigate their retaliation. Now, there are too many Master Class fighters on this world to make it viable even if we wanted to try it.

"At least not alone."

Roxley stares at me and shakes his head. "I cannot commit my Duchess to such an action. Not without her prior approval. Not even for you."

"But you can advise me on the political environment, can't you?"

"I can." Roxley waves and a screen appears, hovering between the two of us. It's a simple pie chart next to the map of the world. I frown at the map then realize why it's bothering me—it's not the usual one we see but a different one that rebalances the landmasses to their actual sizes. The Peters map. And yeah, it's my higher Intelligence supplying stupid facts dredged up from a *West Wing* episode. "This is how I would break the votes you seek up."

41.2% Human-Controlled Settlement Votes

8.8% Galactic Edge

17.6% Irvina

8.6% The Fist

2.14% Artisans

14.7% Miscellaneous powers

6.96% Unclaimed Settlement Areas

108

"Huh," I say and stare at the more detailed breakdown of the "miscellaneous powers."

"The Galactic Council is made up of four main and two smaller factions. Now, while what I speak of is in generalities, it is wise to remember that these are generalities. Not all races and individuals will 'fit' within these categories. Still, it's a useful shorthand." When I nod, Roxley continues. "The first major faction is the Galactic Edge—a group dedicated to expansion in System-registered planets for additional resources. You'll find many of the more recent additions to the System part of this faction, including races like mine. The Galactic Edge is the third largest faction in terms of seats on the Council.

"The Irvina—named after the main solar system and planet from which the Council operates from—is the largest faction by number of seats. They consist of a limited number of races, however, as they consist of races introduced to the System the longest. They include the Movana, a few active dragons, and your dwarves. Obviously, their close allies are all included in the displayed number."

I frown at his words, trying to recall the image of the Galactic System. "But don't the Truinnar have as much space as the Movana?"

"Space, yes. But like your world, we face the issue of votes on many of our planets. We either have not covered sufficient landmass, in many cases, or are forced to deal with interlopers or split votes. My people are not very altruistic, and as such, politics can be dangerous on our home planets," Roxley says.

"Right. So geographic space and number of worlds aren't the same as number of seats," I say softly.

As the Movana are older, they have more seats because they've managed to concentrate power without giving up their settlements. It makes sense then that the older races manage to get away with it too—even if older planets become uninhabitable due to the flood of Mana, they have the existing resources to flood a new city with people and Credits and establish their dominance. And it's not as if the all-out fights happen as much on non-Dungeon-World-designated planets.

"The third faction has a long, cumbersome name which will not translate well. Most know them as the Fist. They are made up of individuals and particularly warlike species and kingdoms, like the Hakarta and your Erethran Empire. Their goal is to push for further exploration into the Restricted Zone near the Mana Spring, designate more Dungeon Worlds, and increase support for combat Classers in general," Roxley says.

"Were they the ones pushing for our conversion?" I ask softly, my eyes narrowing in anger.

"Yes. As were the Irvina," Roxley says. "You must understand, each new Dungeon World relieves the level of Mana buildup in every other world, slowing down the process."

"I know. So why don't you just open a dozen more?" Having been stuck on a Restricted Planet for the last four years, I can understand why they'd prefer to slow down Mana buildup. Dealing with the ever-increasing monster hordes at ever-increasing Levels is an impossible task for a society. It's one thing when your average monster is Level 20 and increases to Level 30. It's another when same increase is to 130.

"System limitations and politics," Roxley says. "Like most things, opening a Dungeon World requires a significant amount of resources and also specific circumstances. It's only possible to designate a Dungeon World when a planet is first introduced to the System. The world should also be pre-inhabited, preferably by a sentient species, to handle the increased Mana load which will be directed to the planet. Failed integration will result not only in the loss of the world to the System but also a loss of all the resources dedicated to its creation.

"And, of course, the entire Council must contribute to its establishment. As the greatest benefits of the Dungeon World are seen by those closest to it, it can be politically difficult to justify such an expenditure, even if it is best for all parties."

I grunt, making a mental note. Those two factions are on my shit list.

"The last major faction is the Artisans. They're the second largest, with numbers close to the Irvina, though their individual power is somewhat limited by their lack of Combat Class Masters and higher. The Artisans do receive significant support from various corporations, so it would be foolish to underestimate their strength," Roxley warns me. "As for the two minor factions, the Technocrats seek to explore the limits of pre-System technology—your 'normal' physics and chemistry—within and outside the bounds of the System. They're a small group but have a pair of members on the Inner Council, giving them a greater level of prestige than they would have otherwise. And lastly, the Systemers are not an official faction, but their religious belief in the System is widespread among the Galactic System."

I nod slightly. The Technocrats are a known group for me—many of the writers I read in my continuous quest for knowledge about the System come from the group. It seems the Venn diagram of Technocrats and Questors has significant overlap. They're also known to be one of the few groups who would voluntarily leave the radius of the System, venturing into the deep unknown to explore, learn about non-System technology from before the System took over, and test older technology. Overall, they're considered kooks of the highest order—but dangerous and useful kooks.

"As you can see, the Artisans have little presence on Earth. Of those here, they're not truly organized, their presence more based on individual desires rather than a group effort. Of course, the Fist has significant presence, with Ares and a few other Corporations and the Hakarta Legion owning the major cores," Roxley says, gesturing to the hanging notification.

"This makes a lot more sense." I tap my lips, doing the math in my head. "But we need eighty percent of the vote, and that means we'll need the vast majority of the people on the board to vote for us. Including getting the majority of those you labeled independents, assuming I'm missing out on either the Truinnar or the Movana."

"Yes. It is possible, I believe, for you to gain either of the pair's backing for your endeavor, but not both."

"Figures," I mutter, shaking my head. The way the numbers read, I'm not even sure there's a way to make this work. Getting so many independents would mean speaking with a large number of disparate organizations. "Why are they indies anyway? Doesn't it make sense to join together with the factions?"

"While there are four major factions, there are numerous other, smaller groups. Some are allied with the major factions on major topics, but not on others. Others have too-contrasting beliefs or just are not interested in joining the larger factional politics on a regular basis," Roxley says, smiling slightly. "Some prefer to be independent, no matter the cost."

"*Ali, make a note to have Kim filter for objectionable moral and cultural practices, will you? If we're going to have to stomp on some ankles to get our votes, might as well make it count.*"

"*You know, boy-o, Kim's upgraded enough for you to tell him yourself. At least up here,*" Ali sends back.

I grunt, sending the note directly to the AI. I get a confirmation, though I send a reminder for Ali to double-check the list. While Kim's smart, he is still a program and I'm not entirely sure his views on morality line up with mine.

For that matter, neither do Ali's at times, but he's been with me long enough to understand my intentions.

"Knowing all this, you still intend to continue your quest?" Roxley says, leaning forward as he places his hands on the armchair rests.

I find myself nodding even as I twirl my now-empty glass. Roxley shuts his mouth as the drone servant comes in to pour refreshments for both of us. Afterward, it leaves, gliding away silently on its anti-gravity jets.

"And you wish for our help?"

"If your Duchess will offer it. I'm assuming there are others I'll need to speak to within your kingdom?" I say. While they might all be the same race and kingdom, the Truinnar are rivals to some extent, peers fighting one another.

"May I make a suggestion?" At my nod, Roxley continues. "If my liege agrees to your request, it might be best to allow her—or specifically, myself as her representative—to speak with the others on Earth. Your time is limited and your understanding of the politics limited."

And of course, it also means we'll end up owing a much larger boon to the Duchess. But the offer is tempting. Roxley's right. We are short on time here, if I want to meet the deadline of the next vote.

"Very well. If she'll agree to help us," I say.

"Good." Roxley taps his lips. "You will find it hard to gain support from most without some concessions. I won't ask what you are willing to give up, but it is something you must consider. The Fist, for example, would be raring to have you in their camp. It is not an all-too-disagreeable notion for the Edge, as we vote together quite often."

"But doing so will put us at odds with the Artisans," I say, running my fingers along the edge of the wine glass. "And they're the second most powerful group who might be willing to work with us. Certainly one of the most economically beneficial for humans."

"Yes," Roxley says. "Though the Edge has some additional benefits. For example, have you considered the benefits of colonization?"

I blink at Roxley. I'm about to protest about the sheer number of hurdles involved in a proper colonization effort before I realize the System wipes out so many of these problems. Hell, given enough Credits and Mana, it's possible to terraform a planet in days instead of decades. Never mind the fact that our bodies can handle a much, much wider variety of environments with minor issues under the System.

"Touché," I say.

"One last matter, John," Roxley says. "Have you even confirmed your support among your race?"

"No. I needed a better understanding of the situation first," I say before shrugging. "They're next on my list."

"Then you'll understand why a minimum prerequisite for us to take any action officially would be for you to gain their agreement?" Roxley says, and I find myself nodding. Roxley smiles before he waves his hand toward the notifications, pulling up the independent list. "Then in the meantime, there are a few groups I feel you might be able to work on."

I glance at Roxley's list, making mental notes of the names as the Truinnar speaks. Still, while he talks, I make note of how he says what he says. Because while I know he is unlikely to lie, where and at whom he points us is suspect. For all the friendliness he and I might share, the Truinnar always has more than one goal.

Even so, I listen. Because any information is better than nothing. And I've got about four years' worth of local and thousands of years of Galactic history to learn.

Chapter 9

When I walk out of the building later that evening—much later—I find the city still humming with activity. Between tech, Skills, and spells, there's little to stop an ambitious adventuring team from working through the night. In fact, most nighttime quests pay significantly better than daytime quests, no matter the type. Part of the reason is that nocturnal monsters are generally tougher, but it's the loss and inconvenience which probably keeps nocturnal-based quests better paying.

As I stare at the scurrying adventurers, I touch my lips absently. Sometimes, I really wish I was like these others. Able to focus on simple tasks, simple quests. Go out, collect a dozen claws. Kill a few monsters, clear a couple of dungeons. Escort a bioorganic researcher who wants to check out how the Mana overflow has affected our ecosystem. Simple. Easy. Uncomplicated.

Not like planet-wide politics. Not like running a settlement. Or a handsome dark elf kissing you on the lips as you leave, then shutting the door on you.

Simple.

"So, Paladin, are you done?" Ayuri says.

I blink, tilting my head to see the champion standing beside me. I frown, prodding my memory and realizing she's been there for minutes now. A slight shiver runs through me at the thought that I'd let someone this dangerous so close to me. But there are no indications of danger from her, none of the subtle signals one learns to pick up on to indicate killing intent. In the end, she was just standing there.

"For now." I sigh and drop my hand. "Why are you here?"

"It was pointed out to me I was a little hasty," Ayuri says, glaring backward at Unilo. The female Guard waves at me in greeting, slitted purple eyes dancing with ill-concealed humor. "Just because you have the Class means little."

"I see," I say, shifting slightly as I eye our surroundings.

Just over a score of people are out and about on the streets, most of them adventurers thankfully. Any collateral damage from Skill use is probably survivable. Blink Step down the road to the other side of the river will pull them out of danger too. So long as I head left after the Blink Step, away from the hospital, I should be able to pull the resulting battle away from most civilians. Of course, the Kapre live there, but they've got their own protections.

"Come." Ayuri points at a gaping black Portal which offers no information about where we're going next.

"You know, it's been a long day already…"

Ayuri drops a hand on my shoulder and guides me to the Portal. Her strength is significantly higher than mine and continuous, as inexorable as tectonic plates shoving me forward. The Portal widens even further, allowing the two of us to walk through side-by-side. We're followed by Unilo and Mayaya, who is looking as bored as ever.

"Plenty of use you were," I send to Ali as he pops into existence over my shoulder just before I step into the Portal.

I could fight this, but my gut says that whatever their intentions, it doesn't include putting a bullet in my head in front of a self-dug grave. The mental shrug I get back from Ali is insouciant enough to put my teeth on edge as the darkness takes me.

***

The other end of the Portal is in a small settlement, somewhere on the North American continent as we're still on Earth and the sun still hasn't risen. I look at the buildings, dismissing those with Galactic architecture and spending time staring at the 1960s brick-and-wood construction for clues. All of it is written in English, so Canada or North America. The air conditioning units makes me guess somewhere down south. Well, that and the lingering heat from the day. Of particular note though is the population striding around the town, many still dressed in their uniforms.

"Yours?" I ask Ayuri as she releases me. The happy nod she gives me makes me grunt, but I follow her passively down the street, heading for a newer Galactic building. "Don't recall seeing the Erethran Empire on the list of settlement owners."

"It's because it's not. It's owned by Unilo directly," Ayuri says.

When I look at Unilo, she smiles sunnily.

"We're still waiting for the requisitioned Credits for the space," Ayuri adds. "Since Unilo's a d'Cha, she's got the Credits to spend on this till my requisition comes through."

Ali chuckles, floating alongside us in his pint-sized form. "Galactic bureaucracy. The same wherever you go."

"Except the M453-Xs the Gnumma, the Vassalee, the—"

"Okay, okay, fine. Not universal," Ali says grumpily and glares at Mayaya, who continues to ignore the Spirit.

I chuckle softly, letting the pair distract me as we walk into the building. Within, it's surprisingly spacious and empty, hosting but four shimmering blue cells. Within one of those cells, a pair of Erethran grunts spar, one wielding a knife and the other what looks like brass knuckles. The pair are Basic Classes and not particularly skilled from what I can see.

"You going to put me in there to fight a bunch of your men?" I say, taking a guess at her intentions. I'm hoping it's this option, because the other one is much more painful.

"Of course not. What would the challenge be there?" Ayuri says with a snort. "No, I'm going to fight you."

***

Standing across from Ayuri in the middle of the reinforced fight ring, I feel my heartbeat slowly speeding up. All four shield walls have been allocated to our single cell, providing the ever-growing audience greater protection. Crouched slightly with my hands by my sides, I watch the purple-haired Erethran casually stretch across the ring.

"Rules?" I say to break the silence as Ayuri continues to ready herself.

"No leaving the cell," Ayuri says. "Five taps, audible indication, or five percent remaining of your health is a loss. The building is tracking our health. There'll be an auditory and visual cue to stop fighting."

"Okay."

I could protest, but truth be told, a part of me is looking forward to this. It's been four years and a lot of experience since we met. Now, I'm curious to see what the gap is. Ayuri isn't like me, having skipped an entire Class. She has over eighty Levels' worth of attributes and Skills as an advantage and countless years of experience. In a straight duel like this, I have no realistic chance of winning. But still, I find myself grinning in anticipation even as I activate Mana Sight. Because this is going to be fun.

"On your signal, Unilo," Ayuri says.

There's a tense silence as Unilo stares between the two of us, a silence which grows as the seconds tick by without a signal. "Now."

Ayuri reacts first, appearing behind me, but it's a move I've anticipated. I'm already dropping and kicking backward even as I conjure a Soul Shield around my body. My attack connects as Ayuri refuses to dodge, bouncing off her Soul Shield. It's only when I'm rolling away that I catch a glimpse of Ayuri's soulbound weapon. The short, flame-bladed sword flicks downward, sending a Blade Strike that I barely dodge by continuing to roll. The shorter blade allows Ayuri to swing the blade back, sending another successful Blade Strike at me even as I recover. The single strike drains nearly half of my Soul Shield, making my eyes narrow. Christ, she's put a ton of points into the attack Skill.

She blurs, charging me as I watch the streams of Mana collect and swirl around her body. Haste. A Basic Class Skill that speeds up her movement at the cost of a tremendous amount of Mana and Stamina while active. She crosses the distance between us in seconds and I find myself blocking the flurry of thrusts and cuts with my own sword.

Even as I fall back, I call forth my Thousand Blades Skill, adding the floating blades and complicating the space between us. Now, not only does she have to work around my initial attack, she also has to move around the flowing follow-up blades. Each block cuts off an area of attack, each additional blade reducing her angles of attack. Rather than avoid the angles though, Ayuri blocks and beats aside my floating weapons, forcefully opening up angles. The ring of blades, the shuffle of our steps, and the harsh grunts of exertion fill the room as we clash. Within seconds of our clash, I've been hit a half dozen times, leaving my Soul Shield with a sliver of health. It's only when I activate the Haste spell that things begin to stabilize.

The champion twists her hand as we clash again, triggering a Skill and breaking my grip on my sword, disarming me. I block the next thrust with my left forearm, the last of my Soul Shield dying in a flare as the blade opens up my forearm. But the sacrifice pushes the blade away from my chest and gives me time to point and fire my beam pistol at her face. The attack flares as it impacts against her Soul Shield, but more importantly, it blinds her for a second to allow me to scramble backward.

"Your sword skills have improved," Ayuri praises me with a grin. She tosses the wavy short blade from hand to hand as she stalks me around the ring, giving me time to replace my Soul Shield.

"You ready to get serious?" I say.

"You noticed?"

"Obviously."

"Good. I'm coming then," Ayuri says, her eyes twinkling with amusement. Even before her words end, she's on me, Blink Stepping to cover the short distance.

I throw a reverse lunge, dropping to one knee with my back leg extended and catching her directly in her chest. Her Shield bursts, the momentum of her charge and Blink added to my own Skills and attack shattering her protection. But it doesn't stop her. The champion uses the momentum of my attack to spin around, a hand trailing along the edge of my blade as her other hand conjures another sword. I retrieve my sword into my left hand to block her attack, but she twitches her original hand and tosses her short sword at me directly. Behind the attack comes another and another.

Within seconds, she's pulling copies of her soulbound blade and throwing them at me, cutting through my blocks by sheer volume, each blade unerring. Under repeated assault, my Soul Shield fails again, the newly conjured blades breaking past my hasty defenses. Even as the first blade plunges into my shoulder, I trigger my Skill.

Blink Step.

Beneath me, Ayuri spins around then looks up, spotting my falling form. She smirks, already throwing knives to intercept me and the grenades I've thrown. Falling as I am, I can see when recognition catches up with instinct, just before her first blade pierces the first grenade.

A chaos grenade.

Fish explode from the grenade—barbed, slimy fish that rain down around us. Another grenade detonates, consuming her conjured blade and leaving a small hole in space. A third grenade lands by her feet and a horde of sizzling, molten fire elementals manifest. Ayuri lets out an involuntary yelp as she sinks, pushed deeper into the swarm as she blocks my falling attack. Already, I can see her Soul Shield flaring as the elementals eat into it.

"Chaos grenades?" Ayuri snarls, gripping my arm as I recover from the fall and blocked attack.

She twists and tosses me away, dodging my follow-up blades at the same time, her movements barely hindered by the elementals. I spin through the air and slam into the side of the cage. By the time I recover, she's cast an Ice Storm, slaying the newly formed elementals and catching me in the back blast.

Even as I stagger, the Soul Shield reforming with a thought, Ayuri is stalking forward. With a thought, I trigger the mines I laid when I dropped, the expanding Tier II foam surprise only barely catching the fast-moving champion at the edges. Long enough for me to cast a Freezing Blade on my sword.

"Freezing Blade. Good choice." With a shrug, Ayuri snaps the restricting foam. "But useless."

I snort, ignoring her taunts as Ayuri darts forward more cautiously. Our blades clash once again, the ice creeping up along her hand with each attack. But as fast as they connect, the blades are dismissed, the freezing barely given time to act upon the champion. And what does appear on her hands seems to be dismissed by a swirl of Mana around her body. Another Skill—probably one that removes Status effects.

She shatters my defense in a few strikes, my Soul Shield failing once more. A Disarm opens up an avenue of attack, allowing Ayuri to snap an elbow strike at my temple. I stagger backward, a cut opening above my eye even as I try to move away from another flung blade. I twist, throwing a half-formed Blade Strike to push her away. I split my focus for a second, throwing Blade Strikes without care as I attempt to buy time to finish forming my spell. It works and Mud Walls forms, rushing upward ahead of me to block her view.

"You're getting your ass kicked, boy-o," Ali says, chortling.

"No shit. I barely have time to use my Skills."

Through Ali's viewpoint outside the ring, I can see Ayuri casually dodging my last Blade Strike before smirking at the Mud Walls. She raises a hand, forming a glowing ball of power in it—a charged Skill, it seems. I'm vaguely curious if it's a Master or Basic Class attack, but mostly, I'm focusing on the flow of Mana as seen by Ali. It's not as effective as viewing it directly, but it's good enough.

When she releases the attack, I Blink Step, appearing behind Ayuri. Immediately, I cast Army of One, hammering her with everything I have. The blades send slashes of power into her back, blood erupting from her body as the attack tears through her Shield and defenses. The champion immediately twists and dodges some of the attacks. My Master Class Skill makes a difference here, making her numerous defensive Skills useless. Ayuri is sent spinning into the Mud Walls, her health plummeting as each attack shaves off a visible chunk. By the time the attack is over, the champion has lost half of her health and I've lost the element of surprise.

"That hurt," Ayuri says, her bloody smile widening. "Now I'm really going to kick your ass."

***

My head slams hard against the floor and I slide backward, slamming into the sparring ring's force fields. The first two have dissipated from the concussive force of Ayuri's last attack. The third shatters as I'm forced into it, piles of rubble building up around my sliding body and being turned to dust under the force. The last and strongest field holds though, leaving me bloody and shattered. The room is dyed red, a warning klaxon shattering the air as it marks the end of our sparring match.

For a moment, I focus and cast a Major Healing on myself, pushing through the pain. The spell is insufficient for the sheer amount of damage done to me, but it fixes the major problems, stemming blood loss from ruptured organs and open wounds. The force field drops, and more healing magic descends on my prone form.

"*What... Skill?*" I send the thought to Ali, barely coherent even as my body patches together.

Rather than answer me directly, Ali flashes me the Skill information as a reminder from the Champion Class information we purchased.

The Will of the People (Erethran Champion Class Skill)

Drawing upon the trust and respect earned by a champion, the user unleashes a single devastating attack to remove all threats to the Empire.

Effect: Attack form and damage done dependent upon user and the amount of Reputation the champion has developed in Erethra. Each 10 points of Erethran reputation deals an additional point of damage.

Cost: 1000 Mana

I snort slightly and regret it immediately, the motion making my chest ache as broken ribs grate upon one another. A single attack my ass. Ayuri formed a million and one separate, spinning decahedrons of blades with the Skill, each of which honed in on me when fired. And a hundred reputation points seems like nothing until you realize the damn Erethran Empire is a multi-system, multi-planet juggernaut. Even a mild level of fame for a champion makes this attack ridiculous. If Ayuri hadn't purposely held back the vast majority of her attack, I'd be dead, even with my damage reduction and Spell resistances. As it stood, the final attack had actually increased my Mana by an appreciable amount.

As the spells rumble through me, I have a sudden urge to cough. Twisting over my side, I hack and cough, pain ripping through my body at each motion, but eventually, the misplaced, shattered bones and mashed tissue comes out. I stare at the bloody mess, my nose wrinkling as my sense of smell comes back, bringing with it the harsh scent of melted concrete and roasted flesh. A Cleanse fixes some of dirt and smell even as a last spell lands on me, leaving the longer-term healing pulses and my own regeneration to finish the job.

"Damn. You just keep ticking, don't you?" Ayuri says as she strides up to my prone form. "Were you trying to get me to use my ultimate Skill?"

"Pretty much." I peel myself off the floor, stare at the tattered remnants of my clothing, and chuckle suddenly.

"What?"

"Just a funny cultural realization." With a shrug, I tear off the remainder of the armored jumpsuit as it is doing nothing for my modesty and get dressed in something new. None of the Erethrans even blink. Then again, considering how uncovered I was before, they had more than enough time to get over their shock.

"What did you learn?" Unilo asks, her head cocked to the side as she watches me. After a moment, she brightens. "Oh! You are speaking about your embarrassment of being nude! We are too."

"You are?" I look at the shreds of my clothing as I pull on my new jumpsuit.

"Yes. But only among those of the same species." Unilo makes a face. "Who'd care about what other species wear? It's not as if you're biologically compatible."

"*Unless you're Truinnar or Movana or Dwarven or boy-o—*"

"*Not. Now.*"

"Right," I say out loud.

Unilo continues, oblivious. "It'd be like watching a cruppa and being—"

"*Cruppa?*"

"*Domestic animal.*" An image flashes up in front of me, a six-limbed, furred on the top and scaled on the bottom creature who is about knee height with a barbed tail. "*Erethran equivalent of a dog.*"

I flush slightly, glaring at Unilo, who continues to blather on without noticing the look I shoot her.

"Embarrassed. Or worse, aroused. We actually don't condone that kind of perversion on Erethra, though I know on some of the other planets… well, it's a bit more uncivilized."

"Unilo." Ayuri's single word cuts off Unilo's ramblings.

Ayuri gestures for the exit, and as I'm now presentable, I'm happy to comply. We stay silent as we push past the crowd, my head cocked to the side as I read lips and listen to the whispered Erethran-filled conversations all around me.

"*You sure he's a Paladin? I hear they're even worse than champions—*"

"*Never saw anyone take more than a twentieth of the Will before. His damage reduction must be insane!*"

"*Well, he did have two-thirds of his health. His regeneration rates were ridiculous. And he kept on buying time with the Soul Shield.*"

"*You think the d'Quam are going to let him live?*"

"*He got her down a quarter health. Shit, I think I'm going to have to buy his profile from the Shop.*"

"*Krell's nipples the Shop. I got a broker for that. Get you a real deal—*"

Ayuri stays silent until we enter a new building and enter what I presume to be her office. It amuses me how, even with a mostly paperless society, Ayuri has managed to clutter her office with junk. I see knickknacks everywhere, from snow globes, lava lamps, a bagpipe, and numerous magnets to other, less identifiable Galactic souvenirs. And trophies. Lots of monster part trophies. As Ayuri slumps in her chair and puts her feet up on the table, I gingerly move aside the half-shattered skull of a particularly large Goblin.

"Hob," Ayuri says, as if it's an explanation. "I was trying to make a cup out of his head and well…"

"Cup?"

"Well, you humans have this interesting saying—"

"Hyperbole. It's hyperbole!" I say, waving.

"Oh. Huh. That'd explain it," Ayuri says. "Well. You passed. Barely."

I nod slightly, my eyes narrowing. She didn't need to drag me all the way here to tell me all this. In fact, she didn't even need to bring me to this town. Any relatively empty zone would have done just as well. Except, of course, her objective had never been to test my combat ability.

"We're done. You should go eat. Unilo, get him some chow," Ayuri says and gestures for me to get up.

I blink, staring at Ayuri then back at Unilo. Oh. Right. "Grub?"

"No, we do not eat insects, but we could find some for you," Unilo says as she leads me out of the office toward what I assume to be the officers' mess.

It takes the rest of the walk to explain the misunderstanding. It takes another few minutes for me to find something to eat, and I'm not surprised when Unilo joins me. Or when Mayaya, who has been quietly shadowing us, drives away the few other patrons.

"The settlement vote," I say after we have both dug into our food for a bit.

"It's yours," Unilo says, then cuts me off when I open my mouth to thank her. "On one condition."

"Of course there's a condition," I say grumpily.

Ali, who's hovering above Mayaya invisibly, rolls his eyes at me.

"It's a simple one. Just a minor favor," Unilo says.

"A favor."

"A minor favor."

"*Some help here?*" I ask Ali.

"*Erethran nobles trade favors. Trivial, minor, major, blood, life, and family in order of importance. A minor favor is generally considered an action which does not significantly inconvenience or danger you. A single vote, an appropriately Leveled dungeon run.*"

Unilo waits for me to answer, digging into the noodle-like substance before her with a weird utensil that adheres to the noodles with the barest touch. I bury my face in my food, barely tasting it even as my newly healed body craves the calories, while my thoughts spin. So. I'm paraded around, my Skills and Class shown off to a group of Erethran soldiers. Obviously the information about who and what I am is now public knowledge for the kingdom. And now, I'm being not so subtly forced to take a deal.

The problem with traps is that even if you recognize them, sometimes you have no choice but to spring them. Sometimes, the best way of dealing with a trap is to bull your way through it. And a trap that is known can sometimes be an opportunity.

"A minor favor. Only after a successful vote," I say, laying down my own conditions.

"Sounds like an open-ended deal on your part," Unilo says.

"Not entirely true. You'll lose this settlement at some point, and I'll lose my vote."

Unilo's lips twitch upward as she cocks her head. "Ah, couldn't slip the time limit past you, could I? Well, okay. Deal then."

I wait, and wait, and eventually frown.

"The food not to your liking?" Unilo asks as she finishes her dinner.

127

"There's no System notification," I say, frowning.

"For our deal? It's not System-registered, no."

"What's to stop me from welching?"

Unilo's eyes glaze over for a moment before she flashes me a smile. "Welching. What a nice word. And if I cannot trust a Paladin to keep his word, well, the Empire is in grave danger."

For a moment, I sit there, somewhat disoriented by the statement. Is she assuming my Class forbids me from breaking deals? Or is there something in my Class that stops me from welching? Are there Classes like that? Or is this a cultural artifact? A belief that anyone who is a Paladin can't break a deal? Or a deeper understanding of me?

I shush the inquisitive, almost panicky thoughts while another corner of my mind points out that I might need some rest. Getting beaten to a pulp can't be healthy, no matter how many resistances I have.

"Fair enough," I say with a sigh then look at Mayaya. "Mind giving me a ride home?"

Mayaya doesn't answer directly, but the next thing I know, I'm falling through a Portal that opens up right beneath my feet, taking me and my chair with it.

Right. Don't ask him for a favor again.

Chapter 10

After I recover from being so ignobly deposited back in Vancouver—and return the chair, hopefully directly on Mayaya—I spend the next few hours sleeping. Between the constant rush of the past couple of days, I've barely had time to catch my breath and it has been over twenty-four hours since I had time to rest. While my higher Constitution allows me to function quite, quite well with no sleep for days on end in normal conditions, normal is not what I'd call my last day. And so, by the time I get up, it's nearly three in the afternoon.

Over the next few days, I spend my time studying. First, there's the delayed meeting with Ali and Kim to receive their findings and research. While it's significantly more detailed than what Roxley provided, the gist of it is familiar. It does, however, provide a few settlements we could target for objectionable actions if I'm so inclined. Sadly, just taking over the City Cores is insufficient. I need people to guard the core and make the settlement actually work. As experience has shown, leaving a City Core unguarded has a bad tendency to create city-wide System-created dungeons if given enough time.

Afterwards, I've got Lana and Katherine in large chunks, bothering me with questions and details about the settlement. I suffer through those discussions as best as I can, mostly because they at least provide me some context to the world. We tackle numerous issues, ranging from zoning and building applications to judicial rulings, all of which require more than knee-jerk decisions. It's frightening how much power I have as a settlement owner, a minor feudal lord who rules by right of might. And so, I spend my time studying and learning, doing my best while I wait.

Because the next big step is talking with the champions, but due to their busy schedules, I've been forced to cool my heels for a few days till their "regular" meeting.

Their meeting time finally arrives, and I find myself porting with Mikito to Hong Kong, appearing on top of the Bank of China tower to survey the city. A quick glance at the notifications informs me the settlement has managed to develop into a full City, a remarkable achievement in the short timeframe. Especially considering only seven percent of their population survived. High population density and a high Mana density combined to create an explosive growth of monsters that trimmed their numbers in the first year. Even from my view, I can see the gaps where entire neighborhoods were razed, their buildings shattered by titanic monstrosities and the battles to subdue them.

"Welcome, Mr. Lee," a voice calls to me in Cantonese, and I turn to meet the gaze of a tiny old man.

Grandmaster Chang Jing Yi, the Iron Gate of Hong Kong, Seventh Dragon of South China (Kung Fu Master Level 2)

HP: 4310/4310

MP: 1080/1080

Conditions: Iron Shirt, Iron Bones, Heaven-and-Earth connection

"Tai Tsifu Chang," I greet the man in Cantonese while bowing slightly. "If you don't mind, I don't believe Mikito understands Cantonese?"

"Baka. *Of course I do. I visit here often enough,"* Mikito says, speaking up before Grandmaster Chang can say anything. *"But you didn't need to meet us yourself."*

"I wanted to meet the famous Redeemer of the Dead," Grandmaster Chang says. *"His recent exploits have been quite eye-catching."*

While Mikito and the Grandmaster speak, I bug Ali for an explanation. Especially for the place-specific titles.

"They're reputation- and achievement-based titles. Available only if you manage to gain both the achievements and the reputation. Similar to Capstan's First Fist. As for his Heaven-and-Earth connection, it's a flowery translation for a unique awareness Skill."

"You do me too much honor," I say to Grandmaster Chang in response to his earlier comment. Huh. I wonder if that's the right word—would face be better? *Mien* is more commonly used. But it's not exactly the same. This is why I hate talking to old school or China Chinese. Being a damn banana, I'm always second-guessing myself. At least my higher Intelligence seems to have increased my versatility with the language. *"My achievements are small compared to yours. I didn't kill a water dragon with my bare hands in the early years."*

"It was a small one and I had help. A lot of it," Grandmaster Chang says with a smile and gestures for us to follow him toward the fire exit.

"Still, I'd love to hear about it," I say.

With a little more prompting, I manage to extract the story of the Grandmaster's fight with the water dragon that had preyed on Hong Kong during the early part of the apocalypse. It's quite a thrilling tale, and one that keeps me riveted until we reach the meeting room. At the door, the Grandmaster leaves us with a bow.

"How come he's not part of the group? He's got the Levels," I say, gesturing to the Master Class Grandmaster's retreating back.

"Not everyone who has the Levels is accepted. Or desires to tramp around the globe," Jessica says as she fades into being right next to us.

Mikito starts slightly, a hand flexing as she begins and dismisses calling her weapon. As for myself, I smile at Jessica. It's not as if my new Class Skill hadn't helped me pick her out of the shadows a while ago.

"I thought you were a grouping of the most powerful on Earth?" I say with a frown.

"Not exactly," Mikito says. "We're the ones willing to join and have been accepted. A lot of settlement owners and others who might have the strength—like Grandmaster Chang—aren't interested. Or available. Not all settlement owners are as hands-off as you are."

"Ah. So you're what? The spearhead? Or the figurehead?" I say.

Jessica laughs at my description, pearly white teeth flashing across dark skin before fading. "Yes. Come on, we're the last."

She pushes the two of us in, a hand on each of our backs. I follow the urgings of the Southern girl, glancing around to see that she is correct— everyone I know is here. And two others I've yet to meet.

"Bipasha, Graham, John Lee," Jessica introduces the two newcomers for me while Mikito stays silent, eyeing the room. "Bipasha's a Weaver and focuses on healing and restricting attacks during combat. She's also the driving force behind BP Fabrics, one of the largest-growing clothing corporations on Earth."

"If you ever want a custom-designed costume, do let me know," Bipasha says, flashing me a smile.

Her long black hair, a slightly prominent nose on top of a large, inviting smile, and gorgeous brown eyes have me stopping for a second, reminding me that it's been years since... well. Since. That she's dressed in a stylish pink-and-cream Indian-inspired variation of the armored jumpsuit is a good reminder that not everything has to look the same. I'm suddenly not surprised that she's managed to garner such a following—a successful businesswoman intelligent enough to use her non-Combat Class Skills to undertake missions at this Level and with enough Charisma to bowl over a blind man.

"Oy! And what am I? Chopped liver?" Graham Speight, the Level 40 Prop with the New Zealander accent, protests. The mid-thirties man is built like a brick shithouse with arms as big as my thighs and a glower that would intimidate a lesser man.

"Well, you are just a prop," Jamal says, and groans explode from everyone.

Jessica winks at Jamal. "That never gets old."

"It really does." Graham complains, glaring at Jamal, who smirks.

"Anyone mind explaining the joke to me?" I ask.

"Rug—" Graham begins and is cut off by Hugo.

"What is he doing here? We haven't voted him in," Hugo asks, arms crossed as he glares at me.

"I would like to know too," Shao says, fixing me with a considering look.

"Don't worry, not here to join your little club. I actually invited myself along because I need to speak with Ms. Chowdury," I say, nodding to the young lady who flashes me a smile.

"You want to talk about the Planetary Vote," Jamal says, an aggrieved tone filling his voice. When I raise an eyebrow at him, he snorts. "What, you think we all don't get hit up on that topic? Most of us own a settlement or two. And those who don't, know most of those who do in our countries."

"Or continents," Shao says, crossing her arms.

"Oh good. That means you'll be useful to getting the vote passed." When I make that statement, I watch for the champions' reactions, trying to judge who is open to the idea and who isn't. Unsurprisingly, Jamal looks pained, Rae is an unreadable hunk of metal, and Jessica and Shao look slightly interested. As for Bipasha, she's unreadable but charming.

"As if we haven't tried that," Hugo says with a snort. "But you need eighty percent of the vote, and that's an impossible number if you don't own the entire planet. Hell, we don't even own fifty percent of Earth. It's bullshit politics."

"You're right," I say, my admission taking the wind out of Hugo's sail for the moment. "But it doesn't mean I'm not going to try."

"Waste of time," Hugo says with a huff. "You can talk to Bi once we're done. But we've got real work to do here."

"Of course," I say and step out of the door.

With the initial bait thrown, I'm sure Bipasha will find me next. And if I'm not wrong, Shao and Jessica will at a later date. As for Jamal, the man I need to speak with to get in contact with Ikael, well, I'll just have to track him down later.

***

When Bipasha finally finds me, I can't help but sigh in gratitude. After leaving the conference room, I'd meant to take a look around the newly remodeled Hong Kong and perhaps even visit their City Dungeon. Instead, I was intercepted by Grandmaster Chang and "invited" to have tea with him and his friends. For the last couple of hours, we've been seated in their favorite tea shop, drinking tea, eating fried donuts and steamed buns, and swapping war stories. Or in my case, listening to war stories.

"Bipasha!" I wave to the young politician urgently while standing and bowing to the group. "Thank you so much for your time. But I should speak with my friend."

"Of course. *See you again.*"

The group of seniors sends me on my way, though not before I make sure to pay the bill. There's an intrinsic terror involved in dealing with the elderly, especially if you've been brought up, like me, to respect them. It'd be too impolite to interrupt them, and so you get stuck in a never-ending series of stories.

134

"Mr. Lee." Bipasha looks around the restaurant at the jade-inlaid faux windows and the wooden chairs, a lip quirking slightly as she spots the mostly elderly customers. "I did not expect to find you in such a place."

"I was invited," I say, taking hold of her elbow and guiding her down the stairs. "Let's walk and talk, shall we?"

"Of course," Bipasha says.

Outside, I feel some of the tension disappear from my shoulders. "Is Mikito…?"

"Off on another delve. There's a dungeon on the outskirts of Monaco that is threatening to spill over. The settlement owners haven't been able to clear it and offered the team a Quest to deal with it for them," Bipasha says.

"Ah… I hope I'm not keeping you from that then," I say.

"No. My Skills would be of little use. It's an aquatic dungeon," Bipasha says as if it explains everything.

I just nod, deciding to pursue questioning about her Skills later. We walk through downtown Hong Kong, the streets achingly empty for a once overcrowded city.

"That's good," I say, then gesture for us to head toward the coastline. I'm curious to see the fishing industry I've heard much about. "So you're attempting to have yourself voted as our representative."

"Yes," Bipasha says. "And you?"

"Not my style."

"Kingmaker, are we?" Bipasha asks as we cross over to the nearby railing overlooking the harbor. We stare at the waters lapping against the ground, the occasional bobbing jellyfish monster that floats along the shores, and the numerous small boats that work the harbor and the monsters for parts.

"No. Yes." I shrug in resignation when I decide to just go with it. "We need to get on the Council. How we do so…" I frown, shaking my head. "Well, I won't say it doesn't matter, because even I'm not that naïve. But I'm willing to concede a lot to get it done."

"And why is it so important to you?" Bipasha asks, her eyes narrowing at me.

"Self-interest." I look around us. "Every planet, every species, that lacks a seat on the Council are second-class citizens. They have no say in the politics, in the direction of the Council. They barely even get notifications."

"Sounds like governments everywhere," Bipasha says, playing devil's advocate.

"Maybe. But once we have the seat, Earth also gains access to the Planetary System, allowing us to tax everything that happens on Earth. We can levy duties on specific industries. We can set up visitor fees and even channel the growth of settlements and dungeons." Channel is, of course, the right word, since doing so is akin to building rocks in a river—the water still flows, but at least you might divert a little bit of it here and there. "But why am I telling you this? You obviously know it all."

"I do," Bipasha says. "But it's always good to understand the motivations of your allies."

"And are we? Allies that is," I ask, tilting my head to the woman.

"Perhaps. You haven't decided to support me yet," Bipasha says.

"I don't even know you," I say with a slight smile.

"And you haven't met the others either," Bipasha says. "But you should know, Shao has managed to convince the Chinese to back me."

I blink, doing some mental math. That'd put her at nearly the same number of votes as Ikael. "Interesting. How'd you manage that?"

Bipasha smiles then. "It's contingent on there being an actual vote that matters, but Shao didn't want it. Their golden boy was never going to get the vote, not after he ran in Beijing. And no one wants the Americans to have it."

"No one?" I say, cocking my head to the side.

"Ah…" Bipasha pauses, as if she's suddenly remembering that I'm from Canada. Yet a part of me doubts that a consummate politician like her would make such a mistake. No, she wanted me to know that. Wanted me to understand the antipathy she and the Chinese and probably a bunch of others have against the Americans.

"Why?"

"Did you ever wonder what happened to the Galactic Envoy?"

"I think I'm about to find out," I say. A part of me is already guessing Area 51. It would make sense…

"The Envoy teleported into the middle of small-town Kentucky. And then the farmer who came out shot the Envoy. And since the Envoy didn't look remotely human, he skewered it, hung it up, and took photos," Bipasha continues. "You can see the photos in a few tabloids. The first real sign of alien life, and some backcountry hick shoots it, strings it up, and takes photos before gutting the corpse and selling the parts for money."

"Well, I'm sure it wouldn't have worked out any better in most places," I say, protesting the rather rude characterization. Frankly, why the heck would it teleport to Kentucky?

"*Teleportation was meant for New York—the UN building. Someone interfered with it.*"

"*How do you know?*"

"*What do you think I do when you're playing kissy-face with Roxley?*"

"*I'm not…*" I send a mental growl while Ali sends a chuckle.

"Maybe. But they're the ones who brought this hell on us," Bipasha says. "And many are tired anyway, of the Americans lording it over us all. Almost anyone would be better."

"Almost?"

"Well, Ikael isn't much better."

"Seems like he's got a lot of support," I point out, recalling the large number of votes he'd managed to engender. Well above her own.

"Bought and paid for, all of it," Bipasha scoffs.

"And you're above that?"

"No. But what he's promised is destructive. Corruption at that level is impossible to sustain."

I blink, staring at the Weaver, piecing together her meaning and the underlying beliefs. Then again, she is Bangladeshi—the level of corruption she's probably run into over her life is significantly more than I have. Which, probably, means she'd be open to bribes and allowing corruption in her own government. But… well, if it works, who am I to complain. Once more, I find myself weighing my own morality against the pragmatism required to keep the damn world running and find that I just don't care enough. Not over something like this.

"Well, good to know," I say for something to say.

"For now, understand that I'm willing to work with you. With your settlements and your prestige, along with mine and the influence of Mikito and other champions, I believe we can sway a large number of the undecided," Bipasha says with a smile. "The benefits could be significant. For all of us."

Bipasha lays a hand on my arm—briefly, but I can feel the lingering heat, the sensation that manages to take away my breath.

Mental Influence Resisted

Right. But like with Roxley, I'm not entirely sure if it's a by-product of her high Charisma or something more focused.

"I'll let you know, after my other meetings," I say eventually.

Bipasha offers me a nod and waves goodbye, pulling away and leaving me standing there on the dock, overlooking the bay and the numerous fishing boats. As I stare, I spot one particular fisherman tug on a glowing blue rod, his boat rocking dangerously as he struggles against a monstrous fish, the pair of them battling for dominance. An empathic flash rushes through me uncharacteristically. But for a moment, I'm not entirely sure if I'm the fish or the fisherman.

Chapter 11

"Mr. Lee, a pleasure." The man who offers me his hand looks no older than I am, somewhere in his mid-thirties, with few lines and close-cut, light brown hair. But there's a look to his eyes that speaks of having lived for much longer than a mere thirty years. It's no surprise. The ex-Secretary of Agriculture had been old before all this happened. If not for luck and the work of his security detail, he would have never survived the first month.

"Mr. Markey," I say, shaking his hand.

Behind him, one of his aides twitches, his lips tightening.

"Rob. For someone who has done as much as you have, Rob will do," Rob says, and I nod. Ex-Secretary turned acting President, now duly elected President. It's an impressive rise, if you don't consider the number of deaths that it required.

"I'm surprised you recreated this room," I say, glancing around. Not that I've ever been in the actual building, but I've seen enough movies to figure that this recreation of the Oval Office looks pretty close. Up to and including the large rug.

"It was recommended," Rob says with a self-deprecating smile. "It helps with the public and reassures them that we're continuing to hold to our ideals. Even if the actual building is a dungeon."

"Level 120 I understand?" I say, rubbing my chin. It'd be fun to try to run the dungeon, though I'm sure certain historic resonances might occur if a Canadian ran amok with sword and flame.

"Level 120 Elite dungeon, yes," Rob says. "The champions tried clearing it once, when it was only 100. They managed to make it a quarter of the way in before the rose bushes got them."

"Rose bushes?" I say.

"You should ask Ms. Sato. It's quite the story," Rob says. "But you didn't come here to speak to me about that."

"No." I cock my head to the side, surprised he already wants to get down to the brass tacks.

"I was never much of a politician. The posting was, well, horse trading and a goodbye gift. I've always preferred to be blunt," Rob says with a slight downward gesture of his hand, as if pressing down or cutting something beneath his body. "And General Miller has indicated you are quite blunt yourself."

"Blunt." I shoot the general a look where he sits with new stars on his shoulder epaulets. Five stars. Pretty sure that's as high as you can get. Not that I begrudge the soldier his accomplishments. I note that another thin, dignified African American man is here, listening to our conversations. The Secretary of State, as Ali has informed me. "That's one way to describe it."

"So. The Planetary Vote," Rob says. "You want to know if I intend to run, and if not, if you can convince me to influence those under me to vote for someone else."

"Pretty much," I say.

"The simple answers are yes and maybe," Rob replies. "I feel, we feel, that the seat should be held by me. But as it stands, we do not have the votes. Ikael and Bipasha have managed to engender significant global opposition to us. And the difficulties even if we did manage to achieve human majority is significant."

"The Envoy," I state flatly. "Is it true?"

"Of course," Rob says with a wry half-smile. "What use is it lying about something so simple? Especially when the truth is so effective. But I fear many of the policies of my predecessors alienated many others before that."

I grunt, shaking my head. Nope. Not touching geo-political history with a ten-foot pole. Still, I'm glad that my intuition—augmented with Eye of Insight—was correct about the Envoy. I'm still getting a feel for using that new Skill, since the Skill only removes other Skill effects and not "normal" lying. Of course, my own intuition and ability to sense when others are lying are significant after all this time, especially with my Subterfuge Perk.

"You said maybe?"

"Yes, my apologies. I sometimes get distracted," Rob says again, flashing me that good old boy charm. I don't even need the notification to tell me he's Charisma stacked, or that he's using it—consciously or not—against me. I'm even willing to admit that some of that charm might just be intrinsic to the Maine politician. "As you know, my position is precarious. We are still attempting to gain the agreement of other breakaway cities and states to rejoin us. Many of the settlements that have joined us would be loath to vote for a non-American."

"But you can force them," I state.

"It is within the amended Constitution to give me that power. But it is not something I would use lightly."

I sigh, bracing myself mentally. In other words, and as much as he might protest not being a politician, he's looking for the right trade. I can feel a small headache coming along, one that grows as we get down to discussing the details. It's only now, when we've gotten past the initial pleasantries and into the horse trading, that the new Secretary of State gets involved.

***

Hours later, Miller and I end up walking out of the room together, the president left to do his own thing. The walk is silent at first, the pair of us making our way past the numerous guards and bureaucrats that make up the nation's bureaucracy.

"Thank you for getting me in," I say to Miller after a time.

"No need. I just greased the wheels. It was your actions and reputation that did most of the work," Miller says.

"I somehow doubt that," I say with a snort and a smile. "How's Wier?"

"Well enough," Miller says. "He's in LA right now, dealing with the border. The dungeon along the border—the Wall—keeps growing. We constantly have to blast it apart, but so far, we've yet to find its center."

I grunt, shaking my head. Sometimes I get the feeling that the System has a sense of humor. Or perhaps a sense of irony. Of course, the scientific reasoning was that the System was using a resonant concept to create dungeons, forming them based off ideas, concepts, and ecological niches. Thus the living libraries with their flying attack books or the giant border wall that keeps growing.

"Glad he's doing okay," I say.

"He's a good man." Miller's lip twitches slightly as he spots my hesitation. "And the president is doing the best job he can. But he was underplaying how tough things are. He's spending as much time talking to those within the union as those who aren't, all to keep us together and out of a civil war."

I nod slowly, grimacing. "Anything I can do to help?"

Miller chuckles. "No. In fact, it's best if you stay out of it entirely. Having a Canadian come in and save our asses—well, it hurt more than a few egos."

"Okay," I say, clapping Miller on the shoulder. "But if you need me to send down some polar bears and maple syrup, just let me know."

Miller rolls his eyes, stopping at the entrance hallway. "I will. And John, be careful about the kind of deals you make. Ikael... he worries me."

I offer one last nod as we reach the designated teleportation zone where the quantum locks around the settlement ease. As I look back after casting my Skill, I see Miller frowning and lost in thought already.

In my office, I flop down in my chair and put my feet on the desk, grateful that Katherine has given me back my old office. She's moved to the office next door, leaving me alone to stare at the wood-paneled interior.

"What do you think, Ali?"

The Spirit lets himself appear, floating backward at a forty-five degree angle. He's still in his traditional orange jumpsuit, though he can conjure almost anything else. But really, jumpsuit, mankini, or plate armor, it all shares the same defense rating for the Spirit, so it's just a matter of convenience and looks. "About what?"

"The meeting. You think he'd be someone worth backing?"

"Doesn't matter what I think. Can you get others to back him?" Ali says with a snort. "Or can you get the others who back Rob to back someone else? Way the votes played out, he got most of your first world countries to vote for him, at least those who were voting for anyone not themselves."

I grimace, nodding. Ikael drew his support from around the African, Middle Eastern, and South American settlements, as well as a wide range of single-city settlements. Bipasha basically had southeast Asia and the Indian subcontinent. Outside of China and Siberia, which had mostly done their own thing. Most of Russia and eastern Europe had split their votes between themselves and Ikael, while Australia had lost so many of their settlements that they weren't even worth talking about.

"Eh, you humans are strange. Still clinging to your old concepts of countries and nations, to old grudges," Ali says with a shrug. "The vast majority of the people who had any say over things before are dead. But you're all still complaining about Western domination and oppression, about shaking off colonial ties. As if you aren't being colonized by Galactics right this second."

I chuckle, mostly because if I don't laugh at it, I'd have to cry. The Spirit isn't wrong. But I can see everyone else's concerns. It's not as if the States and the other western powers hadn't used a very heavy hand for a very long time to keep other countries in check. It was only in the last few decades that the other countries were pulling themselves together.

Now, in many ways, the sheer population numbers and an arguably better ability to cope with the change has led to a higher number of surviving settlements and an overall stronger position in non-Western countries. Few people are willing to give up the power they've earned, especially a position of power earned over the corpses of friends and family.

Whereas the Galactics have it easier. For many, they understand the need to work together, to ally with existing factions. And many of those factions are already culturally set, already guaranteed. Through race or creed, the settlement owners who have come to Earth often have a game plan. We're so busy fighting everyone, we're slowly losing, no matter how hard the champions fight.

The scary thing? I can see it all, read it all, in the histories of other species.

"Fine. We're idiots," I say, echoing my thoughts out loud. "But they're my idiots."

Ali nods and I rip open a Portal, stepping through to move to the Shop.

***

Locating Cheng Shao took but a single expensive trip to the Shop. Teleporting to her took even more money, especially considering I had to port in to where the woman was grinding a hundred miles west of Hainan. It kind of amused me that no matter where you went, if it was up high, the zones were higher. You'd think that Mana would pool lower down, but nope. It was the mountains and deep caverns, the extremes, that generated the differences in zones. Outside of certain notable plains and deserts.

"Mr. Lee." Cheng Shao stares at me as I walk up to her.

I opted to teleport a kilometer away so that I could make the rest of the journey on foot. I figured that'd give her more than enough time to notice me, compared to appearing right next to her. Certainly, it's a somewhat less hostile maneuver.

"Why are you stalking me?"

Okay, maybe not.

"I wanted to speak with you. I come in peace," I say, holding up my hands while giving her a hopefully disarming grin.

Unfortunately, Cheng Shao doesn't return my smile at all. "I am training." She turns away. "Perhaps another time."

"Look, it's about the Planetary Vote—"

"Training."

"Ms. Cheng." I pause then growl. "I just need to know if Bipasha's telling the truth. Will the Chinese settlement owners support her?"

"I do not comment on the Party's decisions," Cheng Shao states flatly while speeding up.

I hiss in frustration as the woman throws up a wall in front of me when I attempt to follow. I could break it or Blink Step through it. But I can't actually make her talk to me, so I stand there, glaring at the metallic silver wall.

"What Party is she talking about?"

"Do you never read anything we give you? The Communist Party of China. The same one that was around before your System. One of their leaders managed to get the Mandarin Class. Utterly useless for direct combat, but it has a wide range of buffs for everyone below

him. Between that and having a few bodyguards with good Combat Classes, they managed to hold things together in Beijing and expand from there. It's not really a Communist Party anymore, but like the Americans, they're keeping the same name. For now."

"And doing the same old terror campaign shit, eh?" I say softly, looking at where Cheng Shao has disappeared over the ridge.

I consider blinking over to her, but Ali flashes some of the dots on my minimap. Of course she's being watched. She might be able to get away with certain things because of her strength, but personal strength means little if you've got friends and families to worry about.

"Damn it. Now what do I do?" I need confirmation of what Bipasha has said, but I don't actually have any contacts in the bureaucracy.

"If you're thinking of walking in and demanding an audience, that might not work out that well."

"Was not."

"Uh-huh. I think this is a Katherine problem."

I roll my eyes slightly but have to agree. The woman probably is the best option to get confirmation. Between being a banana and a North American, I'd probably be looked down upon even more than Katherine.

"I hate wasting my Credits." I let the wind take my words before I open a Portal to the nearest city to tackle the next damn human idiot.

***

Of course, meeting Ikael isn't as easy as Portaling into his office and demanding a meeting. For one thing, I don't even know where he is. For another, I have no waypoints in Ethiopia. Which is why I find myself bouncing from long-range teleportation portal to long-range teleportation portal till I finally end up being pulled apart molecule by molecule and reformed in Addis Abba.

"Off the platform," the guard orders me immediately.

I follow his orders without complaint, craning my head back to take in the view. I'm surprised to note more than a few guards hovering in the sky, guns pointed down at the rectangular teleportation platform, flanked by even larger beam cannons. In fact, I spot more than fifty guards on the ground, each of them armed with at least Tier II beam weaponry. I absently note the increased ambient temperature and the higher humidity, but neither is a major concern. They've set up the teleportation platform in what looks to be an old football stadium, though the grass is rather trampled and worn from all the traffic. All around us, hovering trucks and cranes pick up and deposit teleported goods with crisp efficiency while labourers sort goods like chipmunks on speed.

"Are you deaf?" the first guard snarls at me, bringing my attention back to him. "Newcomers are to report to an intake officer immediately."

"Sorry." I move to the area as directed by the first guard.

Thankfully, the line isn't long, so it only takes me a short while to find myself in front of one of their intake officers. Standing in front of the new guard, I notice one of his eyes gleams with internal light. The slightest tracing of metal around the iris indicates this might not have been the eye he was born with.

Dark skin slightly flushed against the pale brown army uniform, he puffs up before he speaks. "Reason for visiting Tafar?"

"Tafar?" I frown.

"You're in the Republic of Tafar," the guard snaps, eyes narrowing. "Do you not read your notifications?"

"Haven't had the time," I mutter. I call back the notification, watching as other newcomers stroll right past the intake area. Either my tardiness drew the ire and attention of the guard or they've got a way to tell who is a newcomer or not.

You have entered a Safe Zone (the City of Addis Abba)

Mana flows in this area are stabilized. No monster spawning will occur in this region.

Runic enchantments have increased skill growth by 1% in safe zone.

This Safe Zone includes:

- *City of Addis Abba City Center*
- *Shop*
- *City Dungeon*
- *Guilds (Tier III * 4, Tier IV * 2, Tier V * 14)*
- *Armory*
- *More…*

You are now in the Republic of Tafar

Current reputation with the republic: 04 (0 local + 0 regional + 4 global)

Current fame: 222 (0 local +11 regional + 211 global)

Do you wish to review the local laws & ordinances? (Y/N)

"*What is the difference between fame and reputation?*" I send the thought to Ali. I haven't dug into that entire area, which I really do need to.

"Well, make time," the guard snarls. "Now, reason for visiting?"

"I'm looking to speak with Jamal. Or better, Ikael," I say, deciding to not beat around the bush.

Instead of angering the guard, my words make him burst into laughter, which is joined by his friends when he repeats my words to them.

I sigh, waiting for the group to fall silent. "My name's John Lee."

In the background, Ali answers my question. *"They're Galactic measurements. Reputation indicates their favorability toward you, mostly affected by the Contracts and interactions you have with an individual or corporations. Fame is an indicator of how well-known you are. They're like your skills—reported numbers on factual data. A stock ticker for your reputation and fame rather than something that directly affects reality. Put another way—what you do makes it go up, versus your Skills which go up and then change the way the world works. Not that you have any Skills that make use of either of these figures."*

"That supposed to mean something?" the guard says with a snort.

"Looks like it does to some people." I nod over the guard's shoulder.

The guard turns and sees his boss waving him away from me even while muttering orders to another of his subordinates.

"Report this to Kofi immediately," I lip-read the officer's order before he strides forward and takes the blowhard guard's place. He flashes me a smile, his pearly white teeth a stark contrast to his almost obsidian skin. "I am Lieutenant Amadi Worku. I have informed my superiors about your arrival. Would you like to wait in some place more appropriate?"

I nod, and the close-lipped lieutenant takes me to a small waiting room, making sure I have cold tea and snacks to nibble on while I wait.

I take the time to bug Ali. *"And my numbers?"*

"You've entered a few Contracts or facilitated the signing of a few. In addition, as you're a ruler, you automatically get reputation points for, well, governing effectively. Local reputation adds up to give the number on your sheet, but local reputation is significantly decreased when taken out of its geographic bounds. Basically, it's less effective away from where you generated the reputation. In addition, the change in reputation is dependent on the respective fame and reputation of the individual or organization you conduct deals with. Since you're outside North America, your local reputation translates down to that four. As for your fame, do I need to explain that?"

"No. Is there Galactic reputation then? Or Solar System level?"

"Yes, but they're pretty much zeroed out. Earth isn't connected enough on a planetary scale that Galactic reputation has started crossing over significantly. Or that your Galactic reputation would affect matters locally," Ali says.

I grunt, poking at the Fame and Reputation bars and, after a while, find where it's located in my sheet. I barely glance at it these days, especially things like the giant list of skills that are mostly hidden, so I'm not surprised to find that I haven't even noticed the new tab for the two statistics. There's no real surprise in any of the information, so I shut the entire thing down. Though I do have one question.

"Why was it locked till I left and came back?"

"No useable Skill, remember? Also, it's a Galactic achievement thing for those who don't have a use for it. No point in making it available for the hicks who never leave their neighborhood, you know? Or the ones who don't survive their first trip to another world," Ali says. *"If you aren't smart enough to survive a pleasure cruise, you aren't worth wasting the Mana on."*

"Pleasure cruise?"

"Eh, most Galactics don't visit a Forbidden Planet for their first inter-planetary trip. As usual, you're all kinds of special."

I can't help but chuckle at the teasing tone in Ali's mental voice. To pass the time, I pick up one of the snacks, taking a bite of it, and wince before placing the dessert back down. Right. They're trying to kill me with sugar. On second thought, I wave my hand and deposit the entire thing in my Altered Storage. Maybe Lana…

My brain hitches and I pause, my hand over the now-empty plate. Right. Katherine. Katherine might like this.

"Would Katherine have access to a Skill which could see the Reputation and Fame of others?" I send to Ali to distract myself.

"Definitely. Be hard to be a good gatekeeper if you can't tell who's reputable or not, no?" Ali replies. *"I'd bet her new Class gives her other Skills too. Probably an upgraded Contract Skill which allows her to use her higher Reputation to enforce the contract. I could dig into it..."*

"No. That's good." I was just looking for a distraction. No reason to spend good Credits when I can just ask her.

I settle down in my chair and slow my breathing, taking the small break to meditate.

Breathe in. Take the tension, the stress which is flowing through my body, and wrap it up.

Breathe out. Let the world and the stress fall away.

Repeat. Ad infinitum.

Chapter 12

It takes hours before they finally let me out of the luxurious cell they have me waiting in, long hours that I spend meditating and letting the information I've been gathering settle. I've gained a lot of data recently, and while my increased Intelligence has let me gather the information and even process it to some extent, it's something else to grasp it on an intuitive level. Sometimes, letting things settle and allowing your unconscious mind to do the thinking is the best option.

When the door opens, they find me awake and refreshed. There's a whole guard troop here, but nothing in their body language—no overt tension, no angling of bodies to give me a smaller target—indicates what I'm seeing is anything more than an honor guard. Within minutes, we're in an armored and luxurious hover car and being flown over to Ikael.

They show me into his office, an ornate thing with gold décor, gold trimmings, and yes, even a gold lamp. If not for the expensive wooden table and the green plush chair—outlined in gold—the entire place would have been truly too overbearing. As it is, it's just painful to look at.

Seated in the chair till I enter, Ikael can only be described as solid. Dressed in a white-and-grey checkered silk shirt, he has numerous chunky gold rings on his fingers and a shaved head. Ikael's welcoming smile does nothing to hide the predatory look in his eyes.

Ikael Tafar (Level 41 Aksumite Leader)
HP: 1380/1380
MP: 2170/2170
Conditions: Aura of Command, Coin of the Empire

"Aksumite?"

"Can't offer you much. It's a semi-unique, culture-based Class. Closest I've got is like a Celtic Warrior or Roman Counsel, something the System registered a while ago and he somehow decided to choose. Base Skills are definitely more combat-oriented. His Advanced Class here is more kingdom-driven. Coin of the Empire, for example, gives a minor boost to tax collected in his settlements. It literally generates Credits from the System."

Mental Influence Resisted

I grunt, my eye twitching slightly as his Aura clashes with my own mental resistance. I'm surprised at how strong it is. The man must have put quite a few points into it. I feel it push against my mental boundaries. Push—but not win.

Sometimes I wonder about those who use Auras all the time. The more and more people I encounter with the Skill, the more I'm forced to wonder about their effects. Not just on those around them in the short term, but on the long-term effects on interactions. After all, constantly warping the minds of those around you can't be healthy. Earth has a long history of emperors and celebrities changing by being constantly surrounded by yes men. How much worse would it be when even the most ordinary interaction is infected by a Skill like this? And yet, so many decide to leave it on.

Once the initial introductions are done, I take the seat I'm offered. "Thank you for seeing me."

"I'm happy to speak with other settlement owners, especially one who has access to a number of high Level zones," Ikael says, smiling widely. "The wild flame pine sap your settlement produces is quite a useful herb."

The name sounds familiar, but nothing comes to mind. *"Ali?"*

"Kelowna's third most valuable export. Useful for basic and medium fire resistance potions."

"Well, I'm sure we can discuss an increase in trade between our settlements." I pause as I get ready to switch topics.

"Oh, how forgetful of me. I had a gift for your visit," Ikael says in the gap I left. He drops a small ivory-inlaid box in front of me.

I smile slightly at the box, a memory of Mikito mentioning that elephants are no longer on the endangered species list surfacing briefly. It seems those gentle giants are no longer gentle. In fact, there are numerous zones where the Alphas are mutated elephants.

Perhaps mistaking my smile, Ikael's lips twitch slightly as he pushes the box to me. I take it, curiosity warring with mild disgust at the bribe. Still, I'm involuntarily impressed by what I see within.

Ring of Greater Shielding
Creates a greater shield that will absorb approximately 1000 points of damage. This shield will ignore all damage that does not exceed its threshold amount of 50 points of damage while still functioning.
Max Duration: 7 Minutes
Charges: 1

I stare at the small box and the ring within, picking it up and turning it over. The ring itself is made of bone, a curious, almost brittle-looking bone that refuses to bend even under significant pressure. All around it are small glyphs, letters, and drawings I cannot understand. A mental prod makes Ali drag further information about the ring from the System, and my initial guess pans out. This is an Earth creation.

"This is a very generous gift. And an amazing piece of work," I say. "The Artisan is highly Skilled."

Ikael beams while gushing, "He just managed to reach the third Tier of his Advanced Class. It's taken a lot of resources, but Marcus can produce work like this once a week now."

I'm not much of a crafter, but my talks with Lana and others have indicated this would be a brutal workload. Creating enchanted works is difficult, prone to failure, and requires a high Level of Mana. Each inscription, each enchantment requires more than a hundred times the amount of Mana to cast a similar spell or Skill. At the very least. Layering multiple enchantments or more powerful Skills adds to the cost in ever increasing amounts.

"Well, thank you. And him." Under Ikael's urgings, and after verifying there's nothing to be worried about, I slide on the ring. It's not exactly my style, but it's still a powerful accessory. "I don't really control any of my people, but I can certainly see items like this being useful for our police or security force. If you have a list of what you can offer, I can make sure my people send the information to the right people. I'm sure they'll be happy to have a more local customer."

"My thoughts exactly," Ikael says, his smile wide. "And there's another thing I was hoping to speak with you about."

"Oh?"

"The Planetary Vote. Your settlements took little part in the previous vote. Your orders, I presume," Ikael asks cunningly.

"No," I say, shaking my head. In fact, at the time, Lana was looking into how they could potentially put enough votes together. But with the weight of the entire settlement on her shoulders, she and Katherine had decided the task was too impossible to handle. So they'd taken the most minor of actions, gathering information rather than actively participating. "I was incommunicado at the time."

"For a long time, I understand," Ikael says. "It is dangerous for one of us to go away for such a long period. It's amazing you were able to hold on to your settlements, even after such time. Your people must respect and fear you greatly."

I shrug at the statement, unsure of how to answer him. Fear me? I rather hope not, though it might be a tad naïve to think so.

"Then, if you are not looking to abstain, perhaps I can convince you to vote for me."

"You could, but it seems to be a pointless move. There're no benefits to having more votes, not unless we can get the Galactic Seat," I say, leaning back to stare at Ikael. Interesting how Ikael hasn't asked me why I came, instead happy to guide the conversation to his own desires. But if he's willing to talk, I'm willing to listen.

"I see you understand the matter," Ikael says, pounding on the table slightly. "The aliens have taken too much of our land. But it is a small detail. I'm already moving to secure additional votes—including from the aliens."

"Oh?" I say softly, curious if he'll elaborate. He disappoints me though.

"Yes. While I don't expect to win during the next vote, I expect a strong showing will convince even more humans to side with me. I might even manage to get the American to vote for me. I know he's in desperate need of more help," Ikael says with a smirk. "I'm sure with my army, we could convince some of his more stubborn members."

I blink, turning over his words in my head. As I do so, I freeze, my heart rate spiking as a sense of danger shoots through me. In another second, I see a shadow-cloaked figure step out of a gap in space and slam a blade into Ikael's back. His force Shield flares, blocking the attack, but the assassin doesn't stop, her movements a blur as she strikes again and again, each attack tearing apart layered Shields.

"Assassin!" I yell, standing swiftly and lunging forward.

The reaction is automatic but predictable, and shadow tendrils grab hold of my feet, yanking me off balance and pulling me back to the end of the room. Strong as I am, the attack catches me entirely by surprise and it takes me a second to tear the shadows apart. As I do so, the door slams open, Ikael's guards pouring in.

The assassin doesn't stop. A swift twist of her body cuts into Ikael's flailing arm and pins it to the desk as the last of his defensive Shields go down. As I raise a hand to throw a Soul Shield around Ikael, his guards are opening up their attacks. A projected Power Strike, a Molten Beam, and more lash out at the assassin. Before the Soul Shield can take effect, the entire room plunges into a darkness that even the beam rifle's attacks cannot disrupt.

"Ali! How is Ikael?"

"Nearly dead. But uhhhhh... boy-o..." Ali's voice is hesitant, almost confused.

Another second and a new notification pops up.

Ingrid Starling (Level 43 Shadow Assassin)

HP: 643/2780

MP: 754/2330

*Conditions: Shadow Body, Death God's Embrace, Shadow Doppelganger * 2*

"What...?"

My surprise is more than sufficient time for the other notification floating in front of me to flatline. Ikael's dead, slain by an old friend of mine. Right in front of me. I kneel there, blinking in surprise even as the guards scream and shout, attempting to pierce the darkness. In a minute, the darkness fades, revealing the headless body of Ikael, stripped of his rings and other enchanted items.

Within seconds, I find guns and hands pointed at my face. A few hasty guards even take potshots at me, which bounce off my Soul Shield and do little other than shake me free from my surprise. The guards shout and scream orders at me and finally, rather than cause any further issues, I comply.

Thankfully, my Soul Shield keeps the rough handling to a minimum. Still, I'm treated like a dangerous prisoner, one forced to sit in the middle of an empty courtyard where they're able to point field cannons at me and cluster multiple Advanced Classers as guards. I absently note they've strengthened the quantum lock around me, shutting down my escape options.

Through all their barked orders, I comply. I play the good guy, the polite and self-effacing Canadian who definitely did not assassinate or take part in assassinating their leader. And all the while, I'm chatting with Ali.

"How the hell did I not see her come in?" I ask Ali.

My answer comes in another notification.

Shadow Plane

User is able to travel through the shadow plane, a dimension that exists between most other dimensional planes. Quantum lock and other dimensional-locking effects are less effective against users of the shadow plane, for shadows exist everywhere. Spending too much time in the shadow plane can have adverse effects on an individual and attract unwanted attention from residents in the Shadow Plane.

Effect: User may enter or exit the Shadow Plane. Dimensional-locking Skills, spells, and technology have a 50% reduction in effectiveness.

Cost: 500 per entry / exit

"So she wasn't sneaking in, she just walked in through another dimension. And paid the extra cost to punch through their lock. Must have been where she lost her health too," I say, musing to Ali.

It makes sense. I'd noticed the quantum lock they were using in the city was a disruptive one, rather than a stasis lock. It's the cheapest quantum lock method, but anyone willing to take the damage can punch through such a lock, unlike a stasis lock which basically blocks all such movements. Of course, the negative of stasis locks are that if you have enough Mana or strength, you can pierce them and appear without incurring any further damage.

"Good day, Mr. Lee," a small, wiry Caucasian man in a full light-grey suit and tie comes up to me, conjuring a chair and a table before sitting across from me. "I'm so sorry about the delay, but I'm sure you understand how busy it's been?"

"Of course," I say, inclining my head.

A servant comes up with a jug of iced tea and a pair of glasses, which he sets down between us.

"I'm Inspector Jacques Lamar," Jacques says, flashing me a smile as he fumbles in a pocket, pulling out a small notepad and a pen. He grins at me slightly then nods at the jug. "Do you mind? I've been talking non-stop…"

I blink, then shrug and pour the man a glass and myself one too. I push it toward him and watch him drink before I sip on mine. No poison then, or truth drugs. Of course, neither of those things are something I'm terribly concerned with, with my resistances, but it's always something worth noting.

"Thank you so much," Jacques says. "And again, for your patience. Now, I understand you arrived four hours ago?"

After glancing at the clock, I say, "Five and a quarter."

"Right, right." Jacques scribbles on his notepad and begins to question me seriously.

162

I note that he keeps bouncing back and forth, asking questions sometimes out of order or returning to previous points, but eventually, he drags the entire story out of me. I hold nothing back. After all, nothing Ikael or I spoke of was particularly surprising or secretive. In one of the breaks between questions, I find time to ask my own questions.

"Why don't you buy all this from the Shop? I can't believe you can't afford it." I say, my brows drawn.

"We tried. Unfortunately the assassin has a Skill which makes such purchases extremely expensive. As a mere inspector, I cannot approve an expense of such magnitude," Jacques says with a self-deprecating smile.

"And Ikael's successor?"

"Has yet to do so," Jacques replies. "He is extremely busy right now."

"There's rumblings of a civil war, boy-o. I'm picking up quite a few skirmishes going on outside of the compound, and data sieved about the kingdom's status shows substantial swings in all tracked statistics from Credits to safe zone areas. I'm guessing they're losing territory," Ali supplies.

Question done, Jacques moves on to the trade deal, probing into the details of our discussion. Of course, since we had barely even begun speaking about it, I don't have much to say. That becomes a long-winded explanation about how I'm a lazy-ass settlement leader who leaves the real work to his subordinates. Which of course leads to another question.

"If you aren't involved in the settlement affairs, why did you come? It doesn't sound like you were looking for a trade deal."

"I wasn't," I answer truthfully. "I was hoping to speak with Ikael about the Planetary Vote."

"Ah," Jacques breathes the word, scribbling on his notepad.

I wait while he scribbles, patiently until the inspector looks up and raises an eyebrow.

"What?" I grump at him.

"Nothing. I thought you had something more to say on the topic," Jacques says.

"Nope," I say with a shrug. "I'm trying to understand where everyone else stands on it." A beat, then I decide to be fully truthful. There's little reason to hide it. "I want us to win a Galactic Seat, but we need to sort out the votes."

"Eighty percent, yes?" Jacques says after flipping backward in his notebook. I absently note how he goes well past the point where he began writing at the start of our interview to find this information. Obviously this has come up before. Though I have to wonder the context and reason.

"Yes."

"But Ikael would never agree to anyone but him being on the seat," Jacques says, his voice neutral with just a little hint of curiosity. Charming, without the Skill. A subtler use of his attributes, a self-effacing manner rather than an overt push with his attribute. But I see the notification that he's actively using it to affect my emotions and thoughts. "How did you intend to convince him otherwise?"

I consider his question and the context of our interview. Right. Motivation. From the outside, this looks like really good motivation. Crap. I take a moment to be more careful about what I say and how I say it, but I note the slightest tightening around the eyes as the inspector processes my hesitation. Crap.

"I didn't. I hadn't thought of it. I wanted to talk to him first, get an understanding of the man himself," I say. "Maybe he would have been fine to be the person on the seat. If so, I'd throw my backing behind him."

"You didn't want it yourself?"

"Not my style," I say, shaking my head. "The settlements are more than enough work as it stands. I just want Earth to have the seat."

"Why?"

"You should know why," I say.

"Indulge me?"

"Taxes. Duties. Control of the Mana flow. Access to information," I say, chanting the answer I've given to everyone else as if I'm bored by the topic. Which, truth be told, I am. But it also helps conceal the other reason, the most important reason for me, for Earth to get a seat. Access. Access to Irvina, the capital of the Galactic System, which has gated entry. Sure, if I receive sufficient Galactic reputation or fame, I might be able to get in. But the likelihood of that, in the short term, is incredibly low.

"Ah, a patriot then," Jacques says with no derision in his voice, even a touch of admiration. But I'm fast realizing the inspector is smart and gifted. He's an interrogator who knows he'll get more information playing nice, taking his time and asking questions rather than trying to strong-arm his way through this.

"No. A humanist maybe," I say with a smile.

"Then you'd be happy to inform us who it was who killed Ikael."

"Sorry. Information was blocked," I say.

"Really? Because your Spirit is known for being able to call up such information," Jacques says, suddenly going on the attack.

"He is. But the assassin's skill was good enough to stop him. It was a bit hectic in there."

"Really? Because the guards said they could get some information on his Status."

"Well then, why ask me about him?" I say, playing along.

"Because the information they got from her wasn't complete," Jacques says, flipping backward a few pages.

"Her?" I frown, cocking my head to the side. "I thought you said him."

"Oh, yes. I did." Jacques shrugs before sipping on his iced tea.

I can't help but chuckle at his antics, even as I look around the area and note how the guards are being changed out again. They've been rotating portions of the guard around me this entire time, keeping their people rested on the off-chance I'll do something.

"*Well done, boy-o.*"

Interrogation resistance skill increased

Deception skill increased

I blink away the notifications, chuckling within as Ali shows off the results of my hours-long interrogation. It's not something either of us bothers to directly track on an on-going basis since skills—unlike Class Skills—are statistics tracked about actual skills I possess. While my Perk Subterfuge allows me to develop certain skills—like the above deception, interrogation, or stealth skills—at a greater rate than normal, it seems more an ability to accumulate experience faster rather than a sudden surge of information which gets planted within me. So instead of taking say a month of classes to learn something, I only need a few weeks. It's a gradual change over time, but the actual statistics of where I am don't matter. I'm kind of glad there's no weird information download. It'd be even weirder Leveling up something like dancing and finding myself able to do the cha-cha even though I've never taken a class.

On second thoughts...

"Penny for your thoughts, Mr. Lee?" Jacques says, interrupting my musings.

"Just thinking about when this is going to be over."

"Do bear with me. I have just a few more questions..." Jacques says, and I don't even bother hiding the roll of my eyes.

But I stay seated, happy to play along for now. The last thing I need is to be associated with an assassination attempt while trying to get other settlement leaders to meet with and vote for me.

***

The interrogation continues for another couple of hours, but eventually Jacques gives up on getting any further information from me. He shows an amazing amount of Willpower and commitment, but I somehow get the feeling the entire interview process isn't much different than what he's used to. Unfortunately, the interrogation ending doesn't mean I'm released, so I get to sit in the courtyard for a few more hours.

As I'm guided out of the courtyard, I receive a rather sternly worded statement that boils down to "Your presence is not wanted" before I'm sent back to the teleportation portal to be bounced out. They don't even bother paying for a long-range teleportation, dumping me at the nearest settlement outside their borders. It's a bit annoying actually, considering it probably cost them nearly as much to drop me in a non-padded location as it would have to send me back properly. It'd be a major inconvenience if I didn't have my Skill.

For a moment, I stare at the notification that informs me I'm in the Town of N'Djamena with the usual listing of facilities. A quick perusal of my map shows I'm pretty much in the center of Africa, my sudden appearance already attracting the attention of the locals.

"About time," a familiar voice drawls, making me crane my head to the side and back to spot the First Nation woman and ex-party member.

"Ingrid. Are you the one who got me deposited here?" I say, putting two and two together.

"Yup. Amazing what happens when your entire society is built on corruption," Ingrid says with a smirk and drops from the squat building she was sitting on, landing beside me. "Hungry?"

"I could eat," I answer, eyes narrowing as we walk toward the conveniently located restaurant. The paranoid part of me points out that this could be dangerous, but I push it aside. Ingrid's a friend.

"Thanks for not interfering too much," Ingrid says as we get a seat. She holds up a hand as I look to speak, instead ordering in rapid-fire French. "Hope you don't mind me ordering. Their Chef here is amazing, but limited."

I wave to dismiss her statement, instead wanting to focus on the more important part. "Why did you, well, do what you did." I pause, realizing we're still in public. A part of me winces as well, considering everything we could say could be purchased. But she's got her Skills and I've got my necklace. So it should be fine. Right?

"Relax. I didn't just choose this restaurant for its food," Ingrid says, seeming to read my mind.

Sometimes, I really hate how the women around me seem to be able to do that with such ease. Then again, maybe I should stop worrying about the obvious things and trust my friends.

"The owner has a Skill that blocks information gathering in this restaurant." When I raise an eyebrow at Ingrid, she smirks. "I'm pretty sure he's connected. If you know what I mean."

I grunt, waving her on and ignoring her bad mob talk.

"Right. Always so impatient. It's simple really. I got paid," Ingrid says.

"Paid. You a merc now?"

"With the mouth." Ingrid smirks then sobers up when I don't react. "Yeah, not funny. Real pity he died… but yes, I do some jobs when I'm free."

"Who paid you?" I ask, a slight amount of heat in my voice. "And how did you manage to do it when I was right there?" The level of coincidence involved seems way too high.

"Firstly, don't know. And even if I did, wouldn't tell you. I do everything via cut-outs," Ingrid says, tapping her fingers. "Safer that way. Secondly, it wasn't a coincidence. Well, not exactly. I'd been planning this job for days, waiting for him to use that office. That isn't his usual one—his other office is even more secure but a lot less pretty. When you showed up, I knew he'd be meeting with you in his show office, so I made sure to sneak in while they kept you waiting."

"Just my luck that I showed up instead of someone else," I say, grimacing. "How many days?"

"About three," Ingrid says.

So after I got back and started making my presence known. Interesting timing, but there's not much I can do about that, beyond keeping it in mind.

"Any guesses on who?" I ask.

"I don't make guesses. Bad habit to get into," Ingrid says. "But the people I take jobs on? Most of them have a very long list of enemies. A very, very long list. Even if you take out those who can't afford me, it's still a lot of people. My targets are really not nice people."

I smile slightly, glad to hear that Ingrid's still got some form of morals. I'm actually a bit surprised at myself that I'm not angrier or more upset at her. Perhaps it's the apocalypse, perhaps it's the time on the other planet, but I find little outrage in me at her actions. A trace of disappointment, but even that fades at her proclamation about her targets. I know some might discuss the sanctity of life, of how important giving people a chance is, of allowing karma or a higher power to mete out judgment. But the truth is, there's been so much blood on my hands that I find it hard to throw stones of any kind. So long as she isn't coming for me or mine, I'll give Ingrid the benefit of doubt.

I wish she hadn't killed Ikael. After all, his murder set his entire kingdom aflame and destroyed the coalition he had been building. That leaves me with having to contact the numerous individuals under Ikael's banner individually. It's a waste of time, one that frustrates and angers me. I push down the frustration and anger, reminding myself that what is, is.

"Fair enough," I say. "Any particular kind of list for Ikael?"

"Political enemies. Sons, daughters, fathers, and mothers wanting revenge. Workers tired of being forced to work overtime for no benefits. Frustrated businessmen." Ingrid shrugs. "And that's just those in this kingdom. Ikael's been making noises about a war against some of the other settlements nearby. Galactic and human. Anyone who wasn't willing to play ball."

Before I can speak further, the dishes arrive. The cuisine is a range of high-falutin' French cuisine and more traditional African fare with beans, mashed meat, and vegetables I can't even name. Potentially because they might be Galactic. We dig in, our discussion turning to less contentious subjects. Ingrid fills me in on her life while I was gone, one that mostly encompasses a lot of fights, occasional assassinations, and even more scouting missions.

"Sounds like you've been busy."

"Things have changed a bit since you've gone," Ingrid says as she shifts peas around on her plate, separating a single pea before stabbing it with her fork. "Cheaper and more effective to deal with a single asshole and make him an example than to go in and take over entire settlements. You can always do that later if they haven't learned the lesson." The fork shifts, separating another pea. "Or you can just repeat the process if they don't get the lesson. You'd be surprised how many don't."

I cock my head to the side, considering what Lana mentioned to me about Ingrid hanging out with Miller more. Sounds more like what the CIA would do than the army, but without the CIA any longer, I wonder if Miller's taken over those tactics. Or maybe I'm giving them too much credit. There's no reason Ingrid isn't picking these targets herself with this idea in mind.

"Well, this was enlightening," I say finally when the dishes are finished.

"And you?" Ingrid asks, then points at Ali, who's taken a seat at the bar and is imbibing glasses of spirits like a college student on St. Patrick's Day. "I see the Spirit got bigger."

"He did. Consequence of my new Master Class." I consider what to say about my time away. I haven't spoken of it much. Not to Lana or Roxley. Not to anyone. But somehow, I have a feeling that Ingrid might understand. Her experience in the last few years parallels mine, being lonelier and bloodier than most. "It was difficult. I was thrown into a Forbidden Planet..."

I outline the basics. Long years of fighting, of not Leveling. Of having to learn to use my abilities in ways I'd never considered before, of upgrading my spells because I had to learn to manipulate Mana without the aid of the System. By the time I'm done, it's late and we've finished another pair of bottles of wine.

"And that's it..." I say when I see Ali yawning, floating off his chair and staring at a pair of visible System screens. This time, it's a baking reality TV show. "I guess we should get going."

"Hold up." Ingrid twists her hand and a watch I had last seen on Ikael's wrist hours ago appears.

"What is that?" I frown.

"Ikael's dimensional storage chain and AI," Ingrid says, tapping the watch. "The storage is locked, but it can be broken."

"And the AI?" I ask, curiosity getting me. If Ikael used the AI anything like I did Ali, this could be a huge boon.

"Maybe," Ingrid says with a shrug. "I can't. Sam… might have been able to." We fall silent at the old man's name, his death still a little raw. But soon enough, Ingrid looks up. "But I'm almost certain the details of the settlements he had deals with are in here."

"What do you want?" I ask with a frown. It's obvious that she mentioned all this with a purpose.

"I can have it cracked, but you'll owe me," Ingrid says. "One request at a later date. No questions asked."

"No. I don't do open-ended favors like that."

"*Really…?*"

"*Hush, you.*"

"Just ask me," I say to Ingrid, meeting her gaze directly.

She grimaces, not meeting my eyes for a time. Eventually, she looks up with a harsh exhalation. "Fine. I want to join you. On the trip out."

"Trip?"

"To the capital. I want to be part of the entourage," Ingrid says, glaring at me. "Deal?"

I consider her question then raise a finger. "One thing. No killing anyone I don't agree to other than in self-defense on the trip."

"Deal."

I nod and point at the watch. "Then get it cracked and we'll see what we can do about getting that seat."

Ingrid flashes me a smile and I return it. Curiosity bids me ask though…

"Why do you want to go?"

"Why not?" Ingrid says with a shrug. Something dark flashes through her eyes before she looks at me, her lips twisting slightly. "I know you're not going to go sightseeing. I figure if there's violence to be had, you'll bring it. And those bastards, they need to be paid back."

I know which "those" she means. And truth be told, I agree with her. Damn Council. For a time, I stare at my friend and see the shadows of the past, the losses she's suffered. We've all lost friends and family, but Ingrid lost her entire town, her entire tribe. She's the last survivor of Dawson City, maybe even the last of her people. For a moment, I see the gaping hole she covers up with sarcasm. Then she smiles and stands, making the watch disappear, followed by herself.

"Now what?" I ask the open air, considering what more there is to do.

Ali appears beside me, picking at the remnants of the meal. "The usual of course, boy-o. Just more work. You've met the human players. Now it's time to talk to the Galactics."

I let out a low groan, but Ali's right. Still, I decide to push it aside for a bit. Better to Portal home first. There's going to be some fallout from this assassination. And truth be told, there's an elf I need to speak to in Vancouver, if I want to speak to the Movana.

"Home."

Chapter 13

As I guessed, the fallout from the assassination spreads almost immediately. While others have been killed before, it was always cross-species or smaller fry. Ikael is the first true leader to be killed by another human, and the new threat throws everyone into a tizzy. It takes me ages to convince Katherine and Lana firstly, to take additional precautions, and secondly, that I don't need any additional security measures. It's not to say I think I am invincible, but my particular Skillset as an Honor Guard gives me significant defenses against an assassination attempt. It would be really, really tough to lock me down long enough to end me, not unless they throw the kitchen sink too.

Once matters calm down, the next few days are spent on the phone, if you will. Long-range communication towers have been set up all across Earth, linking City Cores to one another. While communication is still limited to City Cores, at least now humanity is once again connected. It makes everything, from commerce to relationships, so much simpler.

My job, over the next little while, is extending a friendly hand to these human settlements. Truth be told, it isn't even my plan. Within a few hours of my return, I receive one call after the other. It seems that a side effect of being involved in Ikael's murder—however peripherally—is that I have become significantly more popular among the more spineless settlement owners. In their minds, it makes more sense to befriend me than face a possible assassination.

"Then we've got a deal. I'll have a pair of bodyguards sent to you once the Contract is finalized," I say to the dark-haired, big-nosed gentleman who smiles nervously.

"Good. Good. I'll have it signed right away. I'm sure your bodyguards will keep the assassins off," the man says.

"They're all very well trained. We've doubled down on training with both ex-members of the US Secret Service and members of the Erethran Honor Guard. I'm sure they'll do well."

A few more words of pleasantries pass before the man fades away. I slump back in my chair as I stare at Ali, who is seated across from me, feet up on my table.

"I believe a major export of ours has become bodyguards," I say, chuckling. "Good thing Ayuri agreed to let her people train ours."

"You're not exporting bodyguards. You're exporting peace of mind," Ali says. "I'm proud of you, boy-o. You've even got that insinuating silence down to an art form in the last few days. Dropping Ingrid's name once in a while is doing wonders. Let's just hope she doesn't take a job on any of them."

I snort. No surprise, but Ingrid's identity was eventually revealed. Of course, I then had to deal with demands to come back for another interrogation, which I refused. I knew the investigator had a Truth Tell Skill of some sort, otherwise he'd never have let me go. And so I repeated my denials of having anything to do with the murder. But somehow, no one believed me. It didn't help that the actual source of the contract is yet to be found.

"What are we at?" I ask Ali while Lana strides in, looking at the pair of us, the bowl of snacks on the table, and the mess of carvings I've left on it.

"Eight point seven percent. Another four percent are wavering from Ikael's people. They're probably waiting for an actual bribe," Ali says, ticking off on his fingers. "And the rest of his supporters are actually angry at you. I doubt you'll get them. Not directly."

"Good thing I'm not looking for them to vote for me directly then. I'm sure Bipasha and Rob are making their own moves too," I say before turning to Lana. "Problem?"

"No," Lana says, shaking her head. "But we do have a visitor. Wynn's here."

I grin slightly. Finally. The damn elf has been off running a dungeon delve for the last few days, which is the other reason I've been stuck waiting. "Show him in."

"Of course."

"And stay, if you can," I add.

Lana smiles at me at the invitation and disappears around the corner.

While we wait for Lana to get Wynn, Ali looks between the door and me. "You guys doing okay?"

"Of course," I say softly. "I'm a big boy. She's moved on. It's more than fair, especially since, well, you know." I point upward.

"I notice you haven't asked anything about her boy toy," Ali points out.

"Don't need to know that," I say snippily and then exhale, shaking my head. "Just because I'm okay with her moving on doesn't mean I need the details."

"If you say so," Ali says doubtfully.

As footsteps near, Ali fades, turning invisible once again rather than be forced to actually participate and pay attention to this meeting.

"Wynn," I greet the Guild Master with a smile as I stand.

Wynn a Maro is the Vancouver Guild Master of the Burning Leaves, a powerful Tier II Guild whose members originate from everywhere but who are headquartered in the capital of the Movana Kingdom. They might not be directly backed by the Movana Kingdom, but they certainly draw a large number of their people from the noble class. In fact, the surnames of their Guild leadership could read like a Who's Who.

"Redeemer." Wynn bows, smiles, and takes the indicated seat.

Lana slides into one too, angling the chair so that we each sit in one corner of a triangle.

"You wished to speak with me?" he asks.

"I'm not going to beat around the bush," I say. "I'm looking to get enough votes for Earth to gain a seat on the Galactic Council. To do that…"

"You'll need the support of many Galactics," Wynn says. "But I'm surprised you're speaking to me and not your Lord Roxley. I am, after all, only a minor guild leader."

"I have," I say flatly. "But I'm an equal opportunity opportunist. If your people can and are willing to work with us, I'm willing to talk. And you can drop the garbage about your position. We both know you're more than just a minor guild leader."

"It is troublesome," Wynn says simply. "Your actions against the Zarrie before you left angered some. Your close relations with the Truinnar are another concern. Even if I were to open lines of communication, it would be extremely troublesome."

"But if you work with us, you can help decrease our reliance on them," I say, offering him a half smile.

Wynn returns it and doesn't directly contradict my words.

"Earth is caught between your kingdoms," Lana says, drawing Wynn's attention to her where she sits demurely, hands crossed on her lap. "But all we want is the right to choose our future. We're willing to work with whoever is willing to help us achieve that goal. And we'd love to have the Movana as an ally."

"And the addition of humanity as allies is something I wish for," Wynn says, laying a hand over his heart. Which, in Movana is actually more toward the right and down than in humans. "I've grown to like your people in my time here."

"And for that, we are grateful. If you can speak with others," Lana says beguilingly. She's not simpering, that'd be too weak, but it is a pointed and heartfelt request. It's enough to make Wynn nod slightly, unconsciously. "And help us pitch our hopes."

"I shall do what I can, Lady Pearson," Wynn says, smiling back at her.

"Just Ms."

"Not in my eyes," Wynn replies, and I almost roll my eyes. "But I cannot make any assurances. I can only speak with those in power here."

"That's all we can ask for," Lana says.

I watch Wynn preen and I wonder if he's even realized he's fallen for her. Or if he does, if he cares. After a few more pleasantries, Wynn takes his leave.

Lana returns to the office after showing the Movana out, slumping in a seat next to me. "Are you sure you want to go with the Truinnar?"

"Pretty boy making you think they're a better choice?" I say.

"I don't know if better is right, but have you done any research about either group? Beyond the people you've met?" Lana asks.

"I have. For all their bitching, they're actually very closely aligned. No surprise, when the Truinnar are just a branch that decided to run off a millennia or so ago. The Movana are a little looser with their noble structures, more free-flowing with those who move up or down their society. The Truinnar are more stratified in theory, but their entire army division allows the ambitious a respected and serviceable method to gain influence and position.

"Geographically—if that's even the right word when we're talking about star kingdoms—the Movana have fewer solar systems under their control but higher populations and higher build-out. The Truinnar have a more scattershot approach, with a large number of so-so areas. Roxley's old domain was one of those scattershot areas, great at first and then, well, not so much. Economically, the Movana are better off, but the Truinnar have a stronger standing army. Not that it matters as much to us. Of course, the last few decades have seen the heating up of their old cold war."

"And they support different factions, which means it's unlikely they'll ever work together," Lana adds. "And one of those factions probably made us a Dungeon World."

"The Movana," I say. "Sounds like a bad option to give them what they want then."

"Except for the fact that if they're willing to send more than six billion of us to hell, what makes you think they'd let you do what you want?" Lana says.

"I've considered it," I say, looking at my hands, framed as they are by the dark walnut wood. I shrug, giving her a half smile. "But they'll find out I'm a lot harder to kill than they think."

"Maybe. But I don't trust the Truinnar either. You know they're willing to backstab to get what they want," Lana says. "Roxley might be trustworthy, but he's not acting alone."

"True. In the end, we're just waiting anyway," I say with a grimace. "If neither group is willing to work with us at all, this is just theoretical."

Lana nods, but her troubled look doesn't go away. Not even when we switch to more productive topics. As the redhead walks out, I can't help but consider that maybe she's right. But in the end, I've got to try.

***

Movana and Truinnar done, I need to hit up the other Galactic groups. Amusingly enough, the warmongering, weapon-building Ares Corp is the easiest to handle. Almost immediately from the initial call, I'm put forward to their planetary head of operations. And after that, it just becomes a matter of horse trading. Thankfully, I drag Katherine and Lana into the actual negotiations, since I find myself well out of my depth within seconds. After all, tax structures, preferred supplier status, and duty rates are all things I have no real experience at. In a surprisingly short amount of time, the entire negotiation is wrapped up, a contract in place and signed. When it's done, the three of us share a glass of champagne around my office table.

"So. Did that seem a lot easier than it should be?" I say, staring at the contract notification floating in front of me.

Lana glares at me, running a hand through her hair. Even with her bountiful Constitution and Charisma, she looks slightly frazzled after the umpteenth marathon negotiating session. "Easy? You didn't just spend the last three days in continuous negotiations."

"It did," Katherine asserts, denying Lana's assertion. "And that last request…"

"Something tells me that was the whole point of the negotiation," I say.

"Are you sure you're new at this?" Katherine says, her eyes narrowing.

I shift uncomfortably, uncertain of what to say. It's true that I wasn't apt at managing office politics in my previous life, but I've had time to reflect on my past mistakes. And between my Intelligence and Willpower attribute increases and my Subterfuge Perk, I have a feeling that some information is leaking in. I'm beginning to get a weird intuitive sense for backstabbing politics. Underhanded dealings, those I can handle. I have a feeling I'd be floored if I ever had to deal with an honest, upstanding politician. Thankfully, the Galactic variety are similar to ours—they exist, but they're rarer than hen's teeth.

"New enough," I answer, breaking off from my musings. And my, somewhat justified, concern about what exactly is leaking in under the influence of the Perk. "In either case, we agreed to it. I need to speak with the Fist anyway, and this is as good a time as any. I'll be back in a few days."

Katherine offers me a nod while Lana grimaces, tugging at her messed up dress.

I stand, considering. "Think Mikito would be up for a trip?"

***

The answer was yes. Once we contacted the Samurai, she managed to catch up with us at the teleportation pad. Of course, part of that was because Lana took an hour to catch a cat nap and change. Mikito looked almost eager to be coming, a light smile on her lips as she gives Lana a hug before playing with the various pets. Once the requisite greetings and licks have been dealt with and a discreet Cleanse cast, Mikito turns to us with a smile.

"It's almost like old times," Mikito says, looking around. "Now if Ingrid was around and Carlos could be dragged out…"

"Huh. I think you'd have better chance with Aiden," I say. "He seems to have gotten over his fears."

"A bit," Mikito says, shooting a look at Lana. "It might have been because Lana kept bugging him while wearing a tank top a couple of summers ago."

"Mikito!" Lana says, apparently scandalized at first before she breaks into a grin. "If you've got them…" She gives a pointed look at the tiny Japanese's rather flat chest.

"Low blow," Mikito says with a growl, crossing her arms reflexively.

"Who says Ingrid isn't here?" I say, looking about and heading off the dustup by changing the topic. "Not as if we could ever tell."

"Har. No. She's too busy making Credits to hang out with us," Lana says with a frown.

I hear the slight bitterness in the redhead's tone and mentally grimace. Damn it. Topic change—fail.

"Come on, we're holding up the line," I say eventually, waving up the group.

It amuses me how the pets go first. All of them, including Lana's griffin, are transported before the three of us get on board. A slight shiver, a twisting in the folds of space, and we're suddenly there. I snort slightly, noting the usual greeting notification and the now prevalent icon indicating a quantum lock in space.

You have entered a Safe Zone—the Town of Scarborough

Mana flows in this area are stabilized. No monster spawning will occur in this region. Stamina and Health Regeneration increased by 2% in this zone. Please note that unauthorized teleportation is forbidden.

This Safe Zone includes:

- *City of Scarborough City Center*
- *Shop*
- *Arena*
- *Armory*
- *…*

"Duelist Lee. Spear Sato. Mistress Pearson," the apelike, barrel-chested creature who greets us uses our titles.

It's the first time I've ever heard anyone called Lana by her title—abbreviated or not—of the Mistress of Flame and Beasts, but obviously, it means something to these people. Which is interesting, since most combat titles are rarely used in greetings. From what I've gathered, it's a bit of a social faux pas.

"Champion Emven," I greet the Galactic while making sure that Ali remembers to send his Status information to my friends. Not that they probably don't have their own Skills, come to think of it.

Emven Iz, Champion of the Purple Sands, Greater Meatshield (Shield Guardian Level 38)

HP: 5430/5430

MP: 870/870

Conditions: Vulcanized skin, Organ sheath, Reflexive Shield

"Good call, boy-o. The Fist care more about combat titles than anyone else. Frankly, your Redeemer title holds no weight here. Though I'm getting an inkling of what we can expect," Ali says.

"Well, spit it out."

"Nah, this will be more fun," Ali sends back with a smirk.

And despite repeated prodding, Ali refuses to divulge anything further. All the while, I'm listening to Emven as he leads us through the reconstructed city where the looming, giant oval structure dominates the city. Emven waxes lyrical about the many historical battles fought over Tobago in its Earth history, and most recently, by the Galactic colonists. I find it all quite interesting, but the big building even more so.

"Where are we going?" Lana asks during one of the few breaks.

"Ah, we walk toward the arena. The governor is holding court there as usual," Emven says. "He also felt warriors like you would find it of great interest."

"Really now," I say, looking at the looming building. Cheers echo out from the open air building. Loud. So very loud, the clash of blades and the hiss of spells ringing through the air, almost as if a heavy metal band had taken to the stands with their amplified instruments. "Sounds like there're a lot of people there."

"It's the major form of entertainment. And training," Emven remarks. "There's normally between five to six thousand, but today, the governor made sure to have a few favorites show up to spice up the regular lineup. I hear we're at nearly ten thousand."

Lana cranes her head from side to side, noting the numerous pedestrians and the busy hum of vehicles which float along the street below and above us. Even at a glance, it's clear Scarborough is as busy as Vancouver, even with the large audience in the arena.

"Mostly humans out here," I send to Ali, judging the difference between the settlements.

"Want to bet the Galactics are at the arena?" Ali says with a smirk.

"No bet."

I get a chuckle from Ali as we are led inward. There's only a brief moment of awkwardness as we deal with Lana's various pets. Eventually, the security personnel compromise, allowing Roland to accompany Lana within while the rest of the pets get housed with other pets and mounts. Grey corridors made of a stone-like substance, marked with light green and blue trimming, encompass us as we go up, finally ending at the skybox. A part of me is amused how certain architectural structures are the same no matter the culture—give the important people luxurious space, a high viewing area, and privacy. I'm sure there are species who would abhor some of these concepts, but here, it's the same.

"Welcome, friends! You are just in time for Umma of the Two Blades and Whirlpool Donnie. The Whirlpool is one of your compatriots and a very entertaining fighter."

The jovial greeting hits us the moment we walk into the room. The speaker is a sight to behold, standing just over eleven feet tall and nearly as wide, his body a mass of firm grey fat, large long ears hanging down his elongated face, and tiny, beady eyes. For a moment, I wonder if anyone ever considered the concept of a werehippo, which is what the speaker looks like.

Asgauver Heindra, Boneshaker, Master of the Sands, Lord of the Fell Reaches, Survivor of the Marrik Raid, (more) (Level 21 Absorber)
HP: 13980/13980
MP: 1230/1230
Conditions: Altered Gravity, Healer's Wrath, Force to Bone, Flayed Nerves

"Thank you," I say and shake Asgauver's hand. For the first time in a while, I feel tiny, my hand disappearing in the werehippo's larger one.

The thirty-by-thirty room is filled with probably the widest array of Galactics I've ever come across in a non-violent fashion. A rolling ball of cables and tentacles, a siren, a sylph, Truinnar, Movana, Hakarta, and Yerrick are all easy to spot. There are other, less commonly seen Galactics in the crowd, including a pair of little grey men.

"What is he?" The notification pops up in my interface, tagged Lana.

"Kudaya Delta. Interesting world—there were four separate species on it when the System arrived, just starting out as agricultural civilizations. Each species is designated by a number type after the planet name. Nearly all their technology is Galactic owned. The Kudaya just decided to abandon creating their own technological culture and focused on being the best damn warriors they could be," Mikito sends back almost immediately.

"How'd you know that?" I can't help but send.

"Know your enemy."

"Sit, sit." Asgauver waves us to a trio of scaled down seats next to him. I absently note that instead of a chair with backing, Asgauver uses more of a leaning apparatus whose structure supports his lower back and butt. "Did you wish to place a bet? If so, you must do it quickly."

"Uhh... maybe later," I say even as Mikito adds a yes.

I blink as the usually reserved Japanese lady waves over at the attendant with a tablet. A few seconds of interaction later and the attendant moves away. Lana watches all this with a light curl on her lips, stroking Roland, who's curled up next to her. I wonder what she thinks of all this.

Directly ahead of us, the window screens flash, shifting to showcase the pair of fighters entering the arena. Immediately, the din of conversation drops off as everyone focuses on the fight. Now that Asgauver and the Galactics around me are a lesser concern, I take in the arena. Perfectly white sand surrounds the otherwise empty arena, whose borders are protected by expensive and nearly perfectly clear force shields. Stadium seating goes up around the arena with a second layer of flying, floating, hovering, and otherwise airborne Galactics watching the fight. As we guessed, there aren't a lot of humans in sight.

The fighters themselves are interesting. Like her name hints, Umma is a Movana who wields a pair of glowing short swords. One burns red hot, and the other seems to freeze the air around it. A plain black armored jumpsuit is covered by a gaudy yellow tactical vest where a series of smaller blades sit. On the other hand, the Whirlpool—short for Elemental Whirlpool—is a short, tanned human with shocking pink hair, a rapier at his waist, and a single glove on his wielding hand. Contrary to his appearance, the man is actually Classed as a Battle Mage. In terms of Levels, both of them are within a couple of points of each other, giving no clear advantage.

At the slug-like referee's signal, the pair battle. Like the rest of the viewers—with the exception of Lana—Mikito is leaning forward, watching the battle with rapt attention. Umma dashes forward immediately, blurring across the ground. Donnie responds by conjuring waves of water. When Umma attempts to jump over the waves, tendrils of the liquid grip her legs, pulling her downward. Immediately, the water twists, transforming into the Battle Mage's namesake.

"Ah, so fast!" Asgauver says, his tone full of disappointment.

"Har! Don't count your Credits yet. My cousin is not so easily dealt with." A Movana walks up to us, his smile wide and relaxed. "Care for a side wager?"

"Twenty thousand Credits," Asgauver offers.

The Movana nods, the pair tapping their left shoulders to seal the deal in what looks like to be pure reflex.

"But this is rude. Friends, will any of you take on Quityan's offer as well?" Asgauver asks.

Lana shakes her head again while Mikito visibly considers the question before shaking her head.

"Let me introduce myself. I'm Quityan o'Shea," Quityan says.

It doesn't take us long to introduce ourselves to the Forest Ranger, who then turns back to the fight. During this period, the elemental water conjured has transformed, icicles forming as they cut at the helpless figure within. Yet Quityan does not look concerned at all.

"Boy-o, focus on the body in the whirlpool with Mana sight."

I call forth the ability, frowning slightly as the colors shift and change. Instead of the heatmap-like viewpoint a normal body would provide, what I see is a more solid figure, one which glows a light yellow.

"Doppelganger?"

Even as I finish asking the question, the body abruptly disappears. The real Umma appears behind Donnie, her blades slicing downward. They shatter against an invisible Mana Shield, one which absorbs both impacts but sends the Battle Mage staggering away. The Battle Mage's reactions and recovery are amazing though, as Umma's next attack is met by the rapier. Within seconds,

188

additional tendrils of water and fire appear, joining Donnie's defense as the pair duel at close quarters.

"A new Skill is it?" Asgauver says, contentment lacing his voice even as it looks as though he might lose the bet.

No one answers Asgauver, not that one is needed. The battle rages on, Donnie managing to pull away a couple of times, but never far enough to completely disengage from Umma. Eventually, the Mage's greatest weakness tells and his Mana bottoms out, leaving him defenseless against Umma's blades.

"Damn. A pity," Asgauver says then gestures toward Quityan, who inclines his head after his gaze goes faraway. "Next time."

"Not much of a Battle Mage," Mikito grumbles, her arms crossed. But I note the bouncing in her foot, the way she's leaning forward slightly as the next fight is announced.

"I believe none of you have visited us before, have you?" Quityan asks.

"No," Lana answers him with a polite smile.

"Then I look forward to your fights," Quityan says.

"What fights?" Lana says.

"*And here we go, boy-o.*"

"It is customary for first-time visitors to the arena to fight in it," Asgauver says, then looks toward Emven. "Did you not inform our guests?"

"My apologies. I must have forgotten," Emven says. His wooden delivery almost makes me choke with laughter.

"Well, as punishment, I'll have to have you fight them," Asgauver says, shaking his head.

"Of course."

"*Why are they doing this?*" Lana sends the notification to all of us, and I shrug.

"Probably because they're battle-crazy idiots. If you want a treaty with them, you're going to need to be 'worthy,'" Ali sends.

"I'm not so sure about that," I send back.

Something about this setup doesn't sit well with me. I can see Lana is perturbed, the slight crease in her eyebrows and the slightly longer look she gives Asgauver the tells. Nothing anyone who didn't know her very well would notice.

"I'll be your first opponent," Mikito says, bouncing up from her seat and staring at Emven.

Lana and I are somewhat startled, staring at the little Japanese who looks ready to start the dance right this second.

"Ah… I'll make arrangements," Asgauver replies then looks at the pair of us.

"Lana's here at my request. And while she can fight, I'd like to make a different offer," I say, a coil of anger running through my stomach. They want to manipulate us and make us dance, make us fight for their entertainment? Fine. We can play.

"Offer?"

"I'll fight you."

Silence spreads at my pronouncement, the guests within the skybox turning toward our group. Asgauver gapes at me before bursting into a long, rumbling laugh that shakes the chair next to me.

"Done! Emven, make the arrangements."

"Of course," Emven says and taps his left shoulder before walking off.

A sharp pain erupts from my left ankle and I turn to look at a furious Lana.

"I don't need you to protect me!"

"Wasn't about you. I just don't intend for them to get their way entirely."

"I got to admit, boy-o's got it right. The Fist are all about strength. This, this is strong."

"So long as he wins."

"I'll win."

"Show-off," Mikito says, crossing her arms grumpily and staring at me. I laugh at her words, and she cracks a slight smile. "Baka."

***

It takes an hour for Mikito's fight to be arranged. In the meantime, the unlucky Samurai ends up losing all the matches she bets on. At Asgauver and Quityan's urgings, Lana and I eventually partake in the betting after receiving contradictory advise from both Fist members. Toward the last couple of fights, Lana and I just decide to bet against Mikito's choices, much to the mock outrage of the Samurai. If it wasn't for the fact that some of the duels are multi-party free-for-alls, this might have been a winning strategy. It's Ali who does the best, the Spirit quietly placing bets and winning a large number of his wagers.

While we wait, a few aspects of the arena battles which had puzzled us are explained. For one, use of grenades, portable shield generators, and drones are disallowed for most Classes. There are exceptions made for those who are not direct combat Classes, to make the fights a little fairer. Another thing we learn is while the arena can and does change its geography and features, providing everything from semi-permanent urban structures to even an aquatic environment, for today, a more sterile approach has been decided—a mano-o-mano fight. Unsurprisingly, many long-range, rifle-, and bow-wielding fighters have declined to fight in this kind of boring terrain. Without cover, portable or pre-made, they are in danger of being rushed by the melee fighters. And in this System-enhanced world, it is all too easy to close in on long-range fighters. My Blink Step is only one of the many teleporting abilities available.

All of this and the various safety procedures are explained to us while we wait for our friend's fight. Eventually, it arrives.

Mikito walks out on the sand, her naginata already summoned and in her hands. She's changed into a simple red-and-white armored jumpsuit, one that provides her full coverage and flexibility, with a simple helmet covering her face and hiding her long hair. Surrounding her body is the Ghost Armor of her Skill, giving her another form of protection similar to my Soul Shield, if more Mana intensive.

I stare at my friend, curious to see her really let loose in such a setting, before looking at her opponent, the shield guardian wielding a halberd-and-shield combination. Except the long blade of the polearm glows with an ominous light.

"What kind of Skills are we looking at with the Guardian?"

"In their main Class, mostly defensive Skills obviously. Two major builds that split along passive and active. Emven has a passive build, so while he's got a significant health pool, he has a really low Mana pool and regen rate. He's going to be able to soak up damage like a troll eats rocks."

"I see you have bet heavily on your friend," Asgauver says. "An admirable show of support."

"I was looking more at taking you to the cleaners," I say.

"Har. A nice thought, but he is not a champion for no reason," Asgauver says. "She is good but young. Inexperienced. All of you humans are."

Before I can answer, the referee signals the start of the fight, focusing everyone's attention. Unlike Umma, Mikito takes her time edging toward the other melee fighter. Emven hunkers down low, his body clad in bulky, plate-mail-looking armor. Without warning, the champion fires a beam of brilliant purple energy from the head of the halberd. To my surprise, Mikito swings her naginata at the beam, cutting the attack apart and leaving the diffused beam to splash harmlessly against her armor.

"What the...?" I stare. It doesn't make any sense. You can't cut light.

Even with his initial attempt failing, Emven is willing to try again, firing another pair of blasts. Interestingly enough, just before the beam reaches Mikito's attack range, they twist in mid-air, curving. Mikito casually cuts the pair of beams apart, her polearm spinning with blinding speed. As if deciding she's had enough, the Japanese woman darts forward, seeming to appear beside Emven in a moment. My eyes widen slightly as she displays her Flash Step ability. She swings her polearm immediately, each strike somehow being blocked by Emven.

"What is that weapon?" Asgauver hisses, leaning forward.

I hear the whispered threads of conversation growing louder as Mikito's repeated attacks begin to tell, each strike leaving larger and larger gouges on the shield, almost peeling back the reinforced shield.

"Mikito's. I believe it's soulbound," I say, lying with a straight face. Inside, I'm sweating a little. Her weapon is more than soulbound—it's a growth weapon. One which can gain strength over time. While we've taken steps— and I'm assured she has too—to hide the nature of it, there's only so much you can do in a System-run world. If she attracts too much attention...

"Impressive. She has at least two Skills improving the weapon itself, but to do so much damage against Emven's shield is astounding," Asgauver says. "I have seen Master Class Skills do less damage."

"Cleave and Reaver if you're wondering. Though I'm pretty sure the second is actually part of the weapon," Ali says.

I say nothing, though a thread of worry grows in my stomach for Mikito. The Soul Drinker Skill of her naginata means it will, eventually, become an Artifact. It's the kind of weapon people get killed for owning.

"I have a feeling... there," I say, watching as Emven gives up on waiting for Mikito to exhaust herself and attempts to fight back.

Shield Bash, Shield Charge, Disembowel, Vortex Swing. The names of the Skills he triggers pop up in tiny notifications from Ali, each attack thwarted. But as Mikito ducks the spinning tornado that Emven's last attack created, the Shield Guardian stomps, creating a minor earthquake. The attack only unbalances Mikito for a fraction of a second, but it's sufficient for Emven to land a Shield Bash, disrupting Mikito's balance further and stunning her.

The champion chains his attacks, each blow timed perfectly with a step, his movements keeping his body right next to the stunned Samurai. Her Ghost Armor bleeds light, cracking under the assault even as wide open wounds send splashes of crimson blood to the white sand.

"Inexperienced, as I said," Asgauver says, almost smug satisfaction in his tone.

"Come on, Mikito," Lana whispers, leaning forward and gripping her knees tightly.

I place a hand on hers, giving it a quick squeeze for reassurance. "I wouldn't count her out yet."

The halberd rises and comes crashing down, caught by Mikito's naginata. But as she recovers, the shield is moving, smashing the body of her naginata into her body. A leg steps forward, striking the tiny Japanese woman's knee and knocking her off balance, forcing her to block another strike. This one sends her tumbling to the ground, where she recovers with a roll. As Emven steps forward, an explosion of sand and smoke makes him blink, flame blinding him. When he recovers, Mikito is standing unsteadily, her weapon held sideways above her left shoulder.

"A good move. But not enough," Quityan remarks.

Mikito's down to five hundred Mana and barely four hundred health. Not enough, normally, for a powerful Skill. Of course, Emven's Mana is in the low hundreds too, but his health is still two-thirds full.

I stay silent as Emven moves forward cautiously, Mikito holding still. It's a stillness that sets the hair at the nape of my neck tingling, a tension which tightens my chest as primal fears rise up. Emven sees it, moving cautiously, but he can't delay too long. Each moment allows Mikito's greater regeneration levels to top up her Mana. And so he nears her, his halberd moving forward in low feints which elicit no response.

With a roar, the champion stabs the halberd forward, the weapon shooting its beam of purple energy at Mikito. The Samurai moves then, flashing forward as her naginata arcs downward, cutting through Emven's shield and armor in a single motion. Emven staggers backward, his arm and halberd clattering to the ground as gravity takes hold and he slumps. Mikito herself sways, her health down to fourteen percent as she sacrifices her life for Mana.

The crowd exclaims around us, in multiple voices and languages.

"It is called Gi," Asgauver says, surprise tingeing his voice.

"The first tenet of Bushido." I lean back in my chair, a little of the tension I felt for my friend draining away as I read the details of the Skill Ali displays.

Gi (Exclusive Skill)

The Samurai exemplifies commitment with their next attack. A single strike, without hesitation or doubt, with full commitment must be made. If completed, the Samurai can deal significantly more damage in exchange for their own life.

Effect: Doubles Base Damage of attack. Health of user may be traded for damage dealt to recipient at a 1:1 ratio, but user must decide on amount of health traded before attack is made.

Cost: 200 Mana

Asgauver laughs, roaring in amusement, followed by everyone else. The group cheers, chatting about the battle. Lana stares at those around us, her eyes wide.

"Aren't you worried about your friend? He lost his arm," Lana says.

"Better than a head. They'll reattach it and he'll be ready for battle in a few hours," Quityan says, waving away her protests. "Pity it's a friendly match though. In a title fight, they'd continue until one really lost."

"He lost his arm!" Lana sputters.

"Emven can fight without it," Quityan replies unconcernedly. "He's an elite member of the Fist. If he couldn't fight without an arm, he wouldn't deserve to be on the team."

Lana shakes her head, looking toward me for support. I smile slightly at the redhead, shaking my head. She looks disappointed by my reaction, and truth be told, I am in hers. But then, she hasn't spent the last four years in a Forbidden Zone. I can't even count the number of limbs I've lost over the years.

"I find myself looking forward to our fight now," Asgauver says, his wide mouth pulling apart to show those large teeth. I can't help but notice that he probably could fit my entire arm in his mouth without a problem.

"Me too."

***

No surprise our fight is at the end of the day, as the sun begins to set. Attempts by Lana and Ali to bring the discussion toward the reason for our visit—to an alliance or agreement for their vote—are firmly and politely rebuffed. After her return, Mikito is swarmed by the attendees, many requesting to see her weapon. All are rebuffed. None take offense, understanding the reluctance of a warrior to show a personal weapon, which is for the best. We can only hope that they'll be fooled by the information we have left public, assuaging their interest in the weapon when they buy it from the Shop. If they do.

With no progress on the actual point of our visit, I find myself standing on the sand, knowing it's likely the results of this match will dictate how much progress we make today. The arena is surprisingly quiet, the roar of the crowd a muted buzz in the background. The light within is just right, diffused and soft so that it never gets in the way. The sand gives way slightly, a bit more unsteady than I'd prefer but nothing so loose as to make purchase impossible. And the smell... well, the smell is of old blood, sour sweat, spent adrenaline, and other, more exotic chemicals.

I find myself raising my sword to my head, offering Asgauver a salute. It suits the mood; it suits the stadium. And it obviously suits the audience, as roars erupt. The werehippo before is big, tough and a Master Class with more years at fighting than I have. Odds of me winning are an astounding nine-to-one. Odds of me lasting one minute is seven-to-one. Barely better.

Pity I can't bet on myself.

The chime, the slight shift in light and the referee's voice is all the signal which is needed. Asgauver dashes forward, his movement so explosive a hole is left behind him as his strength is focused on approaching me. The giant monstrous hippo is here before I can dodge, but then, I wasn't trying to. A single step takes me within the arc of his torso-sized fist and I raise my own, palm out. It hits his giant nose, squishing it slightly as my legs flex and I'm forced backward. A part of me reaches out backward, reinforcing the sand I'm standing on while my body braces against his attack. On a pure point basis, Asgauver probably has a higher Strength stat than me, but he doesn't know how to use it, doesn't know how to apply it fully. In the air, my arm extended before my body, Asgauver slams into the equivalent of an unmoveable object and bounces backward.

The hush from the stadium is gratifying. I grin, shaking my hand slightly while keeping my face smooth. The shake also hides the minor trembles going through my arm as over-abused nerves and a cracked shoulder joint slowly regenerate.

"Impressive!" Asgauver roars as he rolls himself upward, laughing as blood pours from his two large nostrils. He swabs at the blood with one hand, stomping the ground as if to set himself. A second later, his fists shimmer, fields of energy wrapping around them and setting my teeth on edge. "But a trick is trick."

"Then let's dance," I say and salute him once more.

When the werehippo approaches again, this time it's with a lot more caution.

***

"Done. Yet?" I say as I husband my breath. A flick of my sword sends droplets of blood flying, recoating the white sand with the Kudaya's blood.

"And stop all this fun? Never!" Asgauver says but ends up coughing and spitting a gob of blood.

The damn hippo is covered in cuts and stabs, my attacks having scored and torn at the monster again and again. But his Class is an upgrade of your typical Guardian, a tank which can absorb punishment and turn it into Stamina, Mana, and yes, even Health. He's a juggernaut who just keeps ticking, no matter how much I damage him. His health keeps sliding upward, now at sixty percent, yo-yoing with his Mana.

The last thirty minutes has seen me go from using Spells and Skills to cut him down to a more husbanded approach. None of my Spells harm him, not even Enhanced Lightning. His resistances are high, his Class Skills making the little damage that leaks through negligible and even helpful to him. Next, I switched to more mundane attacks, backed up with the Thousand Blades. He ran through the blades, using his greater bulk and defenses to punch his way through them.

And punch he can. His Title is not for show. Boneshaker. His fist, encased in a wall of sonic attacks, hurts even when I block or dodge. My entire body feels as if it's been holding on to a jackhammer for the whole day, my tongue a mess after having been accidentally bit so many times I almost consider a ball gag. My health is down to about forty percent, my Mana doing better at seventy. But Mana's useless because my attacks just don't do enough damage, not against him.

"Fine," I growl and beckon the Kudaya on.

He rushes forward and I meet his fist with blades, a pair in hand as I dance and duck, my teeth and bones shuddering at near misses, my blades cutting into tough flesh. I have to use bigger motions, twisting and pushing against Asgauver's Skill that robs my attacks of momentum, that threaten to stick my blades. I have to duck and dodge, stabbing and moving, my Stamina slowly grinding down, along with my health.

I fall for a feint of a retracted straight, the hand returning and dropping straight down. I get my sword up in time, but it doesn't matter. The hippo drops his body, crushing me beneath his bulk. The earth flattens beneath me, a depression forming as Asgauver activates a Skill which triples his weight. I cough out blood, crushed and trapped.

And I have him exactly where I want him.

As the Kudaya pins my arm with one hand, the other rising to crush my face, I focus. Portals take a few precious moments to appear, the time required depending on the distance. And the interference at the other end. In this case, the other end of the Portal isn't far. Just a hundred fifty feet or so. Directly above me. And the first one is directly below me.

We fall through the Portal and appear above where we were, above the arena and its exclusion from the quantum lock surrounding Tobago. Pain erupts through my body as molecules which were meant to align after teleportation get shifted ever so slightly, the System helping to fix the damage after having enforced the initial damage in the first place. We fall, picking up speed, and I fend off one more punch before Blink Stepping away from the damn Kudaya, just a couple of feet away so that I can nudge him back into the center of the Portal.

"Give up?" I shout.

"*Never!*"

Asgauver falls, twisting in the air, and hits the open Portal and reappears high above the arena to take damage again. And drops downward as gravity takes effect, falling through the Portal again to reappear above, his speed ever increasing. As for me, I stand to the side of the open Portal and focus, keeping an eye on the stubborn hippo's health, occasionally using my spells to bounce him back into the center.

Once again, the silence through the stadium tells me I might have stunned the crowd. This time, when the noise comes back, it's more muted, less boisterous. I might win, but I obviously didn't win the "right" way.

***

"I told you you needed more movement Skills," Quityan is saying to Asgauver.

The giant hippo is less boisterous now, arms crossed, his lips twisted upward in what I would call a snarl while the jaws move, masticating food. Once the Kudaya had finally been deemed too damaged to continue, I closed the Portals. Since then, the Kudaya has yet to say a damn word to me.

"You might have overdone it," Lana says, elbowing me in the ribs. "You could have given up after putting on a good show."

"Bugger him if he can't take losing," Ali says, playing with a string of glittering little spheres on a vine before he pops one into his mouth. "He shouldn't have mocked boy-o."

"He'll get over it," I say semi-confidently.

Whether he likes it or not, the System seems to agree that the win was mine, dumping a ton of experience onto me. It's one of the facets of an arena which makes it popular. Everyone watching within the arena makes a minor experience donation. It's generally pretty low per person, but with so many attendees, the amount stored and distributed is significant. As the headline act, the two of us receive a large chunk of the experience siphoned off during the day. As the winner, I get an even larger portion, enough so that I skip two Levels, putting me at Level 18. I'd assign my attributes and Skills, but it'd be considered rude to do so right now. No rush really.

Mikito nods, then grins slightly. "John could always beat him into it anyway."

I cough as Quityan shoots us a look, obviously having heard Mikito. But she has a point. This is the Fist after all. In fact, I probably should have just wagered their vote on the fight, but truth be told, I hadn't been that confident

I'd win. If he had a Flight or other movement spell he could have used in mid-air, he would have been fine.

Lana rolls her eyes but stops when she sees another well-wisher come up. As usual, they greet Mikito first then me, congratulating us on our arena battles. Once again, I feel the undercurrent of disrespect, a dislike for my methods. By the time he's gone—after extending another invitation to Mikito for a fight at a later date—Quityan is next to us.

"My apologies. Asgauver does not like losing. He'll be better after he's healed. His Skill takes a lot from him, no matter what he says," Quityan says, looking back at the large hippo with a tenderness in his eyes that I didn't expect.

I blink, thinking back to the casual touches, the body language… huh. Well, how would it work? After a moment, I wish I could scrub my brain.

"At a later date. If you're willing?"

"Pardon?" I say, shaking my head. I rewind his words in my brain and catch up. "Oh. Yes, definitely. We do need your votes."

"And you'll have them. For a few small considerations." There's a slight pause before Quityan adds, "We seek little from your world, but individuals are interesting. Your strength, your experience in the Forbidden Zone…"

I nod slightly, mentally wincing. Right. I know now where this is going. They'll want details, explanations of monsters and my experiences. Might even want me to go on a trip with them to a zone, just to power-Level themselves once again. I can see it in his eyes, in the way he speaks.

"Of course. Tomorrow then?" I say.

"Tomorrow," Quityan says. "If you'd like, I can have you shown to your rooms. You must be tired."

Murmured agreements ring out. Lana begs out too, indicating a desire to take her pets for a run. Her words elicits another delay as others offer to show her to a nearby dungeon. In the midst of the hubbub, Mikito and I extract ourselves, glad to leave the fight-crazy Fists alone.

"So how'd you do?" I ask. "On your wagers."

"About forty thousand Credits down," Mikito says happily. "Be better if I had bet on you winning like I thought you would."

"You bet on me losing?" I groused.

"Well, I didn't want to jinx you," Mikito replies, eyes twinkling.

Silence extends between us before we break out in laughter, the attendant showing us the way to our temporary accommodations staring at us as if we're crazy. The look the attendant gives us only drives us to laugh harder.

Chapter 14

"When you said you wanted to spend some time together, I was thinking a nice gastropub. Or maybe a yoga session," Aiden, the skinny-jeans-wearing, goateed, manbun Mage, mutters. His hand twists and a lamppost bends and catches the flying monkey creature in mid-air, crushing it. At the same time, his other hand swings a wand, carving runes of light in the air, which float away to stack up in front of him.

"This is a lot more fun," I say, impaling another downed monkey.

Hitting open settlements and dungeons have become a thing in the last couple of weeks, between conversations with panicked humans and snooty Galactics. I've stepped back somewhat from negotiating with settlement owners while I wait for more information, letting Lana and Katherine take the lead. Part of the reason we're out as often though is because many of the completed deals have included helping out with dungeon population control, monster swarms, and sweeping areas to develop new land. So going out and killing monsters has actually helped strengthen our negotiation power as we show we're not all talk. I do get moments of déjà vu though, when I Portal in another attack team to another strange city before traveling to the next damn location to do the same again. At least this time I've got access to much faster transportation.

All this fighting has provided a nice boost to my experience bar, gaining me another Level. In many ways, my Leveling speed is a bit ridiculous, but I did just spend four years fighting over-Leveled monsters on an on-going basis, so the resulting banked experience is significant. At some point, the banked experience will run out, but for now, I won't be complaining.

"Your definition of fun needs work," Lana calls, shotgun in hand. She hasn't shot it yet, mostly because the Aura of the Red Queen which surrounds her is sufficient to keep the monsters away. That, and her pets do a bang-up job of taking down anything that even remotely threatens her. Her griffin is particularly frightening, though right now, the griffin's fighting a pair of flying snake-like creatures.

"Come on, this is a walk in the park," I say.

"I have a Fireball," Aiden says, holding up his hand.

"I do not understand," Capstan growls between taking shots at the flying monkeys. They mostly bounce off the temporary force shields the Yerrick have erected around our Portal site, only a few managing to make their way through the gaps the Yerrick have positioned.

Every second, more Adventurers are streaming in from Vancouver, parties gathering and receiving their marching orders from Capstan's people while Carlos hands out small bags filled with his latest creations.

"We're in El Chaten, which is located in Los Glaciares National Park. John was punning with the idiom," Aiden says, his left hand still not stopping. "Nearly…"

"What are you casting?" Lana says, cocking her head to the side.

"A localized teleportation spell which is anchored here and linked to my life signs with a secondary healing and regeneration component," Aiden says as he jabs the wand forward.

The last rune floats into the air, coalescing into a giant ball of spinning light before it splits into two parts. The smaller portion strikes Aiden in his chest, the larger sinking into the ground, where it disperses and embeds itself, leaving runic marks that slowly fade away.

"Whoa…" I say, looking at Aiden with admiration. "We can do that?"

"I can," Aiden says, shaking his head. "It's a ritual spell which takes about a week to cast. What you saw was just the engagement process."

I blink, scratching the spell off the list of things I needed for regular dungeon runs. Still impressive though.

"Mikito not here?" Aiden asks.

"No. She's running another dungeon."

"With the champions?"

"No. Americans," Lana adds unhappily. "Howard says the borders are secure. Nothing major in the next few blocks, though he smelled something disturbing on the other side of town. Howard's insisting someone else do the killing as he doesn't want to bite it."

Her words gets a chuckle from Capstan before he barks a few orders. A party of Yerrick run up and are soon sent off to meet with the reluctant pony-sized puppy, Ali helpfully supplying everyone with coordinates. The Spirit is standing next to the Portal, tagging all the newcomers and sharing updated information maps. It still amazes me how smart Lana's pets have gotten. It's rather frightening the Level of power she can wield. Each of her animals is nearly the same strength as an equivalent Leveled individual, making Lana a walking party by herself. It makes her Class over-powered in some ways, but also a bit lopsided. It'd take a single semi-skilled assassin to take her out.

While everyone else is busy, I'm just holding the Portal open, so I take a moment to look around. The earth and our surroundings are all dusty brown, dry in the Argentinian summer. The mountains which ring the tiny town have the lightest of remnants of snow, a stark contrast to the unceasing whiteness of the Yukon this time of year. Most of the—few—buildings around us are broken down, missing windows and occasional walls, weird pitted holes and half-dissolved bricks opening up the interiors. Even the asphalt is damaged, torn up and melted, giving further clues as to the cause of destruction. Monsters. Lots of monsters.

While the town itself hasn't become a dungeon, it's a Level 80-plus zone out at the borders with obviously higher Level zones as you move further in. The town once thrived post-apocalypse but made the crucial mistake of not consistently clearing the surrounding alphas and dungeons, leading to a monster swarm which promptly killed everyone. Since then, no one's taken the town, leaving it unclaimed. It probably didn't help that there's literally nothing connected to it for hundreds of kilometers. Of course, the lack of access is partly why it's the perfect settlement for us to claim back.

"You sure about this, Capstan?" I say again, frowning at the big minotaur.

He chuckles, clapping me on the shoulder. "Whitehorse cannot hold all three clans which have arrived. With support from you and Lord Roxley, we should be able to develop this Village quickly. And I understand the Spear will be leading the champions to clear a few dungeons next week. We will be fine."

"Fine," I say. A moment later, I get the all-clear from our last entrant into our game of whack a monster. I drop the Portal, glancing at my slowly regenerating Mana, and tap Aiden on the shoulder. "You're with us."

"Dungeon clearing?"

"Yup. There's a Level 90 dungeon which needs clearing," I say and point in the right direction.

Aiden grumbles, more out of habit than actual objection it seems, as he follows along. Capstan and Nelia fall in with us after Capstan finishes speaking with the other Fist—a shorter female minotaur who wields a whip and Gatling gun. Lana refuses to come, busy running her puppies and coordinating with the new settlement owner.

Our tiny party makes it about a hundred meters away from town before Ingrid makes her appearance next to us, letting the others know of her presence.

"Ms. Starling," Aiden exclaims. "I did not expect you here. Lana said you weren't coming."

Ingrid sniffs. "Lana's stuck-up and judgmental. I figured I'd hitch a ride quietly. It's been ages since I've done a proper dungeon delve."

"You're welcome to come along," I say with a chuckle, my invitation echoed by the Yerrick.

With Ingrid settled, we pick up the pace, headed for the dungeon. Should be a breeze, with the group as it stands.

***

One of the things any Adventurer learns about dungeons is that they don't hold to the normal laws of physics. Given enough Mana, dungeons have a tendency to warp the space around them, like a heavy metal ball on cheesecloth, stretching it under its weight and density. The dungeon we enter is a simple cave from the outside, but inside, it transforms to something truly immense, large enough to rival the Mammoth Cave system perhaps. As we delve, the initial few rooms are filled with poisoned fungi, warped insects, and mutated bats. Easy kills. Pedestrian even. Afterwards, things get disgusting.

"Acid slimes," I announce, swiping the dripping mucous-like substance from my Soul Shield.

The corpse of the slime slowly dissolves, its Mana core destroyed.

"Flammable oil slimes here," Aiden says, floating as he sprays his own opponents with a burst of freezing cold from his arm. Beneath him, the slimes twist and stretch in an attempt to reach the mage.

"Acid," Nelia calls, her hands shifting as roots explode upward from the ground, piercing the slimes and draining them of their fluids, leaving crystalline remnants and Mana stones.

"More fire slimes," Capstan growls. The large Yerrick looks to be the most perturbed, his usual loadout less than useful against these gelatinous opponents. Even so, he brute-forces his attacks, slamming his axe on a slime and using the concussive force of his attack to blast the slime's body apart.

"Gah. I feel like I'm in a bad Japanese porn video." I shake my head and cast a Blade Strike to rip apart a trio of slimes who drop from the ceiling right above me. Positioned as I am in front of everyone, I'm being swarmed, the slimes preferring to go for quantity over quality. As my Soul Shield keeps ticking down no matter how damn many of these things I kill is a good sign it'd work if we gave them enough time.

"Think you're repeating yourself there," Ingrid says with a chuckle before fading out of sight to reposition.

"Repeat?" Capstan swings his axe and sends out a burning energy strike from the head of it.

"Girlie means there ain't no good Japanese porn. Repeating bad and Japanese, see?" Ali explains happily.

"That's not what I meant!"

"Aiden," I call to the mage, ignoring the byplay.

The Mage rolls his eyes but turns toward me, casting Polar Zone centered around my body. I watch as he does so, my Mana Sight wide open as I study the way the spell twists and shapes Mana in front of me, altering the temperature in my surroundings. Aiden abbreviates some of what would be the normal casting method, short-cutting sections and replacing it with knots in other areas, the final spell-form different from that which I purchased. Different and so much more powerful.

The temperature drops by dozens of degrees in a second, the spell sweeping over all of us. Acid slimes freeze from their edges inward, their struggles shattering their gelatinous bodies and exposing unfrozen parts to the cold, speeding up their demise. Within tens of seconds, the monsters are dead and Aiden cuts the spell. Not a moment too soon—my own Soul Shield has fallen, exposing me to the full effects of the Spell. Not that I can't take the damage.

"Damn…" Ali says, eyeing the numerous, fallen Mana stones "Someone's been working out."

"Thanks, Aiden," I say, grinning at the Mage. It was the right decision, conning the man into coming along. His wide-scale area effect Spells will be useful against the wide variety of slimes that have been reported in this dungeon.

Once Nelia drops a drone to do the pickup of the Mana stones, we head in deeper to hunt down the remainder of the monsters. And of course, the dungeon boss.

***

"That's not a slime," I say, staring at the dungeon boss.

"Well, it technically is," Aiden mutters, his eyes narrowing. "Those crystals that make up its body are slime cores. We're going to need to shatter or separate each of those cores. I'd also assume that a large enough portion broken from the main body would still be functional."

"So. Weird," I mutter.

Crystalline Slime Hive (Dungeon Boss Level 94)

HP: 18318/18318

MP: 7337/7868

Conditions: Hivemind, Ablative Armor, Dispersed Core

"Har. Better than a titan slime," the Yerrick says with a snort, hefting his axe. "My sire fought one of those before on Regis III. Burnt off all his fur, ate his hand and one horn before he blasted it apart."

I shudder at the description, my mind considering what a slime thirty or forty feet tall would be like. The maintenance bill of dealing with one of those things must be ridiculous. Especially if it ate you.

"So, recommendations?" I ask while the party splits apart.

Nelia stays close to Aiden, her hands weaving as she piles together new roots and earthen walls to protect the pair of them while Capstan and I flank the creature. I'm assuming Ingrid's somewhere around, waiting for her chance to do some real damage.

"Hit it hard, shatter it. Then we'll use area effect spells to mop up the shards," Capstan says after a moment's consideration.

The creature is just standing there, little pools of slime swirling around its body.

The moment he finishes speaking, Ingrid drops out of the shadow plane to launch her attacks with her blades. Each strike digs into the body, shattering a core, but doesn't penetrate. As she finishes her first flurry, the slime rises from the ground and wraps tendrils around her body. Ingrid throws herself backward, breaking free briefly, though the remaining pieces of slime continue to burn her legs. I eye the monster's health and wince, noting how Ingrid's barely done more than a few hundred points of damage. This could take a bit.

Capstan charges, using the distraction my Blade Strikes generate to close the distance and smash his axe into the creature's side. It pierces a foot into the creature's torso before it gets stuck. As Capstan tries to yank it backward, the Mana stones shift, trapping the axe head.

"Mine!" Capstan growls, his body glowing red. But the increased Strength from his Skill is insufficient, and already the pool of slime is attacking him like it did Ingrid. Wisps of smoke rise from his feet.

"I'm feeling neglected here," I mutter and form more blades with a thought.

I get ready to swing a massed Blade Strike when instinct has me duck. From all around the cavern, globules of slime fire from the wall, splashing against shields, bodies, and the ground.

"Owww!" Aiden snarls, his casting interrupted as one globule somehow manages to make it past the Mage's Mana Shield.

He raises his hand, reforming and reinforcing his shield, while Nelia works her magic to plug up holes in their joint defense. The wide-ranging, indiscriminate attack also hit the stealthed Ingrid, her body forced out of the shadows, smoking and bleeding.

"Someone kill that thing!" Ingrid says as she ducks another shot.

Worryingly, some of the Mana stones that were initially chipped off from Ingrid's and my attacks are forming new slimes, each of which turn to attack us.

"Working on it," I growl and skip the upgraded attack to go for the ultimate—Army of One. The formed blades shift automatically, giving themselves more space as beams of force shoot outward. Thirteen strikes, each of them thrice as powerful as normal, hammer into the body of the giant Crystalline Slime Hive, shattering pieces off it. I can't help but smirk, noting how much more damage I can do with my Penetrate Master Skill added to my attacks.

"My turn," Aiden says. Instead of attempting a single large-scale spell, the mage flicks and twirls his wand again and again. Small fireballs fly, each about half the size of the one I cast. In seconds, dozens are hovering before the Elemental Mage.

"Don't!"

Ingrid's panicked shout reaches our ears, but no one has time to answer the Assassin. We're all throwing up our own defenses or activating defensive Skills as we ready for the oncoming blast.

When the fireballs land, the flame-filled explosion rocks us during the initial hit and again when the walls of the dungeon compress the explosion inward. And then outward again, the concussive force finding few escapes in this enclosed cavern. My newly recreated Soul Shield fails, my armor barely useful as my flesh cooks and my hair burns off. Even through my resistance, I see hundreds of health points drop, my body burning for what seems like eternity.

Then silence.

"Everyone still alive?" I cough around the smoke, my throat dry.

A low pair of rumbles from the Yerrick indicate their well-being. Ali pops back out of the semi-dimension he's used to and I realize my instincts failed me this time. Having not used the Quantum State Manipulator for so long, I'd forgotten I even had it. I frown, realizing that both Aiden and Ingrid are silent, which is a bit concerning. Less so with the former, since it was his spell. But...

"Oops," Aiden croaks, his clothing smoking slightly as he pushes his way out of the earth-and-ash fortress. "Forgot we were in a cave..."

"*Baka!*" Ingrid reappears behind Aiden, smacking him on the back of the head.

The Mage staggers, rubbing his head, and blinks. "How did you do that?"

"Reaper's Touch. It's a Skill that lets me ignore Shields."

"New?" I ask, and Ingrid nods.

"It's an exclusive Class Skill, but it's worth it." The Assassin's eyes grow dark as I recall Ikael's assassination.

His layering of multiple Shields thwarted her first flurry of attacks, putting her in greater danger than normal. With this Skill, she could bypass some of the problems. How much, I don't know. Since it's an exclusive Skill, the details aren't exactly on the public System net, which means I'd have to buy it if I was really curious.

Ali, smirking at the pair's antics, says, "Oy! I haven't received an experience notification that the Boss is down."

"What?"

We spin back toward the smoking center of the cavern where it's true, Mana Stones smoke and hiss but are intact. As we watch, a few roll back together, joining into smaller clumps. As everyone aims their weapons and spells at the ground, I note something more disturbing on my minimap.

"Incoming!" I warn. Dozens of fast-moving dots are converging on us in my map. With a thought, the minimap in my vision enlarges, giving me a clearer view of the surroundings, but it's of little use since the damn slimes seem to be moving through the walls as far as the map is concerned. "A lot of incoming. Get away from the walls."

Everyone moves to comply, Nelia using a solid earth equivalent of my Mud Walls to sweep the slime cores aside as we rush forward. Simultaneously, the first of the slime reinforcements appear, many of them splattering as we blast, cut, and freeze their bodies apart. Surprisingly, the cores which have survived race toward the largest concentration of slime core shards and join together with them.

"It's regenerating," Ali says, wonder in his voice. "I've got to record this."

"Record later. Electricity now!" I snap, raising my hand.

Ali ignores me, which annoys me, but I don't have time to focus on him. Instead, I pull on my Mana, the spell formulae and the Mana forms twisting around in my mind and around my extended hand as I cast Lightning Strike. It's my own modification of the Spell, an Enhanced version, as I reach outward and inward at the same time for my Elemental Affinity.

Electromagnetic Force, one of the four principle forces that form our universe. While the System might break the rules, while Mana seems to be the fifth overlying force over everything, the laws that they break still exist. My

215

affinity, gifted from my Link to Ali, allows me to sense, feel, and yes, manipulate it. In the four years I was away, I explored the use of this affinity even further, but in this instance, the basic Enhanced Lightning Strike is sufficient. I let it rampage a little more than normal, expanding its range of motion by relaxing the pathways I normally control and increasing the differences in charge at the slime cores.

I play the lightning across the ground, feeling the electricity jump and ground, burning and crisping even as my Mana drops and drops. But it's working—the Slime Boss is taking damage faster than it can recover. It works. Until the ground under us gives way, cutting off my spell and dropping us in a pool of goop.

"Ugh!" Ali says, safely in the air. He stares as the rest of us floundering in the suddenly formed pool of slime, our skin burning as the slime grips our bodies and attempts to drag us deeper.

By the time Nelia manages to use her spells to drain the slime and reinforce the newly created crater's walls to ensure we aren't surprised again, the Boss has reformed.

"I'm really beginning to hate this dungeon," Ingrid says as she pours a bottle of Greater Healing across her face, the enchanted potion healing the red and raw skin while neutralizing the slime.

"Agreed," Capstan growls.

I look at the now nearly nude monster, his fur repeatedly burnt and scorched off. Even as I watch, patches grow out as the Yerrick's regeneration kicks in.

"I don't think we're going to be able to win this quickly. I will conserve Mana for a long battle." Neila suits action to words as she casts a Group Healing Pulse on us all, a long-term healing spell.

"Ditto." Aiden waves his hand, a small floating blue ball forming above his head. When a slime core rolls closer toward us, it sends a single Mana dart at it. A few seconds later, the Mage has cast a second sphere as he begins to ring our new defensive position with these spheres.

"And I'll…" I shrug and jump out of the pit, realizing I'm out of witty things to say. "Kill it."

***

Later on that evening, we're seated at the newly rebuilt City Center with Carlos, Lana, and the rest of the settlement team. Capstan is regaling those interested with the story of our fight, seeming to take great pleasure in emphasizing the disgusting aspects in particular. As for me, I'm seated in my own corner, tucking into the slab of Auroch ribs the Yerrick have kindly supplied me with, along with the bowl of mashed potatoes that have been drowned in gravy.

"May I join you?" Lana says, gesturing to a seat across from me.

Ingrid, who is seated beside me, looks at Lana and nods companionably if slightly coldly. The redhead returns the nod, but I can tell there's a distance now between the two. Still, at my assent, Lana sits down without seeming too discomfited.

"It should take the Yerrick about a week to get settled and meet the Town requirements," Lana says. "I believe that puts us at just over twenty-two percent of the vote. We're still working on some of the other settlement owners in Africa, but our ability to field a focused and effective fighting force and our ties to the Hakarta, Erethrans, and Yerrick have convinced many we can provide the security they're looking for.

"But we still haven't heard from Roxley. Or Wynn. And Rob and Bipasha are at loggerheads over the candidacy. If the situation continues, we might need both Roxley and Wynn for any chance at this."

"Wynn has requested more time. And Roxley…" I frown, shrugging. "He's been quiet so far, but he did get us those two votes from the Okres."

Lana makes a face, obviously less than impressed. I am too, since the Okres were basically a group of slightly more civilized ogres. But at least they don't eat their enemies, and right now, we need every vote we can get. It's a compromise which grates, but it's one I'll live with. At least this way we've managed to get them to banish their human criminals to us rather than the wilderness. It's not a perfect solution, since a good two-thirds of their criminals are real asses, but the third we save for not finishing all their food or not training in the town square every day makes it worth it. Or so I tell myself.

"Nothing like the actual votes of the Movana," Lana says before she puffs out a breath. "We won't be able to get all the human settlement votes on our side. We need to speed up our discussions with the Galactics."

"I'm assuming you have a recommendation?" I say.

Lana nods. Her hand shifts and a list is sent to me. "I've spoken with Kim and Ali as well as Ayuri. Based on their information and analysis, this is how I recommend we tackle it."

I look over the list, then I note Ingrid is staring at us instead of blankly into space. With a mental twitch, I share the information with the Assassin, who flashes me a smile. Lana's eyes narrow slightly but she doesn't protest, so I don't bring it up. I don't have time to deal with the pair of them.

"You're handling the Artisan faction?" I say, looking at the meeting scheduled two days from now. "Should I be there?"

"No. Katherine and I are the better options," Lana says. "I'll bring Carlos too. They're more likely to listen to those of us not active on the battlefields."

"Like appreciates like?" I say with a smirk but shrug, accepting her analysis. It does leave me with a ton of individual meetings, most of them via telecommunications towers, though I see a few in-person meetings marked as required. "I assume Kim's going to brief me before these?"

"Yes." Lana sighs. "You know, this will be a lot easier if you could make up your mind between Rob and Bipasha."

"I know." I scan down the list and frown as something jumps out. "This doesn't cover everyone."

"No. Some are grouped, but the greyed names at the bottom, we won't want to work with. Or they just don't want to work with us," Lana says.

Ingrid hums, tapping a few of the names and sending it over to us. "I know these asses. Want me to kill them?"

"You're talking about murder," Lana says coldly.

"When a state does it, it's called good policy." Ingrid grins at me. "Right, boss?"

I want to shout about not being dragged into this, but... "Can you?"

"Wouldn't have offered if I couldn't. But I will need some help," Ingrid says.

Lana looks upset, crossing her arms over her ample bosom.

"Done. Talk to Kim," I say, making a note which will download to Kim when we're back in range.

Ingrid nods while Lana stares at the pair of us before she walks away without a word.

I watch the redhead disappear, my lips pursing slightly. "Maybe we should have had this talk another time."

"She'll get over it. Lana understands, but she's still a middle-class white girl at heart," Ingrid says, lips twisting wryly. "She still thinks, deep down, we can play nice. We've tried to keep her from getting her hands dirty, but it doesn't mean she doesn't need to know it's happening."

I switch my attention back to my food, which suddenly has lost its luster. A part of me wonders what happened to the innocent, quiet programmer I used to be. But another, more honest part of me knows I was never that empathetic. It's perhaps my greatest strength and flaw in this world. I care, in the abstract.

Chapter 15

"We want another settlement," the mantis-like creature on the opposite side of the projection demands for the umpteenth time.

"And we can help you take an open settlement. But you can't hold it," I say, folding my hands across one another.

"You will help."

"Not going to happen."

"Then we will not vote."

"Okay," I say and kill the connection with a thought.

"I think now's when you come back with a counter-offer," Ali says helpfully and sarcastically.

"Nope," I say, shaking my head. "They'll call back. It's called playing hard ball."

"And if they don't?"

"They will."

"And if they don't?" Ali repeats.

"Then I find someone else, perhaps one of their neighbors, who wants two new settlements. And we kick their asses together," I say heatedly.

"And time! Bits for brains, delay all calls," Ali says. "Boy-o needs a blood sugar transfusion."

"Oh, come on…" I growl, but Ali's raised eyebrow makes me subside.

I sigh, fishing out some chocolates while Ali makes arrangements for a snack to arrive. Just because I'm angry doesn't mean my blood sugar is low. I learned to regulate my blood sugar levels and those issues with the enhances in my Constitution a long time ago. A good thing too, since I ran out of chocolates in the first two months on the planet.

"Want to talk about it?" Ali says.

"No."

"Good. I didn't really want to listen."

We sit quietly for a time before I finally break. "I hate this. The horse trading, the negotiations. It was so much easier earlier. When it was just our swords, our spells, our Skills. And I can see it in them, the greed, the desire to take everything they can just because we need it, I need it."

"Way of the world, boy-o," Ali says.

"Maybe. But I don't have to like it," I say softly. "And I don't like how far I'm willing to go."

"But you're not going to change."

"No." I meet the Spirit's eyes. There's a shared understanding there, one we cannot speak about. Not here, not where others might learn of it. We both saw what would happen, could happen in the Forbidden Zone. The consequences of being too liberal with our knowledge, our goals. The price of failure. And the disastrous future which awaits every race, every planet. A world, racked with Mana, where even the callous benevolence of the System is missing.

"Eat," Ali says softly. "Then we've got another four calls. Afterwards, we'll run a dungeon for the evening till you grind that last level."

I nod, staring at the thread of my experience bar. Just a little more, then I'll hit Level 20. Just a little more. But first, a snack.

***

"I can have your settlement added to our trade list and the teleportation portal's coordinates. We'll also designate a minimum of two tons of the brew for your settlements," I say, tapping my fingers slowly. "But you're going to have to guarantee delivery of at least six tonnes of that Limehouse Barley you have there."

"Five," chirps the bird-like creature.

I've given up on names by now, beyond the usual glances at the floating information when I need to actually name it. It doesn't help that Chirp here has a name I actually can't say.

"Done. Contract will be on the way."

***

"No. We won't ban the Hakarta from this world."

"They are untrustworthy and deceitful." A merman speaks now, floating in inky darkness, illuminated only by the light of the communication screen. One thing they don't tell you about the ocean is that it's pitch black down there, if you get down far enough.

"Those words mean the same thing. But they already have a deal with us," I say. "And three settlements."

"Useless. I knew you were our enemies like them. We will burn you humans out!"

"Feel free to come after me. Or my settlements," I say, leaning forward as my voice grows cold. "But touch a hair on any innocents and I'll be coming for you."

"You think I fear a new Master Class like you? We are the rulers of the ocean!"

"Maybe not today. Or tomorrow. But in a year? Two? You've seen my Leveling speed. How long do you think it's going to take for me to become a real threat?"

My threat shuts up the merman, gills at the side of his neck opening and closing as he flushes water out. Rather than speak—and really, it's more of a mental command to an integrated communicator in his head—the notification cuts out.

I lean backward, huffing out a breath as I shake my head. Idiots. "Let's add one of their settlements to the hit list, will you?"

"DONE."

"Cancel that, bits for brains," Ali says and crosses his arms, glaring at me. "You are not starting a war with the mermen. Not over one phone call."

"They only have six settlements," I say grumpily.

"Right now. Unless the Waz or the Loom arrive in greater number, they will have full run of your coasts. And unless you intend to go swimming constantly, there's little you can do to slow them down," Ali points out.

I can't help but let out a little shudder. Months underwater? Ugh… "Fine. We'll look into another way of dealing with them."

"Good. And they were the last one," Ali says. "But overall, well done."

"No comments about how I handled myself today?" I blink, finding the sudden turnaround surprising.

"None from me," Katherine speaks up from the door.

I blink, realizing I must be more tired than I thought to have missed her. Or else I unconsciously file her away as a non-threat.

"I'm surprised," I say, scratching the side of my head. "I figured I was playing it too rough."

"Do you think every party should be handled the same way?" Katherine smiles slightly as she walks forward. "Negotiations are multi-faceted, and the tactics employed differ depending on the party. Some, a more genteel approach is required. Others, a longer, slower, and more circuitous route"—Katherine places a hand on her chest as she makes the last statement, almost as if indicating that's her specialty—"while others need a firm, some might even say aggressive, approach to get the best results."

"You split the list to me for people I could pound on," I say, my lips twitching upward slightly.

"Crudely put, yes. Though I would recommend some moderation. We are seeking allies, not enemies."

"Fair enough." I stand, stretching. "Did you need anything or…?"

"Just the casting portal at your desk. Kim informed me you intend to train?"

I nod and slip aside. Katherine walks over and casts a Chill spell on my chair before she sits down and adjusts it to ensure the vidcaster catches her just right. I smirk slightly at her vanity, then realize perhaps it's not vanity. After all, looking good might actually be important. Or perhaps, giving off the right impression rather than looking "good."

As I muse about the line between vanity and practicality in diplomacy, I wander out, headed for another dungeon and more violent concerns. Time to grind.

***

I spit out a tooth, grateful that one of the advantages of a greater-than-human Constitution is the replacement of teeth. Otherwise I'd be walking around with dentures, clicking them at little children on the street and giggling as they run away screaming. Actually, that doesn't sound so bad…

"You can stop kicking it," I say to Ali, the Spirit growling as he wails on the dead Ice Drake.

We're near the edges of my domain, in the northern part of British Columbia where the Rockies meet, helping to trim down the number of monsters. Unfortunately, the dungeon I expected to find had actually been cleared by an enterprising group of Adventurers. Still, the Level 90 zone has enough regular monsters for me to get in some decent training.

"You overgrown pair of boots. You're supposed to eat the human!" Ali growls, kicking the drake one last time before he makes it disappear in my Altered Space.

I get a notification a second later, laughing as I read Ali's comments.

Wannabe-Dragon Hide (Drake Hide)

4 * Good Quality Pieces

11 * Damaged Pieces

Perfect for making a pair of high-quality boots

Wannabe-Dragon Teeth (Drake Teeth)

2 * High Quality pieces

Only desired by crazy alchemists and tasteless collectors.

"I figure that's it?" I say, cocking my head at Ali.

The Spirit disgruntledly waves at me, and my notification belatedly blooms.

Congratulations! You have reached Level 20 as a Paladin of Erethra

Attribute gains automatically assigned. You have 67 free attribute points and 6 Class Skills.

Perfect. This time around, I look at my Class Skill options first. At Level 20, I get access to the second tier at last, which is all I'll have access to till Level 40, when I'll get the third and last tier. In some ways, having fewer tiers of Skills is actually better for me, since I'll be able to focus my Class Skill points rather than having my Skills spread out like in my previous Class. It's a good combination, versatility in my Advanced Class and more focus in my Master.

I still dump a point into every Skill available at this newly unlocked tier. Just because I want to focus doesn't mean I don't want a taste of everything first.

Beacon of the Angels (Level 1)

User calls down an atmospheric strike from the heavens, dealing damage over a wide area to all enemies within the beacon. The attack takes time to form, but once activated need not be concentrated upon for completion.
Effect: 1000 Mana Damage done to all enemies, structures and vehicles within the 20 meter column of attack
Mana Cost: 500 Mana

I'm rather tempted to toss another point into the Skill, but I'm a little concerned the attack might be limited to certain environments. Of course, this is the System, so while the Skill describes the attack as coming from the heavens, it might just port the attack into the center of a dungeon without tearing through the surroundings. It's something I'll have to check out, but I finally have my first area effect Skill. This is perfect for dealing with large groups of enemies. Especially since the damage is direct Mana damage, which bypasses most resistances.

Eye of the Storm (Level 1)

In the middle of the battlefield, the Paladin stands, seeking justice and offering judgment on all enemies. The winds of war will seek to draw both enemies and allies to you, their cruel flurries robbing enemies of their lives and bolstering the health and Mana of allies.
Effect: Eye of the Storm is an area effect buff and taunt. Psychic winds taunt enemies, forcing a Mental Resistance check to avoid attacking user. Enemies also receive 5 points of damage per second while within the influence of the Skill, with damage decreasing from the epicenter of the Skill. Allies receive a 5% increase in Mana and Health regeneration, decrease in effectiveness from Skill center. Eye of the Storm affects an area of 50 meters around the user.
Cost: 500 Mana + 20 Mana per second

Aura of Chivalry makes everyone look. Eye of the Storm makes everyone charge. It's a nasty on-going taunt, though it's not as powerful as a direct taunt Skill would be. But considering it's on-going, does damage, and affects a wide area, I'm not complaining at all. It also has the side benefit of boosting health and Mana regeneration, though I do note there's no indicator it can be stacked. That generally means it either won't, or the benefit will be significantly lower. Better than nothing though.

Vanguard of the Apocalypse (Level 1)

Where others flee, the Paladin strides forward. Where the brave dare not advance, the Paladin charges. While the world burns, the Paladin still fights. The Paladin with this Skill is the vanguard of any fight, leading the charge against all of Erethra's enemies.

Effect: +30 to all Physical attributes, increases speed by 50% and recovery rates by 30%. This Skill is stackable on top of other attribute- and speed-boosting Skills or spells.

Cost: 500 Mana + 10 Stamina per second

My first major Skill that uses Stamina. Most of those I purchase don't use Stamina since I like not running out of breath and being too tired to move my arms in a fight. It's amazing how many monsters and individuals go for the burst damage approach, then they get caught out after a few minutes and realize they can't finish off their opponent. Vanguard is a nasty, nasty burst Skill, giving me a ton of benefits which can be stacked on top of other Skills and spells. But at the rate of drain, it's something I only want to use in short bursts. It's perfect for shattering a battle line, getting behind your opponents, and then getting down to business.

Society's Web (Level 1)

Where the Eye of Insight provides the Paladin an understanding of the lies and mistruths told, Society's Web shows the Paladin the intricate webs that tie individuals to one another. No alliance, no betrayal, no tangled web of lies will be hidden as each interaction weaves one another closer. While the Skill provides no detailed information, a skilled Paladin can infer much from the Web.

Effect: Upon activation, the Paladin will see all threads that tie each individual to one another and automatically understand the details of each thread when focused upon.

Cost: 400 Mana + 200 Mana per minute

This is another of those Skills which I'm going to have to spend some time exploring. Thankfully, I can attempt to figure out what the heck it does outside of a dungeon. Though I'll admit I'm curious to see what it does in a dungeon. I mean, do dungeon monsters have a Society's Web? If so, what would it look like? But I picked up this Skill on a hunch it could be of use during the negotiation process rather than any expectation it'll help me Level.

In truth, I'm finding that more of the important parts of my life are revolving around political and social battles than the next settlement or dungeon I have to clear. Sure, those are important, as my ability to kick ass and take land are the pillars which reinforce my ability to negotiate with political parties. They are not, in themselves, the orbit of my life anymore. In some ways, I'm grateful for the de-emphasis in violence in my life. While I'm scarily skilled at dishing out damage and calculating the flow of a battle, I spent too many years recently being nothing but a kill-monger. My future, our future, cannot be one soaked in blood.

With the Skill points allocated, I dismiss the Skill information. I still need to figure out what to do with my extra points, but I want to see the effects of these Skills first. Afterwards, assigning attributes is a simple enough matter.

I've got such a large surplus of free attributes now, I can use them to iron out some of the areas I feel are lacking.

I start by adding a few points into Luck, Perception, Intelligence, and Strength. Luck because the gradual effect on loot drops generally pans out. I've noticed the difference between the quantity and quality between myself and Ingrid or Mikito, who both have focused on other Stats. It's not exaggerated, but an extra high quality material or two every couple of drops does eventually add up.

Sadly, Luck, much like Willpower, is one of those attributes I've yet to understand how to manipulate. It's a failure of knowledge and understanding, of course. While I can, say, push my Perception to increase or dull my senses as needed, I'm not sure what I'm doing with Luck or Willpower. And I'll admit, I'm a bit concerned about testing out either.

Perception is easy enough to understand. In the middle of combat, I rarely have time to adjust how I'm shifting the emphasis of my attributes around, which makes a higher base stat important. It lets me keep up with speed builds like Mikito and, heck, my own body. As for Strength… well, if fighting the damn hippo was anything to go by, I still need to hit harder.

Once I've allocated over ten points to each of those attributes, I dump the remaining four points into Willpower because I desperately need more Mana Regeneration. All my recent purchases of Skills have seriously hampered it. In fact, I sometimes wonder if I would be better off increasing my Willpower more.

Once done, I pull up my character sheet to admire myself for a moment.

Status Screen			
Name	John Lee	Class	Erethran Paladin
Race	Human (Male)	Level	20

Titles			
Monster's Bane, Redeemer of the Dead, Duelist, Explorer			
Health	3320	Stamina	3320
Mana	3100	Mana Regeneration	229 (+5) / minute
Attributes			
Strength	215	Agility	295
Constitution	332	Perception	160
Intelligence	310	Willpower	334
Charisma	98	Luck	65
Class Skills			
Mana Imbue	3*	Blade Strike*	3
Thousand Steps	1	Altered Space	2
Two are One	1	The Body's Resolve	3
Greater Detection	1	A Thousand Blades*	3
Soul Shield	2	Blink Step	2
Portal*	5	Army of One	2
Sanctum	2	Instantaneous Inventory*	1
Cleave*	2	Frenzy*	1

Elemental Strike*	1 (Ice)	Shrunken Footsteps*	1
Tech Link*	2	Penetration	2
Aura of Chivalry	1	Eyes of Insight	1
Analyze*	2	Harden*	2
Quantum Lock*	3	Elastic Skin*	3
Beacon of the Angels	1	Eye of the Storm	1
Vanguard of the Apocalypse	1	Society's Web	1
Combat Spells			
Improved Minor Healing (IV)		Greater Regeneration (II)	
Greater Healing (II)		Mana Drip (II)	
Improved Mana Missile (IV)		Enhanced Lightning Strike (III)	
Firestorm		Polar Zone	
Freezing Blade		Improved Inferno Strike (II)	
Mud Walls		Ice Blast	
Icestorm		Improved Invisibility	
Improved Mana Cage		Improved Flight	
Haste			

"Now what, boy-o?"

"Find me another drake or two," I say, grinning as I bounce on the balls of my feet. Best to test out my new attributes and get used to them now.

A look at the night sky which still shroud the mountains indicates I have maybe another couple of hours before dawn. Enough time to trim the population a little more.

***

"*I said one or two,*" I send to Ali as we crouch low, staring at the family of five drakes sleeping in the cavern. Damn Spirit even hid most of their signatures till I had sneaked into the cave, revealing the other three once I was within.

"*Whine, whine, whine.*"

I don't bother answering the Spirit, rubbing my chin in thought. These aren't shadow drakes, they're astral drakes. From what I recall, they have lower hit points but are even sneakier, able to shift dimensions and attack while half-corporeal. It makes them incredibly tough to see when they're active, making them powerful ambush predators. They even have a ranged attack of sorts, an attack which basically sends disruptive energy from the Astral plane into this world. The attack ignores most defenses, which makes it even more dangerous. A single astral drake would be a tough fight for any Advanced Class team.

Unfortunately for them, I'm not an Advanced Class any longer. And they're asleep.

Step one, test Beacon of the Angels. Since the drakes chose a relatively high and steep cave to rest in, it makes the amount of earth the Skill has to blast through—if it does come straight from the heavens—minimal.

Rather than potentially wake the monsters with the use of Mana, I skip activating my usual complement of buffs. Instead, I focus within and reach into the new bundle of knowledge in my mind, caressing the information for a moment before I activate it.

Mana surges through my body, pulled from my pores in such a violent fashion it churns the air around me and reveals my location. The drakes wake even as my mind is cast thousands of meters into the night sky. I float, seeing the formation of the beam of light, and a part of me suddenly understands. I can let it come down like the wrath of a Greek god, a column of fire and flame, of the inexplicable force that is Mana, and let it destroy everything as it does. I can be flashy and make a statement, which is how a Paladin should do battle.

Or I can adjust the Skill, the attack coming from the heavens but manifesting only when it nears the ground. In this way, the attack will bypass the stone and trees and strike through terrain without damaging what is between, all for a minor loss in effectiveness. Subtler, but useful in an indoor fight.

I choose the latter of course. It all takes less than the blink of an eye, knowledge understood and decision made. The Skill manifests as a cylinder of pure energy, a column of destruction which burns and tears as it strikes. The drakes scream, thrashing as the Mana rages, while I channel a firestorm.

When the Beacon is over, the drakes are only just beginning to recover from the surprise attack before the firestorm lands, sweeping them up again in further hellish flame. Fast as I am though, a pair of drakes disappear into the Astral Plane.

I snarl, Blink Stepping into the center of the cavern, appearing on the shredded wing of one miserable, semi-conscious drake. I feel the space around me then shut it down, locking everything into place with the Quantum Lock Skill. The strain on my mind is incredible. The necessity of understanding and holding every single aspect of reality together is almost enough to make me buckle. Almost.

The pair that escaped are forced back by my Skill, reappearing in meat space halfway toward my ex-hiding spot. But I'm busy, chopping at the neck of the nearest drake, cutting into its burnt and dried flesh, blood dribbling out from the wounds and hissing in the volcanic heat of the cave. I spin, savaging its neck and moving within the periphery of its body, allowing the injured drake to block the attacks of the others. I grunt, staring at my dropping Mana bar.

I need to finish this. Fast. With a grin, I call upon the Vanguard of the Apocalypse. Immediately, I feel my attributes increase, my strength and speed growing even as I see each movement of my attackers even clearer. I can sense where attacks are going, almost chart each movement, as my sword appears in one hand and a beam pistol in the other.

The injured and enraged drakes, too angry to run and forced to fight in the cramped quarters of their cavern, are no match for me. I jump, run, and spin, cutting and stabbing with one hand and blasting with the other. It's a dance through the dark, the cavern fitfully lit by the remaining flames from my previous attacks, the walls and floor of the cavern the canvas for my painting of blood and violence.

When it's over, I'm left panting and on my knees, my Stamina drained, my Mana the barest sliver left. But I'm grinning. Because for all the pain and sorrow this world has brought, it's also brought an understanding which I would never have received in the previous world. Among the winds of the apocalypse, I have found my place.

***

I use a full hour to test myself, pushing my body and my new Skills to the limit. For all my bitching at Ali, he's right. The only way to improve is to push the boundaries, to test myself. Not with a single drake or two, but with a flight. To push and push until all there is blood and pain, because it's at the limits where you find yourself.

But as much as I might wish to train, to indulge my penchant for violence, the dawn comes. Time and responsibility grind inexorably onward, ignoring the needs and desires of pitiful mortals. After I pack up the Mountain Giant's corpse, I look around the snow-covered land one last time then gesture, opening a Portal back to civilization and responsibility. Time to go.

Chapter 16

I Portal in, not back to my office but just off Granville Street in downtown Vancouver. The once-vibrant main street has become so again, shedding its mixture of hipster bars and sex stores for a more eclectic mixture of stores. Gyms cluster on the top floors, training grounds for those looking to brush up the edges of their skills. Everything is taught, from human martial arts to newer Galactic combat forms that focus on the development and integration of Skills. Below, retailers hawk their System-integrated wares, offering anything from monster-hide leather armor to combat and utility drones. I see a Potioneer flashing passersby as he hawks his wares from within his trench coat while a Busker plays for an appreciative audience of people who tip and wait for the buffs to take effect.

The street bustles with life, both Galactic and human. A small metallic ball rolls alongside a towering Yerrick, his green-skinned Hakarta date leaning into his arm with a smile and eye-popping cleavage. In a clothing store, a mother smacks her child's hand, casually disarming him and taking away a newly bought survival knife. All around, Adventurers bustle and get ready for their next great expedition while others run their mundane routines, buying groceries and clothing, offering Skills and skills.

"Quite a difference, eh?" Ali says, walking beside me with a slight smile.

I cock my head to the side, considering his tone. I'm surprised to hear pride. Huh. Who'd have thought?

"WE HAVE SEEN A 14.3% INCREASE IN ANNUALIZED GDP IN THE LAST MONTH."

"Nice…" I have nothing to say to Kim's statement. It's not as if I really understand what it means, beyond the obvious signs before me.

"Why'd we Portal back here, boy-o? Not that I mind getting out of the office, but…"

"Skill training," I say. A moment of focus and Society's Web activates. All around me, glowing threads erupt, stunning me for a second. There's so many, in such a wide variety of colors and sizes, it looks like a knitter's stash after a barrel of kittens and a tornado had been let loose.

"Oy! I'm walking here," Ali roars as he is nearly squished by a landing hover taxi.

My little brown man gets into a spirited argument with the driver while I stand stock still, taking in the new view. I admit, I struggle as I attempt to grasp the intricacies of my new Skill. The Skill is strange, with some individuals bursting with threads, some so thin they're no larger than a spider's web and others as wide as a door. The child has few threads, her thickest to her mother and a few other large ones spreading out of sight. All but one other—a thin, light grey thread which runs from her to me.

I look down and realize tens of thousands of these grey threads lead to my body. They overlap with other, brighter-colored threads that lead to me, but thankfully, when I concentrate, the grey threads become more prominent, pushing the colored threads to the background. Some of the grey threads are as thin as the child's, others as thick as my wrist. With a shift in perception, I push away all the grey threads and focus on the others. I frown, focusing on a dark-red-and-green beam of light about three inches thick which moves toward the northeast.

Lana Pearson

Love, lust, debt, gratitude, jealousy, guilt, joy, confidence, pain...

I see, I sense the words, the emotions which I hold for her and her for me. I sense the long string of obligations incurred and the aid she has given me over the years, the unspoken social contract we've indulged in. Love, lust, guilt, and hurt. Favors traded, time employed. Kisses given and tears shed. It all comes to me, the weight and depth of our connection, stunning me as I realize something.

Thousand hells.

I'm an ass.

The thought is enough to pull me away from her beam of light, for me to regard my body. I cock my head to the side, one particular shiny black thread catching my attention. There's a darkness to it that draws me close, forces me to focus.

Un Bair

Contract. Obligation. Death.

I shudder, feeling the coldness that radiates from the thread, and look to the side. My eyes widen, seeing the thread disappear into nothingness a bare foot away.

Then a pair of knives plunge into my chest, stealing my breath.

You are Poisoned!
47 Health per second
Duration: 8 Minutes, 9 Seconds

You are Poisoned!
Mana and Health Regeneration reduced by 18%
Duration: 11 Minutes, 12 Seconds

Dimension Locked
All movement skills which require teleportation are blocked

Mana Lock.

Mana flow in your body has been disrupted. You are stunned for 3.8 seconds (resisted)

I stagger backward even as the daggers come out and plunge toward me again. The second attack hammers into the Greater Shield I trigger from the enchanted ring with a mental command, an act I can still take. It buys me a second as the blades skim and shatter the Shield before they pierce my chest again. The Poison notifications flash on my interface, resetting the clock as even more of the poison floods my system. Pain erupts through my body as my nerves finally catch up, even as the daggers are taken out again, flipped overhand, and plunged into the ball sockets of my shoulders. I scream as much as I'm able to, muscles locked as the Skill keeps me frozen.

Crippled!

You have received a crippling blow. You will not be able to use your arms until you are healed.

Three seconds might seem like a blink, but in a fight, it's an eternity. As the blades rise again, his hands crossing as he moves to behead me, I feel a hand yank me away. Too slow to avoid the attack entirely though. The blades cross across my neck, leaving me gurgling on my blood.

Bleeding!

You have received a bleeding debuff. You will lose health so long as the wounds are not treated.

-3 Health per second

Warning! Health below 15%

"Oy!" Ali shouts as he pulls me away with one hand while he thrusts forward with the other.

The assassin doesn't hesitate, a dagger punching toward Ali's glowing red hand is wrapped with bolts of lightning. The attack lands, forcing the Spirit to lose control of the spell. The ensuing explosion of raw plasma released into air throws all of us apart.

My body tumbles, crashing into a pair of passersby. I try to push myself up, but my arms aren't working and I uselessly flop to the side as I scramble to my feet. A hand grips my shoulder, hauling me to my feet while a green light bursts upon my body, healing wounds. I blink, tilting my head to see the mother with her child held behind her, bleeding from a head wound but focused on healing me.

"Come on there, no lying down on the job." The rough hands which grip me belong to an older Adventurer, his face cragged and lined, his vest filled with potions of healing and stamina.

A part of me is trying to figure out why these people would risk their lives to help me, to step up when it'd be easier to hide. The other is scanning the surroundings, searching for signs of the assassin. I see nothing, not that I did before.

"*Ali?*"

"*Son-of-a-Gremlin! Youch!*"

"*Master Class?*"

"*Definitely.*"

I snarl, staring around me, waiting. But no matter where I look, how I look, I can't see him. It's obvious his stealth Skill is stronger than mine, even as I layer Soul Shield on myself.

Quantum Lock released.

I exhale harshly then Blink Step directly upward. A moment later, I've ascertained his thread leads off into the distance, fading away in the horizon. I briefly consider going after him as I fall to the ground, triggering my Flight spell to land lightly. I absently note the healing light has cut off, probably shaken by my abrupt motions. Better not follow him. If he's as good as I think, I'll be walking into a trap.

"Anyone hurt?" I say, looking around.

The older man stares at me as blood drips from my numerous wounds. The pain is pushed to the back of my mind, a part of me but not hampering my motions. The mother ignores my silly words, again bathing me in healing spell after healing spell. I incline my head in thanks while casting a Major Healing on myself too, pushing my health up to a quarter and giving me some movement in my arms.

"Other than me," I clarify.

But I can see the answer is no. The violence, abrupt and explosive as it was, is taken in stride by many. Already, the hole in the ground is being patched by the System. Many others are brushing off their clothing, casting healing or cleanse spells or waiting for the System's regeneration to fix them. It's frightening how even the "civilian" population of my city has such a blasé attitude toward violence. Only a few glance at me curiously, and I can't even say if it's because I'm their technical settlement leader or the target of the attack.

"Thank you. Both of you," I say.

My words get shrugs and muttered words of acceptance before they leave. I try to press Credits, gifts on them, but the pair refuses. As the mother guides her daughter away, I see the child look back and flash me a comforting smile. It's a bit of a thunderbolt, that smile, one which pierces through the self-delusion I've created.

The lonely hero, perched above the throngs of humanity, their guardian and savior. The all-seeing protector is such a common depiction even I had taken it for truth. I've molded myself around the image, pursued the idea as if it were a truth I needed to grasp. I set myself apart from the members of the society that I wanted to protect. And only now do I realize what a lie it was. Because you can't protect what you can't understand, and you can't understand without taking the time to know. And being above it all doesn't just give you perspective; it makes you miss the details. In the end, it's the details that are important.

The child who can smile after a moment of scary violence. A mother who will step forward to protect others even while her child stands by her side. The couple fighting and making up, their passion burning so bright it makes others mock them silently in jealousy. The daughter crying over the loss of her parents. The politician turning down a bribe. The good and bad which make up who we are.

Somewhere along the way, I'd forgotten this, missed it because I was too busy playing the cool, aloof hero. And only now do I understand. They don't need another remote hero, a lord who oversees them all and gives nothing but cold reassurance. These people, they need someone who cares about them, day in and day out.

***

"You called?" Lana says, finding me in the most guarded place in the city a minute later.

"Yes. Give me your hand."

Lana frowns, walking toward me and cocking her head to the side. I take her hand and place it on the core, stopping the automatic jerk the Beastmistress makes when I do so.

"What are you doing?"

"What I should have done from the start," I say and release her hand once the notification appears. Luckily, I turned off the global notification option. Otherwise, everyone in all the settlements would be getting this warning.

"John…"

"You're the right person for this. Always have been," I say softly. "I was being greedy and selfish. And perhaps a little scared."

"I'll take the first two, but the last?" Lana says, her voice forcibly light. But I note she doesn't move her hand away from the City Core.

"Scared that I couldn't trust you. Or anyone else." I sigh. "Scared that somehow, if I didn't do it, no one else could. That I'd be giving up control to another person who would make a mistake. But it's stupid, isn't it? Because you've been in charge this entire time anyway. So… sorry."

Lana nods then she opens her mouth and says slowly, "John, this gift…"

"Has nothing to do with us. The us that… well, you know. And it's no gift. Shackles maybe," I say, my lips twisting wryly. "You've earned it either way."

"Oh. Real nice."

You have lost your settlement of Vancouver voluntarily. Would you like to transfer all owned settlements to Lana Pearson?

(Y/N)

Of course. In for a penny, in for a pound. While I'm confirming, double confirming, and then triple confirming that yes, I really, really wanted to do this, Lana goes over her own notifications.

"Why am I only now receiving a report that there was an assassination attempt in the middle of Granville Street?" Lana's voice has an edge to it, and I wince.

"Would you believe I forgot to mention it?" I say, giving her my best wide-eyed look of innocence.

"Am I being put out as bait?"

"What? No!" I glare at the woman, my hands on my hips.

The redhead breaks into a little giggle at the sight of my face. "Sorry. I shouldn't even have asked. But it was too good an opportunity not to."

"Truth be told, I think they've been waiting for boy-o." When we look over at the Spirit, he continues. "Kim and I have been going over footage from various security cameras, searching for his attacker. At best, I'd say he's been around for just over four days. But since boy-o either Portals himself to wherever he needs to go or directly to the heavily guarded teleportation station…"

"No opportunities." I say, frowning. It makes sense. My office is significantly reinforced against assassins, including multiple shields, sensors, and even a teleportation circle which has been triple reinforced. Heck, the entire City Center building has a security system. Even if my assassin managed to kill me there, getting away might be significantly more difficult. "Why'd he run?"

"Probably didn't expect me or other people to aid you. He probably expected to get you on the first pass," Ali says. "Assassins gear their Skills toward a quick attack, doing enough damage to kill in one strike. Once you survived his first pass, he probably figured it was time to go. He probably didn't

245

realize you'd picked up a number of damage reduction Skills on top of your health pool."

I nod slowly, deciding to accept the explanation for now. It sounds a little shallow, but since I have no other suggestions or evidence to prove otherwise, I can't argue.

"Am I going to have to worry about this?" Lana says, concern tinging her voice. Not as though she hasn't already been targeted, but there's a difference between an Advanced Class assassin and a Master Class one.

"Possibly," I say. "Your pets should provide significant protection, but you might want to consider letting your bodyguards know. And upgrading your defensive enchantments."

"Do you know who hired him?"

I shrug. I have a few guesses, the Movana being highest on my list. They have, after all, the greatest motivation to ensure I don't succeed. The name I had noticed drew a blank from the System. It likely had been altered by a Skill. Ali wasn't able to get any further information from the System either. Even the attack designations we were provided just had a series of question marks for personally identifiable information. In the end, the reason you hire a damn assassin is to stay hidden.

Before we can continue the discussion, Katherine walks in, hands on her hips, and glares at me. "It would really be useful if you informed us before you took such actions." I open my mouth to apologize, but Katherine's already turned to Lana, offering her a slight inclination of her head. "Congratulations, Ms. Pearson. It's about time. I look forward to the development of these holdings in an orderly and efficient manner once again."

"Hey, I'm right here!" I protest.

"Yes." Katherine sniffs at me then relents, inclining her head while offering me a slight smile. "You have done well with the resources at your disposal."

"Sassy. Been repressing much?" I say with a smile.

"It looks like I've got a lot of work to do in the next little while. But this change, it'll affect how we're going for the seat," Lana cuts in before we get into it.

I don't miss the amused glint in Katherine's eyes before she turns all business.

I rub my chin while answering Lana. "Not a lot. We never qualified who the vote would be for. In fact, some might assume I'm looking to be voted in, no matter how much I protest. They might even side with us because of that. Who knows, it might also make things easier. I could just pay a visit to anyone who's really being an obstructionist..." At the pair of glares and overdramatic sigh from Ali, I wave. "Kidding. Mostly."

"Well, I can use you as the rebellious caveman," Lana says. "But Rob and Bipasha will need reassurance."

"Fair point. I'll make sure to visit them."

The ladies nod, then both twitch as their eyes glaze over. With hurried farewells, the pair head off, leaving me alone in the City Core room.

"MY LORD. MAY I ENQUIRE ABOUT MY CURRENT STATUS?"

"What... oh. Right. What do you want to do?" I say, realizing the awkward position Kim is in.

He's a settlement AI after all—with politic upgrades perhaps, but still a settlement AI. But while he's been running the settlements, I purchased him directly to give me more control.

"I AM PROGRAMMED TO CONDUCT SETTLEMENT SERVICES. IF I HAD A PREFERENCE, IT WOULD BE TO CONTINUE TO WORK WITH MS. PEARSON."

"Done," I say and take a few seconds to transfer ownership. "Just keep feeding me politic updates and tips and we're good."

"OF COURSE. MS. PEARSON HAS INDICATED THAT IS ALLOWABLE."

I chuckle softly and dismiss the notification, leaving me with Ali. Even with my new resolution to stop being an ass and think I'm doing all this by myself, there are certain things only I can do.

Chapter 17

"Mr. Lee," Bipasha greets me, standing with a smile.

I absently note her addition of a couple of silent guards, individuals in business suits and shades. Which almost makes me want to smack them over the head since we're indoors. But then again, those shades are probably high-tech ones with toys like flash suppression and auto-targeting. Or at least, I hope so for the Weaver's sake.

"Thanks. And yes, tea would be great," I say, nodding to the assistant who comes in to serve us. After I let go of my settlements, I spent a full day reassuring everyone I was still alive, that I would take more precautions, and no, Lana had not decided to launch a coup. Or, in some cases, that the redhead hadn't snapped. "I thought I'd swing by to talk to you about recent events."

"I'm grateful for your consideration. But I hadn't realized we were that close." Bipasha's eyes glint with humor and a slight barb.

"We aren't, but I should have come by sooner," I say, leaning back in the plush chair. "Things have been hectic."

"Gathering the votes."

"I've also been considering who might be hiring assassins to knock off the competition. And it made me realize, you know, you and Rob have good motivation to do so." I stare at the woman, seeing if I get any reaction.

"I have no hand in the attack on you," Bipasha says.

Eye of Insight doesn't even twinge, so she's not using any Skill to conceal her words. Well, nothing beyond the usual array of charm-based passives. Then again, Eye of Insight's not like Nelia's Skill, which can ascertain the actual physical truth of a statement. All I have is my own skill and intuition.

"I am still waiting for your answer."

"About who I'll support?" I say softly. Instead of answering her, I pick up the cup of tea and blow on it while activating Society's Web. Hundreds of threads run from her. I've realized many of the thinner ones are from her ownership of the settlement. Lana gained so many more in the transfer, the additional responsibility multiplying the already exhaustive threads. Yet for all that, I'm getting the hang of this Skill and find myself sorting through them with one part of my mind while continuing the conversation with the other. I've stopped reading the individual information pieces but instead "feel" the threads. "Still haven't decided yet."

"Do you intend to wait till the day of?"

"Maybe. Or maybe I'm holding off till I know we have a chance. I'm still waiting for word from the Truinnar and Movana." My hands open slightly, as if a shrug. "Till we get either or both of them, we have no chance."

"True. I had hoped your relationship with Lord Roxley would be of use there," Bipasha says.

"Me too."

"Assuming this goes through, we have yet to speak about what you wish for your help," Bipasha says. "Unless you are doing this for the betterment of all?"

I hear the lightest derision in her tone at the last line, a hint of what she thinks of the idea. And perhaps for those who might act for others? Hard to say. Still, I do note a trend among the threads. The largest and strongest threads lead to many whose names I know, some of whom I've actually spoken to. They're all individuals of power and import in this new world. The feel of those threads is mostly cold, analytical. A weighing of debt and obligation, of resources traded and favors gained. I find a few—very few—threads which glow with emotion, but I almost choke on the intensity of those emotions. When and to whom she feels, she feels with passion.

Thankfully, I'm not one of those. When I finally find the thread leading to me, it's thin, barely larger than many of those leading to her staff. There is no great emotional baggage related to me, no hidden desires. As far as she's concerned, I'm just another business transaction.

"No, I'll want something. But as an acquaintance once said, let's leave it be for now. Call it a favor for later."

"A favor."

"Nothing which will harm you or your settlements. It'll be within your grasp to grant, and it won't be too onerous," I reassure her.

Huh. She has a thread to Lana. Again, not much, though there's a touch of jealousy there. Envy. But respect too. And another for Mikito, this one tinged with similar feelings as she has for the other champions. Those threads are all thick, deepened by their repeated interactions and numerous times saving each other. Nothing untoward there. Another one to Roxley. Again, a business relationship, though there's a touch of lust there. I feel a twinge of jealousy which I squash by locating another thread, this one for Ingrid. It's not thick, but contracts and obligations abound. Interesting.

"Well then, I'll just have to take your word on it." Bipasha's lips curl upward and she leans forward, her armored jumpsuit pulling tighter against her chest, outlining her body. "Tell me, Mr. Lee, am I that beautiful?"

"Huh?"

"Well, you have been staring at me fixatedly this entire conversation. If you would like time alone…" Bipasha says, touching her lips gently. "You are not entirely hard on the eyes either."

In the corner of my mind, I hear Ali laughing. The damn Spirit is invisible, floating around and inspecting the surroundings, occasionally sticking his tongue out at the guards who cannot see him.

"No. Nothing like that," I say, shaking my head.

"Oh? Pity."

I pause, realizing that my automatic rejection might have been idiotic. And then I realize that I'm thinking of sleeping with a woman who might have ordered my assassination. The incongruity of it all breaks my concentration and I let my Skill drop, allowing my Mana to recover while I stare out a nearby window at the changes to Dhaka.

"You've done great work here. I'm surprised so many of the Galactics have integrated their designs so well to your architectural theme."

"I imposed no theme," Bipasha says and gestures outward, encompassing the many Galactic buildings that have stuck a variety of domes, detailed carvings, and tall towers to their buildings. "The Galactics appreciated some of the local designs and copied it. At least it's better than the wave of slum architecture."

I raise an eyebrow and Bipasha gestures, a series of notification images popping up. Four-, five-story buildings with radical overhangs, balconies, and a cluster of faux air conditioners dominate the images. All of the design elements contrast with the silver-grey sheen of System-enhanced material and the alien-required modifications like too-wide or too-tall doorways, filtered window shades, and the like. Buildings that look sleek and elegant under Galactic architectural now look ugly and distorted, a mockery of what came before.

"Oh…" I make a face while Ali laughs softly, muttering something about damn *noveau riche* idiots.

"Bad enough I've been trying to convince the council to repurpose those neighborhoods for agriculture, but now we've got Galactics saying we need to preserve it for historical and cultural reasons," Bipasha says scornfully. "As if anyone actually wants to live and work in those areas anymore. They've all moved into the center."

"All?"

"All but a few fools," Bipasha says with a dismissive wave. "Sentimental fools."

I keep silent. Watching Bipasha at work, airing her beliefs, is interesting. It gives me insight into the woman, but I have no place to comment. After all, I ignored such issues in my own settlement, leaving the final resolution to others.

"But that's not what you came to speak about," Bipasha says with a smile. "And while this has been interesting, I do have other work. Unless there is more…?"

"Just one. What would it take for you to support Rob? Hypothetically."

"Hypothetically, I might agree if there was an arrangement to rotate the seat," Bipasha says. "And I'd have to have a Contract outlining what he'd be allowed to do, on-going reports of his actions and the meetings he conducts, and of course, political, economic, and military support for my expansion."

I fall silent, considering her words, and call up the map of the country once again. Bipasha has, between herself and her allies, conquered a large number of settlements in Bangladesh and its neighbors. There are glaring spots Galactics have managed to hold on to through a mixture of military or diplomatic maneuverings. But somehow, I have a feeling it's the non-aligned human settlements that Bipasha is eyeing in a bid to solidify her hold of this area. Certainly, from what I've learned, her leadership has been significantly compromised by the simple fact that she's a woman. It's a misogynistic viewpoint and one that ignores the reality of the System, but old habits die hard.

In the case of some of her ex-enemies, very hard—or so it's rumored. That is, perhaps, one of my major concerns of any long-term alliance with this woman. Even if the rumors had reached me before, the insight I've gained through my Society's Web has underlined that fact. But perhaps a cold, merciless, and ruthless leader is what we need. Is Rob, someone who literally stumbled into his position of power, any better?

"Good to know," I say. "I'm glad to hear that there's some leeway to discuss things."

"Some. I'm giving you the benefit of the doubt that you seek a better future for us all. Do not push that too far," Bipasha says.

With that warning, the meeting comes to an end. For all that I've learned of the woman, I can't help but consider that she has been extremely frank with me thus far. At least on the surface. A nice change, compared to some of the more obscure political maneuverings I've had to deal with.

God damn Truinnar.

***

Next stop, China. I appear on top of the Bank of China once again, looking over the high rises of Hong Kong. I'd Portal into the teashop, but sadly, I'm blocked. Annoying, but in truth, it isn't that far. A quick elevator ride and jog later and I'm ready for my meeting with Grandmaster Chang.

"Mr. Lee," Grandmaster Chang greets me.

"Grandmaster." I take the seat before I pick up the teapot and top off his cup, then I pour myself one, taking the time to regard him with Society's Web. I split my mind as I consider the various threads and carry on the initial pleasantries. "Thank you for meeting with me."

"Not at all. Food?" Grandmaster Chang asks, gesturing at the waitress.

Over my protests, a series of snacks are ordered. I sit back, flicking my gaze away from him occasionally so that I'm not as obvious in my use of the Skill.

"Thank you. I actually came by to speak with you about the Chinese," I say.

"There are a lot of us."

"Yes. There are," I say, acknowledging his point. Interesting. Obligations, contracts, a chain of responsibility flows from his chest further west, into China. There are a few, but one is certainly larger, more prominent by far. "And that's why I'm surprised that Bipasha is being supported."

"I do not indulge in politics," Jing Yi says firmly.

My lips tighten as I recall Cheng Shao's flat denial as well. "I am not asking you to. I'm just trying to understand things. And you are much closer to the matter than I am."

"Again, I don't comment on politics," Jing Yi says firmly.

My eyes narrow slightly as I consider what a man with this much power could be concerned about. Yet I somehow don't sense concern, just caution. I wonder if it's a holdover from before the System, a desire to keep his head down. After all, the curse "May you be recognized by those in high places" might be apocryphal, but it sure as hell exemplifies Chinese views of the government. The last thing the common man wants to do is deal with them.

"I see," I say and fall silent while I consider how to push him. The old man is smart and stubborn, so I doubt a straightforward approach will work. However, I have to admit, I hadn't actually thought through my plans for this meeting.

"Ah, good. The food has arrived. Eat, eat!" Jing Yi proclaims, pushing the plate toward me.

I take his prompts with alacrity, mulling over and discarding various iterations of the same question. It's only when a truly unfamiliar dish plops down that my concentration is broken.

"Roasted and seasoned Junaar Beast," Jing Yi says and points at the small, anteater-like creature that sits on the table. Except its skin is crispy like a roasted duck and the set of six feet are certainly not common. The chef has even used the head and its oversized eye sockets to place dipping sauces.

"Quite the treat. They started appearing a year into the apocalypse and have spread all across China."

"Oh?" I serve him a chopped piece of the meat before picking one up myself, savoring the chewy and surprisingly boneless dish. Its meaty taste is a cross between flavorful young lamb and crispy, crunchy, fatty pig. In other words, delicious. "It's good!"

"Very much so. It's a pity they're so hard to catch." At my polite hum of interest, the Grandmaster continues. "The beast actually is interesting. It raises small creatures—Junaar Mice—and sends them out in front of it. The mice act as bait and distractions for the Beast itself. A very pragmatic approach to life. Don't you think?"

I pause while chewing on the latest morsel, staring at the smiling old man. I look at the alien creature then the man, before chuckling softly. "Yes. Very practical. Here, have another piece!"

It's only when I walk back out of the teahouse, after stuffing myself full of good food and trading more war stories, that Ali pops back into existence. The Spirit sniffs, floating alongside me as we fast-walk back to the teleportation pad.

"Not the subtlest of analogies," Ali says.

"But it works."

So. Bipasha is the mouse and the Chinese consider themselves the owner. Well, I can live with that, so long as they vote. And after having one attack set on me, their strategy might not be the worse one I've seen. Keep your name hidden, keep your head down, and let others attract the attention. Until you need to strike. Not a bad strategy, but not for me.

***

"Mr. Lee." Rob smiles, offering me a hand as he stands.

We meet once more at his faux-Oval Office, though this time a half-dozen Secret Service members are standing around. I'm amused, somewhat, by the increase in security.

"Didn't think me nearly getting killed was that big a deal."

"Gods, your head is big. You do recall that Ikael got killed while speaking with you, right?"

"You mean, they're here to protect him against me?" I send the thought back, almost scandalized. Then, realizing there're a half dozen Advanced Class bodyguards in here, a significant portion of any settlement's fighting force, I decide that maybe it's a nice compliment. Of sorts.

"President Markey," I greet the man and take the offered seat. I'm a little amused that the chair is nice and plushy and still not as comfortable as the Galactic nanoweave chairs I have in my office. But tradition dictates that these chairs look this way, and so here we are. The moment I take my seat, I throw up Society's Web and begin the sorting process.

"Your decision caught many of us by surprise," Rob says. "I'm glad to hear that it was voluntary."

"It was, and it made sense," I say with a half-smile. "Lana was doing the job anyway. And this leaves me more time to talk with people about the Vote."

"I thought you might be here for that." Rob opens his hand. "I'm sorry to say, but if you wish our support, you'll only receive part of it. Our representatives will all be conducting a conscience vote."

"Huh. Your free media really does put the Shop to shame. Seems like they had a house— senate?—vote and they forced Rob to agree to that. Good news is that they picked up most of southern Texas by agreeing to that though."

"Ah…" I lean backward. "Any ideas of the numbers?"

"If they were to vote for Ms. Chowdury? Maybe half," Rob says.

That means we'd lose two percent of the vote. Not huge, but still significant since that's about ten percent of what we can afford to lose. It doesn't help that so much of North America is already taken by the Truinnar and their allies, forcing Rob's half-formed government to work around it.

"What do you want if you do throw your backing at her anyway?" I say softly, doing the math in my head. It's still not enough, not by far. Not without the Truinnar and more of the independents. Which probably dictates my next trip.

"Nothing major. We've already spoken somewhat about this. But I can sell a further portion of my people on supporting her if she would commit to lending her support on an expedition."

"You mean war," I say, cutting through the bullshit. "Where?"

Rob doesn't say a word, gesturing and flicking a map to me, highlighting the state of Oklahoma. I don't ask why that state—I'm sure there're good reasons. What I'm more concerned about is who owns the settlements there. Sadly, I'm once again right. He's looking to clear the Truinnar from Oklahoma, which would put us in direct conflict with people whose vote we probably need.

"That's not going to work," I say, my eyes tight. "Or I don't think it will."

"I understand."

I sigh, standing and offering my hand to Rob. He seems a nice man, but with the state the country is in, the wars he must fight, I'm not sure why I came now. Perhaps I'm intrinsically biased to think of the Americans as a major power, but in this new world, they're too scattered. When Rob stands, there's a little of the same understanding in his eyes. A tiredness and a resignation that I never noticed before.

"Thank you. And good luck."

"You too, Mr. Lee."

***

East. The Portal to Whitehorse drops me off in the lobby of the City Center, startling more than a few Adventurers. A part of me wonders what it means when I've got full access to Portal anywhere I want within Roxley's settlements. Not just Whitehorse, but even all the way up to Alaska. Well, theoretically at least, since I don't have any waypoints in Alaska yet. Another, more cowardly, portion decides, as always, questions like this about my relationship with the Truinnar should be set aside for a more appropriate time. Like never.

"John," Roxley greets me with a smile at the elevator after I ascend. "I was wondering when you'd arrive."

"Well, I've been thinking you'd tell me when you're ready, but tick-tock, man."

"Tick-tock?"

"The sound a clock makes…" I shake my head. "No distractions. I need an answer. Are we going to make the vote this time, or am I going to have to plan for another six months of politicking?"

"And settlement conquest?" Roxley asks, an enigmatic smile on his lips.

"If necessary."

"Very well," Roxley says. "I'm glad that I read you right. The Duchess has agreed to backing your efforts, with certain caveats. Firstly, we'd like Earth to officially join the—"

"Nope."

"You didn't let me finish."

"Didn't need to." I place my hands on my hips. "You didn't spend all this time to make an offer you knew I would turn down immediately."

"I did not. But I had to try," Roxley says, giving me a belly-flopping, stomach churning smile.

Damn it. I check my notification logs but don't see a damn note, so either his Charisma and other Skills worked or it's all just me.

"*It's just you,*" Ali sends to me, obviously having seen me open my notification logs.

"*Get lost,*" I send to Ali then fix Roxley with a look, pushing my other thoughts and feelings aside. "So?"

"We will require you to vote with us for certain bills. Ten such times, we will compel your votes—and those will not be negotiable," Roxley says. "In addition, we will want you to levy additional duties and taxes against the Movana and their allies. Truinnar are to be exempt from entry charges, while—"

"You want us to double or triple the charges for the Movana and their allies." I wave. "If those are the biggest sticking points, it doesn't sound horrible if we can get all of you on board. We'll want to adjust them a bit, like making sure those bills don't directly impact us too badly and maybe set a time limit on those duties and taxes, but it's something for Lana and Katherine to handle." I hesitate but add, "And Bipasha."

"You have made your decision then?"

"I'm actually more interested in what took you so long," I say, tapping my foot. "You obviously have been considering this for a while."

"The delay has been for your benefit. Our meetings have been of particular interest to our enemies. Confirming the agreement before this would have placed you and your efforts in greater danger."

"But now we've got less than two weeks to get the rest of your people to agree, then they're going to have to argue about what we've decided."

"The agreement you make with me will be sufficient," Roxley states confidently.

"How...?"

"Can I be confident of the matter? It has already been agreed on."

"You've been talking to them already? But if you were, won't our enemies know?"

Roxley looks slightly miffed. "Please, John. My compatriots and I have been politicking under the System all our lives. This is a minor matter."

I pause, then shut my mouth. Fine. They know how to game the System and their opponents. And I'm the blunt idiot who was kept in the dark for his own good. I grit my teeth, drawing a deep breath and exhaling slowly, forcing calm on myself. When Roxley puts a hand on my arm, squeezing my bicep for comfort, I growl and shrug him off, stalking away to stare out a viewscreen which acts as a window.

"John...?"

"One second," I say, holding up a finger.

I force myself to breathe, to run through the emotions and slowly, slowly push down the anger. Because in the end, they were right. I just hated being handled.

When I have better control of my emotions, I say, "Why are we having this talk now?"

"The assassination attempt on you has escalated matters. It is obvious our stall tactics have been seen through."

"By the Movana." I say without inflection, curious to see what Roxley thinks. I turn back to the Truinnar and open my Skill. Threads appear, dozens, hundreds. I avoid the obvious one, the thread which leads to me, and instead focus on the others.

"Most likely," Roxley acknowledges. "Of the factions present, it is only theirs which would be threatened by Earth. Facing the Fist directly and winning their respect has blunted the danger from their faction. So long as you allow them access to Earth and its dungeons, they should not act against you. In fact, they might support humanity's growth. After all, you and Ms. Sato are prime candidates for recruitment."

"What? A battle maniac and a cheat?"

"Yes. But to return to the point, the Artisans do not care enough to act against you. And well, you have a deal with us."

"Which leaves the Movana," I say. "Or other humans who don't believe I don't want the seat for myself. Or any independent Galactic group who's willing to blow enough Credits to hire a Master Class assassin."

"Which are few."

I hate to say it, but the logic is impeccable. In fact, outside of Bipasha and perhaps Rob, I can't think of any group who might want me dead that badly. Among other things, while I'm important to this movement, I'm not the only mover and shaker. After all our efforts, it'd take a lot of assassinations and Credits to stop this train.

"I will speak with Ms. Pearson about the details of what we require and the number of seats I can guarantee. It is, of course, not everyone," Roxley says.

I nod in acceptance of his warning. No surprise there. As much influence as the Duchess might have, as charming as Roxley might be, and as much as the species is going to vote for its betterment as a whole, there will still be those who disagree. But most is good. Most is better than none.

"Thank you," I say, flashing him a grateful smile.

With the Truinnar votes and the ones from the Fist, we should be close. At some point, I need to push Cheng Shao again, just to make sure what I heard from Bipasha is true, but if so, we might have this. Or close enough. But still,

I see the message in my notifications, the request from Wynn for a meeting. And I find myself wanting to give him the benefit of the doubt.

"You're welcome, John." Roxley visibly hesitates, looking uncertain for once.

I wait, knowing he has something to say. I wonder what kind of bomb he's about to drop.

"Would you care to join me for dinner?"

"Nah, I'll just grab a bite in Kamloops—"

"John." Roxley's voice grows slightly heated. "Would you like to join me for dinner?"

"You just…" I stutter to a stop at the way he said it, the hesitation and uncertainty and yes, the slight blush. Oh. Oh… "Ummm… right. Got to go…"

You Are Quantum Locked

"What!?!"

"No running away," Roxley says, crossing the distance to me and staring at me heatedly. "I want an answer. A real one."

"And if I don't give one, you'll keep me trapped?" I growl. "Very *Misery* of you."

"Wha…? No. You will not divert me from this. I know of your plans. If you succeed, you intend to leave Earth. I have responsibilities which will not allow me to go. We have danced around this matter for years. I wish—no—I require a resolution."

"Roxley…" I shake my head. "I'm leaving. Gone. Stars away. And what happens next, I have a feeling it'll be worse than taunting a dragon. There's no point to this. To us."

"No point?" Roxley says softly, almost gently. "No point in joy? In happiness? Are you so fixated on the future you will avoid the present? What is your Taoism then, your pursuit and acceptance of the now?"

"Not fair," I mutter. "You aren't supposed to use our conversations against me. And joy isn't the goal..."

"No? Well, perhaps you could educate me further. Over dinner."

Roxley is right next to me now, so close I could touch him with the barest motion. But he doesn't move to cross those final few inches and neither do I. With his last sentence, Roxley lets the silence take over, giving me time to think.

I hate this. Hate contemplating this giant ball of emotions, the fear, the worry, the desire. The immediate, chemical reaction to the man—the alien!—before me. But... what is, is. Isn't that what I've tried to embrace? Sometimes, the right choice isn't what I think or what I believe. Sometimes, to see the whole, you need to step outside of the boundaries of your own views.

And hell, I haven't been laid in four years.

***

I don't make it out of Whitehorse till the next morning. Late morning. But when I leave, it's with a smile and a secret from Roxley. Because for all the logic, all the clear and indisputable circumstantial evidence pointing to the Movana's guilt, I can't believe it. The teleportation portal to Paris rips me apart and dumps me out in the City of Lights, in the square right outside the Notre Dame de Paris. It's not exactly how I ever expected to revisit the city, but at least I managed to come back.

Paris is beautiful. There's something about the city which gives it a certain charm, the grey block buildings, the picturesque centuries-old architecture, the giant bestial mounts. It's a city which demands attention, even after the ravages of the System's arrival.

"Wynn." I greet the Guild Leader with a smile.

In the corner of my eyes, I note the multiple Quantum Lock symbols, denoting the numerous teleportation barriers in place. Over the entire city, a Settlement Shield is in place, lightly flickering as the occasional low Level monster flies into it. Numerous flying mounts glide and flap above me while flying cars float among the hovering beacons, taking their passengers through the large metropolitan. Hundreds of Galactics and humans move around me on their feet, ducking between gigantic beasts of burden and larger humanoid feet, treading to jobs, schools, or Quests. It's an amazing show of prosperity, though a part of me knows it's a false front too. Paris is the center of the Movana's push. Outlying settlements are not nearly as busy.

"Redeemer," Wynn says with a smile, offering me his hand. "I'm glad you accepted my invitation."

"Color me intrigued. I hadn't expected to be invited to Paris of all places." After all, the guild master's guild is based in Vancouver.

"It was considered a better option," Wynn replies and waves me toward a waiting hover car. "If you will, we have only a brief window."

We take off, giving me a view of the sprawling city. Like Dhaka, I notice how many neighborhoods have retained their older, human architecture. Of course, not all of Paris is made of heritage-worthy architecture, nor do all Galactics care. And so, the city is dotted with the occasional incongruently placed building, like the floating oval, the hexadecimal-structured building, and one I swear was made by Dali himself. Strangely enough, it suits the city.

"A beautiful city," Wynn says, waving below. "We were able to restore much of it after the initiation. It seemed to satisfy many of the locals. As well as our adoption of their language. I am told it is linguistically similar to our native tongue, though with less gender definitions."

I open my mouth then shut it, declining to comment. While I took French in school like any good Canadian, I have to admit, mine is beyond rusty. Add the fact that Canadian French is not really considered "real" French by the French themselves, and well, I'm not one to comment. Come to think of it, I'm finding myself holding my tongue more and more. I wonder if it's a sign of maturity or cowardice?

"How many?"

"Pardon?"

"How many humans are left?" I ask, looking below. "I know the Movana purchased the settlements a little after the apocalypse. And even took a few Cores by force. So. How many?"

"For the region? Just under a million. But we've had significant immigration from outlying areas," Wynn says without sugar-coating the truth.

I shut my eyes for a second, pushing away the wave of emotion. It's too complex, too dense for me to pick apart right now. Though the aching grief over all the loss is still there. Still. A million. That's a lot.

"Chatter on the local boards indicates they're relatively happy. And Wynn isn't telling the whole story—there's been a constant level of immigration from the city too. They're using more and more of the locals as go-betweens in other cities to help mollify the local populace."

"How's it going?" I'm trying to imagine the conversation between a Frenchman and German, then I decide perhaps I shouldn't be basing my imagination on bad Hollywood movies. After all, they are neighbors and were in the EU together for ages. Surely it isn't as much of a farce as Hollywood would have me believe.

"Insufficient data to provide a statistically relevant conclusion, as bits would say. It's not as if the local boards go into exhaustive detail over something like this."

I send a mental affirmation back to Ali. Since I'm here anyway, I open my new favorite Skill, staring at the numerous threads that criss-cross the city. Rather than give myself a migraine trying to actually understand the information before me, I just watch the shift and twist and let it seep in. Hopefully my subconscious mind will be able to make use of it. Or not.

"I am somewhat surprised you agreed to come," Wynn says, breaking the silence.

I turn back to the guild master, staring at the halo of threads around him, and do a brief check on the thread which leads to me. It's not particularly thick. The obligations we initially shared as settlement owner and guild leader have disappeared, leaving just our normal interactions. While there were traces of friendly, even respectful interactions, it's mostly a business relationship.

"Why? Because it's rumored the Movana are the ones who set the assassin on me?" I say bluntly.

"Yes."

"I figured if you really want to kill me, I'd make it easier. Rather get stabbed in the front than the back."

Wynn bursts out laughing. "Oh, you definitely are an Erethran Paladin."

"You've met one before?"

"Once. A long time ago, when I was still a child," Wynn says.

Damn. Our legends are right—these elves live for centuries at least, considering what I know of the Paladins.

"It was on a space station above Linx 4. He had been chasing a crew of space pirates and finally found their ship docked at the station. The pirates had switched out the transponder beacon on their ship and fled to Movana space. But the Paladin refused to let it go. He took on the entire station's security forces and the pirates by himself."

My mentor had spoken about a few of my predecessors, told stories and discussed what was expected. But she'd never mentioned anything like this—just major battles and sometimes a few illustrative events. So was a fight with an entire space station's security team and a gang of pirates considered a day in the life for a Paladin?

"Did he win?" I ask.

"Depends on your definition. He tore up the space station, killed all the pirates, and destroyed their ship," Wynn says. "But he also hurt relations between Linx and the Erethrans for a century and forced the Empire to pay repatriations higher than the damage the pirates could have done in a decade of raids."

"A blunt instrument," I say, letting the Skill drop and allowing my Mana to regenerate.

Yet I detect a hint of admiration in Wynn's voice. A fond recollection of the unnamed Paladin. For the rest of the flight, I ponder the contrast between the pragmatic and the emotional, the needs of the now and the future.

***

No towering, hollow trees greet me when we finally arrive. Instead, the building is what I call Galactic-norm, a stylized grey rectangle thrust into the sky without care for physics or decorum. I absently note even more quantum locks in place once I enter the building, shutting down any chances of me porting in or out of this area. I'm not surprised.

You have entered Paris City Center

Facilities available:

- *City Core*
- *Shop*
- *Meeting rooms (+18% experience increase in administrative skills)*
- *Training rooms (+8% experience increase in skills trained)*

We're led into one of those meetings room, a large board room which hosts four different Movana. Three men, one woman. Like Wynn, the leader and the female look like *Lord of the Rings* extras, thin and slim and perfectly coiffed. One of the extra males is, interestingly enough, portly and unkempt with a mohawk for a hairstyle and nose piercings which gleam in the diffuse light. As for the last man, he looks like an elf given steroids, sporting a sleeveless tunic to show off his arms.

"Redeemer. It's a pleasure to meet you," Bhale a Bhode, the leader of the group, says as he stands and offers his hand to shake.

I take it while activating Society's Web and watch as the thread between us grows. Within seconds, I'm introduced to the rest, whose names I forget almost immediately in exchange for an interesting insight into the interpersonal politics among the group. For example, Mohawk's jealous of everyone in this group as he's the only non-Combat Classer and non-Master Class. He's also slightly afraid of Musclehead, who in turn has an extremely thick, twisted thread to the female elf. It's filled with numerous dealings over a long course of years, with familial and personal feelings messed up in it. I'm scanning through it all, gathering as much information as I can, while we do the small talk thing.

"Once again, we have to thank you for being willing to meet with us directly," Bhale says, waving around the meeting room. "It shows a degree of open-mindedness which is refreshing."

"You're being too generous," I say.

Wynn coughs slightly, hiding his movement behind a sip on the blue juice we're drinking. Quite tasty actually.

"But I do think we should talk about why I'm here," I say.

"The Planetary Vote," Bhale says. "We are willing to provide you the votes you require. All our votes."

Surprise obviously shows on my face because Bhale smiles and continues. "We understand the position you are in. And ours. So we do not ask for much."

I find myself leaning forward, listening to Bhale as he lists their demands. In the end, they come down to a series of small concessions, none of them much greater than what we've provided to other independent and smaller kingdoms thus far. At least, none are much greater individually, but as a whole, it's a significant package of concessions. Still very reasonable considering they're offering nearly nine percent of the votes. More interesting is the way they're asking for it. Most of those we've spoken to have requested immediate benefits —economic and military concessions which take effect immediately, Credits and materials sent over. Here though, the Movana are basing their concessions on a future where we win the Vote. A show of confidence perhaps—or of good faith.

"It's relatively reasonable," I say once he's done. Smiles cross all their faces, but I hold up my hand. "Details can be argued by those under us. But the problem is, your votes aren't enough."

"It is all we have," Bhale says. He doesn't look surprised by my words at all.

"Aye, and the Truinnar want you out," I say, opening my hands. "You see the position I'm in?"

"We do. It's why we're willing to compromise on what we will accept. And I'm sure the Truinnar have requested significantly more," Bhale says. "I can offer nothing more."

"Nothing...?" I say.

Bhale meets my gaze calmly, refusing to back down from his words, and I let out a low huff of exasperation.

"Yah gots enough. Yah want our baybies next?" Musclehead speaks up, his arms crossed as he flexes the large biceps and leans forward. "I told y'all it ain't worth speaking to the damn monkeys."

"He got a speech impediment or something?"

"I think it's an accent. An affected one." Ali is looking at Musclehead a little incredulously, and I admit, I'm embarrassed for the Movana too.

I close my mouth and run the numbers, using the Neural Link to aid in the calculations and the voting scenarios. With the Truinnar, and assuming Bipasha is telling the truth, we've got roughly seventy-five percent of the seats. With the Movana, the number drops by nearly eight percent, putting us at sixty-six percent. We could, with a little elbow grease, eke out another percent of space by taking some of the unclaimed spots. I might even be able to get a percent or two from the independents, but in both cases, I'll still fall short. With the Movana, it'd just be a little shorter.

"Thank you for the offer," I say softly. "But it's not just my decision. I'll pass it on."

Musclehead frowns, but Bhale raises a hand, quieting the other man before he can say anything. He, however, leans forward and fixes me with those turquoise eyes of his. "Redeemer, we are not your enemies. No matter what the Truinnar have told you, our actions were not personal."

"I'm imagining a giant but here," I say.

"But if you persist in declining our overtures of friendship, we will have to take action."

"And the blades come out," I say, smiling at the quartet who sits opposite me. Wynn shifts uncomfortably in his chair, his presence a footnote here. Bhale doesn't back down, not that I expected him to. "We'll let you know."

On those foreboding notes, I'm allowed to leave. Wynn is quiet when he sees me out and back to the teleportation pad. I don't bother using their pad though, triggering my own Portal once I'm inside the exclusion zone. As I nod goodbye to the troubled-looking guild master, I can't help but feel somewhat satisfied with what I've learned.

Unless the Movana are really playing a deep game, they aren't the ones who set the assassin on me.

Chapter 18

"You're going to have to explain that again for us," Lana says while handing me the basket of bannock.

I take two pieces and reach for a third before my hand gets slapped and the basket stolen by Carlos.

"What are you doing here?" I grumble at the man. "You weren't exactly invited."

"Bannock," Carlos replies and puts a piece on his plate before the bready, doughy goodness is taken by Mikito.

"You don't think the Movana are the ones who set you up. Because you didn't see anything connecting them to you in an aggressive way?" Ingrid says slowly as she waves a pair of long wooden chopsticks while standing over the pot full of oil. "Am I right?"

"Sort of," I say. "It's also because they were willing to work with us. Even if they know they can't get the vote."

"Could be a ruse," Lana says, waving a drumstick to punctuate her point. "You know, make you think they're your friends while sending assassins to kill you."

"See, that's the other thing. Killing me won't stop the vote. We've done enough groundwork, you guys could finish the job," I say. "I'm not that important."

"Then who sent the assassin?"

I shrug, not having an answer. I could put together a million and one conspiracy theories, but in the end, I just don't know.

"I don't think it matters," Ingrid says while we all sit there, considering matters. "There's not been another attempt as yet. And no one's reported an attempt on them."

"Good. Just one problem," I say. "If we confirm with the Truinnar, the Movana have pretty much guaranteed they're going to try to stop us."

"Did they indicate how?" Mikito asks, concern in her voice. "If they intend to go after the local human settlements, I'll need to inform Hugo and the other champions."

"No." I shrug. "But you might want to do it anyway."

Mikito nods, and we fall silent for a little while as we dig in.

It's Carlos who breaks the silence. "Are we actually going to succeed at the Vote?"

"Not yet," I say. "We're still short."

"Then..." Carlos frowns as he sees the slight smiles among the team. "What am I missing?"

"There's always a but with John," Lana explains with a smile.

"But with the Truinnar, we're close enough we might be able to get the other independents who have been on the fence."

"If we choose Bipasha and the Truinnar," Lana states firmly while holding up a finger. "Is that what I'm hearing, John?"

I nod reluctantly. I don't trust Bipasha. Something about the outwardly friendly, internally cold woman worries me. Perhaps it's because she reminds me a little of my own father—a man who learned to "fake" the appearance of an extrovert while still being entirely reserved inside. I understood why he did it, and it had been effective at letting him climb the corporate ladder, but still, the dichotomy had made for an unpleasant childhood.

"Damn. Here I was hoping to pick up more work," Ingrid says, sitting down beside me. "But once we've chosen, you know there's going to be a bit of a mess. The Movana will act, as will any other group that thinks you're going to shut them out."

274

That means all the Movana and their allies, as well as a few independent species we'd gotten on the bad side of—or who we'd visibly disapproved of their practices. The entire Serfdom thing still grates against the vast majority of humanity's morals, and the species who twist the rules to make it slavery in all but name know we'll be targeting them. And then there are the species who aren't much better than the monsters out there, killing, eating, and smashing their way through life. Who, even in "normal" Galactic society, are relegated to the edges. Like Dungeon Worlds.

"What do you think they'll do?" I ask the group in general.

"Settlement attacks," Mikito says.

"Assassinations on vulnerable settlement owners. Or where the second-in-command is weak," Ingrid adds.

"Political and economic pressure." Lana raises a finger. "Don't forget many of the Galactics have interests outside of Earth."

"Bribes?" Carlos says, shrugging. "No reason they can't try to entice the others away."

Everyone proceeds to throw out ideas of what might happen, but it mostly boils down to variations of the initially stated ideas. Once we exhaust the brainstorm, we shift the conversation to what we can do. In the end, our plan of action is limited not only by the number of personnel we have and can trust but also our timeframe.

When we finally clear the multiple plates and pots of food, I sum up our conversation. "Right. For the most part, we're going to have stay on the defensive. We target settlements owned by enemy independents with military strikes. That'll be Mikito, the champions, and my job. We use Ingrid and any of her friends—I assume you have friends in the business—to target some of the other groups if we think it'll work. Or at the least, it'll keep them busy and looking over their shoulder. Kim and Lana can provide the necessary list to you, as well as the budget."

Ingrid grins at the offer.

"And as for the rest, Lana, Bipasha, and Katherine will work on reinforcing our contracts and working on the edge cases among the indies," I say.

"What should I do?" Carlos asks after I fall silent.

The rest of us share a look then chorus, "The dishes!"

***

Of course, we don't just delegate kitchen duties to Carlos. Carlos is designated our spokesperson with the Artisan's group and a few other non-aligned Artisan settlement owners. While pigeon-holing the man as a non-Combat Classer isn't really nice, he is likely to have more luck chatting with them than we would. If nothing else, developing a relationship could be beneficial for future trade.

Once we make up our minds, we get to work. And we definitely have a ton of work to do. I find myself bouncing from city to city, settlement to settlement, talking and occasionally fighting while my friends scramble to get their own tasks done.

I find myself portaling back from Kisangani after another fruitful discussion days later. The African city has many similarities to Whitehorse, including the presence of a Galactic owner, a location in a high Level zone, and a major river flowing beside it. Of course, it's located in a temperate forest, had more than fifty times our population prior to the apocalypse, and has an all-round moderate climate. But, you know, outside of those things, it is very similar to my old home.

Amusingly, the Galactic owner is another Kudaya, though it is closer to a giant, stork-like reptile than a hippo. The creature uses a series of thin legs to

276

stand and move about and is not a fighter at all. For a Mid-Level Administrator though, the creature has a clear grasp of the realities of combat, with our major negotiation including a deadline to clear a half dozen of their dungeons each quarter. Luckily, we don't need to commit our own forces to this directly, so the moment I step through the Portal, I issue a series of Quests for Kim to pin to the Adventurer's Board. I even include an all-expenses paid Portal to the location.

When I'm done, I flash a grin at the trio of grumpy occupants in my office. They're all seated in their respective seats, their System screens floating visibly in front of them.

"Sorry. Forgot I gave up this office," I say, nodding to Lana, who lets out a theatrical sigh.

Katherine sniffs slightly, making her displeasure quite clear. As for the last participant, I'm surprised to see him here actually.

Peter Steele (Level 38 Planetary Diplomat)

HP: 980/980

MP: 1780/1780

Conditions: Aura of Temperance, Scale Balancer, Diplomat's Shield

"Peter," I greet the Diplomat with a grin, shaking the trim African American's hand. The man has a great smile which shows all his pearly white teeth while enveloping you in a comforting warmth. In the corner of my eyes, I see the ping of a resisted Mental Influence, his Charisma breaking against my mental resistances. "It's been ages."

"I know," Peter says with a smile. "I was thinking you were avoiding me."

"Just busy," I say, shaking my head. Not as though we're major friends, but we met and talked in my capacity as settlement leader and before, when he negotiated the agreements in San Francisco.

"Of course," Peter says, glancing back toward the ladies who are already chatting on their own calls, dealing with recalcitrant settlement owners.

One of the side benefits of the office is its ability to seal off external visual and audible distractions while on a vidcall, allowing us to speak freely. Even as we speak, Peter is busy eyeing the smaller notification screens for the two young ladies.

"I won't bother you guys. You seem busy," I say graciously.

"No, I have a few minutes. My last call finished faster than I expected," Peter says.

"It went well, I hope?" I say.

"Nope," Ali chimes in as he picks at the snack table the trio have set up in one corner. "I just got their name added to the Ingrid list."

Peter nods amiably at Ali's words, his face perfectly serene. "They were particularly upset we would even consider speaking with them after our recent moves in Brazil. It seems we missed the fact that the Iwik Corporation which owned Lucas do Rio Verde is actually owned by the second brood mate of the Third Head. Taking the settlement was considered a breach of the peace."

"I wonder how we missed that." My voice drips with sarcasm.

"Diplomacy is a matter of knowledge and understanding. A proper diplomatic mission should take many factors into account. Your—our—recent actions have been extremely rushed," Peter says with a grimace.

"You've had four years."

"And hundreds of Galactic parties to investigate," Peter counters. "It is already a miracle we've managed to do as well as we did. Thankfully, greed and arrogance are still universal traits."

I chuckle, a reaction which is obviously to his liking.

"Helps when you and the girls are all Charisma junkies," Ali adds with a wry grin. "And your Skill, the Greater Good, has worked wonders. I never realized the upgrade of the Skill was so powerful."

"It is," Peter says, smirking.

I shake my head slightly, impressed the man was willing to dedicate so many of his Class Skill points to a single Skill. While I know, theoretically, Skills upgrade once you dump ten points into them, I just never had the ability to do so. It takes a certain single-mindedness to be willing to choose one path and stick to it like Peter.

"John, hi. Now, bye. Peter, I want your take on these guys..." Lana interrupts before we can chit-chat more.

I chuckle and deposit bars of chocolate in front of everyone before I head out of the room to the sniff—and crinkling of plastic wrap—from Katherine.

***

I find the Assassin in a room a short distance from my office, in a comfortable chaise lounger, tight pants showcasing her legs, and an ice cream sandwich in her mouth. When I step in, she starts slightly before she relaxes, continuing to chew on the sandwich.

After swallowing, she says, "Want one?"

"I'm good," I say, popping out a chocolate bar of my own and finding a chair to sit on. "You called?"

"Yup. Got the list," Ingrid says and waves.

A moment later, I've got the notification with the list of names for the targets and, most importantly, the cost. My eyes bulge out slightly as I spot the final line item. "Are you serious?"

"I know right? I got a great deal," Ingrid says.

"This is a deal?" I whisper with horrible fascination as I go over the names and Credits. The cheapest bugger to take down is just over two million Credits. I could buy a small spaceship for that much! Of course, it'd be a single-man spaceship which would barely putter around the solar system, but spaceship!

"Yes. What? You think it's easy going after a settlement owner? Most of the Galactics have banked on their positions to purchase a large number of enchanted objects and Skills via loans. Some of the most in-debt fellows have bank-designated bodyguards," Ingrid says. "If killing settlement owners was easy, you wouldn't get a nifty Title for doing it."

"You have a title?"

"Oh, right! I have mine hidden," Ingrid says with a smile then gestures again.

Settlement Killer

Murderer, killer, assassin! Where the title holder goes, other owners will fear. The Settlement Killer is the bane of good order in well-run settlements and the hope of the downtrodden in despotic settlements. In the end, killer and savior are but two sides of the same coin.

Effect: Title owner gains a 5% increase in damage done to settlement owners

"How come I never got one?" I frown. I've killed a few myself.

"Wars and combat don't count. Sort of." Ingrid shrugs. "I got mine after five kills. The number is higher if you receive your kills in a different way. It also depends on the settlement importance and the owners' Levels, as I understand it."

"I could look into it if you want, boy-o. I'm sure there's a 'completion rate' somewhere."

"Never mind. It's not that important."

I turn my attention back to the list and shake my head, closing it out. "I can offer a little bit to the cause, but I don't have the settlement funds anymore. Bipasha might be a better option…"

"Oh, I got the girls and Roxley to cough up the funds for eighty percent of them," Ingrid says with a smirk. "We just want your feedback on the list itself."

I nod slowly, taking a closer look. If we have to cut a bunch of those, we'll want to find those who might be intimidated or backed off sufficiently. It'd help as well to have the settlements near others which might be hesitating. Maybe we could trade one settlement to another…

Thoughts spinning, I balance the numbers, names, and political affiliations with their geographic distance and cost. It's only when nearly a half hour has passed and I've crossed out a bunch of names on the list that I realize Ingrid is still lounging on the chair, eyes half closed.

"Don't you have anything better to do?" I say.

"What makes you think I'm not doing it?" Ingrid smirks. "Ninety percent of assassination is about planning."

I take the rebuke, having forgotten she could easily be staring at her notifications. In fact, it's probably what she was doing. I consider prodding further but decide against it. Instead, I ask a more personal question. "Are you okay with this?"

"With what?"

"All the killing," I say. "I know you've been doing it for a while, but…"

"But you never asked?"

"Yeah."

"It's what I can do," Ingrid says softly. "It's all I have left. They took everything else away." I wince slightly, the movement hidden almost as soon as it started. But it's enough for Ingrid to spot. "Are you pitying me?"

"No!"

"Good," Ingrid says and continues to stare.

Eventually, I look away, my discomfort with the emotional outburst breaking through my self-control. Or perhaps, I let it break. Because among friends, you can be more yourself.

"Because I wouldn't want pity from someone that easily fooled."

"Easily…" My eyes narrow, and the First Nation's woman returns my stare with a slight smile. I wonder if she's telling the truth, if what she said was the truth or a lie after the fact to cover a moment of honesty. "Funny."

"Now, shoo. You're a bit too big and distracting for me," Ingrid says and shoos me out of the room.

I leave, shaking my head. I swear, it feels as if everyone keeps kicking me out of rooms, cities, and countries.

***

Dealing with the settlement owners is mostly a job for the others, whether or not my advice was requested. My task list, as usual, mostly deals with Portaling individuals around, planning, and conducting raids with Mikito. Since things have progressed to this point, the pair of us are doing our best to project force to the various settlement owners and clear up any obligations we can. While it sounds simple enough, not everything is going our way.

"What do you mean the champions aren't going to help us?" I ask Mikito as we stroll through the destroyed town.

We've been porting around so much lately, I can't even recall exactly where we are—some Baltic country with rolling hills and cobbled streets. The destroyed, small stone buildings and the empty streets offer few clues, especially since I don't read the local language. The fact that this is an ex-settlement is even more tragic, the city key sold off at some point in the last few years. Now, it's just a ghost town, a reminder of better days.

"As an organization. Individually, some will back us up. Rae, Jessica, and Jamal are working the Caribbean. But Jessica has to tread carefully," Mikito says, shaking her head. "Local politics. Cheng Shao is saying she has training of her own to do and is refusing to take part except for official business. Hugo is busy getting the settlements ready in Europe for the Movana. And he hates your guts even more."

"Because I set up his people to take the brunt of the Movana's retaliation?" Sadly, since Hugo and his people are literally next to the Movana, their settlements are pretty much guaranteed to get hit.

Mikito nods, and I sigh. We fall silent for a bit as a group of half-owl, half-deer creatures charge out of a cross street, forcing us to focus. When we're done, I make sure to open a Portal for the group of enthusiastic Butchers waiting to collect the bodies.

The small Town on the savannah on the other end of the Portal is probably one of the most pitiful settlements I've come across. Somehow, they've managed to be surrounded by a large number of monsters who are all inedible, a rather impressive feat considering the System makes most meat edible. They'd been surviving off a dungeon that had produced a series of mutated wild boars until a year ago, when a passing team of Galactic Adventurers "helpfully" cleared the dungeon. Since then, they've been purchasing food directly from the Shop. Katherine had contacted them to get their vote and struck a deal to help finance a long-range teleportation pad in the medium term and to supply them with food in the short term.

Which is how I came to be out here with Mikito, dealing with two birds. Killing monsters to cover our side of a security deal for a nearby settlement and providing food for another. It still surprises me sometimes how there are portions of humanity, of human settlements, which have yet to progress to dealing with Level 50-plus monsters. Even with the experience boost in the first year, many struggled to progress not because they couldn't, but they wouldn't.

Fear keeps them down, keeps them from pushing themselves. And it's in those locations which the Galactics come with their Levels and Skills, Adventurers who have chosen to grow strong. Unfortunately, their presence, their overwhelming courage is a mental blow some humans cannot stand. When every single Galactic you meet is strong, powerful, and confident, willing to risk life and limb, and you're struggling to survive another day, well… it's hard to accept. Even if, logically, you understand you're seeing a small, selective sample.

And so, settlements stagnate. People grow weary, focused on going back to living their "normal" lives. They farm out jobs to others in Quests, giving up experience and loot for safety, sacrificing future strength for current comfort. And so, here we are. People like Mikito and me walk the hills while other Adventurers and the gear we've brought releases a multi-kilometer taunt. It's a bit more effective than us running around and hoping to find something to kill.

"Sensors are reporting we've got another horde coming in from the south," Ali reports to us, flicking the updated map to our notifications.

Without a word, we switch directions and jog toward the attack zone. It's nice to hang out with Mikito, even if it's not the best use of our resources at this moment. But with only a few days left before the vote, getting involved in anything too elaborate is probably a bad idea.

The horde of monsters is another weird owl-creature combination. There's an owl-bear, owl-deer, and even an owl-skunk that we have to fight. It looks like Dr. Moreau was working through his owl fixation and left the door to his lab open.

I duck, throwing a series of Mana Darts into a beaked face, watching as the blue projectiles blind the creature. I step in, launching a series of short punches which throws the monster backward before I conjure my sword and cut, ripping a hole through its body and its friend behind it.

A screech resounds, my sense of balance shaking briefly before my resistances and the helmet's defenses kick in, cutting off the noise. Beside me, Mikito is staggering and swinging her polearm. Unlike me, she seems to be going with it, using the induced vertigo and the long reach of her weapon to create an unpredictable vortex of destruction. Anything that gets hit by the blade of her naginata is dismembered and left to flop uselessly on the ground.

An owl-skunk bends over and sprays, sending a visible cloud of fast-moving gas toward us. I hop backward while casting a fireball spell. I let it explode right in front of my hand, the overpressure from the spell battling against the smell. Of course, I get caught in the back-blast of my own spell, but it's a decent trade. Normal skunks are bad enough—a System-enhanced one features in my northern nightmares.

The entire fight takes less than five minutes to finish. It's a scary thought, but fights have become so routine, so simplistic even when we aren't over-Leveled against the monsters we face, the entire damn thing is boring. It's rare now for fights to actually force me to concentrate. I know, having chatted with a few "real" soldiers from before the System, arrogance like this is a good way to get killed. But I wonder if that piece of wisdom is true anymore.

Back then, a misstep meant a bomb going off in your face, a bullet to the chest. Make a mistake and even if you came out alive, you were in for days, years, of permanent pain and reconstruction. Now, ten minutes later, you're good to go. And with the way HP works, what would be a deadly attack for a

Level 10 is nothing more than a scratch for me. So where's the line between the wisdom of the past and the reality of the present? I'm not entirely sure, and it worries me.

"John, head east. Mikito, southwest. We have other teams dealing with the smaller incursions."

Ali's tone of command breaks my musings, bringing my attention back to the present. Whatever my thoughts, they aren't pertinent to our current excursion.

Hours later, Mikito and I meet again in the center of town. Teams of scavengers have gone to pull the many corpses back to the town center, where we'll loot then dispose of the corpses through my intermittently opened Portal. In the meantime, Mikito's showing me a few new forms to play with. When the notification finally pops up, I find the slight tension in my shoulders relaxing.

"And it's on. Mikito, Peshawar. John, Kuala Lumpur," Ali orders once he's assessed the information transferred.

"Damn it." I don't have access to Kuala Lumpur. It wasn't exactly on the list of places for me to visit. Which I guess is why the Movana chose to attack it. Either way, it won't stop me. I can pop down to one of the nearby cities with a long-range teleportation pad and get sent to the city within seconds. It'll just take a little longer. I'm already forming a Portal for Mikito.

"Good luck," Mikito says to me as she ducks through the dark oval.

I hope that wherever I'm sending her, it's safe. Not being able to tell what's on the other side has caused more than one problem for the Erethrans before. It's why, even though I've tried to visit as many new locations as possible to set down waypoints, I've also had to do more than just pop in. Moving around the city and its surroundings enough to lay down sufficient waypoints means that an ambush is much harder to set.

It's only when the Samurai is gone that I realize I forgot to wish the woman well too.

Oops.

I'm sure she'll be fine.

Chapter 19

Sometimes, when you bitch, the world answers. I'm once again reminded of that fact as I—amusingly enough—crouch on top of Malaysia's famous twin towers, the night sky twinkling behind me. No haze today—or any day recently with the decline of gasoline-powered vehicles. I'm crouched right between the two towers actually, on the skywalk they'd created. I chose this spot for a few reasons, including the fact that I didn't expect anyone would think I'd be dumb enough to pop into being hundreds of feet in the air on a gently swaying platform when there're more comfortable, indoor locations.

Good news is, there wasn't an ambush awaiting me. Bad news—the forces the Movana sent to take over the city consist of six peak Advanced Classers, twelve mid-range Advanced Classers, and one brutish Master Class. The biggest problem is, one of the peak Advanced Classers was actually a Mercenary Commander whose Skills boost the entire mercenary company's stats. That left me with the dual problem of locating either of those priority targets and ending them. And deciding who to go for first. I can't let them take the city or we'll lose our vote, but as Mercs, I'd rather keep the body count down if possible.

"*Ali. Anything?*" I call, hoping his answer might give a clue which way fate wants me to go.

"*Still updating. Lots of interference, but data's coming in,*" Ali says, floating above the drop. When I look at him, I feel my stomach lurch a little, but his body doesn't even move under the winds which buffet us up here.

Take out the man who is boosting everyone or the blade driving straight for the heart of the settlement. Normally, it'd be an easy choice—take the Commander because his increase is wide-ranging. But I'll bet they've got a few Advanced Classes protecting the Commander. So not attacking him actually pins down and makes useless a bunch of their men.

As I ponder, the data flashes again and details on the Master Class updates. He's headed straight for the City Core. If he takes it, he can transfer the city's numerous defenses over to the attackers, making the battle even harder. Even if we take it back, this fight is as much about morale and showing that we can protect our friends as much as it is winning. We don't just have to win; we have to win with style.

"Okay, these dots are probably the command group. Lots of data flowing in and out from them, and the comm boys are intercepting a bunch of encrypted traffic flowing towards them. They're trying to shut it down, but well, they're under-Leveled," Ali says.

I judge distances and angles, manipulate my map for a second, and watch as it updates as I plot where to go and how. Without any major waypoints in the city, I need to start setting some down while I traverse the area. At the rate the Master Class is going, I figure I have about eight to ten minutes before he hits the City Core. Maybe more if the resistance he faces is significant enough.

"Can you plot the fastest way in to the command group?" I send over the link while I spend a few moments pulling up the details of the Malaysian defenses to add to the map. Better to have two heads rather than one.

Interestingly enough, unlike the rest of us, the Kuala Lumpur's settlement owner invested incredibly heavily on fixed defenses. Not only is there the usual slew of beam turrets, mobile sentry robots, and settlements shields, there are also explosive wards, lightning, fire and ice orbs located in self-contained and self-managed turrets. The entire city seems to have been restructured to create a slowly shrinking ring of traffic around the City Core. Multiple layers of shields and walls have popped up since the attack, forcing attackers to either follow the route or blast their way through a settlement shield. It takes me a moment to realize what it looks like—a tower defense given life.

Of course, any attacker can punch their way directly through—and the Master Classer is—but the shields regenerate so fast taking them down requires a ton of Mana and firepower. Rather than waste their Mana on fixed, regenerating defenses, the majority of the mercenary corp has elected to run the ring.

"Done. But I don't think they're going to be able to hold against that Juggernaut."

"Then we need to be fast." I share my own plot with the Spirit who does the same with me. Within seconds, we've adjusted the plots to come to a common consensus of where and how we should go.

"Ready when you are."

I don't answer the Spirit, instead bunching up my feet beneath me and throwing myself forward, taking through the air. At the apex of my jump, I Blink Step. I hit the roof with one bounding step, bouncing forwards across the gravel top and push off for the next roof even as Ali zips along behind me. Two more Blink Steps, one right over a dagger-close firefight in a crowded back alleyway, and I'm nearly on them, my speed fully built up.

Momentum and one last Blink Step takes me into the middle of the command group, a human wrecking ball covered in Shields and blades, tossing aside the outer ring of mercenaries. Even at the speed I'm moving, I've got enough time to scan the group for their Classes. In the middle of battle, Ali's simplified them all to say Guardian, Warrior, Paladin, Soldier, Mage, or Mercenary Commander—a guide to what I can expect rather than an unusual Class and title I have to spend precious seconds understanding.

"Now!"

The Mercenary Commander roars the command as the Guardian and Soldier next to him brace and take my charge, absorbing my momentum with their mass and Skills. Even as I come to a stop, the mercs are reacting, some picking themselves off the ground while others are training weapons and Skills at me.

You are Quantum Locked. Teleportation and dimensional shifting is restricted.

It's a trap. Of course it's a trap. I duck low as spells impact, and I drop the grenade from my hand. The obfuscation grenade throws up smoke, metal particles, and chaos Mana in equal order to disrupt senses. A moment later, the chaos grenades I dropped on my way in explode.

Luck. It's on my side this time. A howl echoes through the battleground as a tornado of sound and wind appears where one grenade dropped, incapacitating the nearest merc and driving all of us to the ground. Even through my resistances, the pain is enough to shake me for a few precious seconds. Extremely dangerous as the second chaos grenade had formed a ball of chaos energy. It constantly spits out a stream of random energy and material. I see a single shot tear apart a Fighter's arm like wet paper while a second blast completely heals another Mage. Another merc gets hit with a stream of what looks like soda water while the ground turns into Jell-O around another energy burst.

Fortunately, I don't get hit. In the few seconds of peace I've been given, I begin the next steps, calling down the Beacon of Angels while my other hand forms my sword, trailing weapons appearing behind it. I step forward and lunge at the defensive shields the Mercenary Commander's bodyguards have put up.

"You're trapped, Redeemer. Give up or else we'll tear this city down, brick by brick," the Mercenary Commander says, having recovered nearly as well as I have. I can't even tell what sex it is—if it has a sex—as it uses a voice synthesizer and, like anyone with a pair of brain cells to rub together, it has a full-face helmet with visor. It looks roughly human, even if its arms have webbed wings beneath them.

"I haven't even started," I say, watching as the recovering mercs target me. My swords have punched through the portable shield the Soldier was using, but the Guardian has switched places with the Soldier with a weird push-pull swap Skill. It's not quite teleportation, but it's so smooth it might as well be. That's okay, because the attack was mostly a distraction.

"Say hello to the rain, baby!" Ali crows, making himself visible as he punctuates his words with a thump of a drum.

Those who look up get a chance to see the incoming beam, but everyone else just gets hit. Power pours onto us, my Soul Shield absorbing and displacing the damage before it cracks and breaks. My Hardened and Elastic Skin Skills provide little benefit right now, the damage being direct Mana damage; they only protect me from secondary effects. But Shields and skills are insufficient, especially since I call a second Beacon immediately. A portion of my mind splits enough to toss up a Soul Shield while I stab a Minor Healing Potion into my thigh, recovering my health.

The Beacon is pure Mana, a rip in the plane of existence itself. It overloads the environment's ability to handle the Mana within seconds, setting fire to the air and searing the earth, the asphalt melting beneath our feet and the earth itself smoking. Buildings which have lasted through the apocalypse itself and the battle for settlements become naught but torn ruins, brick and cement vaporizing or shattering under the force of the winds.

Once the Beacon falls—and my Shield along with it—I throw out another Spell—Firestorm. The flames from the attack erupt around me, eating into flesh and bones, searing skin and crisping hair. Choked off screams ring all around me as throats are burned raw, lungs robbed of oxygen.

When I'm done, only the Advanced Classers are left. Almost all the Basic Classers are but crispy corpses, their health insufficient to handle the damage I have laid out. But there's a price for a flashy attack like this— between the

Skills, my Blink Steps, and my buffs, my Mana is down by half. At least my health is mostly there, the small amount taken from my own spell recovering.

"They were good men..." the Mercenary Commander snarls as he levers himself upward. The helmet is shattered, the armor cooked away, the skin-wings under his arms gone. For all his talking, I notice the Commander's hands moving at his belt, probably throwing out commands and Skills. A second later, the helmet drops off his neck entirely, separating and revealing a double-snouted face with tiny beady eyes, a face that is busy consuming a weird red globule. A health potion variant for sure, since the Commander's skin heals right before my eyes.

"Shouldn't have messed with the best," Ali crows from above.

The Spirit twists away as a surviving Soldier opens up with a beam rifle hooked up directly into its arm, sending a spray of electric darts even as the Spirit accesses my storage. Within seconds, more obfuscating grenades are tossed out as the Spirit flies around, dueling the Soldier. I don't have time focus on him as I call back my swords and tear into the pair of bodyguards who are still standing.

The three of us dance, my superior Skills chipping away at their armor and weapons. Unfortunately, both of them are actually more skilled than I am—decades of experience fighting humanoids compared to my half-decade of fighting anything that moves. The two of them are able to dodge a good chunk of my attacks while chipping away at my own health.

The Commander is relaxing a little, seeing as they seem to be on the winning end after my initial display. At which point, I decide to pull the rug out from under him, having sucked my Mana Bracer dry while dueling the pair.

Vanguard of the Apocalypse kicks in with an exertion of will as I throw a sweeping cut boosted with Cleave. The explosion in attribute and speed catches the Guardian by surprise, his hasty block pushed aside and my blade disemboweling him. Another exertion of will and mental energy and a Mud Walls forms behind the pair, pushing them toward me. The Soldier doesn't budge an inch as his Skill Hold your Ground counteracts my spell. The Guardian, on the other hand, isn't as lucky and is pushed forward, right into the Thousand Blades which are still moving.

"Suppressive Fire," the Soldier snarls, triggering a new Skill.

I end up throwing myself sideways, feeling beams burn my calf and ankles as I move a touch too slow. Truth be told, the additional wounds are nothing—our flesh is already cooked from the melted asphalt. I'm just grateful the Soldier feels the need to scream his Skill usage.

As I recover from my roll, pain held at bay by discipline and my resistances, I find my beam pistol in my hand. I've already dropped the Vanguard Skill, the momentary boost having done its job. Instead, I rely on the beam pistol as I move in the obscuring smoke and dust, firing at the Soldier and the Mercenary Commander who has pulled out his own bulky assault weapon. With my last sword passing through the corpse of the Guardian, I dismiss them rather than wasting further Mana, flicking my Soul Shield back on. It's going to be a long fight and these guys are just the appetizers.

The attack comes from nowhere. I sense the movement a fraction of a second before the blades are about to plunge into me. Insufficient time to dodge, insufficient time to block. I try anyway.

Rather than searing pain and repeated notifications of poisoning, my senses process the distinctive ring of blades. Twisting to the side as I move backward, I spot the Master Class assassin in desperate battle with Ingrid even as the bait disappears further into the obscuring smoke.

"About time," I gasp in relief and drop behind a crumpled corpse.

I'd shoot the damn assassin, but the pair are fighting so close and fast I'm as likely to hit my friend. Still, I have to grin as our trap finally worked. I'm even happier to see that the assassin is bleeding and fighting with only a single arm remaining. Part of the reason we spent so much time plotting my route and taking a couple of detours was to ensure our assassin could get in place in time.

"Incoming," Ali snaps, and I stare at the minimap. It's fuzzy and jumpy but slowly getting better as the interference from the massive Mana dumps and the chaos energy disperse. Thankfully, since those are our grenades, we've got their Mana signature stored, giving us a slight advantage in clearing our screens.

I cast the Improved Invisibility spell and scramble upward, putting away the beam pistol. I stalk the Soldier as he comes across Ingrid and the assassin, visibly hesitating to take a shot like I did. The hesitation costs him, for I take his arm then his head with my swords.

"Need help?" I send to Ali.

He sends a mental confirmation, then almost immediately updates me with a new minimap. I growl, realizing the Mercenary Commander has decided to run for it. I do the math and realize I won't reach him before he hits the reinforcements.

"Ingrid, reinforcements soon," I growl and turn back to the dueling pair. Or at least, where they were. I frown, realizing they've disappeared. "Damn it!"

Without any other target, I run toward Ali while trying to figure out my next steps. I needed the quantum lock down, but with the Commander still around and free, it doesn't seem as though it's going to happen. Killing him and his reinforcements should be possible, unless he runs again. The problem is, doing so will drain more of my Mana and the time I've allocated to this.

When I get to Ali, the Spirit is looking much the worse for wear. He's got a floating electric shield around him, which is taking the repeated blasts from the Soldier attacking him, but cracks show up all around. Still, I manage to make my way close enough to shove all four of my swords into the Soldier's back then twist them out, dropping him.

"Feel like an assassin," I growl.

"Kind of the point." Since he isn't in need of his full size, the Spirit is back to his foot and a half sizing. Unfortunately, this particular quantum lock type disallows the Spirit from fading back into the dimension he normally resides within to interact with me. For now, he's as real as I am.

As we speak, reinforcements stream in and blindly fire into the fog. Rather than risk getting shot, we run toward the nearest settlement shield. It drops long enough to allow us in, chased by beam weaponry. A low whoop of happiness appears behind us, one which is cut off as the replacement shield flickers back online.

"Can't do that too often, John. The original shield is now on recharge and refresh, so each section we take down is weakened."

"I know. We just need to get away from the lock," I answer the Spirit as we sprint forward. Hopefully they'll drop the quantum lock once they realize I'm deep enough in the spiral they won't ever catch up. Or perhaps I'll get far enough away I can shatter it with my Class Skill.

Habit has me running in a zig-zag pattern as I attempt to get to the next shield as fast as I can. It's all that saves me when a trio of spells lands where I would have been if I hadn't zigged. Ice erupts from the ground, creating crystalline towers as the temperature drops and lightning discharges futilely.

"Out of the fire…" I growl, ducking into a nearby building to buy myself more time as I realize one flaw with my newest escape plan. I'm now right in the middle of the mercenary company's vanguard.

"Mr. Lee! Where are you? The Master Class is nearly at our core." The shrill, panicked voice of the Austronesian man rings out in my helmet as his priority

message gets through. A small video image also pops up in the corner of my eyes, briefly obscuring the more important health and Mana bars.

"*I'm quantum locked. The Mercenary Commander got away,*" I say, gritting my teeth. "*He had a lot more life-saving Skills and equipment than expected. We did take out four of the peak Advanced Classers though.*"

"*The Master Class is the issue! When will you be here?*" the settlement owner snarls, almost panting with desperation. I see the fear in his wide eyes and I briefly wonder how the hell someone who panics so easily could have gotten and held the settlement. But...

"*I'll be there as soon as I can get out of the field,*" I say then kill the connection. Thousand hells. "*We're going to have to run.*"

"Yay. More running," Ali says dryly. A flicker later, his entire clothing choice has changed to a familiar red-and-gold suit with lightning bolts along the side.

***

"Made it," I say as I use Ali's viewpoint to Blink Step into a peaceful scene. The guard room leading to the City Core is still in one piece, which is perfect, especially considering it took me nearly four minutes to break the quantum lock and get here. I'd been forced to use some of the Mana I'd regained to port to the nearest rooftop and then more precious time waiting for Ali to get in position, which means I'm cutting it too close for comfort. As it stands, my regeneration has only recovered me to sixty percent of my health and forty percent of my Mana.

"Finally!" the Malay man snarls from a monitor set up high on the wall.

He's hunkered down in the room behind us, the last, last line of defense, with a giant beam cannon pointed at the doorway. Even from here, I can tell the weapon is meant more for taking out vehicles than people. Which might make it just about powerful enough to annoy the Juggernaut.

"Ali?" I call. I absently note the heads of the guards behind me turn toward each other, probably trading glances, but I don't explain why I'm talking into thin air. We don't have time. "Open the doors and let me out."

The guards comply, the doors sliding upward to let me out. The moment the doors open, the noise of battle washes in. Screams, the tearing sounds of walls breaking, and the hiss of beams echo through the hallway before me. I duck out even as the settlement leader screams at them to shut it.

Gods, but I hate politics.

My thoughts are cut short as the wall ahead of me explodes, a fist emerging from it. As the clouds disperse, I'm forced to ask, "What is it with me and big creatures lately?"

I stare at the giant who walks in. The creature could best be described as a mixture of an ape crossed with a crocodile and given a pair of sparkling pink horns. Crouched low on all four of its limbs, its scaly Galactic shoulders still brush against the ceiling every time it moves, its horns tearing channels in the ceiling.

Ooi Eea, Contracted Son, The Great Sinner (Juggernaut Level 29)
HP: 16894/17210
MP: 279/750
Conditions: Contracted, Health Drip, Greater Mana Regeneration, Spatial Lock

"Before you ask. It's a sort of summoning Skill, except it shoves the summon inside his body. It's partly why his health is so damn ridiculous. Good news, it only lasts as long as he can sustain the Mana cost. Bad news, he knows it," Ali says. *"You fight him direct. I'm going to disrupt the bond as much as I can, increase the cost."*

I can't help but let out a low groan at the Spirit's words, but Ooi has obviously done enough looking. Naked as it might be, the creature rushes me, barrelling down the long corridor. My hands move, pulling and tossing portable shield generators, remotely activating them the moment they land. Within seconds, I have four generators right in front of me. Even then, I add a Soul Shield to myself as the living wrecking ball picks up speed and grows purple with literal flames erupting from his body.

"Oh hell," I breathe as the first three shields shatter while barely slowing down the Juggernaut.

In fact, as it breaches the third, the damn thing actually picks up speed as it triggers its titular Skill. Time slows as I run through my options and decide on the stupidest one as usual. I form my floating swords in front of me and hunker down low, bracing the original weapon against my body and the floor and casting Harden on myself.

Then, there's no more time. The impact throws me backward, my Strength insufficient to hold it back, even with my new skill in manipulating it. I'm pancaked against the reinforced blast doors, my Soul Shield having shattered all around me. I feel a tiny trickle of health return from the damage as Elastic Skin activates even as the Juggernaut peels its body away from me, low grunts of pain erupting from its mouth. As Ooi moves away, I get a glimpse of the torn-up floor between where I made my stand and here.

Before Ooi can recover, I hitch my legs up, while supported by the blast doors, and kick forward, sending the surprised Juggernaut staggering backward. I push away from the doors the next moment, dropping lightly to the floor. Pain finally catches up, the cracked bones in my legs refusing to cooperate anymore.

"Fuck."

"Master Class. Weak," Ooi says then pauses to spit to the side. The stream of greenish blood is disturbing to see, as are the numerous broken blades jutting out from the Galactic's body. With a thought, I dismiss them all, allowing the wounds to bleed freely. Anything for a little advantage. "Tricks are fools."

"Yeah, yeah. Be glad I didn't drop you from the sky," I growl back.

"Try," Ooi says with a laugh.

"No can do, boy-o. The Spatial Lock Condition? That's him locking himself down. A lot cheaper than locking down the entire area like you do."

"Fine. Bluff called." I stand as I regain control of my body. Each second lets my Skill and Greater Regeneration tick my health up, so I stall. "But tell me something, how much are you guys paid to lose?"

"Don't care. Fight." Ooi lurches forward, covering the ground in a single step and following it with a well-executed and fast jab. Ooi's body is wreathed with lightning which flows from his horns, his body erupting with power and savagery.

If you've ever had to try to dodge a jab the size of a microwave, you realize how difficult it is. I get most of the way away before the jab hammers the edge of my shoulder. The jab carries with it a charge, frying flesh and seizing muscles slightly. But I'm not just standing around, my sword coming upward to cut at the joints at the elbow. One thing spending four years in a hell planet has taught me—if it's got joints, it's got tendons. Cut those, and you buy yourself time.

His arm droops slightly, but he's already pulling it back as his other arm arcs toward me. And stops as reason overcomes instinct. My floating blades are following the motion of my initial attack, blocking his retaliation. He could push through, bash the swords aside, but he'd risk cutting himself apart. Even so, his retracted arm gets sliced up as it gets caught on the first of the attacking blades.

I don't stop, but neither does he. He launches a low kick strong enough to shatter bones. I step sideways into the attack, feeling the edge of his foot brush against my thigh and leaving what will be a humongous bruise. Even as I step away, my arm is swinging down, the conjured blade falling right into my grip as I cut the exposed foot. It skitters along his scales, biting into the muscle and bone underneath and shaving off a few scales. Ignoring the futile cut, I snatch one of the falling blades with my other hand and swing it to disembowel him. My strike is battered aside by an elbow, a precursor to a rising uppercut.

We dance in the cramped corridor, the Juggernaut and I. The Juggernaut blocks, kicks, and punches, using its tough scaly hide and an occasional burst of lightning from its horns to damage and distract. I swing, cut, and thrust with my blades, using my soulbound and conjured weapon to bleed the monster. The blades flow, lunge, and twist around us in patterns of preordained movement, cutting off lines of attack and movement.

Ooi is stronger than me, faster, and with significantly more health. But the style of fighting I use, the blades which never stop moving, which restrict lines of attack and open at my command, is new to him. Numerous times, the Juggernaut has to abort instinct-driven combos. Numerous times, I see him visibly hesitate as he does the shish-kebab math.

In a close quarters fight like this, at the speeds and strength we use, hesitation is a loss. A loss of one punch, one kick, one cut. But the ones keep adding up. Blows land on tendons and ligaments, shredding scales and tearing muscle. Each attack, each movement, drains the Juggernaut's massive health pool, whittling down the Galactic.

But it's not all one-sided. Even through the focus and resistances, the pain from my accumulating injuries piles up. The creature is too big to dodge fully. The Juggernaut isn't the only one restricted in his movements, and I'm forced often to discard a promising line of attack or defense, to dismiss my swords as

I spin and twist away. But fists, elbows, and feet brush past me, chipping away at my health, adding bruises and light shocks with each attack. Each attack replaces a touch of Mana, is reduced by my Class Skills. But only partially.

A hook comes, cutting through the air and leaving a hiss of ozone behind as I'm forced to jump backward. The charge releases as it brushes against my stomach, throwing me backward even further, and I'm brought up short by the gates again. They creak and groan as I bounce off them to fall on my knees. Blood dribbles from my mouth as I'm seized by a coughing fit, the sweet smell of blood and the acrid burn of raw ozone filling my lungs.

"Not weak," the Juggernaut says, held back by the still-spinning blades. The Galactic is bleeding from numerous cuts and on one knee, its opposite hand hanging useless by his side. Tiny eyes glow with power, lightning wreathing its only arm as it punches forward to smash away my blades.

The two of us stare at one another over the distance of only five feet, unhindered.

"No. No, I'm not." I cough.

It's now a question of regeneration. Once its leg is healed, the Juggernaut will rush me. If my Mana recovers, I can recall my blades, cast a Spell. Blink Step to get away. But the low warning thrum through my nerves tells me I'm nearly drained, the pain in my head from Mana loss mixed with that of an abused body. A glance upwards tells me I'm in the low hundreds now, enough for a single spell.

"It's over." Ali floats down, making his body appear. In his hands, a glowing ball of plasma is contained, one which I can see the Spirit compacting further and further with his affinity as he faces off against the Juggernaut. "You're nearly out of Mana."

I blink, then stare at the Juggernaut, at the Juggernaut's Mana pool. Forty-three. Forty-two. The Juggernaut snorts, anger in its eyes as it forces itself to stand, sending fresh blood bursting from its wounds. Ali raises his hands, the glowing plasma ball a clear threat.

"Move and I throw this at your feet. You'll get real stumped then if you don't block with a Skill. Use it, and your Spatial Lock and Contract ends. And boy-o will make you swim the Pacific Ocean," Ali bluffs while my own Mana ticks upwards, nearly ready to make true his words. Nearly.

"Cheating." The Juggernaut sways slightly, but Ali just smirks.

"Tell your Mercenary Commander he's either going to lose his Master Class or he pulls back," I say softly and push myself up. The injuries I carry—the broken ribs, the dislocated shoulder, the bruised and bleeding internal organs—are numerous, but none of them are crippling. Not yet. It hurts, but I've done pain so much, it's just another day in the apocalypse. I turn on my Aura, the beat of power filling the room. I had it off, since I was fighting alone, but now, I use it to make a point.

The Juggernaut growls at me but doesn't move. And every second he waits, his Mana drains and mine rises. "Done."

"*Wait for it… all right. Confirmed. We're seeing a slow pullback.*"

"Good," I say. "Drop the Spatial Lock and the Contract. Once we've confirmed they've pulled back, we'll let you go."

"*No,*" a voice roars over hidden speakers, the settlement owner screaming in rage. "He stays. We'll try him and strip him down, behead him!"

"Ali, shut him up," I say while raising a hand at the Juggernaut, hoping the Master Class understands that this is not my position. I see the Juggernaut tense but not move.

"What do you think I am, a brainless series of bits? I got nothing here," Ali says.

"Fine," I say. "Drop the Spatial Lock."

"Why…?" the Juggernaut manages to ask.

"Or do you want stupid to get you?"

Behind me, I hear the blast doors twist and groan, straining as they attempt to open. But the damage done to them from my body pancaking against them repeatedly must have shorted out something.

"I'm commanding you to stop!" the Malaysian settlement owner's voice grows shriller and higher.

After a brief consideration, the Juggernaut drops its Spatial Lock and I open a Portal underneath our feet, dropping us right through it.

The loud thump and creak of the walkways puts all our teeth on edge. The Juggernaut growls, sitting down heavily as the glass roof—thankfully System-reinforced—creaks again. Together, we stare at the small park and open spaces splayed out before us, the city slowly smoking from the war it just experienced.

"Chocolate?" I offer to the Juggernaut, a hand held out as I continue to stand. Stupid spine—I'm pretty sure I cracked something in my coccyx. But at least no one else has to die.

***

"Why'd you let him go?" Ali asks me thirty minutes later. I'd have kept the Juggernaut longer, since the pullback isn't over, but the increasing calls for aid from other settlements under attack forced my hand. Better to get rid of this hot potato.

"Killing him wasn't a guarantee. Better to get the agreement and pullback now. Even if asshole isn't letting it go," I say, rubbing my temple.

Thankfully, whoever was actually in charge of the defense was smart enough to let the mercs run when they wanted to. It didn't stop the owner from bitching, but I at least had him on mute and feeding into a virtual avatar of myself run through my Neural Link. It wouldn't fool anyone rational, but stupid isn't rational right now.

"It almost sounds logical," Ali says with a snort. "You sure you're feeling well, John?"

"Any word from Ingrid?" I say softly.

When Ali shakes his head, I grit my teeth. *Damn it, Starling, you better be okay.*

"Isfahan's calling again, requesting ETA. Latest update shows they're really getting hammered."

I mentally call up the latest map update, overlay it with my waypoints, and grunt. "Then let's get to work."

I jump off the building, letting myself build up some speed before opening the Portal right beneath me. Time to bring some hell.

***

Too late. Days later, I know I'm too late even as the transition into Prague tears at my health, the molecules which make up who I am coming apart before snapping back into place. My body burns as I transition fully, the world snapping into focus while the quantum lock symbol appears before my eyes.

"You are too late." Musclehead's voice.

I turn, spotting the Movana, his legs spread and a pair of short blades held lightly in his arms. He's gloating slightly, challenging me. All around me and on my minimap, enemies populate as my Skill and Ali stabilize and do their jobs. Dozens, then hundreds. I look sideways, seeing the snipers who have me bracketed in the city square I chose.

Sishin Narato (Level 6 Legionnaire)

HP: 1890/1890

MP: 1080/1080

Conditions: Buff, Rallying Presence, Impeccable Taste

"How'd you get me here?" I ask, refreshing my Soul Shield while I calculate trajectories and plot an escape route. No Blink Step. Portaling would be expensive and I'm not entirely sure how...

"A simple redirection," Sishin says with a smirk. "Your Skill is well-known. A simple matter to find a counter."

"Working on it, boy-o. Stall them."

"I take it you've taken the City Core," I say.

Seven snipers above. Just over two dozen soldiers on the ground, ringed around me and blocking any exits. They're smart enough to space themselves such that they can cut off any route I choose if I do a direct rush. Musclehead is the most dangerous by far, the only Master Class here. But most of those here are at least low Level Advanced Classers. Good enough to slow me down. Good enough to kill me if I stick around to fight.

"Yes. Order your men to stand down. There is no reason for additional deaths," Sishin says, the swords swinging by his side easily.

"Not my men. I'm just a helper," I say.

"Rubbish. They'll listen to you. If you pull them back, we'll let them leave."

"Okay, Skill is called Spatial Twist. It's an area effect Skill, but it triggers whenever a spatial or dimensional rip occurs. It diverts the 'tunnel,' if you will, into a specific location. Bad news—it only costs a little Mana to keep active. Good news—when it actually diverts, it's a huge cost."

"So what? Multiple Blink Steps and hope they run out of Mana before I run out health?"

"Why let them go?" I say out loud. The unasked implication is why he isn't shooting at us already.

"Orders. We are not your enemies, Mr. Lee," Sishin says, the slight grim smile still on his face.

"Pretty sure the word doesn't mean what you think it does." I look around pointedly at the damaged buildings, the guns pointed at me, and the corpses which still line the street.

"This is just necessity," Sishin says. "If your combatants leave, overall damage will be lower. You will lose less, we will lose less. You know you cannot win at this point."

I grunt, but he's right. With them owning the City Core, I'm locked down from bouncing around. We can't even shift people in, not without them getting killed due to their Spatial Twist Skill. Never mind the fact that getting out is a little tricky right now. "Why not end me now?"

"You make it sound like you'd make it easy," Sishin replies, eyes narrowing slightly. "No matter how inflated your reputation might be, you are a Master Class. And any battle with you would prolong the battle in this city."

"Not worried I'd go help somewhere else?" I say.

Sishin shrugs.

"Most likely different factions within the Movana themselves. He probably is hoping you'll hit them and weaken his allies."

"That's idiotic."

"But effective."

My lips thin for a moment before I give the order to Ali. Within seconds, we're connected to the local communication grid and authenticating a pullout. As usual, not everyone agrees with the decision, but when I stress that I'm leaving, it deflates quite a few of the hotheads. Even so, I spend a good fifteen minutes arguing with my people while under the guns of the Movana, a most uncomfortable situation. But when it's done, Sishin offers me a slight nod.

I still dislike the preening Musclehead, but I have to admit, they've allowed us to cut our losses significantly. It's honorable and maybe a little kind. I wish… well, I wish things were different. I could work with them, I think. But I don't have time to think about it, not before Ali pushes another urgent request for help even as I'm "escorted" to the city limits.

***

"What are you doing here?" I cough and drain the water bottle before spitting some of the residual dust from my mouth.

"All hands on deck, remember?" Lana says with a smile.

I snort but look around the short brownstone buildings which surround us in Harlem, just south of 125th street in New York. "Didn't think they'd drag you in too."

"No one dragged me. I volunteered to come," Lana says, her lips curling up slightly. "I always wanted to visit New York. And when the mermen attacked, I couldn't let it stand."

I laugh, wondering if she was imagining bad silver age comics. Her griffin drops down from the sky, depositing the carcass of a mutated narwhal on the street and tearing into it with its beak. Roland slinks out from the shadows, yowling in communication with the hissing griffin as they vie over the carcass.

"Puppies?"

"I left Shadow with Katherine," Lana says. "Howard's organizing the strays to deal with stragglers."

"Pardon?" I blink at Lana, who chuckles.

"Howard has gained the ability to lead other canines," Lana explains. "It seems it's a side effect of his greater intelligence."

"Huh."

I take a moment to stare at the blinking dots on my minimap but see nothing too concerning. The attack was sudden, but the mermen were more enthusiastic and populous than actually effective. We still needed a large number of bodies to deal with them, but on land, their swarm tactics had not ended well.

"Well then…" I say awkwardly when I realize I have no idea what more to say to my ex.

"John, don't. Not yet." Lana places a hand on my arm. I stare at her hand and she takes it back with a wry smile. "Sorry."

"No, it's fine. We're still friends," I say automatically then scratch my head. "Sorry. Just awkward. I mean, I'm good with you and him. Just… you know."

"Are you really? Okay with us not being together?"

I grimace at the conversation we're having now, of all times. But if not now, when? When the next crisis hits? We've got a moment.

"I am," I say truthfully. "We had something good. Perhaps it could have been great. But I think we both knew I was always going to leave. Somehow. Some when. The Erethrans just sped up the process."

For a second, violet eyes stare into mine. Then she snorts. "Are you sure you're John Lee? Not a doppelgänger from the Forbidden Zone?"

I laugh but shrug. "I learned a few things about myself. People change. I think it's about the only thing that saves us from the ghosts of the past."

"Good. I'm glad. You know…"

Before we can continue our discussion, another notification appears, along with an image.

"Are you kidding me? Thousand hells!" I swear, staring at the giant kraken which has emerged from the sea, slithering its bulk towards the shore. Best part—this damn monster seems to have legs!

***

"That. Was. Disgusting," I say, kicking the dead monster corpse. It managed to crawl a dozen blocks into downtown Manhattan. In the distance, I hear continued explosions as the defenders push the mermen incursion back into the water.

"You could have given me another minute!" Lana complains as she prods the body, moving down to its lower body.

"What are you looking for?"

"Eggs."

I stare at the Beast Master and shudder slightly.

"Got you covered, Red!" Ali chirps, swooping down and depositing the loot in her hands.

I shake my head, wondering how the Spirit got around the war loot option. Then again, maybe I shouldn't ask. Some things it's better to be ignorant about.

Kraken Egg

May be raised by particularly insane Beast Masters. See Beast Tamer manual for Level, skill, and habitat requirements.

Effect: It hatches. Maybe.

Oh hell.

"No time to waste, boy-o. Got another call!"

For once, I'm grateful for the call to action in another besieged settlement. As I leave, I watch the redhead settlement owner literally cooing over the slimy egg in her hand.

***

Days later, we're all seated around the boardroom in the public library in Vancouver. Glowing next to us is a projection of the world, the numerous settlements displayed in differing colors denoting their alliances. I stare at the slowly spinning globe, too tired to really see it. Even with a high Constitution and Willpower, the sheer amount of fighting we've dealt with—and the amount of high Level fighting too—has been draining. I haven't slept in days, and I know Mikito has only managed to catch an hour at my insistence. But...

"How'd we do?" I ask, the slow blinking red of some settlements showing where continued fighting still occurs. Of course, they've requested help, but considering the forces arrayed against them, we've declined to get personally involved. One danger is getting stuck—forced to fight till we release a quantum lock, during which another settlement is attacked while we're helpless to provide assistance. It's happened once before, after all.

"We're currently up four," says Lana. "We lost a half dozen settlements to the Movana, but the Truinnar used the distraction to take a few locations themselves. The champions managed to win a few others. The Chinese were particularly effective at re-establishing in Mongolia as well."

I grunt, staring at the estimated votes we'll get. Eighty-two percent. If everything goes well, if everyone follows through and we don't magically lose anyone else. Four successful assassinations, ten more failed ones. Enough fear to make us lose a couple votes. Still, even with our troubles, we're up. Many of the independents and humans who had been on the fence finally agreed to back us, deciding to grab whatever benefits they could get rather than be forced to stand aside and watch others reap it all as we're coming up to the finish line. We might even see a few more defectors. Or so we can hope.

"Well done," I congratulate the group.

Still, our success is not without some cost. There's been no word from Ingrid. We spent a decent chunk of Credits to confirm she's alive, but her Skills make it very, very expensive to learn more. All we can do is hope.

Now there's just one last thing. The actual vote.

Chapter 20

"Incredible," Lana whispers, and I have to agree.

We're standing on the viewing platform of the International Space Station, watching as Earth spins below us in all its blue-and-white glory. Amazingly, the station itself has survived the entire apocalypse and come out the other end bigger and better than before.

"I never get tired of looking at it." The speaker is clad in a simple blue jumpsuit, no armored plates or weapons on him at all, and approaches from my left. The salt-and-pepper-mustached astronaut offers us a smile when he notices he has our attention. "Though the view has changed from the first time I saw it."

"Commander," I say, slightly breathless and wide-eyed. I offer him my hand with a jerk. "Thank you. For letting us on."

Phil Katz, Overwatch, Space Commander, Star-born (Space Commander Level 8)

HP: 980/980

MP: 3780/3780

Conditions: Spatial Awareness, Domain, Gravity Shield

Lana and Mikito cock their heads at me. I ignore their incredulous looks while Commander Phil Katz shakes my hand. After I shake it a little too vigorously for a little too long, he peels his hand away and flexes it discreetly.

"You've done an incredible job on the station. It's a Fort, right? How'd you get the Credits to get it fixed up?" I say as I wave my hand around.

The ISS is no longer the modular, creaky science and exploratory habitat it was before. Now it's a fully functioning, five-kilometer-long space station with multiple docks for spaceships, remote-controlled arms, a greenhouse, and yes, artificial gravity.

"Now that's cool." Ali's thoughts break through my excitement, along with a notification.

Title: Star-born

A unique title available only to those who are born in the stars (or it looks like, were in space when the System came into play - Ali), the title holder gains an intuitive understanding of space. Of course, the Star-born are hampered when on a planetary object, facing greater difficulties than the landlocked.

Effects: +10% increase in all attributes, Skills, and spells while not on a planetary object. Receive a 10% decrease in all attributes, Skills, and spells when on a planetary object.

The Commander smiles, obviously used to answering impertinent visitors, and humbly but concisely regales us with his and the crew's adventures. Very soon, the Commander has a small audience as other humans drift over to listen to his story. It's no surprise. The man is both naturally charismatic and pre-apocalypse famous. But like all good things, it has to end.

"Now that we have more people here," Phil says before he looks around and waves.

A notification blooms in front of us, one titled "Rules of the ISS."

"I'm sure you've all seen this," he says. "But I'd like to remind everyone the gathering held in my station is at your request. There will be no violence during the event. Furthermore, there are specific restricted locations. Individuals found breaking the rules will be ejected from the station immediately. There are additional rules for emergency evacuation as well, which I recommend all of you read and comprehend."

There are nods all around. One of the few advantages of using this location is that up here, the chances of an assassin showing up are extremely low. After all, entry and exit from this station is extremely closely watched. It makes the station a perfect location for the last few hours before the vote. In addition, a number of the settlement owners, including Lana, want to speak with Phil about expanding the station to improve Earth's ability to trade with the wider galaxy.

As a newly developing Dungeon World, we have a strong draw as a trade hub due to all the rare loot and materials which come from the various imported monsters. Add the mutations of our own terrestrial species and well, we've got a lot of trade material. However, the fact stands that not all spaceships are designed to enter atmosphere, so it makes more sense to develop the station to receive incoming freighters and transfer goods back and forth using dedicated transport shuttles. Of course, the upgraded Fort needs a significant influx of Credits to become a fully functioning trade station.

With his pronouncement made, the various other humans dispersed into their own groups.

"Well, nice to meet a group of Canadians, but I've got other guests to see to," the Commander says, flicking his eyes to the clustered groups of Galactics who hang around the large viewing platform.

"Of course, of course," I say, smiling widely.

Once he's moved away from us, Phil gets mobbed by the other settlement owners. I admire the man, the way his easy smile never leaves his face even as he answers a million and one questions.

As I stare at his departing figure, I find my thoughts interrupted by giggling. "What?"

"Nothing. Commander." Lana's lips twitch while Mikito does her best to keep a straight face.

"Never seen you be so respectful," Katherine adds.

"That's Phil Katz," I hiss and wave. "These guys, all of them, they're astronauts. The best of the best at... well, anything. And they built this. Of course I'm respectful."

"I do believe it's a little case of hero worship," Ali crows. "Who'd have thought boy-o had a heart?"

"Not me," a silken smooth voice answers, one which makes me tense and straighten.

Lana's gaze darts to where the tall Truinnar is then back again to me, her eyes narrowing with suspicion and summation. I ignore it while silently cursing my forgetfulness. Why wouldn't the damn man be here?

"Roxley," I say and incline my head.

Roxley raises an eyebrow while Vir meets the inquiring gazes sent his way by Lana and Mikito with his usual imperturbable face.

"Redeemer," Roxley says with a light smile on his face. But I can tell he's a bit annoyed at me.

I draw a deep breath, excuses flashing through my mind. I've been busy. I forgot to call. I didn't think we had that kind of relationship. Then I shut down the line of thinking with an exhalation. Later. We've got bigger things to fry.

"Are we ready?" I say, my gaze flicking around us as an indication of what I'm speaking of.

It's strange. Even though theoretically the vast majority of those here are on our side, I still feel as though we're besieged. Perhaps I just really, really want tomorrow's vote to go through. Even though we'll get another chance in another six months, the fragile alliances we've managed to weave could easily shatter by then.

"I have acquired the votes and agreements," Roxley says. "There will not be any surprises on my end."

"Good." I relax slightly, though I chide myself after a moment. Of course Roxley's got his side handled. As long as I've known him, he's handled his affairs well. Well, except for the Duchess, but we were somewhat out-classed then. If it weren't for my willingness to destroy the entire town to get our way, we probably wouldn't have won.

Sometimes, I still get nightmares from that day. There are times when I wonder exactly how far I would have gone. And other times, I know. I'm not entirely sure which is worse.

We try a few more polite sentences of conversation, but the tension between Roxley and me is so high the group breaks up soon after. Lana moves over to speak with Katherine to check on who's wavering and to press hands. Mikito heads over to the Combat Classers to do much the same, in a more direct manner. Me, I head toward Bipasha to confirm we're good to go.

As I close in on the Bangladeshi woman, I see her in the midst of a discussion with the Chinese representatives. My lips thin slightly, especially as I realize my lip-reading won't be of much use here. Obviously their choice to use Teochew rather than Mandarin is specifically to avoid people like me lip-reading them. It's particularly annoying since I actually went and bought the language package from the Shop.

"Mr. Lee."

"Redeemer."

"Sir."

Various other greetings flow from the settlement owners, Bipasha, and their aides. I return the greetings politely enough, smiling and nodding, but it doesn't take me long to note one particularly young fellow, with a great head of hair and a slight curl to his lips, paying particular attention to me. A quick perusal of his Status offers nothing suspicious.

Fang Lei, Bridge of the Two Rivers (Chosen One Level 38)

HP: 1280/1280

MP: 980/980

Conditions: Shielded, Poison Resistance, Fate's Kiss

"Interesting Class," I say to Fang Lei.

The man's smile grows wider, though smile is a bit generous. Smirk would be a better description. "It's a prestige Class. Much like yours. Paladin. What a... Western... Class."

"Galactic actually," I say with a smile that doesn't reach my eyes. "And I'm not sure I've ever heard the term prestige Class before."

"I would not expect you to have. It is a term coined only recently, to describe Classes which are rarer and have more stringent requirements. Those which are prestigious."

"Fang Lei is the only one in China to have received the Class," an older man says with a smile, patting the younger man's shoulder almost paternalistically. "We are extremely lucky to have him."

"And Cheng Shao," I add, just to see to their reaction. It's everything I expected—a slight flinch here, a tightening in the eyes there. It's clear the champion, while internationally loved, is less favored locally. If not for her skill, I have a feeling they'd sideline her even further.

Bipasha, consummate politician that she is, cuts in. "The champion is a gift to all of us, as is Mr. Fang."

No one contradicts her of course—it'd be impolite, no matter what they might think. I'm still curious about the presence of the kid in the station. It's not as if he's a settlement owner. If he was, I'd know, having spent some time memorizing the faces of everyone involved.

"Any idea about the kid?"

"You do realize he's not much younger than you?" Ali retorts. *"I got nothing. Probably wanted to go on a holiday."*

"It sure is pretty up here." I acknowledge Ali's point, but I don't agree. There's no way his presence up here is innocent.

After the stilted introductions, we switch topics to the recent attacks. Interestingly enough, China—or what we're calling China anyway, since its borders have changed drastically post-apocalypse—only had to deal with a single attack in the last few days. Still, the recent widespread attacks and the desperate battles after years of relative quiet is a topic of interest for everyone.

It's only when the conversation lags again that I bring up my reason for coming over.

"I just wanted to check we are settled for the upcoming vote?" I say to Bipasha. I wish I had a better, less blunt way of segueing into this, but… well, I don't.

Bipasha winces ever so slightly, the movement more of a twitch of the eyes, but I ignore it. Lei visibly smirks, but the various settlement owners are quick to voice their support. I can't help but feel a little nervous about them. Unlike many others, we don't have a Contract or any official agreement with the Chinese. Just a guarantee from Bipasha. It's a tad late to be worrying about it, but things have been hectic. I console myself with the knowledge her deal is similar to Roxley's.

"Our votes are with Ms. Chowdury," the Chinese settlement owners reassure me.

Even Bipasha brightens slightly, happy to reassure me she has gotten guarantees from her side of the table. I restrain from asking her to list everyone, mostly because it'd be rude and counterproductive.

Eventually, I take my leave and find a corner near the buffet table. In some ways, I'd prefer to be down there fighting than doing all this. But my new Skills are for more than just show. And so, I open my eyes and let Society's Web appear.

Most, if not all, the threads are what I expect. In time, with more usage, I've learned to discard and filter out the tiny threads which detail the shallowest of connections between individuals. If I didn't, in a room filled with settlement owners, I wouldn't be able to see anything at all. Even now, it's a staggering maze of threads which cluster around the various settlement owners to others of their kind or those below. It's one reason I haven't been using it much within this room and only resorted to it now when I have a quiet moment.

So.

It's as I guessed—Fang Lei is more than a treasured student or someone on a vacation. The threads between him and the other Chinese settlement owners are heavy and almost exclusively one-sided. There's an even heavier thread from Fang Lei downward, one which implies a more powerful hidden benefactor on Earth. Whoever it is, the hidden power is neither a settlement owner nor present. Someone else who does not like the limelight.

There's another heavy thread, one which looks similar to Fang Lei's, which emerges from Bipasha and heads in the same direction. It's significantly thicker than any thread between Bipasha and the other settlement owners, though the thread connecting Bipasha and Fang Lei is interesting. I spend a little time touching each of the threads, finding heavy threads of obligation, duty, and contracts within, as well as a rather interesting amount of disdain. Mostly from Fang Lei toward everyone else.

I purse my lips in thought then turn away, staring at Roxley. Once again, I purposely ignore the heavy thread that runs between the two of us and instead concentrate of the ones surrounding the Truinnar. Nothing seems untoward there. Most of the threads speak of deep contracts and obligations between the Truinnar and others. There's a particularly thick thread which shoots off into space which I linger over, "tasting" the emotions and depth, noting the respect, vigilance, pensiveness, and apprehension surrounding the thread.

I let the thread go and move on, scanning individuals, "tasting" their threads and the webs which form between them and others before moving on. Once again, I feel somewhat stifled by the lack of detailed information, but it is what it is.

"Mr. Lee." Bhale, with his entourage, appears before me.

There's no trace of the friendliness and openness the Movana showed when we first met. Instead it has been replaced with a layer of coldness and professionalism. By his side, Sishin is much more direct as he glowers at me. We met once more after Prague, this time with Sishin receiving the shorter end of the stick. I'd managed to kick his and his team's ass—with the help of a local Advanced Combat team—before the Movana pulled out. That Sishin left a half dozen corpses behind was just one of the vagaries of war. Somehow, I don't think the thought is comforting for the elf.

I quickly do an assessment of the threads leading from them to me and find they are no larger or brighter than before. Other than a layer of hostility in most, there's little change—besides the one from Sishin, and his is no surprise. It's not as if we've had a lot of direct contact.

"Gentlemen," I say with an inclination of my head.

"Your men did very well. I must admit, we were surprised at the effectiveness of the defense and their combat prowess," Bhale says.

"It happens when you try to kick people out of their homes after an apocalypse," I say softly. "What you're facing now are the survivors."

"Yes. Still, you must know we have expanded our holdings," Bhale says.

I snort. Yes. Mostly by taking our cities and one allied independent city. Which reminds me… "Why not just hit the Truinnar? If you had managed to reduce their votes and increase yours, you'd have narrowed the gap."

Sishin snorts and I look at the sleeveless Movana. Since Bhale hesitates to answer me, Sishin decides to do so. "And start a Galactic war? While this might be a Dungeon World, an attack on the bond-breakers would be a direct provocation. Even if we didn't start a war, we'd have to pay significant reparations."

I grunt, crossing my arms. Great. The Truinnar and Movana are like the US and Russia with us poor humans and any non-allied settlements the countries they're happy to wage proxy wars in. But it is a good reminder that as much as Roxley might be friendly, the Galactics are neither good nor bad—just nations looking out for their best interests.

"We are here to ask you, once again, to reconsider your stance," Bhale says. "You ally your Earth with forces you do not comprehend. You meddle in affairs even Legends fear to casually involve themselves in. You are children running alongside the adults during a dance, deluding yourself into thinking you are dancing but are actually stumbling along, making a fool of yourself."

"Whoa. Way to be subtle there," Ali says with a snort.

"Subtle has not worked," Bhale says with a sniff. "You rush matters too much. In a few years, you might achieve what you seek without allying with those you should not."

"Really?" I say, stepping closer. The others tense up, but I ignore them as I lower my voice. "Because the way I run the math, the longer we wait, the less chance we have. People like you and the Galactics, the corporations and the Fist, are all going to chip away at our settlements. Divvying it up. Seems like the longer we wait, the more chance more of your Master Classers arrive."

"It is a possibility. But better to lose your chance than commit your world to politics you do not understand. The Pegasus which flies too high will burn its wings off," Bhale says.

"That's not..." I shake my head. Actually, maybe it is how the story goes for them. "It doesn't matter. It's a little too late for us to change."

Bhale's lips thin, but he inclines his head then walks off. Sishin glares at me for a second more before walking off. I find myself letting out a breath, shaking my head slightly, as tension drains. In some ways, the Movana seem to be nice enough people. It's a pity we've been forced onto opposite sides. But...

But like with Roxley, all I'm seeing is a single facet, a single set of individuals. What they are, who they are, means nothing under the aegis of their respective empires policies and desires. In the end, under the wheels of politics, humanity will be ground away unless we can establish ourselves.

Which is the point of today, after all.

***

Finding a time to speak with Bipasha alone is more difficult than I imagined. It takes nearly the whole night and waiting for her to make her way to the ladies' room. Thankfully, the modified ISS has artificial gravity because while I might admire the astronauts, I'm not inclined to fully experience certain things in zero g.

"Mr. Lee," Bipasha says to me when I catch her in the corridor on her way there.

"Are we really good?" I say, cutting right to the chase.

The woman smiles, her tight, tailored armored jumpsuit shifting as she steps closer to me. "Do you not trust my assurances?"

Her hand lands on my chest. She's so close I can see how flawless the chocolate skin on her face is, smell the exotic scent which wreathes her, sense the swell of her body. In the corner of my eyes, I note how my Mental

Resistances have kicked in even as my hormones rise slightly, but not untowardly. Just enough to remind me that yes, I do like women too.

"Cut it out," I say, glaring at her. "This isn't the time for this."

"Oh, Mr. Lee, I'm sure it's not. But it's what makes it so fun." Humor dances in her eyes as she steps back, the arch in her back relaxing slightly. "In any case, I understand even my charms might be insufficient to take you away from your most recent conquest's side."

"Roxley has nothing to do with this," I say and point at her. "For one thing, we don't have that kind of relationship. And for another, I know you're not really interested."

"Really?" Bipasha says with a sniff. "Thank you for telling me my mind, Mr. Lee." There's a slight pause before Bipasha shrugs. "And perhaps I seek to enjoy what I can, when I can. After tomorrow, many things will change."

"So we're good?" I repeat stubbornly, attempting to drag the conversation back.

"We are good," the Weaver says with a sigh. "All of my contacts have signed and affirmed their Contracts. If there are any concerns, they will not come from my people."

"Great." For a moment, I stare at the woman, sensing something in her. I try to figure out what it is my intuition is telling me, but it eludes me.

"If you are done, I was going somewhere?" Bipasha says waspishly.

I grunt and wave her on, discarding the thought. It doesn't matter. I trust her to be true to her word. After all, we were voting her in.

Chapter 21

Trouble comes eleven hours away from the vote. I'm resting in my room, drained from the constant politicking, socializing, and hand-holding. Rather than snap at another settlement owner, I retire to my room. Having paced, fretted, and attempted to read, I finally gave up and collapsed on my bed to journey to the blessed lands of sleep.

"Wake, Redeemer. The flags of betrayal have flown!"

I jerk awake, sword appearing in my hand as I roll out of bed and scan for threats. The quickly cut-off chuckle from a familiar voice is sufficient for me to relax, though I find myself glaring at the tired-looking First Nation's lady. She's seated on the only chair, head propped on her hands with a smile on her lips.

"Ingrid," I say frostily. I briefly wonder how she could be here and then realize the answer is real simple—

we never did take her off the entourage list for Lana.

"No joking. Wake up, John. We've got problems."

My eyes widen as I stand, dismissing my sword. I almost call it back when the door slides open, but I stop as Lana, Mikito, and Roxley tramp in.

"I really would like to know what is going on. I left Katherine to hold down the fort, but all of us disappearing is not a good idea," Lana says.

"Betrayal!" Ingrid says, adding a little timbre to her voice. Seeing no reaction, she pouts before continuing. "So, good news. I've managed to kill the assassin. Bad news, when I went checking the boards for more work, I found a lot. Not much work which actually pays what I'm worth, but you know, it's kind of the way it's always been, right? You struggle and work hard, but does the rockman ever give you credit? No. Never. It's always, what have you killed today?"

I stare at Ingrid for a second then materialize a carafe of coffee. When I get a few pointed looks, I hand out cups of it, including one to a very grateful assassin.

When she's done sipping it, she gets back on topic. "So I started looking into the jobs. Some of those jobs, they'd been around before, right? And then there are the low-end bids on everyone and their dog. Quite literally. I mean, who hates dogs that much? But there was this whole new set which are serious and have deadlines of, like, ten hours from now. Their targets are all clustered, but they aren't exactly high-profile fellows. Definitely not worth what is being offered," Ingrid says. "I did some digging, and well, looks like the Fist might not be playing straight. Cost a pretty penny, but the contract on you isn't the only one they took out."

I blink, staring at Ingrid, putting the pieces together. One of the facets of the Shop is the need to know the right questions to ask. But once you do, the answers you can get are astounding—if you're willing to pay. Obviously, the information Ingrid collated was sufficient to make her risk asking and paying for the answer.

"Why?" Mikito says with a frown, small hands tightening into fists.

"Politics," Roxley says, a foot tapping rapidly on the ground for a brief moment. It's a surprising amount of loss of control for the normally cool Truinnar. Then again, he's rarely so wrong. "The Fist consider the Dungeon Worlds theirs. Their fears of what you intend to do when you gain a seat—or perhaps of what the other Dungeon Worlds might do with your example— must have overridden their Contract with you.

"It's possible your attack and their betrayal, might have originated from outside Earth as well."

"I thought they'd just stab us in the front…" I muttered. But really, just because they were fight maniacs didn't mean they couldn't scheme like everyone else.

"What do we do now? We can't just let them attack our people," Lana says, frowning. "And why would the Fist risk multiple assassinations? There's no guarantee those settlements will fall the way they want. If they succeed."

"Distraction and disruption," Roxley answers promptly. "I would wager they have forces ready to launch an actual attack to take advantage of any attempted assassination."

I nod slowly. I can see how having someone try to kill you could be distracting. Depending on the targets chosen, it could make a huge difference. With all the settlement owners—or at least their proxies—up here, taking out the second-in-command or whoever is in charge of the defenses could make a huge difference. Especially since most settlement owners are the highest Level residents in any city. I have to admit, it's a decent plan, especially if they intend to betray us. But…

"Why now? Why not wait till the actual vote?"

"Numbers," Ali says. "That was probably their initial plan, but our defense was likely better than what they expected. Even if they walk away, so long as Ares doesn't, we're good."

"Ares is unlikely to break a System contract. Breach of contract for a corporation is a much more significant matter," Roxley adds. "The impact on their rating and reputation would have a much wider impact on their business. No one wants to buy from a weapons corporation which refuses to fulfill their contracts. It is why I believe their change of mind is more recent."

There are nods all around while everyone looks somewhat more unsettled. What was a comfortable margin in case of defection and betrayal has become significantly smaller and tighter. In fact, it's low enough that losing even a couple more settlements would be dangerous.

"Mikito, we need you on Earth. You and the champions," Lana says, the redhead's mind obviously working quickly. "Ingrid, can you liaise with Mikito and the settlement owners who might be affected?"

"About that…" Ingrid hesitates.

"What?"

"I believe Ms. Starling is concerned about letting the source of information be known. I assume the access to such information is often restricted and tracked," Roxley says.

Ingrid swiftly acknowledges Roxley's conjecture then sits in pensive silence, leaving Lana floundering as she rethinks her plans.

"Right, well, the diplomatic group up here will focus on double-checking all our votes again. Hopefully there aren't any additional surprises, but we need to be sure." Lana turns to me. "John…"

"Yes?" I say.

"I'll do it." Ingrid looks at Lana and nods firmly, lips pressed tight. "If we can, I'd like us to hide where the information came from, but worst-case scenario, I lose access. But I'll make sure everyone gets word."

Lana flashes Ingrid a smile filled with gratitude and relief. In it, I can see hints of shared recollection of all the struggles we've faced together. Or perhaps it's just me.

I watch the pair of them for a second before I speak up. "What am I going to do? Should I join Mikito?"

"Ali, how many Master Classes are in play?" Lana says.

"Right now? I got nothing. They've got a bunch, but they're all sitting in their settlements. Probably deterrence to stop us from sending our own forces in," Ali replies.

"Until they commit those forces, sending you down would be foolish," Lana says. "Once you're in play, yanking you out will be difficult. It's unlikely you would be able to finish any fight quickly."

I grimace but nod. True enough. Sometimes, not committing me to a fight is as good a deterrence as sending me down. With the other champions in play, it's not as if we don't have our own powerhouses. But none of them have the ease of mobility that I do. At the end of the day, while I'm a single Master Class and can't be everywhere on the battlefield, the threat of adding a second Master Class to a fight can be an extremely powerful deterrent. "So what do I do?"

Lana and Roxley share a look before Lana asks the Truinnar, "Hardball?"

"Not yet. Let's test their resolve first," Roxley states.

"If it's weak?"

"Then we'll use John," Roxley says, to which Lana offers a nod.

"Hey! I'm right here," I say with my arms crossed.

"We know. We'll send you a list of those you should speak to," Lana says. "If we can reinforce the impression..."

"Viable. But a practical example might be required."

"I'm not going to like this, am I?" I say.

The smiles the pair give me offer little hope.

Hours crawl by as I scramble to complete all the conversations I'm allocated. Between the high Constitutions among the populace up here which reduces or eliminates the need for sleep, the settlement owners from all over the globe, and the myriad rest habits of the Galactics, there's always someone to talk to. Or threaten. Or cajole. Hours of walking, talking, sipping, and drinking. Of playing the social butterfly.

In time, everyone realizes something is going on, though what exactly might not be known. When Lana finally comes up to me during a break, I find myself grateful.

"Any news?" I mutter softly.

"Three attempts. So far, we lost one settlement and are in the midst of fighting for two more. The Movana have continued their push too and even increased their attacks, which have kept the champions busy," Lana says. "We're going to need you to speak with the Fist."

"About this?" I say with a frown.

"Five minutes. In the observatory," Lana says.

"Exactly what do you want me to do?"

"Just be yourself. Convince them, if you can, to keep their word."

I can't help frowning at her words, but Lana gives me a mysterious smile before she walks off.

When I make my way to the observatory, I'm somewhat surprised to note the crowd. Then again, perhaps I shouldn't be—with so few hours left till the vote, most people would be up. Drawing a deep breath, I let it out slowly to calm my nerves before I make my way to the Fist. Interestingly enough, or perhaps tellingly, it's only Asgauver and Emven up here today.

"Asgauver. Emven," I say, trying to remember to stay polite. At this point, the attacks have made it pretty clear they've betrayed us, but we're in polite company. For now, being polite will provide a better image than acting like a screaming, ranting hillbilly.

"Duelist," Asgauver says, feet spreading slightly. "Are you here to confirm our support?"

"No. It'd be a waste of air," I say, the placid, almost insultingly blasé reaction from the pair immediately making me break from Lana's instructions. "I was surprised you chose to outright break your word and Contract rather than turn us down directly. Not the bold and honorable image of the Fist I had been led to believe."

"What do you know of the Fist, Duelist?" A spark of anger rises in Asgauver's voice at my insult. "You might have lucked into a few Perks and fought a few wars, but we at the Fist are true warriors. And there are no rules in war but the most important—a blade must always be sharpened. You and your dreams for Earth would block our people from testing ourselves on your planet, in some misguided attempt to better everyone."

"And you think we shouldn't?" I say softly, my eyes narrowing.

"You cannot Level those who refuse to fight. You need only look at the average Levels to realize the Artisans' way of growth via production is a lie," Asgauver says. "The Artisans bleat about how important they are, but in the end, they rely on us, hide behind us. Without the Fist, without our trips to the Forbidden Zone, without us clearing dungeons for them, their precious cities would be overrun. The Fist is what holds the Galactic Council together!"

"And so to hell with us on Earth and our hopes of not being dragged into your cycle of war and death," I say. "Keep the doors open, give you guys everything you want, and vote to send even more worlds to hell."

"Yes," Asgauver says. "Because if not, we all die."

"Ah, of course," I say. "Even if you could have designated another world, like Mars or Neptune, as the new Dungeon World. It's too damn hard, isn't it, to build up a non-populated world? So rather than do that, you'll sacrifice billions for some imagined future. The tyranny of the future justifies the sacrifice of the present in your eyes. Well, pardon me if I'm not going to lie down and take it."

Asgauver snorts, shaking his head. "I knew you were useless. You Paladins, you champions and Guardians, you all think you're better than us. Doesn't matter what species. You refuse to accept your place in our System."

"Our System?" I scoff, scorn filling my voice. "This System forces us into a world where the few grow at the expense of the many. Master Classers lording it over Advanced Classers who lord it over Basics who do the same to Artisans. Settlement owners who own and gain experience and Credits and power over those under them, dictating taxes and lives without recourse.

"The System is broken from the beginning, meant to provide only for those on the top. You think because you've struggled to the top, it justifies it all? You think, because a few can progress and climb to the peak it's sufficient proof the System works? Garbage. On the way, you've crushed and killed, taken and discarded hundreds, thousands of others. We're all victims of this damn System. But you'd rather bend to it than make it bend to you."

My hands clench as I stare at the giant Kudaya, the hippo's nostrils flaring at my challenge.

"You speak as if this is new. As if what the System offers is somehow wrong. But it is what it is."

For a moment, I falter as my own words, my own thoughts reflect back at me. But there's a lie in those words too.

"What is, is. There is no justice, no mercy inherent in this world. Entropy takes. Without recourse or consultation, it devours our hopes and ignores our despair. All true, all correct," I say then look at the Kudaya. "But what is, is not what may be. It lies with us to build the world that we desire, to shore up the sand castles of our beliefs against the tide of necessity.

"So yeah, I'll stand right here and tell you and your Fist to get back on board and keep your word. Because if not, if we lose this vote, the first damn thing I'm going to do is open a Portal and take all your settlements."

"Threats are useless without the force to back it up. And I would crush you," Asgauver snarls and leans forward, his giant snout inches from my face as he speaks.

334

"Pretty sure the score's 1-0, ugly."

Asgauver snarls and shoves, a giant meaty arm hammering my body. I'm forced to step back, unable to soak up the full force, a low throb in my chest as my ribs creak. Before I can even draw a breath, Phil is there, between us.

"*Enough*," Phil Katz says, his voice filling the room. "You know the rules. There is no fighting here!"

"Of course you would side with your human," Asgauver says with a snort.

Phil's eyes narrow as he looks over the Kudaya, then he speaks, his voice still calm. "I am siding with no one. You were informed of the rules when you arrived, as was Mr. Lee."

I consider pointing out it was Asgauver who hit me, but decide against it. Something about the way Phil holds himself tells me he would be less than happy with my meddling.

"I agreed to allow the station to be a center point for such events under guarantees from all parties that such altercations would not become violent. If that has changed, then your presence on this station is unwanted," Phil says.

"Please, Commander Katz. It is a small argument. We will all hold to the agreement." Katherine slides in with a smile, gesturing to the others. "No one else has taken any action, and even Mr. Heindra has stopped his actions."

"I'll allow it. As Mr. Lee was provoking the incident to begin with," Phil says then raises a single finger. "But no more. You leave your fights down there."

I grunt and my agreement is echoed by everyone else. At Phil's insistent wave, I move aside to find Roxley and Lana standing side by side, speaking softly.

"Was that what you were looking for?" I growl.

"Almost exactly," Roxley says with a smile. "It would have worked better if you were able to fight, but your surprising eloquence will do. I take it you've been considering the matter?"

"Had four years to think about it," I say.

"Interesting. We'll have to speak about that, but for now, we need to capitalize on your little display." Lana steps aside swiftly, disappearing into the crowd. Leaving me and Roxley alone.

For a time, we stand in awkward silence before I finally muster enough courage to deal with this. "Look, Roxley. About us. It wasn't a mistake, but it wasn't smart. There's…" I hesitate before pushing on. "Something there. It might be more, but after this… if this works…"

"You intend to leave. And my duties require me to stay." His lips twist slightly as he sighs. "Oh, John. Did you ever, perhaps, look into Truinnar relationship norms?"

"No…"

"Oooh… I do think tall, dark, and elfy is talking about paired bonds."

"Then be assured that I understand the context. For us, there is a distinct difference between those who are chosen from duty and those from desire. Neither holds greater value, but they do differ significantly in what is expected of one another."

"Desire?" I cough.

Roxley snorts. "You really are adorable at times. But we can speak of this later. Dinner, after the vote?"

"Uh…" I pause, realizing numerous eyes are fixed on us. I glower at the others before deciding to ignore them all. As difficult as I find our relationship, with all its political, social, and personal implications, it's none of their business. "If I don't have to Portal down and take a few cities, sure."

Roxley laughs lightly and walks off to tackle another figure while I find myself standing alone for a few seconds. I turn when I feel a glare behind my back and find myself smiling at Asgauver as the werehippo glares at me.

Three hours to the vote.

***

Rob finds me soon after, a slight smile on his face. The ex-Secretary of State looks relaxed, in his element out here. As much as he might act as if he's not a seasoned politician, the man knows how to maneuver among the throng with ease. It's something I've had to learn, mostly by watching people who are better than me, but it'll never be something I'm comfortable with. I sometimes wonder if I'm holding myself back and that's why I'm not improving as much—or as fast—as I should.

"Evening," I greet the man.

"Is it, really?" Rob says, looking out into the pitch blackness.

"Pretty sure it is somewhere," I say.

Rob chuckles and tilts his head toward the robot server that comes over, carrying a pair of glasses. He picks them up and hands one to me. "Well then, if that's the case. Cheers!"

I snort but down the drink. It's something a little bitter, a little strong that burns going down the throat and burns even hotter when it hits my stomach. My eyes widen slightly even as I'm notified that I've resisted a poisoning effect. Bah! Once again, my innate resistances make a mess of things including blocking alcohol's effects on me.

"Nice. I'll have to keep this in mind," I say while looking around for Ali.

I spot the damn Spirit a short distance away with a glass in hand, regaling a group of Galactics with a story. I decide not to lip-read or listen in. It's rather embarrassing listening to the damn Spirit talk about our adventures, especially since he seems to feel that our "regular" adventures are nowhere near exciting enough and thus carefully shapes the truth.

"So we never talked afterward. But are you okay with this?" I say, gesturing toward Bipasha.

"Couldn't really ask for more. We're not what we were," Rob says. "Vice-chair is more than sufficient. Surprised the Chinese let it go actually."

"As am I," I say. "But Bipasha says they'd rather have their tenterhooks directly in her."

Rob can only shrug before he points at where Asgauver stands. "Heard what you said. I have to admit, I was impressed. Reminded me a little of a little piece of paper dear to my heart. All men being equal and all."

I nod, deciding not to comment. The ideals his country was built upon, which were consciously chosen, are hard to argue against. Yet those ideals, those beliefs—like so many other things—are easy to betray in application.

"We do what we can," I say.

Rob flashes me a half smile before offering me a salute with his glass as he wanders off. Once again, I think it's a pity the man doesn't have the votes to win this. But needs must.

Chapter 22

For all the drama leading up to it, for all the nail-biting tension and the last-minute discussions in political realities, the vote itself is entirely banal. When the time comes, even those who have chosen not to come up to the station may cast their vote from the safety of their cities. Our presence on the station is a matter of convenience and preference, a desire to meet and mingle, rather than need. Even the proxies here are mostly proxies for networking, not voting.

During the vote, Lana's eyes defocus as she reads through the notification, then they slightly tighten as she makes her decision. It happens quickly. By the time I look at Roxley and the Truinnar, most of them are done too. It's mostly the humans who take their time, reading through the notification in detail. Perhaps it's our concerns about things like predatory contracts and terms and conditions or just a general distrust of the System. In either case, results show up on the simple bar charts and globe Phil has taken the time to set up.

"Looks like the Fist really did betray us," I say softly. Damn them. They'd managed to take a couple more close-by settlements in the interim.

"They're not pulling back either, boy-o. I'll keep an ear out, but I don't see them backing down. You might have to miss your dinner."

I'm amused to see that Asgauver, for a brief moment, actually has the highest number of votes—before the votes for Bipasha arrive. Immediately, her bar eclipses Asgauver's and even the Movana's.

"Do we have enough?" I ask, turning to regard the globe as lights shift and turn on. "And any variations?"

"Nothing yet," Lana says as she tilts her head. I'm not surprised to see her doing so, probably listening to her AI and getting an update.

Another jump as a slew of others finish their voting and Bipasha's numbers push past fifty percent.

"Come on…"

I shift from foot to foot as the bars creep upward. I'm just grateful the vote is done by the System. Even then, seconds seem like hours as I wait. Around us, whispered conversations of Galactics and humans dominate, while the low hiss of the ventilation system underlines every word. In one corner, Bipasha stands, her lips slightly parted, anticipation radiating from every inch of her body. Beside her, the Chinese settlement owners wait, a sardonic, imperious look on Fang Lei's face. I blink and realize the deeper shadows in one corner of the room contains a friendly assassin.

I draw a deep breath, and by the time I exhale, the numbers update.

"That's it?" Katherine says beside me.

I understand her feelings. Where's the swell of music from the orchestra, the drum roll? The crash of thunder or the cheers? Instead, there's just a floating bar chart and a single notification.

Congratulations to Earth (Planet XVI.1928813) for voting Bipasha Chowdury as your representative to the Galactic Council.

Your representative (or a designated representative) has 94 Standard Days to arrive and take her seat.

Additional details and benefits will be provided when you have successfully completed this mandatory quest.

"That's it," I say. Eighty point one percent. Thousand hells the vote had been close.

I look around, spotting the few who voted against Bipasha. The Movana look unhappy and are moving toward Phil as a group with haste, shoulders hunched and eyes gliding over the groups as they looked to leave. The Fist are standing in their own corner, focused on perusing notifications of their own.

Probably from the on-going fight below. A part of me wants to head down there immediately. Now that things have played out, Ali is already feeding me notifications about the state of affairs on Earth. How the Movana have pulled back their forces while requesting a cease-fire and how the Fist are still fighting. Since I'm not the only Master Class in play, I should be able to go down, right?

"Just wait a little bit," Ali says, obviously reading my mind. "I'm pretty sure Bipasha would be annoyed if you left during her victory lap."

I find myself grunting in acknowledgement. The Bangladeshi woman is radiant, all smiles and glowing with the light of victory as other settlement owners gather to offer their congratulations and suck up a little. I find it amusing—until Rob lets loose an exclamation of surprise and stomps over.

"What the hell is this?" Rob is waving one balled fist as he stalks nearer to the crowd.

Fang Lei moves to block him off, his smirk growing.

"*Boy-o...*"

Your Planetary Governor: Bipasha Chowdury
Your Planetary Deputy Governor: Fang Lei
Your Planetary Vice-Deputy Governor: Rob Markey

...

"That's not..." I exhale, understanding why Rob is angry.

It's not what we agreed on. Not what she told us she had agreed on. And I get why Fang Lei has been smirking, so confident. The threads make sense now, the choices they made. In the corner of my eye, new notifications appear as Bipasha's reputation takes a hit. Contracts set up between us flicker warning signs as her reputation plunges.

"Why?" Rob snarls over Fang Lei's shoulder.

"Because you people are unworthy dogs," Fang Lei says.

My eyes narrow at something in his voice... I look toward Bipasha, but I'm too slow. Phil, sensing something is wrong, is turning too, but he's too slow as well.

The first attack comes from a hand that lands ever so lightly on her arm. It bypasses her inactive shield because Bipasha doesn't expect the attack. The twist and rip warps her skin and the bone in her arm before it detaches, removing her rings of protection. Behind her, the other Chinese settlement owners attack.

Daggers appear in hands and dart toward Bipasha's body, wreathed in flame and lightning, the blue glow of Mana, and the twisting winds of compressed air. They impact against her secondary defenses, the other enchantments they didn't manage to strip out, the weaves of her jumpsuit as they harden. It's not enough. Her defenses fall one after the other even as spells and Skills trigger. Blades plunge into her lithe body, which is attempting to escape, tearing holes in her clothing and flesh. From the daggers, energy flows, green darkness spreading from her wounds.

I see her choke as another attack, this one from a newly generated metal gauntlet, smashes into her face, crushing her cheek and unleashing pure energy into her skull. Even as these attacks pile on, the crowd reacts. Bodyguards moving to protect her are outnumbered and blocked by other members of the Chinese congregation, Bipasha's men falling under the surprise attacks. Phil takes a more direct route, tapping into his control of the station and banishing settlement owners. But it takes time to locate and target individuals, and each moment sees another attack. The Soul Shield I throw up and my Two are One Skills do little to slow the damage, even as a quantum lock hinders Phil's ability to remove the assailants.

The Indian woman falls, poison, chaos magic, weaponized nanites, and more spreading through her body. By the time I Blink Step to her, a Major Healing spell already forming, it's too late. The pain from the shared Skill is gone, Two are One deactivating as its target disappears. Healing magic cast on her body flashes and disappears as it finds nothing to grasp. Her brain is fried, her nerves torn apart, her body poisoned.

At first silence dominates the room—no screams—then there's more than a little cursing. And laughter from the Fist. Death comes in a blink and it staggers us survivors. The Chinese bodyguards fall backward, but Bipasha's don't. The lock disappears. With a heavy sigh, Phil banishes the remainder of the guards. When he reaches Fang Lei and his pair of bodyguards, he frowns.

"It's done," Fang Lei says, raising his voice to project. There's a timbre to it, a commanding presence that actually makes people listen. "I'm sorry you had to see that, but we didn't want her to change her mind."

"You bastard…" Rob snarls, his fist clenching.

"Now, now. You've got what you wanted. Deputy Governor," Fang Lei says with that irritating smirk.

"You double-dealing scumbag," Rob says. "If you think…"

I step up and clap my hand on Rob's shoulder. The American halts, meeting my eyes and seeing the warning in them. He growls again, but I ignore it as I turn to Fang Lei.

"What exactly do you think you're doing?" I say softly. "In five years, you are up for re-election. And you just lost all of the Indian continent's votes at the very least."

"Five years is a very long time," Fang Lei says. "Much can change in that time. Much can be changed. Those who stand against us will learn better."

My eyes widen at the implications. At what he is suggesting he is willing to do. For the first time, a pit of cold fear opens up in my stomach as I realize who I've inadvertently gotten into bed with. I step forward, my hands clenching, but a look from Phil makes me stop, the warning clear. As much as I might dislike Fang Lei, Phil has already warned me once. I doubt he'll warn me again. Before I can say anything else, a blinding light flashes out from around Fang Lei. My eyes slam shut too late as our sight is overloaded on purpose.

"You dare!" Fang Lei's voice rises in a shout. Dull clinks and clanks resound, the noise all too familiar, as is the low hiss of smoke being released from an obfuscation grenade. "Commander, do your job!"

"I can't see," Phil growls, his voice fading slightly as I sense him backing off. Mana flows erupt from around his body as he piles on defensive measures.

All around me, people are reacting to being blinded. My Mana Sense is flaring like crazy as people trigger even more Shielding Skills to protect themselves from a potential attack. But from what I can hear, what I sense, the attacks are all concentrated on one location. My sight comes back relatively fast, but the smoke that permeates the room obscures most everything.

Most. I see Phil pushed back by Emven, who has launched himself at the Commander. I try to Blink Step to Phil's aid and feel my body lurch forward only a few feet as a Skill degrades mine. I jerk in surprise, turning in time to see a fist come flying toward my face. The fist is as large as my body, and as it impacts, I'm thrown backward. I groan, pushing myself up as my head swims slightly.

You are Dazed!
6 Seconds Remaining

"Why...?" I ask, not understanding why the Fist would act now. This doesn't have anything to do with them...

"For many reasons," Asgauver says as he throws a hook that I barely weave under. Another punch and another as I duck, the hippo refusing to stop talking as he does so. "The new Governor seems to be quite open to negotiation. But mostly because you threatened us."

Spells and Skills flare as I call forth my sword and the other blades. A new notification tells me that Asgauver has learned his lesson, locking me in place with a Skill. Frustration pushes at the edges of my self-control when I see that notice. I'm still not sure who is fighting Fang Lei, how Phil is doing, or where the rest of my team is. I don't have time for this, but I'm not exactly given a choice.

Blade against fist. But I'm eating more punches this time, unable to move as smoothly as I'd like, as the hippo hems me in on the observatory. I snarl, watching as the integrity of my Soul Shield and the Shield from the ring drops, smashed away by the overpowered bruiser. His attacks are simplistic, focused on adding to the damage quotient. But damn is it effective.

Another punch, this one shattering my Shields and throwing me into a pile of screaming Galactics. Their soft bodies soak up my painful landing, though I get shocked by a few reflexive Skill uses. I roll aside before the giant table that Asgauver throws hits, using the smoke, dust, and confusion to buy myself a few precious seconds.

I can't win this. Not like this. But the good news is, I don't need to.

"Point into Penetration. Another into Vanguard," I snarl.

Then, remembering where I am, I trigger the Eye of the Storm. I have no idea where my friends are or who they're fighting—if they're fighting—but if they are, I'd best make their lives easier. At the same time, I let my Aura loose, going all in as my body shudders slightly from the Class Skill changes taking effect.

"There you are!" Asgauver says as he stalks forward. His hands glow again, built up charge filling those meaty bulldozers.

"Yes. Here I am."

Idiot takes the time to talk and let me speak, so I take the time to cast Haste then trigger Vanguard. Everything slows down even further as the spell and Skill boosts my attributes and speed. Then I move.

I'm beside Asgauver before he realizes it, my sword cutting upward into the gap between his arm and chest, right into his armpit. The four other swords follow, spongey flesh that is inordinately hardened by Skills tearing apart under the assault. But I'm moving, not stopping as I pile cuts and slashes across his body. The hippo howls, slamming his hands together and sending a shockwave that pushes me, the smoke, and everyone else back.

I slide backward, panting, as I see the entire room has erupted into battle. Katherine is cowering with other non-combatants in one corner, a series of portable shields safeguarding them. I spot Peter—the Planetary Diplomat—with them, standing at the forefront, ready to trigger his ultimate skill if necessary. Diplomatic Immunity will give him, and hopefully everyone behind him, temporary immunity from all damage. Roxley, Vir, and the rest of the Truinnar are caught in a skirmish with the Movana and their allies, though it seems to be a stalling action rather than a predatory one. Phil, in the small gap provided to him, has actually gained the upper hand on Emven and is literally beating him into the floor with a pipe wrench. And surprisingly, Ali is dealing with both of Fang Lei's bodyguards while Ingrid stands over Fang Lei's prone form, her dagger slowly inching its way toward his brain.

"Ingrid…?" I say in surprise.

The First Nation's woman is bleeding, one side of her body fileted, the bone and a few organs visible. Her foot is half-removed and she's squinting through a haze of blood, but there's grim determination on Ingrid's face. Even as Fang Lei uses his hand, straightened and sharpened with Mana, to slice and stab into her body to throw her off, she attacks.

I raise a hand, ready to trigger Two are One even as I drop out of Haste, but I'm interrupted. Asgauver gets in the way with his bulk, throwing a roundhouse kick so strong it could bring down a building. I do the lambada, dropping beneath the kick and popping back up to stab my sword into the hippo's body. I snarl, shoving forward as I conjure my other blades, twisting and cutting to get around my opponent and cast my Skill at Ingrid. But even though I'm boosted with Vanguard, the damn hippo is too big and wide and the few glimpses I get of her are insufficient, especially as the smoke rolls back in.

"Can't hold on much longer, boy-o."

"Damn it." I snarl and give up, focusing on finishing this fight.

The werehippo's massive health pool and passive regeneration is a problem, as is his ability to lock down my Portaling abilities. A punch comes in and I hop upward, landing on a blade that still sticks out of the Kudaya's body. I cut with one sword into his shoulder to give me even more of a lift before I thrust the sword in my hand. The attack plunges into his eye, blinding Asgauver. As he staggers back, Asgauver unleashes another scream, the sonic attack throwing me into the ceiling.

The ceiling crumples under my body, steel and more exotic metals warping. Phil is distracted for a second, taking a blow from Emven.

As he struggles to his feet, another voice echoes, "We got the station, Commander. Kick his ass!"

Reinforcements pour in, the remainder of the ISS's crew appearing. Like Phil, they've got the Levels and Skills to make a difference, and the moment they arrive, my Skill boosts their attributes. A purple light bathes Asgauver, and I note his Mana bar shrinking visibly under its effects. As the air scrubbers kick into overdrive with a whine, clearing the smoke, the werehippo focuses in on me.

"You will not win!" Asgauver howls.

I release myself from the crumpled metal and get my feet bunched up behind me. I propel myself past the Kudaya, aiming for where I last saw Ingrid. A part of me is swearing, wishing I had her on my party info. But it never occurred to me, not during what should have been a peaceful, even joyous occasion.

"Ingrid!" I slam into the floor next to their prone bodies.

Fang Lei has a dagger stuck in his eye, the victim of a fatal dose of metal poisoning. And real poison too, if I know anything about Ingrid. But it's the First Nation's woman I'm concerned about.

I push against her still form. "No!"

I hear movement behind me and my body reacts, reaching backward and conjuring my sword to block the blow. It smashes into my angled sword and keeps coming, the floor beneath my feet buckling as my hand collapses. But even as the blow lands on my body, I hold myself up and away from the charred, flayed, and still corpse.

"You idiot. You should have run..." I swear at the corpse, tears filling my eyes.

Another blow, the physical pain a dull reminder that a fight is going on around me. But it's distant, a minor ache compared to the loss of another friend. A stupid, senseless loss. She could have survived if she had run. She could have tried again. I don't even know why she acted, what prompted her to kill Fang Lei. We could have...

Another blow, this one so hard it cracks a few ribs. My head throbs, muscles groan, and I touch her body, dumping it into my Altered Space. As another attack comes, I twist and dodge, rising to my feet. My hand conjures a plunger of Mana Potion that goes into a torn, exposed section of armor.

"Face me, you coward. I'll show you why the Fist are not to be angered!" Asgauver swings again, his hand burning with power.

"Ali, have everyone leave."

Then I let it loose, the anger that sits in my soul. The pain I keep hidden. He took my friend away. If he hadn't blocked me, I could have saved her. He cost me a friend. So I'm going to take his life. And his friend's life. And his city.

The world turns red as Asgauver learns what it means to deal with the fury of a Paladin.

***

Frenzy. It's an old Skill, one I rarely use because while it reduces the pain I feel and increases the amount of damage I can deal, along with increasing my Stamina regeneration, my Mana regeneration drops. With the huge drain on Mana most of my Skills have, Frenzy isn't as suited for me as it would be for like someone like Asgauver. But there's a much more important reason to keep it off—the damn Skill doesn't let me retreat or back off until all my enemies are slain.

Interestingly enough, the first time I activate Frenzy after my Master Class upgrade, I realize I'm actually able to think. Previous usages of the Skill reduced my conscious decision-making ability significantly. Luckily, for one reason or another, I have a little skill at fighting and so much of my unconscious decision-making is correct. But against a Master like Asgauver, reacting rather than thinking might be deadly.

All of these thoughts flash through my rage-filled mind in the time it takes to slip his punch. I'm inside his guard, my sword cutting sideways and moving. Because now, I'm no longer fighting him alone. A half dozen others are here, individuals who are part of the Fist or chose to act when they did. The Chinese bodyguards are my first target, a Blade Strike catching one high while I dash toward the next.

Vanguard of the Apocalypse thrums through my body even as my Aura of Chivalry works on them all. I can feel the attention that is drawn to me, the anger and focus targeted at me, and I find myself grinning. Grinning wide.

A cut, a punch, then I grab and toss the other Chinese guard at Asgauver. The giant hippo bats the man away, his body flying into the windows and causing a spider-web of cracks. The hiss and hum of over-worked ventilators surround us, as does the acrid smell of urine and spilt blood. I open fire at other fighters with a newly conjured beam pistol, using the attack to disrupt formations rather than for pure damage. A shot takes Emven in the back of the head, giving Phil the opening he needs to put his fist through his opponent's chest.

Ali is cajoling, pulling, and at times throwing people out of the room. Lana is guiding out Katherine and the other non-Combatants, Shadow and Roland somehow having made their way up here. I'm curious how that happened, but only in an abstract, clinical way. I'm too busy with kiting Asgauver and annoying everyone else, jumping, sprinting, and sliding across the giant room, blades cutting and pistol firing.

Blood flows and Mana drops, my body feeling the strain of my actions even as I push as hard as I can to stay ahead of Asgauver. I don't always succeed, the hippo being larger as well as fast and smart enough to know when to use his ranged attacks. And as I attract more and more attention, the attacks pile on. I bleed health points and suffer actual damage. But the cracked ribs, the dislocated shoulder, the torn hamstring are nothing compared to the anger in my soul and the pain in my heart.

"We're out! Phil is closing down the observatory. You've got until he's done with Emven out here."

So. Emven's still alive. Surprising. But that's more than enough time.

I skid to a stop and turn, holding both swords I conjure in front of me. Muscles creak and my hands tremble as I cross the weapons to soak up the most recent series of attacks, my legs buckling and tearing up the floor beneath me. A pause, a fraction of a second to clear my mind. Time enough to conjure a Skill.

Light explodes from nowhere, filling the room via the windows before the Beacon tears through the ceiling. Metal vaporizes and bathes all of us in the raging inferno of the Beacon's attack. The Advanced Classers in the room die, pain ripping through their bodies as the Mana-based attack ignores their defenses. Air rushes out, picking up and throwing debris into the endless void, while the thumps of blast doors through the soles of my feet inform me the station is taking steps to protect itself.

Asgauver shoulders his way through the pain, grabbing me and lifting me to slam my body into the floor. A part of me is thankful for his actions, for I call another Beacon down on us. I'm sheltered from the direct effects of my own attack by the hippo's leaning body, close enough to see his eyes widen as skin flays and burns away, exposing bone.

When the Beacon dies off, Asgauver has one hand held over me, the other pinning me. He's bleeding, skin burned away, flesh cut and muscles chopped apart from our repeated clashes. The Kudaya is in pain, conscious through a sheer exertion of will. But I'm not much better. I drop all my other Mana-intensive Skills, staring at the bar of my Mana pool. Not enough. But that's okay.

"Any last words to pass on to your friends when I bring your corpse out?" Asgauver taunts, slamming me back into the floor when I twitch.

I cough, feeling something snap in my back. "Yeah. Army of One," I whisper and activate the Skill, watching my health plummet as the Skill takes from my body what it cannot from Mana. Another 'gift' from my time away, an understanding of how the world, the System works.

Blades appear around my prone body even as I conjure the original in my hand and stab upward. Blades, glowing with ethereal power, launch into Asgauver's body with such force he is ripped from my body. I stagger upward, staring as the giant Master Class is pushed outside of the range of the artificial gravity that holds us to the station.

My head throbs with a pain that would probably cripple me if I wasn't in my Frenzy state. I stare at the helpless Asgauver floating in space, his blood frosting over as the giant hippo twitches. Even the Master Class's monstrous health pool and his numerous damage-soaking Skills aren't enough.

"Should have taken their advice," I whisper then gesture, pulling a beam rifle into my hand. I open fire, just in case.

Chapter 23

When I'm finally done, I find myself standing in the silence of space. Ali is darting back from Asgauver's corpse, having flown over and stripped the giant hippo of his gear. A part of me is surprised to note the Spirit's already done the same for the various other corpses, but I shake off the thought as my senses return to me slowly with no additional threats around me.

There's no hiss of escaping air any longer, just the throb of warning sirens beneath my feet and strobing red warning lights which indicate the room has been depressurized. My lungs ache from the lack of oxygen, eyeballs burning and frosting over under the cracked helmet. My body aches with the lack of oxygen, my lungs clawing for much-needed sustenance as my Skill flickers off and pain returns.

I look upward, seeing the gaping hole I created when I called forth the Beacon of Angels, melting armor and damaging the Galactics within. If not for the floor being reinforced by the Commander and an unconscious flexing of my own Skill, it might have torn through the floor too. For a moment, the silence of the vacuum consumes me, the unhindered view of the stars and Earth below bringing with it its own sense of peace.

"*Eh, boy-o. I can keep throwing Heals on you, but you're running out of health here either way.*"

"*Sorry.*" I tap the helmet and toss it back into my storage then pull out another one and clip it on. It's not as good, but for a spare, it does its job perfectly.

A second later, it covers my face, the warmth from my body heating up the tiny sealed space. Oxygen, stored in a small reservoir within the helmet, pumps in, filling the emptiness in my lungs. It's barely enough for a minute of normal use and my body consumes it hungrily.

"*Not even the sense to put on a helmet in vacuum.*" Ali's mental grumbling is comforting in my numb state. A familiar refrain.

With a shake of my head, I walk toward the exit. At the door, I frown, realizing I have no idea how to get in without depressurizing the rest of the station.

"*One second.*" The Spirit darts through the door, phasing right through it before his vision is impressed on me.

A moment later, I Blink Step into the warm, oxygenated corridor. The sudden shift in temperature is comfortable at first then painful, as dead nerves regenerate and cold flesh warms. I grunt through the pain while Phil stands in front of me, blocking my friends.

"Mr. Lee," Phil says. "Take a moment to gather yourself. Say goodbye to your friends. Then I expect you to leave."

"You're banishing him?" Lana says, her eyes wide.

"He continued fighting after he was ordered to stop. He caused significant damage to the station. Be grateful I'm only banishing him for a period and not permanently," Phil says.

When Lana opens her mouth to argue, I shake my head. It's more than fair. And I've got better things to do on Earth anyway.

"Where's Rob?" I ask.

"He's back on Earth, under serious guard," Lana says. "I dispatched Roland and Shadow to join them too. He should be safe enough."

I nod. I know his security detail, and while they might not be Master Classes yet, they're not that far away. If it weren't for their need to constantly guard their charges, with the talent and dedication those men—and women—have, they'd be much higher Leveled. "Roxley?"

Lana shakes her head. "He had to leave. The Truinnar are busy reorganizing and discussing the fallout and keeping an eye on the Movana. There's a lot of fighting going on on Earth now, with the Indian and Chinese settlements mobilizing and the Galactics getting ready to pick off anyone still left standing."

I grunt, closing my eyes, then open them. My voice, when it comes out, is cold and aloof, the emotions shoved aside for now. "Ingrid's dead."

"I know." Lana's voice is laced with pain but carefully controlled.

"Katherine, can you liaise with Phil? Let's see what we can do to help him fix up the station. And make sure this never happens again," I say, and the older woman gives a short nod. I turn to Lana, my voice growing colder as my mind turns. "Get an occupation force ready."

"John…"

"Don't worry. I won't do anything stupid. But they're down a Master Class and are stretched thin. I'm going to take back those cities," I say firmly. "And then, I'm going to take one of theirs."

Lana's brows furrow, but she nods as I knew she would. I turn to Phil, giving him a grateful nod. He didn't need to give me the few minutes.

A second later, Phil engages the station's teleportation matrix and I'm gone to another blood-soaked battlefield. War may be an extension of diplomacy, but it's also what happens when greed overcomes diplomacy.

***

Days later, we're gathered once more, up north. Not Whitehorse, because she didn't come from the city. No, we went further. It took us hours to fight our way up, hours of dealing with creatures that once were a deadly threat and now are nothing but an excuse to vent.

We find ourselves at the remnants of the old cemetery a few kilometers upriver of the settlement. The cemetery is part of the Tr'ondëk Hwëch'in's gathering place, a cultural center that is now barren and desolate, the few buildings shattered and grown over. The cemetery itself is on the top of the hill, overlooking the frozen Yukon River, older headstones and the white picket fence hidden beneath the snow. It takes a little time to clear the snow off the ground and form the grave. Afterward, we deposit her body within.

In minutes, I have a Portal open and friends stream in. People whose lives that quiet, sarcastic, and jaded woman touched. Jason and Rachel, Andrea and Mike, Vir and Capstan. A few of the champions. General Miller. More. People that I don't know but who have requested an opportunity to say goodbye. And so, I open Portals and people stream in. Some who weren't able to reach the waypoints I have available port in.

I have no words, no way to speak of the loss of another damn friend. But luckily, I have friends and they know what to say, what to do. And so, when the grave is closed, people speak.

Some of fond social times. Others, so many others, of times when Ingrid appeared in battle to save them. And some, a select few, of the woman behind the mask. Of the times when Ingrid let her guard down and laughed, when she smiled. When she forgot about the loss of her people, of all her friends and family. And then it's my turn.

"I'll miss her bannock," I say, feeling the weight of the crowd's attention on me. But I ignore them, staring at the small mound of earth that holds my friend. Such a small amount of space for a woman who had been larger than life. "I'll miss her ribbing me, her attempts at keeping me grounded. I'll miss her practical approach to problems…

"I'll miss my friend. But I know, I believe, she died doing what she wanted. I believe she died because sometimes, some things can't be accepted. She died giving us a chance to make Earth better."

There's silence before someone else speaks. I listen half-heartedly while staring at the grave. It's strange. I'm not exactly sure why her death has hit me so hard. Perhaps it's because after coming back after so long away, seeing my friends became more important than I thought. Perhaps it's because I was stuck in hell for so long, and till now, I've not yet had time to relax. Or perhaps, perhaps, I miss what could have been.

***

Time passes and people slowly leave. I Portal nearly everyone away, leaving only a few of us standing in the cemetery. In the corner of my eyes, I see the blips inching their way in, monsters growing slowly bolder as the gathering disperses. Scavengers and opportunistic predators, hoping for the weak or distracted. I briefly consider showing them how wrong they are.

"President Markey called and asked if I would accept the position of Deputy Governor," Roxley says, his voice cutting through the ashen haze that fills my mind.

"Pardon?"

"President Markey called—"

"I heard you the first time," I cut Roxley off and wave. "Why?"

"I believe he's looking for assurance and backing. With the splintering of your other human factions, humanity's position has grown more precarious. We spoke of acting against the groups of Independents within North America, as well as ceding certain territories to regain his United States," Roxley says.

"He asked me for help too," Lana confirms, a slight twist in her lips. I wonder what it means, but don't find the motivation in me to pursue the matter.

"India and China?" I ask softly.

"Already fighting at the borders." Mikito sighs, rubbing her temple. "The champions have their hands full trying to keep the dungeons and Galactics at bay. Cheng Shao is doing her best to slow down China, but there's no equivalent in the Indian sub-continent. They're all—"

"Fighting. Trying to become the top dog. If it wasn't for the internal strife, they'd be in all-out war," Lana says. I have to admit, I'm grateful for human idiocy.

"Can Rob get the votes?" I ask, and looks are traded around. In five years, we're going to have to do this all again. With the current state of affairs, we might get less than fifty percent of the vote if we're lucky.

"Five years is a very long time…" Mikito voices the only hope we have.

Though I took back every settlement taken by the Fist and one of theirs, it's not enough. Not by far. I know more and more of their people are pouring in, an aggressive stance they've taken which hasn't broken into outright war. Yet. Even the additional taxes and entry fees Rob has thrown up are doing little to slow the Fist.

"President Markey also asked if I had a recommendation for the envoy," Roxley adds, and I twitch. "It is just a term, not a designation."

"Heh. Just don't want them returning the favor," I say.

"No. We have rules," Roxley says then smiles grimly. "Though the fact President Markey hails from the same country as the perpetrator has less than desirable optics."

"No shit." I scratch my head, thinking about Roxley's question.

I look at the two ladies, and Mikito gives me a shrug. Yeah, fair enough—the lady is an even worse choice than I am. Most of Mikito's contacts would be less than suitable. Lana on the other hand…

"Stop looking at me like that," Lana says, her eyes narrowing.

I offer her a light shrug and look away. Fine. Maybe I do put a lot of hopes and burdens on the lady. On the other hand, I do note how in the months I've been back, I have yet to actually meet her boyfriend. I'm not exactly sure what it says about what she thinks of me, that even now she refuses to introduce us.

"It's not as if I have a list of people who should go," Lana adds. "It was supposed to be Rob... but..."

"But he's Governor now." I grimace. "And there was no guarantee he'd go. Doesn't he have anyone on his staff he can tap?"

"Probably busy," Lana says with a shrug. "Anyone good enough to go would be good enough to run a settlement. And we're a little pressed on that front."

I can't help but agree. The need for good, competent, trustworthy individuals is not small. In some cases, I know we've had to compromise and go for two out of three. And once in place, not many settlement owners are willing to give up their spots.

"What about Peter?" I say, recalling the Diplomat. After all, we're literally talking about a diplomatic mission. And his work has been good.

"He's on the team, but Rob has suggested we find someone else if possible," Roxley says. "I agree. It would be best to find a Diplomat who is not tied directly to the Governor. This is meant to be a mission for the entire planet."

Fair enough, though I'm not entirely sure asking us is much better, considering we're from Canada. If half the world before the apocalypse couldn't tell the difference between the two countries, I'm not sure it'd be any different now. Still, perhaps we could find a settlement owner with a competent assistant like I had. Of course, people like Katherine...

"Oh. Duh."

"You thought of something, John?" Roxley says.

"Katherine."

Everyone pauses, their brains working on overdrive before there're a few curses for forgetting such a simple answer.

"Exemplary suggestion. I shall endeavor to inform President Markey and allow him to extend the invitation," Roxley says.

"And I'll inform Katherine beforehand so that it's not a complete surprise," Lana adds.

I nod. With that major issue dealt with, Roxley asks for a Portal back to Whitehorse. Lana departs next, leaving me with Mikito and Ali as the monsters close in. The Samurai tilts her head, looking at me.

"So. What now?" Mikito asks.

I consider her words. There are still settlements in doubt, dungeons close to overflowing, a space station commander who needs to be repaid. People to say goodbye to, arrangements to be made. But glancing at the grave, I find a sardonic smile crossing my face as a wave of exhaustion runs through me.

"What do you think of bannock?"

***

A few days later, after Katherine had—politely—bitched about being tossed into the deep end, the Erethrans find me in the middle of clearing a dungeon by myself. With the champions stretched thin by the various conflicts and my reputation for killing settlement owners and taking settlements, I've been banished from dealing with the politics. It doesn't help that my Reputation took a bit of a ding when I wasn't able to completely cover all the deals I'd made. The agreements I'd had with Bipasha were voided after her death, and while Rob was thankful for our help, he was also less willing to play ball. Sadly, the man is smart enough to realize I can't and won't do anything to him, so he's gone ahead and screwed me over a bit to get what he wants. I can't complain too much—it's not as if I didn't sacrifice him earlier to the altar of expedience.

I admit, I'm still surprised to see the Erethrans. The champion looks around the Level 80 dungeon with a sniff and waves at the team of Erethrans, who rush forward at her command. Within seconds, we're left alone except for her usual shadows.

"Champion," I greet Ayuri before I nod at Unilo and Mayaya. "Shadows."

I get a slight smile from Unilo, but Mayaya just stares at me with his blank expression. I roll my eyes theatrically before Ayuri coughs into her hand, drawing my attention back to her.

"I wanted to meet with you before you left," Ayuri says.

"Calling in your favor?" I say.

"It's Unilo's. And no. I wanted to inform you that we'll be leaving soon," Ayuri says. "Matters at home have progressed. It's possible we might need you to return to Erethra at some point soon. Try not to get yourself killed."

I chuckle but sober up when Ayuri doesn't even crack a smile. She's surprisingly serious—for a woman who doesn't seem to take much seriously.

"You crossed the Fist. And while Asgauver and his cronies were not particularly strong, they were connected," Ayuri says. "Your actions have made your position in Erethra even more tenuous. We are, technically, part of their faction."

"You are?" I exclaim.

"Of course. We're a warrior-based society. The Army by itself has nearly twenty-four percent of our population under arms, and that doesn't include independent Adventurers," Ayuri says. "The only way we are able to keep those numbers viable is via Dungeon Worlds like yours."

I feel truly conflicted now. I always knew the Erethrans focused more on quantity than quality for their defenses, though the Honor Guard is obviously the cream of the crop. Still, the realization hits hard. The Erethran's, the group I've somewhat allied myself with are part of the Fist, a group that elected to cause our apocalypse. With a slight shake of my head, I push it aside for later consideration.

"So you figure I'm going to be forced to deal with hardliners if I ever come to Erethra," I say with a slight twitch of my lips. Well, damn.

"When you come, I expect you'll anger many of the traditionalists and Fist adherents," Ayuri agrees. "I would also consider distancing yourself from your people once you arrive in Irvina. It is highly likely you will be targeted."

"More assassinations?" I sigh loudly.

"Among other things. Be careful. Irvina is a hotbed of politics, and you, Mr. Lee, are as subtle as an orbital strike."

The statement gets a chuckle from Unilo. Warning given, I'm actually shooed away as the Erethrans proceed to hog the dungeon. Left with no monsters to kill, I walk out of the dungeon and Port back home, heading for the Shop. I need to pick up a few things before we leave in a few days and deal with all the loot I picked up from Fang Lei's, Asgauver's, and their cronies' bodies. Bipasha's I've returned to her settlement. There's something about looting your allies that seems wrong, no matter the kind of advantage it might give you. But still, whatever else I had to say about Fang Lei and the hippo, they had good stuff. I'll need to rework some of it to be more suitable for me, but I figure it'll be ready for when I get to Irvina.

As I walk toward the Shop, I pull up my Status Screen, looking at the progress I've made since I came back from the Forbidden Zone. It's been a crazy half year.

Status Screen			
Name	John Lee	Class	Erethran Paladin
Race	Human (Male)	Level	23
Titles			
Monster's Bane, Redeemer of the Dead, Duelist, Explorer			
Health	3470	Stamina	3470
Mana	3220	Mana Regeneration	272 (+5) / minute
Attributes			
Strength	227	Agility	307
Constitution	347	Perception	172
Intelligence	322	Willpower	352
Charisma	110	Luck	68
Class Skills			
Mana Imbue	3*	Blade Strike*	3
Thousand Steps	1	Altered Space	2
Two are One	1	The Body's Resolve	3
Greater Detection	1	A Thousand Blades*	3
Soul Shield	2	Blink Step	2
Portal*	5	Army of One	2

Sanctum	2	Instantaneous Inventory*	1
Cleave*	2	Frenzy*	1
Elemental Strike*	1 (Ice)	Shrunken Footsteps*	1
Tech Link*	2	Penetration	3
Aura of Chivalry	1	Eyes of Insight	1
Analyze*	2	Harden*	2
Quantum Lock*	3	Elastic Skin*	3
Beacon of the Angels	1	Eye of the Storm	1
Vanguard of the Apocalypse	2	Society's Web	1

Combat Spells	
Improved Minor Healing (IV)	Greater Regeneration (II)
Greater Healing (II)	Mana Drip (II)
Improved Mana Missile (IV)	Enhanced Lightning Strike (III)
Firestorm	Polar Zone
Freezing Blade	Improved Inferno Strike (II)
Mud Walls	Ice Blast
Icestorm	Improved Invisibility
Improved Mana Cage	Improved Flight
Haste	

Epilogue

The world spins slowly beneath us, showcasing an endless vista of blue. The Atlantic Ocean is covered in spinning white clouds that earmark the start of another massive hurricane, the islands which make up the Caribbean hidden at this angle. A part of me winces at how bad things will get for my friends below. Ever since the apocalypse, hurricanes have included Elementals and Spirits galore, creatures of fickle disposition and violent nature. Still, the violence which is about to erupt is only in my mind. In my vision before me is only a peaceful blue globe.

"Taking one last look?" Katherine asks as she stands beside me, her hand resting lightly on the railing of the ship's observatory.

I don't blame Phil for putting us on the passenger ship as soon as possible, rather than keeping us on the station. Well, not much.

"Yeah. Trying to imprint it on my mind." Not as though it's particularly hard, not with the Intelligence I have. Some things, like an almost photographic memory, come naturally to me now. Just another damn change.

"You make it sound like you don't expect to see it again." The words are uttered like a statement, as if Katherine knows the answer.

And so rather than answer her, I fall silent. As usual, Katherine doesn't push, for which I'm grateful.

"Eh, I've seen prettier planets," Ali says, standing beside us and sipping on a drink.

"Not all of us live in the elemental plane of stupidity," I reply to Ali.

"Hey!"

"Well, it seems both Ms. Pearson and Lord Roxley would regret it if you did not return," Katherine says.

I grunt, turning sideways to spot Mikito seated on a comfortable chair, staring at a broadcast arena match. The Spear of Humanity just showed up at the teleportation pad this morning, as if her presence was perfectly reasonable. When I inquired about what she was doing there, she simply said "Baka," and walked away.

"Perhaps. But it'll be a lot of years…" I finally say.

"Five. Not much longer than when you were gone," Katherine says. "Did I ever tell you thank you?"

"What for?"

"Hiring me."

I snort. "Pretty sure that's my line."

"No, it's mine. I was lost. In this world, I was nothing. I only survived because others, braver others, sacrificed themselves to save me. I had no purpose, and so when you and your mismanagement happened, I jumped at the chance. I was so scared you would turn me down," Katherine says, looking at me.

I refuse to meet her gaze, focusing on Earth beneath us, the slowly diminishing planet. "I'd have been a fool to do so."

"True." Katherine half smiles. "I never did ask why."

My lips twist slightly, amusement at the sudden change in temperament. Then again, we are leaving Earth—for the first time in Katherine's case. A certain level of sappiness is to be expected. "You've got a lot of work ahead of you. A lot to learn. It's a completely different ball game, and we're minnows in a great big, blue sea. And, Katherine, when we arrive…"

"Yes?"

"Ali and I will be separating from the group. While we have to use you to get into the capital, you need to distance yourself—and Earth—from us as soon as possible."

"What are you planning?"

I straighten, Earth already no larger than a particularly large yoga ball in the viewport. It's strange we don't even feel a touch of the acceleration. Then again, there's artificial gravity too. So hey, what's a little inertia dampening?

I flash Katherine a comforting smile before I turn away. "Remember. Distance yourself."

We have nearly two months to get there on this cruiser. Two months to train, to study, to prepare. And then... well. Then we'll finally be able to start answering the question that's been plaguing me since the beginning.

What the hell is the System?

###

The End

For now.

John and Ali will be back in a new Galactic arc in book 7!

Author's Note

Well, that's it. That's the second arc of the System Apocalypse series. The next arc takes John and Ali into the Galactic arena, with the pair of them having to face a whole new world. John's grown a lot, both in Class and as a person, but the challenges he'll face next will be galactic in scope.

I also wanted to discuss why John's Master Quest was not in this book, but instead we skipped four years ahead. This wasn't an easy decision and one that I struggled with through the entire end of book five, as I contemplated the next book.

As many of you have noticed, John didn't rise in Level at all during his stay in the Forbidden Zone. The entirety of his Master Quest can be considered a very long training montage. And while I enjoy writing fight scenes, an entire book of endless fights without any Level gains might be extremely boring and certainly not very LitRPG. Rather than subject readers to that, I time-skipped the process. In addition, while the effect of the Master Quest was important, the actual process itself is not important to the story.

I **will**, at some point, write book 5.5—the training montage—for those curious, but due to the way the book / quest / world is structured, it will veer much more toward "normal" fantasy. No Level Ups, no Stat Screens, etc. This way, those who are still curious can read it, while those who are more interested in the overall story can continue to enjoy the series.

Hopefully, that gives everyone some context.

If you enjoyed reading the book, please do leave a review and rating. Not only is it a big ego boost, it also helps sales and convinces me to write more in the series!

Follow John's continuing quest in:

- Stars Awoken (Book 7 of the System Apocalypse)
  https://readerlinks.com/l/729215

In addition, please check out my other series, Adventures on Brad (a more traditional LitRPG fantasy), Hidden Wishes (an urban fantasy GameLit series), and A Thousand Li (a cultivation series inspired by Chinese wuxia and xianxia novels).

To support me directly, please go to my Patreon account:

- https://www.patreon.com/taowong

For more great information about LitRPG series, check out the Facebook groups:

- LitRPG Society
  https://www.facebook.com/groups/LitRPGsociety/
- LitRPG Books
  https://www.facebook.com/groups/LitRPG.books/

About the Author

Tao Wong is an avid fantasy and sci-fi reader who spends his time working and writing in the North of Canada. He's spent way too many years doing martial arts of many forms, and having broken himself too often, he now spends his time writing about fantasy worlds.

For updates on the series and other books written by Tao Wong (and special one-shot stories), please visit the author's website:
    http://www.mylifemytao.com

Subscribers to Tao's mailing list will receive exclusive access to short stories in the Thousand Li and System Apocalypse universes:
    https://www.subscribepage.com/taowong

Or visit his Facebook Page: https://www.facebook.com/taowongauthor/

About the Publisher

Starlit Publishing is wholly owned and operated by Tao Wong. It is a science fiction and fantasy publisher focused on the LitRPG & cultivation genres. Their focus is on promoting new, upcoming authors in the genre whose writing challenges the existing stereotypes while giving a rip-roaring good read.

For more information on Starlit Publishing, visit their website: https://www.starlitpublishing.com/

You can also join Starlit Publishing's mailing list to learn of new, exciting authors and book releases.
https://starlitpublishing.com/newsletter-signup/

Glossary

Erethran Honor Guard Skill Tree

John's Erethran Honor Guard Skills

Mana Imbue (Level 3)

Soulbound weapon now permanently imbued with mana to deal more damage on each hit. +20 Base Damage (Mana). Will ignore armor and resistances. Mana regeneration reduced by 15 Mana per minute permanently.

Blade Strike (Level 3)

By projecting additional Mana and stamina into a strike, the Erethran Honor Guard's Soulbound weapon may project a strike up to 30 feet away. Cost: 30 Stamina + 30 Mana

Thousand Steps (Level 1)

Movement speed for the Honor Guard and allies are increased by 5% while skill is active. This ability is stackable with other movement-related skills. Cost: 20 Stamina + 20 Mana per minute

Altered Space (Level 2)

The Honor Guard now has access to an extra-dimensional storage location of 30 cubic feet. Items stored must be touched to be willed in and may not include living creatures or items currently affected by auras that are not the Honor Guard's. Mana regeneration reduced by 10 Mana per minute permanently.

Two are One (Level 1)

Effect: Transfer 10% of all damage from Target to Self

Cost: 5 Mana per second

The Body's Resolve (Level 3)

Effect: Increase natural health regeneration by 35%. On-going health status effects reduced by 33%. Honor Guard may now regenerate lost limbs. Mana regeneration reduced by 15 Mana per minute permanently.

Greater Detection (Level 1)

Effect: User may now detect System creatures up to 1 kilometer away. General information about strength level is provided on detection. Stealth skills, Class skills, and ambient mana density will influence the effectiveness of this skill. Mana regeneration reduced by 5 Mana per minute permanently.

A Thousand Blades (Level 3)

Creates four duplicate copies of the user's designated weapon. Duplicate copies deal base damage of copied items. May be combined with Mana Imbue and Shield Transference. Mana Cost: 3 Mana per second

Soul Shield (Level 2)

Effect: Creates a manipulable shield to cover the caster's or target's body. Shield has 1,000 Hit Points.

Cost: 250 Mana

Blink Step (Level 2)

Effect: Instantaneous teleportation via line-of-sight. May include Spirit's line of sight. Maximum range—500 meters.

Cost: 100 Mana

Portal (Level 5)

Effect: Creates a 5-meter by 5-meter portal which can connect to a previously traveled location by user. May be used by others. Maximum distance range of portals is 10,000 kilometers.

Cost: 250 Mana + 100 Mana per minute (minimum cost 350 Mana)

Army of One (Level 2)

The Honor Guard's feared penultimate combat ability, Army of One builds upon previous Skills, allowing the user to unleash an awe-inspiring attack to deal with their enemies. Attack may now be guided around minor obstacles.

Effect: Army of One allows the projection of (Number of Thousand Blades conjured weapons * 3) Blade Strike attacks up to 300 meters away from user. Each attack deals 3 * Blade Strike Level damage (inclusive of Mana Imbue and Soulbound weapon bonus)

Cost: 750 Mana

Sanctum (Level 2)

An Erethran Honor Guard's ultimate trump card in safeguarding their target, Sanctum creates a flexible shield that blocks all incoming attacks, hostile teleportations and Skills. At this Level of Skill, the user must specify dimensions of the Sanctum upon use of the Skill. The Sanctum cannot be moved while the Skill is activated.

Dimensions: Maximum 15 cubic meters.

Cost: 1,000 Mana

Duration: 2 minute and 7 seconds

Paladin of Erethra Skill Tree

John's Paladin of Erethra Skills

Class Skill: Penetration (Level 2)

Few can face the judgment of a Paladin in direct combat, their ability to bypass even the toughest of defenses a frightening prospect. Reduces Mana Regeneration by 10 permanently.

Effect: Ignore all armor and defensive spells by 55%. Increases damage done to shields by 110%.

Class Skill: Aura of Chivalry (Level 1)

A Paladin's very presence can quail weak-hearted enemies and bolster the confidence of allies, whether on the battlefield or in court. The Aura of Chivalry is a double-edged sword however, focusing attention on the Paladin—potentially to their detriment. Increases success rate of Perception checks against Paladin by 10% and reduces stealth and related skills by 10% while active. Reduces Mana Regeneration by 5 Permanently. Effect: All enemies must make a Willpower check against intimidation against user's Charisma. Failure to pass the check will cow enemies. All allies gain a 50% boost in morale for all Willpower checks and a 10% boost in confidence and probability of succeeding in relevant actions.

Note: Aura may be activated or left-off at will.

Beacon of the Angels

User calls down an atmospheric strike from the heavens, dealing damage over a wide area to all enemies within the beacon. The attack takes time to form, but once activated need not be concentrated upon for completion.

Effect: 1000 Mana Damage done to all enemies, structures and vehicles within the 20 meter column of attack

Mana Cost: 500 Mana

Eyes of Insight (Level 1)

Under the eyes of a Paladin, all untruth and deceptions fall away. Only when the Paladin can see with clarity may he be able to judge effectively. Reduces Mana Regeneration by 5.

Effect: All Skills, Spells and abilities of a lower grade that obfuscate, hinder or deceive the Paladin are reduced in effectiveness. Level of reduction proportionate to degree of difference in grade and Skill Level.

Eye of the Storm (Level 1)

In the middle of the battlefield, the Paladin stands, seeking justice and offering judgment on all enemies. The winds of war will seek to draw both enemies and allies to you, their cruel flurries robbing enemies of their lives and bolstering the health and Mana of allies.

Effect: Eye of the Storm is an area effect buff and taunt. Psychic winds taunt enemies, forcing a Mental Resistance check to avoid attacking user. Enemies also receive 5 points of damage per second while within the influence of the Skill, with damage decreasing from the epicenter of the Skill. Allies receive a 5% increase in Mana and Health regeneration, decrease in effectiveness from Skill center. Eye of the Storm affects an area of 50 meters around the user.

Cost: 500 Mana + 20 Mana per second

Vanguard of the Apocalypse (Level 1)

Where others flee, the Paladin strides forward. Where the brave dare not advance, the Paladin charges. While the world burns, the Paladin still fights. The Paladin with this Skill is the vanguard of any fight, leading the charge against all of Erethra's enemies.

Effect: +30 to all Physical attributes, increases speed by 50% and recovery rates by 30%. This Skill is stackable on top of other attribute and speed boosting Skills or spells.

Cost: 500 Mana + 10 Stamina per second

Society's Web (Level 1)

Where the Eye of Insight provides the Paladin an understanding of the lies and mistruths told, Society's Web shows the Paladin the intricate webs that tie individuals to one another. No alliance, no betrayal, no tangled web of lies will be hidden as each interaction weaves one another closer. While the Skill provides no detailed information, a skilled Paladin can infer much from the Web.

Effect: Upon activation, the Paladin will see all threads that tie each individual to one another and automatically understand the details of each thread when focused upon.

Cost: 400 Mana + 200 Mana per minute

Other Class Skills

Frenzy (Level 1)

Effect: When activated, pain is reduced by 80%, damage increased by 30%, stamina regeneration rate increased by 20%. Mana regeneration rate decreased by 10%

Frenzy will not deactivate until all enemies have been slain. User may not retreat while Frenzy is active.

Cleave (Level 2)

Effect: Physical attacks deal 60% more base damage. Effect may be combined with other Class Skills.

Cost: 25 Mana

Elemental Strike (Level 1 - Ice)

Effect: Used to imbue a weapon with freezing damage. Adds +5 Base Damage to attacks and a 10% chance of reducing speed by 5% upon contact. Lasts for 30 seconds.

Cost: 50 Mana

Instantaneous Inventory (Maxed)

Allows user to place or remove any System-recognized item from Inventory if space allows. Includes the automatic arrangement of space in the inventory. User must be touching item.

Cost: 5 Mana per item

Shrunken Footprints (Level 1)

Reduces System presence of user, increasing the chance of the user evading detection of System-assisted sensing Skills and equipment. Also increases cost of information purchased about user. Reduces Mana Regeneration by 5 permanently.

Tech Link (Level 2)

Effect: Tech Link allows user to increase their skill level in using a technological item, increasing input and versatility in usage of said items. Effects vary depending on item. General increase in efficiency of 10%. Mana regeneration rate decreased by 10%

Designated Technological Items: Neural Link, Sabre

Spells

Improved Minor Healing (IV)

Effect: Heals 40 Health per casting. Target must be in contact during healing. Cooldown 60 seconds.

Cost: 20 Mana

Improved Mana Missile (IV)

Effect: Creates four missiles out of pure Mana, which can be directed to damage a target. Each dart does 30 damage. Cooldown 10 seconds

Cost: 35 Mana

Enhanced Lightning Strike

Effect: Call forth the power of the gods, casting lightning. Lightning Strike may affect additional targets depending on proximity, charge and other conductive materials on-hand. Does 100 points of electrical damage.

Lightning Strike may be continuously channeled to increase damage for 10 additional damage per second.

Cost: 75 Mana.

Continuous cast cost: 5 Mana / second

Lightning Strike may be enhanced by using the Elemental Affinity of Electromagnetic Force. Damage increased by 20% per level of affinity

Greater Regeneration (II)

Effect: Increases natural health regeneration of target by 6%. Only single use of spell effective on a target at a time.

Duration: 10 minutes

Cost: 100 Mana

Firestorm

Effect: Create a firestorm with a radius of 5 meters. Deals 250 points of fire damage to those caught within. Cooldown 60 seconds.

Cost: 200 Mana

Polar Zone

Effect: Create a thirty meter diameter blizzard that freezes all targets within one. Does 10 points of freezing damage per minute plus reduces effected individuals speed by 5%. Cooldown 60 seconds.

Cost: 200 Mana

Greater Healing (II)

Effect: Heals 100 Health per casting. Target does not require contact during healing. Cooldown 60 seconds per target.

Cost: 75 Mana

Mana Drip (II)

Effect: Increases natural health regeneration of target by 6%. Only single use of spell effective on a target at a time.

Duration: 10 minutes

Cost: 100 Mana

Freezing Blade

Effect: Enchants weapon with a slowing effect. A 5% slowing effect is applied on a successful strike. This effect is cumulative and lasts for 1 minute. Cooldown 3 minutes

Spell Duration: 1 minute.

Cost: 150 Mana

Improved Inferno Strike (II)

A beam of heat raised to the levels of an inferno, able to melt steel and earth on contact! The perfect spell for those looking to do a lot of damage in a short period of time.

Effect: Does 200 Points of Heat Damage

Cost: 150 Mana

Mud Walls

Unlike its more common counterpart Earthen Walls, Mud Walls focus is more on dealing slow, suffocating damage and restricting movement on the battlefield.

Effect: Does 20 Points of Suffocating Damage. -30% Movement Speed

Duration: 2 Minutes

Cost: 75 Mana

Create Water

Pulls water from the elemental plane of water. Water is pure and the highest form of water available. Conjures 1 liter of water. Cooldown: 1 minute

Cost: 50 Mana

Scry

Allows caster to view a location up to 1.7 kilometers away. Range may be extended through use of additional Mana. Caster will be stationary during this period. It is recommended caster focuses on the scry unless caster has a high level of Intelligence and Perception so as to avoid accidents. Scry may be blocked by equivalent or higher tier spells and Skills. Individuals with high perception in region of Scry may be alerted that the Skill is in use. Cooldown: 1 hour.

Cost: 25 Mana per minute.

Scrying Ward

Blocks scrying spells and their equivalent within 5 meters of caster. Higher level spells may not be blocked, but caster may be alerted about scrying attempts. Cooldown: 10 minutes

Cost: 50 Mana per minute

Improved Invisibility

Hides target's System information, aura, scent, and visual appearance. Effectiveness of spell is dependent upon Intelligence of caster and any Skills or Spells in conflict with the target.

Cost: 100 + 50 Mana per minute

Improved Mana Cage

While physically weaker than other elemental-based capture spells, Mana Cage has the advantage of being able to restrict all creatures, including semi-solid Spirits, conjured elementals, shadow beasts, and Skill users. Cooldown: 1 minute

Cost: 200 Mana + 75 Mana per minute

Improved Flight

(Fly birdie, fly! - Ali) This spell allows the user to defy gravity, using controlled bursts of Mana to combat gravity and allow the user to fly in even the most challenging of situations. The improved version of this spell allows flight even in zero gravity situations and a higher level of maneuverability. Cooldown: 1 minute

Cost: 250 Mana + 100 Mana per minute

Sabre's Load-Out

Omnitron III Class II Personal Assault Vehicle (Sabre)

Core: Class II Omnitron Mana Engine

CPU: Class D Xylik Core CPU

Armor Rating: Tier IV (Modified with Adaptive Resistance)

Hard Points: 5 (5 Used)

Soft Points: 3 (3 Used)

Requires: Neural Link for Advanced Configuration

Battery Capacity: 120/120

Attribute Bonuses: +35 Strength, +18 Agility, +10 Perception

Inlin Type II Projectile Rifle

Base Damage: N/A (Dependent Upon Ammunition)

Ammo Capacity: 45/45

Available Ammunition: 250 Standard, 150 Armor Piercing, 200 High Explosive, 25 Luminescent

Ares Type II Shield Generator

Base Shielding: 2,000 HP

Regeneration Rate: 50/second unlinked, 200/second linked

Mkylin Type IV Mini-Missile Launchers

Base Damage: N/A (dependent on missiles purchased)

Battery Capacity: 6/6

Reload rate from internal batteries: 10 seconds

Available Ammunition: 12 Standard, 12 High Explosive, 12 Armor Piercing, 4 Napalm

Monolam Temporal Cloak

This Temporal Cloak splices the user's timeline, adjusting their physical, emotional, and psychic presence to randomly associated times. This allows the user to evade notice from most sensors and individuals. The Monolam Temporal Cloak has multiple settings for a variety of situations, varying the type and level of dispersal of the signal.

Requirements: 1 Hardpoint, Tier IV Mana Engine

Duration: Varies depending on cloaking level

Type II Webbing Mini-Missile

Base Damage: N/A

Effect: Disperses insta-webbing upon impact or on activation. Dispersal covers 3 cubic feet.

Cost: 500 Credits

Shinowa Type II Sonic Pulser

Base Damage: 25 per second

Additional Effect: Disrupts auditory sense of balance on opponent during use. Effects have a small chance of continuing after use.

Joola Communication Booster (Tier II)

Military Grade Communication Booster able to deliver your message where and when it needs to be. Joola Tech is the only way to go when what you need to say needs to be heard!

Effect: Disregard all communication interference from shields, communication scramblers, Skills and Spells below Tier of communication booster. 50% chance of breaking through equivalent tier blockages (chance decreases dependent on proximity to emanating blockage).

Other Equipment

Ares Platinum Class Tier II Armored Jumpsuit

Ares's signature Platinum Class line of armored daily wear combines the company's latest technological advancement in nanotech fiber design and the pinnacle work of an Advanced Craftsman's Skill to provide unrivalled protection for the discerning Adventurer.

Effect: +218 Defense, +14% Resistance to Kinetic and Energy Attacks. +19% Resistance against Temperature changes. Self-Cleanse, Self-Mend, Autofit Enchantments also included.

Silversmith Mark II Beam Pistol (Upgradeable)

Base Damage: 18

Battery Capacity: 24/24

Recharge Rate: 2 per hour per GMU

Tier IV Neural Link

Neural link may support up to 5 connections.

Current connections: Omnitron III Class II Personal Assault Vehicle

Software Installed: Rich'lki Firewall Class IV, Omnitron III Class IV Controller

Ferlix Type II Twinned-Beam Rifle (Modified)

Base Damage: 57

Battery Capacity: 17/17

Recharge rate: 1 per hour per GMU (currently 12)

387

Tier II Sword (Soulbound Personal Weapon of an Erethran Honor Guard)

Base Damage: 218

Durability: N/A (Personal Weapon)

Special Abilities: +20 Mana Damage, Blade Strike

Kryl Ring of Regeneration

Often used as betrothal bands, Kyrl rings are highly sought after and must be ordered months in advance.

Health Regeneration: +30

Stamina Regeneration: +15

Mana Regeneration: +5

Tier III Bracer of Mana Storage

A custom work by an unknown maker, this bracer acts a storage battery for personal Mana. Useful for Mages and other Classes that rely on Mana. Mana storage ratio is 50 to 1.

Mana Capacity: 350/350

Fey-steel Dagger

Fey-steel is not actual steel but an unknown alloy. Normally reserved only for the Sidhe nobility, a small—by Galactic standards—amount of Fey-steel is released for sale each year. Fey-steel takes enchantments extremely well.

Base Damage: 28

Durability: 110/100

Special Abilities: None

Brumwell Necklace of Shadow Intent

The Brumwell Necklace of Shadow Intent is the hallmark item of the Brumwell Clan. Enchanted by a Master Crafter, this necklace layers shadowy intents over your actions, ensuring that information about your actions are more difficult to ascertain. Ownership of such an item is both a necessity and a mark of prestige among settlement owners and other individuals of power.

Effect: Persistent effect of Shadow Intent (Level 4) results in significantly increased cost of purchasing information from the System about wearer. Effect is persistent for all actions taken while necklace is worn.

Ring of Greater Shielding

Creates a greater shield that will absorb approximately 1000 points of damage. This shield will ignore all damage that does not exceed its threshold amount of 50 points of damage while still functioning.

Max Duration: 7 Minutes

Charges: 1

Made in the USA
Las Vegas, NV
18 December 2021

38548614R00236